Malina

Penny Perrick

D0928355

BANTAM BOOKS

LONDON · NEW YORK · TORONTO · SYDNEY · AU

MALINA
A BANTAM BOOK: 0 553 40720 1

Originally published in Great Britain by Sinclair-Stevenson,
an imprint of Reed Consumer Books Ltd

PRINTING HISTORY
Sinclair-Stevenson edition published 1993
Bantam Books edition published 1994

Set in 11½pt Monotype Bembo by
Phoenix Typesetting, Ilkley, West Yorkshire.

Bantam Books are published by Transworld Publishers Ltd,
61–63 Uxbridge Road, Ealing, London W5 5SA,
in Australia by Transworld Publishers (Australia) Pty Ltd,
15–25 Helles Avenue, Moorebank, NSW 2170,
and in New Zealand by Transworld Publishers (NZ) Ltd,
3 William Pickering Drive, Albany, Auckland.

Printed and bound in Great Britain by
Cox & Wyman Ltd, Reading, Berks.

For Caradoc King,
who said yes you can

Acknowledgements

I am grateful to all the following for their help: Ann Henning, Anne de Stacpoole, Emma, Jill and Rod Teck, Geoffrey Boothroyd, Mary Hobart, Anthony Clare, Vera O'Dowd and Michael Barrett. Steve MacDonogh helped me with Irish words, Anne Walsh gave me comfort and hospitality in Oranmore and her son John sang me the songs I needed to hear. Caroline Upcher was a sympathetic and scrupulous editor, Beth Humphries copy-edited the manuscript with daunting intelligence and Joanna Duckworth reworked it with patience and gaiety. Most of all, I should like to thank the people of Roundstone who, in the true spirit of Ireland, have always offered me a hundred thousand welcomes.

Penny Perrick
London 1992

Author's note

This is a work of fiction so, except for the political and literary figures who appear under their real names, nothing is fact. Even the Connemara I describe is, in some part, an imagined countryside. In an act of literary landscaping, I have transposed whole tracts of land so that my heroine is able to ride to hounds without sinking in the bog and brought forward the Clifden pony show by more than a decade. Malina does not exist but houses like it do, although their number was depleted during 'the troubled times' of the 1920s, and by change of ownership. Those that remain are the most beautiful examples of domestic architecture that I have seen, their extraordinary atmosphere bringing to mind W. B. Yeats's line, 'A dance-like glory that those walls begot.'

All fiction is fastened on to fact in some way and this novel could not have been written had I not read the work of two writers whose concerns are to do with the real Ireland, rather than an imagined one. I owe an enormous debt of gratitude to R. F. Foster for *Modern Ireland 1600–1972* (Allen Lane, The Penguin Press) and to Tim Robinson for *Setting Foot on the Shores of Connemara* (Lilliput Pamphlets) and *Connemara: Introduction, Gazetteer and one-inch map,* published by Folding Landscapes, the publishing house which Tim runs with his wife, Máireád, from Roundstone, the village that I am always homesick for when I am somewhere else.

Penny Perrick

'But what use is it to cry, even if
ye dhragged the hair out of yer head?
Ye might as well be singin' and dancin'.'

Norry the Boat in
The Real Charlotte by Somerville and Ross

Some Irish words used in the text

bainin (báinín): an oatmeal–coloured frieze jacket.

borheen (boreen): a laneway.

bowsie: a ruffian.

crubeen (crúibin): a dish of pigs' feet.

currach (curach): the traditional fishing boat of the West of Ireland.

drisheens (drisín): black pudding.

poitin (poitín): an illicitly stilled spirit made from barley and potatoes.

pookawn (púcán): a small sailing boat.

sennachie (seanchaí): a storyteller.

PART ONE

1

My husband's first wife threw herself off the dunes at Horam's Cove and died. It's a beautiful cove. At low tide, the sand follows the curve of the dunes in an almost perfect half-circle, and, just above where the sea licks the shore, there are curved rows of shells, some of them looking like sweets, lemon-yellow curls and purple and white striped ones, and, sometimes, in the summer, a rim of jellyfish appears, glassy pink blobs winking in the sun.

But when Harriet died the tide was high. The dark, thrashing sea hit the dunes again and again, the Atlantic waters were deep, ready to welcome suicides in a black grip. There was no lantern found on the dunes the next morning when the body was recovered, carried sweetly by turquoise waves and put to rest on the warm sand. How had she followed the track on that moonless night with no light to guide her? The track turns off the coast road, six miles from the village and almost ten miles from the town. At all times it is narrow and sandy, there are places where it is a permanent puddle entangled with reeds and other places where the rocks have remained uncleared and difficult to avoid even in daytime. There are six cottages built alongside but.

that late at night, there would have been no candles in their windows and the glow from their oil lamps would have dimmed long since.

Of course, Harriet knew the path to the cove well. She took the governess cart from Malina to where the track joins the coast road every day in fine weather. She would unharness the tubby Connemara pony and let it graze by the side of the road, watched by John-Jo Doolan, who lived in the first of the cottages. She left the trap there too, and walked to the cove, spending hours collecting the shells and bits of feathery seaweed which she would use to make shell pictures, fashionable at that time in the 1880s, when fussy, decorative things were more to people's taste than they are now, at the beginning of the new century.

On those fine, summer days, rare treasures in Connemara, this wet, wild region, Harriet looked gilded, like a buttercup. Her pale, gold hair shone in the sunshine and the small diamonds in her ears beamed light. I never felt sorry for Harriet then. The winters were when she seemed pitiful, her long, narrow back hunched against the cold, her hair dulled by turf-smoke, her fingers beginning to look knarled around the blue knuckles, her ears chapped to a hard redness.

The architect who designed Malina was English like Harriet and her husband Charles, who is now my husband. It was Charles's idea that the house should rise straight and sheer from the edge of the lake, so that the wooded slope behind it, twittering with birdsong, seemed like a green backdrop to its dove-grey grandeur. Malina exposed its great, grey flanks to the damp, chilly winds which gave it no shelter. A local man would have known better. He would have nestled the house further back into the crook of the woods, made it turn some gentle corners to trick the wind of its prey, created snug, little nooks to sit in and get warm. But Charles and his English architect had no notion that in the west of Ireland a house must offer protection against the rough climate as well as display beauty. They made huge, vaulted rooms with doors of imported mahogany which swelled and then warped in the changeable temperatures, letting cruel draughts nip along the polished floors and chill Harriet's thin limbs that shivered, I was certain, under her heavy skirts. In those high, cold rooms, which only warmed through when the sun smote directly on the vast south-facing windows, even the great fireplaces that the architect had installed looked toy-sized, as though they belonged in a doll's house. Charles Trewin would have nothing of the local marble, a pale, white-veined green stone, splodged with deeper green. He says it reminded him of the soap in his dormitory at Rugby school, a school he loathed. Instead, he ordered snow-white marble from Carrara and brought over English stonemasons to carve rich designs of swags and fruits and angels on the mantelpieces. The fireplaces blazed with turf, popped and crackled with wood from the trees behind the house. Whole tracts of bogland were cut into neat, dark sods to heat that house, scores of young lads spent hours on the bog road, their donkeys, with reed baskets strapped to their sides, quietly waiting until the boy had filled the baskets with turf. And all for the B

House, for Malina, the house that would not grow warm.

I have made Malina seem like an unwelcome and chilly place. In fact, it is magical. Charles Trewin started building it for his bride, Harriet, in 1865, and, by the time I was born, a few years later, in the whitewashed farmhouse on the far side of the lake, that grey enchantment was complete, a fairy palace growing out of the glittering water, its winding drive, plushy with rhododendrons in late spring, leading from tall, wrought-iron gates to the massive, oak front door, sturdy within its stone archway.

The wooded place where the house stood had always been known as Malina, an English place name imposed on the older Irish one, Míleac, meaning a place by water. Only twenty years before Malina was built, its driveway was a famine road. Men, women and children, their faces worn away almost to skulls, chewed the grass by the wayside as they tried, pitifully, to follow the winding road as far as the sea, where the ships were waiting, the terrible gaunt ships to take some to a new life in America, some to a wracked death. Where once those skull-faces walked, the rhododendrons bob prettily in their glossy leaves. We have the railway now and the lace school. The ice-ships come to take delivery of the herring that the women salt on the quay. Our marble is fashionable even if my husband, Charles Trewin, still despises it. The men quarry it and then it is shipped to England, Europe, America, even Russia. Rich tourists come to land ur salmon and feast upon our shellfish. Their wives, ppier than Harriet ever was, collect the shells, as she once did, and give them to their children to play with.

My father, one of fifteen children, is the only one to have stayed in Connemara. Long before I was born, his brothers and sisters sailed to America and Australia on the emigrant ships. They were not starving nor destitute. The McCallas are an enterprising family, owners of the house and land where my father breeds ponies, whose coats are the colours of the stones on the beaches after they have been washed by the waves: milky beige, dappled grey, glossy fawn. It is true that my great-grandfather, Thomas McCalla, had been a tenant of an absentee English landlord, a Mr Fortesque, whose family went bankrupt during the famine years, since their tenants had been evicted or had died of the great hunger and the landowner no longer had the rents they paid for their hovels to finance his gambling debts in London and Paris. Thomas McCalla had a restless energy, rare in this region, where the people are sleepy, slow-moving and resigned. He grew bored of digging the pearly-white potatoes out of the dark clay, long before the failed harvest of 1845, when the potatoes were no longer firm ovals but little rotted explosions that smeared the land with decay. Thomas became a boat-builder, stretching canvas over wooden frames to make currachs, our local fishing boats that are closely related to the coracles used by the Ancient Britons in the time of Caesar. He chose and seasoned his wood well, curved the prows so that they nosed confidently through the Atlantic waves. It is said that no fisherman ever drowned in a boat made by Thomas McCalla, and to own one of his currachs was to own something as valuable as a field that was well fertilized with seaweed and bounded by well-maintained dry stone walls. It was easy, in these parts, to marry off a daughter if you could offer as dowry one of my great-grandfather's currachs. Poor as our people were, as most of them are now, the financial arrangements regarding marriage were, and are, complicated and lengthy, involving match-makers and spokesmen for both families. In Ireland, it is thought to be unlucky to marry for love. The Scots, I believe, have a proverb, 'As loveless as an Irishman.'

It is said that, though his currachs made him money, Thomas McCalla made even more from operating an illicit still hidden in the hazel grove at the foot of Errisbeg mountain. My father, Garrold McCalla, refuses to believe this. As far as he can remember, the McCallas have been temperance men, sobriety and hard work being the reasons why we are one of the more prosperous families in the west of Ireland. My grandfather, Brian McCalla, was an only child, Thomas having married late, as is the custom here. He did not inherit his father's boat-building skill but had a gift with animals. The ponies that are indigenous to our heathery mountains and wild boglands are beautiful beasts, their grace coming from their ancestry – the Arab thoroughbreds, brought over by the Spaniards who once settled on this coast, mingled with the local horses to good effect – and their ruggedness from the need to survive in the wind and rain. They have a gentle disposition and those bred and trained by my father are perfect for children to ride, so sweet-natured and obedient and nimble that they could be household pets. It seems that there is scarcely a well-to-do child

18

in England who is not taught to ride as soon as it can toddle, so my grandfather did as well selling his ponies to rich English families as his father did with his boats and the fiery liquor, clear and pure as water, that I suspect he brewed at the mountain's foot.

Indeed, he did so well that he was able to leave the small, limewashed cottage by the crude, stone jetty at Ervallagh, where Thomas had built his boats, sinking them in the sea for the timber to season and, later, painting their canvas skins with shiny, dark tar so that they looked like the seals who basked on the rocks by the bay as Thomas worked. Brian leased the thirty acres of flatland between the sea and the lake, a place called Shanvally, where I was brought up and my father still lives, breeding and training ponies like his father before him. The house that Brian built seems too small to have housed his big family. There are five small bedrooms, all with sloping ceilings lined with varnished planks. Downstairs is the kitchen where, during my own childhood, everything happened and a musty parlour where nothing did. There is a pleasing sprawl of stables, barns and outbuildings, some thatched, some roofed with thin, dark grey slates. My father and his fourteen younger brothers and sisters must have spent most of their lives out of doors: there would never have been room for them in the low-ceilinged rooms with their thick walls and narrow windows. My father doesn't talk about his childhood; I think he was wounded by the departure of the rest, even though he now has seven daughters of his own. His brothers and sisters left, even though there was money and work enough for most of them as the pony-breeding increased, because they had inherited Thomas's restless temperament. My father could never leave Connemara; it is the tradition that the eldest son stays near his parents, looking after them in their old age and inheriting their house and land when they die. My uncles and aunts, so I have heard, hankered after new lives. They have done well in New York and Boston, Sydney and Melbourne. They run textile mills and local politics; they live in fine brick houses in the middle of important cities. They are proud of their children who, their letters say, are planning to go to the university and then enter the professions: law and finance and teaching. But my aunts and uncles have never come back to Connemara. I wonder if they carry pictures in their minds, images of the Twelve Pins, that range of mountains whose shapes and colours change every day, sometimes flaming with gorse, sometimes thundery black, sometimes an almost transparent, gauzy green. And the narrow borheens, dripping with fuchsia and the long, straight ditches where the turf has been cut and heaped into little footings to dry in the sun. As they light the gas jets and blink in the sudden, harsh, unkind light, do they remember the pink glow of the embers in the kitchen fireplace, just before their mother, my grandmother, long since dead, raked them over before going to bed, damping down the remaining blaze so that the embers could be fanned into life again in the morning? Saving the seed of the fire, we call it. Before the embers become a white silky ash, women bake soda bread in their heat. Other women, not me. For at Malina, which is now my home, Charles has installed a patent stove that serves as an oven and heats the water, although it cannot do battle with the draughts that made Harriet suffer so; but not as much as Charles made her suffer.

My name is Rose Erris Trewin, born McCalla. I was named Rose after my paternal grandmother but Erris was my father's idea. My mother would have preferred something more ordinary, I think, Bernadette or Kathleen or Brigid. But my father had always been drawn towards the sight of Errisbeg; its rocky flanks were the first thing he saw when he awoke in the morning and flung open the narrow window. He said that from the first there was an unyielding look in my dark grey eyes that reminded him of the dull gleam on the flinty rocks that pressed into the mountainside.

I should have liked to have inherited my mother's red-gold hair, as three of my sisters, Anne, Betty and Vera, did, along with the fragile, lightly freckled white skins and thin, high noses that are not uncommon in these parts. But I, and the three girls who were born after me, Eithne, Deirdre and Geraldine, have the blue-black curls and tawny complexions flushed with dark rose that are equally prevalent among Connemara people. In summer, we look lightly toasted, the tender brown of hazelnuts, and, even in winter, however biting the wind it cannot take the sunny colour out of our skins. Visitors to this Atlantic shore look approvingly at our dark, almost uncontrollable hair and like to point out that our people are the real Milesians, descendants of Miledh, the mythical Spanish king who seized Ireland before the Normans came, and long before Cromwell conquered in that terrible time when the soldiery speared living babies on their bayonets an roasted them on the fires they had reduced our nobles' houses to. Later than King Miledh, Spanish galleons loaded with cargoes of wine sailed the western seas. We were not always hospitable to their sailors. We lured their ships on to the rocks with false harbour lights, so that the massive decks splintered into beams, which we put to good use in our own houses. We looted their cargoes, and became famous as pirates in the time of the English Queen Elizabeth I, when our own sea-queen, Grace O'Malley, looted her way to power and was proclaimed an outlaw by the English government. Nonetheless, not all the Spanish sailors fled such hostility. Many stayed, mingled and married with us and left this legacy of wild hair and olive skin.

'My damask rose', my mother used to call me, as she gently brushed the tangles out of my black curls. All the memories of my early childhood are happy ones. Perhaps it should have been otherwise. Had I encountered meanness or deception or cruelty when I was a little girl I should have recognized them for what they were later. My upbringing made me guileless. My memories are of my sisters and myself standing in a circle in the flagged kitchen, near the window, so that, in the light that poured through it, we could each plait another's hair. All of us wore our hair in a single, long plait, and my father joked that, when he had the ponies ready for showing with their plaited tails threaded through with bright ribbons, he might easily confuse his daughters with his horses but that the horses obeyed him more readily.

Ah, the sweet smell of hay and ponies that was always at Shanvally. The delicate smell of young, girlish sweat in the attic bedrooms, the smell of bread baking and the lemony smell of the geraniums that my mother grew in old, black trivets set along the limewashed walls of the house. When you pinched their leaves, the scent intensified, clinging to your fingers. Malina is too large, too airy to trap the smells of things. The only persistent scent there is the cologne worn by my husband, Charles Trewin. It has a heady smell like carnations, a smell most foreign to Connemara, where carnations are a rare sight.

My mother was a contented woman. Why wouldn't she have been, married to a kind and sober man who doted on his wife and daughters? He didn't seem to mind the lack of a son. It was perhaps in the back of his mind that one of the American nephews would come back to Shanvally to carry on the breeding and selling of ponies.

There was such order in our lives then, such rhythm, the year pricked out with festivals and ceremonies, birthdays, choir practice, regattas, fair days and pony shows. There was always something to look forward to, even on those mornings when we woke to a day that was black as pitch and to the sound of rain hissing on the cobbled yard. My life was brim-full then. Now I feel as though I am dying alive.

Every day, my sisters and I would follow the edge of the lake to the coast road which led to the one-roomed village school. Miss Gwynn ruled the roost. She was a small, twiggy woman, rather whiskery about the chin and clearly not as old as my child's self took her to be since, twenty years after I first walked into her schoolroom, she is still there, dividing the village children into three groups, according to ability rather than age, and not letting any child progress into a higher group until he or she is able to write a neat and clear copperplate, read fluently in English and Irish, do difficult sums in the head, and recite the stories of our bloody heroes, Cuchulain, Brian Boru, and our ocean god, Manannan MacLir.

The little boys thrilled to these stories of battles and betrayals and recited them proudly like excited parrots, but the little girls soon grew bored. There was too much trickery and deception about our heroes; they were too wriggly, too crafty, too stubborn to appeal to our softer hearts. We preferred the fairytales from across the water, ones in which gorgeously dressed princes hunted high and low for a girl with a small, delicate foot, or cut through hundred-year-old briars to awaken a sleeping beauty with a kiss.

Miss Gwynn was, is, committed to the idea of a free Ireland. Yet she is the first to offer English tourists the hospitality of her whitewashed cottage opposite the school. She admired everything English: their puddingy old Queen sitting in Windsor Castle in her fusty jet and lace, their Oxford colleges, their gilt and red plush theatres.

Miss Gwynn is a woman whose life is too small for her. That is why she is so restless and strung-up with thoughts of rebellion and blood sacrifice. She should have been born a man so that she could have become a politician like Parnell or Davitt. Being a woman, she can only try to instil a sense of the larger world to children who, for the most part, long for nothing but to rush out of the schoolroom door to chase hares in the fields and try to lure conger eels with a bit of rancid meat tied to the end of a fishing-rod dangled from the stone pier.

From time to time, my parents threatened to send all seven of us to boarding-school in County Armagh. For all our pretty copperplate loops and ability to add up compound interest in our heads, we were wild girls, never still. On Sundays, following behind our mother as she came home from Mass (our father, like so many of the men, seldom came with us) we would walk decorously behind her for a while, blue satin sashes on our flounced dresses, matching blue bows on our long plaits. But, as we proceeded up the hill, we itched for action. We would jump in and out of our mother's shadow as it lengthened and shortened on the ground, leap over ditches, stuff blackberries into our mouths. By the time we arrived back at Shanvally, our dresses were crumpled, sashes trailing, flounces grubby with grass stains and splashed with blackberry juice. Our plump arms showed red fretworks of scratches from the briars and blackthorns into which we had pushed and shoved each other, shrieking and giggling, for much of the way home. How was it that there was always so much to laugh about? We were great mimics, of course, especially Deirdre, two years my junior, who could change her voice, the way she walked, even the set of her features, so remarkably that sometimes we thought she was a changeling, a fairy child.

And the person she mimicked most, her 'turn' as it were, was Harriet Trewin, the tall, slender English lady from Malina, whose lovely brows were always slightly furrowed with bewilderment, or so it seemed to us larky little girls as we watched her, all of us huddled, giggling as usual, in a shop doorway as she made one of her rare appearances in the village.

'So meet aye expect you at eet o'clock?' Deirdre would mimic Harriet, leaning and dipping over an imaginary listener as Harriet did, as though she were ashamed of being tall. Poor Harriet. No matter how politely she asked her dinner guests to be on time, 'eet' o'clock came and went with nary a sign of them. Lord and Lady Girdiron from Toombeola, Mr and Mrs Hemming from Ballyconneely, Mr Graves, the Church of Ireland rector from Clifden, all of English ancestry but, after a lifetime in our sleepy country, more Irish than the Irish, like us never bothering to put on their watches in the morning, mindful of the day's ending only when the vibrant sunset threw streaks of orange and crimson across the sky. Charles and Harriet, by contrast, were relative newcomers, their trim and orderly English minds still counting off the minutes, convinced that punctuality was kin to morality. Later, I was to discover that Charles's obsession with time took the place of morality. He did not care what he did just as long as he did it at the appointed hour.

It was told that when the Trewins gave a party, long before eight o'clock, both would be pacing the handsome Chinese carpet in the drawing-room; Harriet in one of her low-backed evening dresses, which revealed her palely gleaming shoulderblades and narrow waist, Charles in a damson velvet dinner jacket, his wide feet crammed into black patent pumps. Charles would march a route between the fireplace and the great windows that opened on to the driveway, alert for the sound of carriage wheels smashing down on the gravel, while Harriet would pause before the window-seat, her long back straight, her knuckly hands twisting a handkerchief into a damp wad.

We learnt all this from Binnie McMahon, one of the maids at Malina, whose father, Thomas, was the blacksmith. On one such evening, Binnie had entered the drawing-room of the Big House to add more turf to the fire, and had found Charles, half-hunter in the palm of his hand, checking its time and then gazing out of the window as though 'he were expecting the Good Lord himself'. Baffled by his anxiety, Binnie had said, 'Sure, Sir, haven't these fine evenings a lot of stretch in them. Them being so long and the light so gorgeous, you wouldn't be wanting to hurry indoors.' At which Charles gave her a chilling look and shook his gold watch as if in disbelief that its hands showed it to be almost nine o'clock. 'Ah, the English people,' Binnie said to us later, when she came over to see the trembly-legged foal that had just been born to our mare, Gormley. 'Did no-one ever tell them that you're a long time lying six feet below the ground, so you may as well enjoy the days you have when you're six feet above it.'

For all his fretfulness over time, you could not accuse Charles of lacking a sense of enjoyment. From the first day I met him, when I was twelve years old, I recognized him as a source of sparkling fun. Even now, in spite of all that has happened, he can make me laugh until my sides ache. My first sight of Charles Trewin was on a sunny June morning in 1885. By then, he had lived in Ireland for twenty years but still smacked of

Englishness. His tweed suit, in shades of golden brown, was beautifully tailored and looked new. As he walked up the gentle slope of the borheen towards Shanvally and saw me and my younger sisters washing our dolls in a tin bath in the cobbled yard, he did not give a sideways jerk of his head as an Irishman would have done but nodded gravely at us and said a formal, 'Good morning.' None of us had seen him before but of course we knew who he was, Englishmen in bespoke tweeds being none too plentiful in the neighbourhood. We stared at him with the penetrating and innocent curiosity of children, Geraldine, who, at the time, was only two, chewing the padded cloth arm of her doll as she always did when she was concentrating hard.

I took in the golden tweeds, a mane of amber hair that streamed backwards, matching amber eyes with narrow, almost slitted, pupils and, most astonishing of all, a nose that seemed to have no bone in it but lay flatly between his cheeks, which were downy with amber hair. He looked so much like a lion in one of my picture books that when he extended his hand to me, saying, 'My name is Charles Trewin, from Malina', I half expected it to be a velvety paw. The hand, definitely not a paw, was warm and dry, and gripped my small, grubby one firmly. While I hung my head and wondered whether I should tell this lion-like man my name, he deftly extracted an egg from my ear, shook out a crimson silk handkerchief from his breast pocket, discovered that it contained two more eggs, and began to juggle them. Eithne, Deirdre and Geraldine began to giggle; I was more cautious, being older and having recognized the eggs, small and brown, as having originally come from the basket of new-laid ones that my mother had taken from the hen coop earlier that morning. They had been counted and there would be the devil to pay if any of them were found cracked on the cobbles. A shadow must have fallen across my face, for, suddenly, this leonine stranger caught the airborne eggs, laid them tenderly with the rest of that morning's gathering in the rush basket propped against the henhouse and dropped down on his haunches so that his eyes were on a level with mine. And what eyes they were. With our faces only inches apart, I could see that the amber irises were scattered with gleaming, tawny flecks. They gave me an itch for possession, as though they had been fabulous jewels or rare birds' eggs. I stared into their fiery yellowness.

'Would you like to touch my nose?' asked the eyes' owner.

Before I could answer, he grasped the forefinger of my right hand and pressed it on the soft blob in the centre of his face. As I pressed, his nose flattened further until it almost disappeared. It felt like the putty that my father used for replacing windowpanes – not unpleasant, just strange. My sisters were laughing so much by now that they could hardly stand, but I was suspicious.

'What happened to your nose?' I asked, too curious to be frightened.

'Fell off a horse in Gloucestershire. The bone needed setting, but when the doctor started to set it, it hurt so much that I leapt out of the chair and decided that a filleted nose would do me. Do you think I was a coward?'

'No. I fell off my pony, and when I had to have stitches in my head I cried. I cried when they were taken out too, even though Doctor Pat Burke let me keep them in a little box. I like your flat nose, anyway. It makes you look like a lion.'

My mother emerged from the kitchen door, looking rushed and flustered, raking her hair back from her shiny forehead with a hand that was lightly dusted with flour. She crossed the yard, and came quickly towards the place where Charles Trewin was crouched beside me. She did not stop to pluck a leaf from the lemon geranium in its black pot and crush it in her fingers, as she usually did. 'You're very welcome, Mr Trewin,' she said, in the traditional greeting, but there was an odd bite in her voice which signalled to her daughters that Charles Trewin was not welcome at all.

2

After that first meeting with Charles Trewin, I hoarded every little bit and scrap of information about him that I could, the way I hoarded the delicate tufts of sheep's wool that fluttered on the hedgerows, which I used to make a soft stuffing for my dolls' pillows.

I had no guile then, as I have none now. 'Tell me how Mr and Mrs Trewin came from England to live at Malina,' I asked my mother that same morning. We were in the back meadow, oiling the hooves of a grey mare with a white-blond mane that my father was going to show in the class for five-year-olds at the Clifden pony show that afternoon. I could smell the sun on the horse's flanks, the calming scent of meadowgrass, the pungent smell of the rag soaked in linseed oil that I held in my hand.

My mother felt for loose hairpins in the coiled plait at the nape of her neck, a gesture she made when troubled. She did not speak until she had rubbed a gloss on the mare's back hoof. 'There was trouble in England, I think. Some argument at the gaming table and a man ended up shot. It's as well the English have Ireland to escape to when things go wrong for them over the water. Not that Mr Trewin was ever blamed for anything, except wildness.' She gave a little snort that made the mare's flanks quiver anxiously.

'Why is it that he is never around the village? I saw him only just this once, although Mrs Trewin is sometimes at Miss Gwynn's. They do be reading some old books together, Binnie says.' (Binnie McMahon was the village's eyes and ears.) 'Why did Mr Trewin come here today?' 'They have visitors at Malina and some of the ladies want ponies to ride. You'd think he'd know there's the show to think about and the best ponies entered. But Mr Trewin doesn't seem to grasp that there's a world outside Malina. He must think that we've all been put on God's earth to service his estate.' She rubbed the already gleaming hoof ferociously, then put aside her rag and took the curry comb to the mare's pale mane. She seemed to be trying to comb out her own distress. When she had seen Charles Trewin in the yard that morning, she had shooed me and my sisters into the house, saying we must change out of the clothes that were wet with the water we had sploshed around with in the tin bath. But it had been a sunny morning and my mother had always let our damp clothes dry on us without fussing.

My mother was not a disapproving woman. She was as easy-going as the mare whose mane she was now angrily jerking into small, tight plaits. That Charles Trewin had wanted to rent ponies on a fair day was not something I would have expected to rattle her so. Her usual way of coping with transgression – when my father had dozed away a Sunday afternoon instead of lifting the hay, or when he spent the money intended for new delft on brass-studded bridles for the ponies

– was to wriggle her plump shoulders and say, soothingly, 'Well, why wouldn't he now?'

'You are angry with Mr Trewin,' I accused her.
Anger was a sin. I wanted to make her feel embarrassed so that she would tell me the reason for the
mockery in her voice when she had bade Charles
Trewin welcome. She began to wind a scarlet ribbon
through the mare's plaited mane. 'You are a child,
Rose Erris. Such things are not for children to discuss.' But as she leant her cheek against the mare's
hot, bright neck, I could hear her mutter under her
breath, 'It's herself I feel sorry for.'

Sorry for Harriet? Why? The tall, thin Englishwoman led a life that seemed gorgeous to the
twelve-year-old child that I was then. Every time
she appeared in the village, about once a week, when
she would sometimes make a fluttery appearance at
Keane's General Stores, to order a new saucepan or a
set of glasscloths, or drink tea at Miss Gwynn's house,
she would be wearing something new. The arrival of
each (unreliable) season seemed to be an excuse for
additions to Harriet's wardrobe. I remember, from
one of my childhood's springtimes, the sight of her
counting pennies from her purse into Noona Keane's
flabby palm, from a hand encased in new kid gloves
the exact colour of buttermilk and of so fine a leather
that the knuckles of her large hands showed through
as a range of bumps, like tiny mountains. Later that
same year she carried a new parasol, white muslin
above and, underneath, rose-pink silk that covered her
face with a blush. Little Eithne loved that parasol; she
cried one day when Harriet was caught in a downpour

and the parasol crumpled into a sodden wreck above her head, irretrievably ruined. Deirdre pestered Binnie McMahon to search the dustbins of Malina for what remained of it and, a few days later, Binnie came panting up the borheen with the crushed and rusting object. But its ribs had buckled and the ivory ring that held them would no longer ride up and down the cane stem. Deirdre laid it in front of the fire and stroked the streaked silk, the way she would comfort an ailing kitten but, like many a kitten, it failed to thrive and one day, in spite of Deirdre's protests, my mother threw it away.

Now my mother put away the linseed oil in the drawer of the kitchen dresser and out of the same drawer took a brush and started to brush my curly hair, quite fiercely. She wished me to look presentable at the pony show. We were standing by the kitchen window, and from where I stood I could look right across the lake to where Malina's vast windows flashed like giant diamonds. I thought of the pony show: the trampled ground, the fumy sweat from men and animals, mingling with the smells of steaming dung and stale beer. There would be clusters of men in shabby suits that were too tight across the back and under the arms. One or two of them would make little weaving movements around me, call me a grand girl and ask for a kiss. Amid such shabbiness, such noise and disorder, I always found it hard to share my father's pride as he won cup after cup, rosette after rosette, proving once again that he was the best pony-breeder in Connemara. He would not drink, even though porter and whiskey would be pressed upon him, but the cries of 'Good man, yourself' and the many slaps on the back would turn his head briefly, and when he returned he would be uncharacteristically boastful until my mother would complain snappishly that he thought more of his ponies than of his family and stomp off to bed, slamming the kitchen door so that the candle flames juddered.

The Trewins and their visitors would not be going to the show, I felt sure. Not for them, such bawdy riff-raff. The gentlemen would go fishing and the ladies would put on their hand-made walking boots and drift through the woods, picking wild flowers which they would later press between the leaves of a book and write the flower's name in Latin underneath. After dinner, one of the ladies would play the rosewood piano in the drawing-room that would not be quite warm enough, even though the evening was fine, and a gentleman would sing 'Let the Toast Pass' in a confident baritone. I fidgeted as my mother tied a piece of the same red ribbon she had used to braid the horse around my glinting curls. It was time to load the cart and follow the coast road to Clifden to help my father lead the ponies into the ring. I did not want to go. I wanted to be at Malina.

Yet I had no need to be there to see again the lion-eyed man who had intrigued me that morning. For, to my surprise, Charles Trewin was at the pony show. I saw him, leaning against the newly erected picket fence that bounded the show ring, as I led Gormley and her colt foal round and round, both horses well behaved, the foal prancing in step with his mother, like a cocky little boy doing his party piece. As we completed the ring's circuit, I handed Gormley's lead rein to my father, who was standing at the entrance ropes, white-faced as he always was until the results were announced, so that he would be able to lead Gormley to the judging stand when, inevitably, the time came for her to have the winning rosette pinned to her harness.

Charles Trewin was there before me. 'You have much to be proud of, Mr McCalla,' he said, tipping his beautiful ash-grey bowler hat towards my father. 'Both your ponies and your daughter have acquitted themselves admirably this afternoon. Since Rose Erris has been tramping around the ring for some time, I wonder if I may have your permission to take her to the refreshment tent for a lemonade?'

My father looked wildly around for my mother. But she was in the field where the stalls had been set up, gossiping with her friends in the village as they examined crocheted lace collars and embroidered firescreens. As for my sisters, those wayward girls were all over the town by now, the younger ones organizing complicated games of hopscotch on the pavement outside the Travellers' Hotel and getting in the way of the crowds, the older ones lolloping on the beach with the Clifden boys, whom they considered more sophisticated than the boys from the village. Of all of us girls, I was the one considered to have a way with horses and so was denied my sisters' freedom. I gave it up gladly. I was proud that I had inherited my father's gift. Nothing pleased me so much as exercising the ponies, training them to look well on fair days, grooming them to the required smartness. Sometimes I longed to be a boy so that Shanvally's ponies would one day be mine, instead of handed over to some hardly heard of cousin from Boston who had always felt a pavement beneath his feet.

'I shall bring her safely back to you within the half-hour,' Charles Trewin said decisively, placing a warm, dry palm on my elbow. And while my father gazed at him in a half-witted way, he led me to where the refreshment tent was pegged clumsily to the spongy ground of a hummocky field. An odd assortment of tables had been set up to wobble in this enclosure. Every household in Clifden must have contributed some of its parlour furniture. The tables were covered with bolts of the local tweed, some the dull gold of dried seaweed and some a bright gorse yellow. Benches from the assembly hall of St Benedicta's convent school surrounded the tables. Charles Trewin motioned me towards one that was in the furthermost corner of the tent and made his way to the trestle table where Binnie McMahon, her mother and aunt were serving lemonade and porter and, for those who knew to ask for it, poitin from Sean Gorham's still in Oughterard. The men standing around where the drink was, frowsty and fractious and already drunk, as much from the heat in the tent as from strong drink, stumbled back a few steps to make way for Malina's owner. Charles Trewin raised his hat to the MacMahon women, ordered a glass of lemonade and one of porter, and walked briskly over the uneven ground to where I sat. He set both glasses down on the glaring, yellow tweed before turning the glint of his amber eyes on me. He said, 'Malina's a lonely place, you know.'

But it was not his own loneliness he was referring to that day, nor that of his wife, although I would learn about that soon enough. That day, in the refreshment tent, it was the too-solitary existence of Harriet's plump, low-bellied pony, Pepper, that concerned him. Under-exercised, except for the short trip to Horam's Cove on fine days, the animal had become both lazy and nervy, snickering nastily at Harriet and the groom, sometimes refusing all food, sometimes clearing the dry stone wall in a clumsy jump to raid the apple orchard next to his paddock. Charles Trewin described these antics sadly, his pale brown eyebrows knitted with worry. 'I have heard, Rose Erris,' he said, 'that you have a way with animals, that you speak into their ears and they listen to you. I wonder whether you would be kind enough to come to Malina one of these days and try to calm this wicked animal. Its behaviour is beginning to alarm my wife.'

I remained silent. I knew that Mr Trewin had no right to be asking me what he had without consulting my father first. I knew this and was troubled by it. Yet my heart sang. This powerful Englishman was treating me as though I were grown up. We sat at the tweed-covered table, sipping our drinks in their smeary glasses, discussing matters of importance just like the boozy pony-breeders and dealers who also sat at tables drinking, though rather more avidly than Mr Trewin and I did. Understanding the reason for my silence, Charles Trewin said, 'Of course, I shall raise the matter with your father directly. But it is you who will be involved. I wanted to mention it to you first.'

He smiled. His teeth were small, square and crowded, and a yellowy-white. It was a smile of complicity; even at the age of twelve I understood that, although I did not yet have the word for it. It was the first of many such smiles, for, over the years, Charles Trewin was to turn me into his accomplice as expertly as he had extracted an egg from my ear the morning we first met. How cleverly he began our relationship by giving me what every child wants: a piece of information that its parents do not yet know about. I felt almost giddy with power and responsibility as I took a long sip of my tepid drink. As I did so I was aware of a commotion at one of the other tables in the centre of the tent. 'I'll bet any man of ye ten pounds, ten pounds, I say, if you can but lift the bottle in your two thumbs.' It was Flurry Joyce, the fisherman from Inishnee. He was a good fisherman but a desperate drinker, and earlier that summer his sleek black-hulled hooker with the rust sails had been taken away from him by the bank since he had drunk away the amount of his overdraft once too often. Now he was holding between his two huge thumbs, whose nails were thickly ridged and blackened at the tip, a small glass beer bottle. 'Any man of ye, any man of ye,' he repeated, and there was a threatening note in his beer-roughened voice. It was a surprisingly difficult feat. At least twenty men tried to lift the bottle and none succeeded. And these men were strong, used to lifting reeking baskets of turf, hauling in nets, heaving boulders out of a field. Flurry caught sight of Charles Trewin. 'And will the English gentleman have a try?', he said wheedlingly. He took the beer bottle off the table and put it in front of Charles Trewin. Everyone must have known that the landowner was a major shareholder in the bank that had sent out bailiffs to remove Flurry's hooker from

Roundstone harbour, otherwise why would the tent have become so silent of a sudden?

People glanced furtively at Charles Trewin's hands. They were broad across the palm with short fingers, not so unlike a lion's paw after all, and his fingernails were not ridged or scored with dirt and hard work but satiny and clean. Charles Trewin removed the gold signet ring from his little finger, massaged his thumbs thoughtfully one against the other and motioned to Flurry to set the bottle in front of him. The bottle seemed to stick to the cushions of his thumbs like a calf to its mother's dug. It rose inches off the table and Charles pointed it at Flurry as though it were a pistol before letting it drop on the grass where it rolled away under a table. 'Give the ten pounds to the Society of St Vincent de Paul,' Charles said airily to Flurry. 'Come, Rose Erris, your father will be getting anxious.'

I followed him out of the tent. 'How is it that you are so strong?' I asked. The amber eyes glimmered down at me. 'I went to an English public school, Rose Erris, where I endured a life of hardship unknown to the poorest, hungriest tinker who ever spent a night huddled on an Irish mountainside. Such a life makes you strong, or else it makes you dead.'

My mother and father, along with the other breeders, were enticing the ponies back into trailers ready for the journey home. So much praise and petting had made the ponies wilful. They whined like spoilt children, refusing to mount the ramp to the trailer. I left Charles Trewin and ran towards them, giving my special low whistle. When I was at their side, I enticed each one into its straw-floored prison by using my own little coaxing tricks. I blew softly into Gormley's ear, stroked the underside of Crystal's sweat-soaked neck, traced gentle circles around Slane's snorting nostrils. By the time I had fastened the tailgate my mother and father were deep in conversation with Charles Trewin. My father looked shifty and uncomfortable, my mother's lips were sucked into a line as thin as a pin. When I came up to them, Mr Trewin was the only one to give me a smile of welcome.

My mother took me by the shoulder, quite roughly, and said that she would be taking me home at once, leaving my father to round up my sisters and the various men who had promised to help him bring the trailers back to Shanvally. This round-up of over-excited daughters and tipsy men was a devilish job, for the girls were reluctant to leave the town and the men reluctant to leave the refreshment tent. My mother had always stayed behind to order everyone into action, with promises of tea and boxty and rashers, once the ponies were safely stalled at Shanvally. But now she almost pushed me into the cart, snapping the reins to make the horse break into a trot so that we bumped and jolted painfully along the pot-holed road that winds between the mountains and the sea.

We were more than halfway home before she let the reins slacken and I dared to ask her what I most wanted to know. 'Am I to go to Malina?'

Her voice sounded hoarse, whether from fear or anger I could not tell. 'It seems that you are,' she said, 'and may God protect us all.' She half-turned her face away from me, a sign that I was to ask no further questions. She hunched her shoulders to shield her face further and the hand that held the reins was trembling. I thought she must be crying.

It was not until five years later, on the eve of my marriage to Charles Trewin, that she told me what had taken place that day at the pony show. She told me in a last effort to make me change my mind but by that time I was too far gone in love to listen and too determined to have my own way to heed anything said against the man I was marrying.

3

'It will be herself who'll be bringing you down,' Binnie McMahon said. She was drinking tea with my mother in the warm kitchen, one of the cats nestled in her wide lap, purring at its comfort. When I had come into the room the same look had skittered over the faces of both the women, a look that combined grief and reproach. It made me feel that I had done something wrong, although I did not know what it was.

In the week that had gone by since the Clifden pony show, my parents had settled into their everyday selves again; my mother's mouth soft and rosy as she washed the new-laid eggs at the pump in the yard, my father's face no longer haunted and moronic, as it had been when Charles Trewin spoke to him, but smiling and slightly sly, the slyness of a man who sold horses for a living.

How soothing the rhythms of a working life are. I know that, now that they are denied me and I may no longer throw grain to the chickens or dig up the pearly onions and plait their stalks into garlands, my fingers nimble as spiders, the repetitive actions stroking my soul into a state of peace.

I had spent that week half-hoping to be summoned to Malina, half-dreading that I would be. Now it seemed that Charles Trewin's plan had not flittered away on the summer wind. The school holidays had begun and on Monday, two days away, Harriet, Binnie told us sourly, would collect me in the governess cart driven by the mutinous Pepper. Later Roddy McMahon, Binnie's younger brother, who kept up the garden at Malina, would bring me home in his trap.

That Sunday evening my mother yanked my scruffy boots off my feet, pulled open the dresser drawer with a force that made the cutlery inside rattle, took out a rusty knife and prised out the mud that had dried in a flaky line between the soles and the uppers. She blacked and buffed them until they shone like black beads and the powerful smell of blacking overlaid their familiar, comforting odour of dung and dried grass.

On Monday morning, the boots twinkled on my feet, my dress was newly ironed and my curly hair had been brushed until it sparkled and then tamed into a plait that I could feel already beginning to loosen. The morning was misty and I heard the sharp clang of Pepper's hooves in the lane-way and the grumbling trundle of wheels long before I could see the governess cart at the end of the borheen. The air was tender and moist, blurring the colours of earth and sky so that both seemed pearly and vaguely melted. But Harriet was dressed as though for a torrent, crushed inside a long waterproof coat, her lovely hair hidden in an ugly black hat that lay splat on her head like a toadstool.

Our conversation on the way back to Malina had a thin, tinny sound. We both knew that this situation was not of our making; I think, young as I was then, I sensed a certain powerlessness in her and was embarrassed by it. She talked of her great admiration for Miss Gwynn, an admiration I certainly didn't share. The schoolteacher was a tiresome gaoler, whose chin was outlined in fine white hairs like a dandelion clock and whose elbows were grey and scaly beneath the cuffs of her dress. Harriet's prattle sounded strained and tinkly and I was relieved when we reached the paddock at the back of the Big House and I could busy myself unharnessing the pony. The grass in the paddock was rich and sweet, bound to make Pepper greedy and out of sorts. 'He'd be better off left on the mountain a while,' I told Harriet. 'Connemara ponies are meant for a rough life. Too much coddling makes them cranky.' I took the long rope I had brought out of the governess cart and fastened it to the pony's bridle. Soon I had him prancing obediently, stopping when I flicked the rope, never stooping his neck towards the dewed grass until, the training exercise over, I stroked him gently just under his eyes, a sign that he could.

While I was disciplining her pony, Harriet sat miserably in her unnecessary mackintosh on the fallen trunk of an oak tree. There was an exaggerated fastidiousness in the way she sat that made me want to shake her. The mist had cleared and the sky was a thin, brittle blue, so fine that a bird's wing might make a crack in it. The sun shone on Malina's slate roof and its tiles glowed sleek as sealskin. The mountains were a magic ring, peaked with violet, sloped in gold. Yet Harriet seemed blind to their beauty. Her eyes were fixed on a pancake of dung, jewel-encrusted with a buzzing army of bluebottles. She swatted feebly at a fuzzy swarm of midges, wrinkled her nose at the rank smell of nettles. Midges love English-born ladies. Their rich diet makes them luscious to bite. Fergus Keane does a roaring trade in summer, charming the English visitors into buying some sticky cure of his own making that smells to high heaven of sour milk and ammonia. It doesn't work. When the ladies return to his shop, nipped and blotchy, he shrugs apologetically and urges them to buy calamine to soothe the angry red dots on their arms and foreheads.

'Will we drive around the lake to see if Pepper is any better behaved?' I asked Harriet. She glanced suspiciously at the sky, convinced herself that the day would be dry after all, and put her hat and mackintosh into the governess cart. She took the reins and Pepper ambled neatly along the road that ringed the lake, turning his head now and then to check that I was there. I raised my chin at him, a warning that he was not to veer towards the rhododendron bushes to rub his flanks against the branches. In the hazy sunshine, Harriet shone like a buttercup. Even her long chin was brushed with gold, slanting up from the frill at the neck of her yellow muslin dress. I looked at her with awe. Love for this handsome, gilded woman had caused a man to build a shimmering grey house. Today, its magnificence was printed jumpily on the lively water of the lake, grey walls turned to liquid silk, great wooden door shape-shifting as it slid on the sunlit surface. But for Harriet, there would be woodland where Malina now stood. Her burnished hair and narrow waist had been the cause of a massive clearance, making plover and linnet rise from their nests in panic, and beetles and woodlice scuttle confusedly about the ransacked earth around uprooted oak and holly. To have a house built for you. Did Harriet realize how astonishing that was? No other woman I knew had had so much as a mud cabin put up for her as a symbol of love. The custom was that a man waited for his last surviving parent to die before he could marry and claim ownership of the house and smallholding he had tended all his life. 'Understandings', pledged when a lad and his girl were young and hale, dragged on for long, unconsummated years, while the girl lost her ripeness and the boy's hopes became wan, and an old mammy lived on, kept alive by spite, snug in her chair by the fire, smug with power, insisting that she would never have another woman in the house until the good Lord closed her eyes for eternity. When she died, love had often died too. A sourness had festered which a late marriage and home ownership could not heal. A wife looked at her husband, lording it on the half-acre that was now his by right, and her eyes were fogged with disappointment.

As we rounded the lake, the governess cart fairly gliding along the road as Pepper proved how silkily he could amble, Harriet looked towards Malina, and I saw in her eyes that same look of disappointment. Although the sunlight sparkled on her long, blond lashes, the eyes beneath them were deadened, as though something had killed off her soul. Never had I seen such bleakness on a face, not even on the face of Nan Lavery, who had waited thirty years for Bertie Corrigan's mother to die. She lived, twisted with arthritis but with a mind that was spry and spiteful, until she was ninety-six and Nan too old to have children. Nan moved into Bertie's farmhouse, which smelt of cabbage and old age, and lashed him with such bitterness that he turned to drink and let the farm at Ballinafad fall into neglect. His cows were scabby and wandered the roadside, his ewes died giving birth for want of attendance, and now the holding had been repossessed and he and Nan would have to emigrate.

Hanging from a fine, gold chain threaded with seed pearls was Harriet's fob-watch, its face thudding gently between her breasts, keeping time with the steady motion of the governess cart. Harriet caught the watch in her palm, squinted at the Roman numerals and then at the sun-flecked walls of Malina. 'Time to go,' she said. There was hopelessness in her voice. The sun vanished and it began to rain, hard, vicious drops, as if her voice had willed the weather to match her mood. The rain banged on the lake so hard that it raised circles where the drops fell. I reached behind me for Harriet's mackintosh and arranged it, tent-like, over our heads and shoulders. I took the reins from her, clacked my tongue, and Pepper, his flanks streaky with wet, quickened his trot towards the house.

Horty O'Goole, the groom, was waiting with Binnie McMahon in the shelter of the arched porch. I drew in the reins and Pepper stopped obediently, sliding his hoofs under the glistening gravel of the drive. Horty handed down Harriet with mocking ceremony and, as she went into the house, punched me lightly on the shoulder and gave me a fat-lidded wink before he led the pony away. Horty had neither the time nor the inclination to look after Pepper. Charles's three carriage horses were what he doted on, Charles's navy and gold phaeton his pride. Every day he groomed and exercised the animals, then took a stiff brush to the carriage's interior, a nest of buttoned, plum-coloured plush. And every night he stabled the carriage in the gloom of the stone coachhouse and, later, when the lights in the great house were dimmed, he led his sweetheart, Agnes MacReion, into the dark, soft depths of the stabled carriage, safe and secret within stone walls that muffled sounds and admitted no light however bright the moon, its dense blackness something that I would discover, horribly, in years to come. Horty was a farm boy, short and stocky with fat, graceless thighs. He never looked comfortable in his uniform of dark blue gabardine frock coat and cream leggings; his barrel chest strained against the stiff, unyielding fabric as though imprisoned by it. But Agnes thought him gorgeous and made him wear his livery to Mass, rather than the old black suit his father had handed down to him. Sometimes, she would finger the cloth of his sleeve or brush a fleck from his tailored shoulder, smirking at her envious girl-friends as she did so. I did not like Agnes McReion then and do not now, but now I have good reason to dislike her.

Binnie put her roughened hand on my back; its heat felt vigorous through my thin dress as she led me down the backstairs to the kitchen. 'I'm to be doing something light for herself only,' Binnie said. 'Himself is off to Carna getting Seanie Boyle to make him a rowboat. Driving Seanie to distraction, too, I shouldn't wonder. Himself is a divil for inventions. Doubtless, he'll have thought up a pair of oars that smash through the water as fast as thunder and will be pestering Seanie to fashion them for him. I've made a fish mould for her, dainty as a moonbeam, it would slip down your throat before you'd had a taste of it. But from the look of her, she won't be touching it. I'd be saving myself time and trouble if I gave it to the cat this same minute, rather than waiting until she's pushed it all over her plate. I'll be making us a cup of tea, so.'

She began to clatter at the stove. The kitchen was enormous, big enough to hold a dance on its flagstoned floor. Hocks of gammon hung lumpily from hooks on the wooden ceiling. Copper dishes in odd shapes – a scaled fish, a turreted castle, a rabbit – were set in tidy rows on white-painted shelves. I had no idea what they were for. Later I would become familiar with words like terrine, pâté and mousse, shaped in these strange dishes and then carefully turned out for a late supper at a ball at which I would be the hostess.

'What makes Mrs Trewin look so unhappy?' I asked Binnie, as we sat at the handsome scrubbed table, blowing on our tea.

She set down her cup with a thump that made the tea slurp over the sides.

'It's himself, entirely. Doesn't he torment her night and day, poor soul that she is. Would I be telling you this, Rose Erris, you being but a child, but that I can see you are part of a plan to vex her further. The divil himself knows why, for I surely don't. The weeping he draws out of her would fill the lake to flooding.'

Binnie was no admirer of men; I had known that since I was very small, a little girl teasing the kittens in front of the kitchen fire, while Binnie tittle-tattled a long list of complaints against various men in the vicinity, while my mother, drying dishes at the sink, shook her head in sorrow and wonderment.

'Take John-Jo now,' Binnie would say, launching morosely into her narrative. 'There's a fortune coming to him from his uncle in Californy and wouldn't you think he'd be shamed to see his wife's Sunday dress all in flitters? Not him, though. Sure he wouldn't notice if the darling woman came to Mass mother-naked. That's men for you. Such mean creatures they'd begrudge you the spit to lick an envelope.'

Seething with rage against the entire male sex, Binnie had never had an 'understanding'. Doing a line with a man was, to her way of thinking, the first step on the road to misery. First they had you slaving away for them, then bearing and raising their children until you were 'wasted away entirely'. And then, while you lay in agony on your deathbed, they'd be guzzling porter in some shebeen, spending money that they should have been saving to give you a decent funeral and wake. 'Get married, is it?' Binnie would say grimly. 'Not for a sack of gold, and that's a fact. I'm telling you now, Nora, there's worse things than being in your own bed of a night.' My mother would blush furiously then and bend her dark face towards the plate she was drying.

The single life suited Binnie well. At an age, somewhere in the mid-thirties, when girls she had been at school with were scraggy and bedraggled by the harshness of conjugality, Binnie was plump and rosy still, lapping up the privacy of her little attic bedroom at Malina, which she promised to show me as soon as we had drunk our tea, so that I might admire the brass bedstead, the pitcher with blue roses on it, and the view right across the lake, over the village, as far as Deer Island, where the cormorants roost. But first there was a question I needed to ask. 'What does Mr Trewin *do*?', I insisted. 'Does he *hurt* her?'

Binnie spread her weight more easily in the chair, scratched at her round arm while considering whether to tell me the cause of Harriet's misery. 'It's he who has you brought to Malina, Rose Erris, so you have a right to know, child or not. I'll tell you so I will, so sit quietly like the good girl you are.' A dreamy look came into Binnie's cow-brown eyes. 'I was here when he brought her to Malina,' she said. 'He carried her over the threshold as though there was no weight in her at all and straight up the staircase, although all the servants were waiting in the hall to greet the new mistress. The shame and arrogance of the man, you'd think he was raised in a sewer, although I've heard that he comes from decent people, over the water.

'The house wasn't finished then, of course. It's said he was waiting for the dowry money to pay all the plasterers and the masons. It's a queer thing to think that it's herself who's paid for the building of her own prison, for that's what Malina is. Those great windows now, for the Missus they could as well be iron bars. She got carried away by love, as surely as she got carried up them stairs. Her family's from Devon, I do believe, and they say the climate is very mild there, very mild, and the grass grows over the gentle slopes like the softest carpet. And all a lady in those parts is expected to do is a small, little bit of embroidery and tinkle out a little tune on the piano of an evening.

'Well, he brought her here and I'm not denying that she was the sun, moon and stars to him, but he wanted her out and about all the same. There were bad times here then, Rose Erris. The famine was over but evictions were still going on. Though I'll say this for Mr Trewin, he never evicted a soul. The rents he gets here would hardly pay for the buttons on Horty O'Goole's uniform. It was Mr Trewin's da made the money. He invested in some stuff they pour over the roads in England so that they're smooth as silk. Macadam, I think it's called, although that sounds like some kind of little almond biscuit that we serve with the ices when there's a big supper party. Anyway, that's where Mr Trewin gets his money, although it would seem the old da didn't leave him enough to finish Malina. The old da loved the Missus as though she were one of his own. He died just before her wedding, heartbroken, it seems, because his son was determined to bring her over here – "that benighted bogland" is what the old man called it. We never saw sight nor shade of *him* while he lived. 'Tis a pity he didn't come over with a pail of his old macadam. A body could drown in the pot-holes on this road of a winter.

'When Mr and Mrs Trewin came here to settle, he had it in mind that, once the house was built, they would both make their mark one way or another. Some say he even saw himself as the Viceroy one of these days, with Phoenix Park for his garden in its entirety. The idea of it! He's no princely gentleman like a Lord-Lieutenant should be, and always has been, and that's no word of a lie. There's telling that he was in the Indian Army when he was young, and there was a baby he fathered on one of his house servants, hardly more than a child herself. But then he bought himself out and came back to England and met the Missus, and that's when all her troubles began.'

Binnie swilled some of the tepid tea around her mouth for her lips were dry with so much talking. She seemed to have forgotten that I was there, speaking her words into the air, looking straight ahead of her without ever catching my eye. And I stayed quiet, afraid that if I spoke, asked a question, I would break the spell, and the extraordinary words would peter out and stop, like a mountain track that suddenly dives into a thicket of gorse and never re-emerges.

Binnie set down her cup again, more carefully this time, and sighed. 'Now the Missus wasn't up to scratch and that's the size of it. He would have wanted her to be something like the Duke of Marlborough's Duchess who set up the famine relief fund, may we never forget her. But the Missus isn't the dashy type. She was brought up to be quiet. She's in mortal terror of people; don't I hear her retching her stomach out of her before they're to go to a party somewheres. It's the wildness she can't be tolerating. The other ladies here, the likes of Lady Fitzhaven and Mrs O'Brien, it's not the small little drawings they'll be doing but the hunting they're mad for, lepping over the ditches with their hair scattering pins over the fields, and then dancing all night with the energy of the divil. The Missus now, she shrinks away from all that. She's frightened of horses, even though I've heard there's good hunting in Devon. Her people were very strict though; they thought hunting was for hoydens, not for gentlewomen like their daughter. Yet, I'm thinking there's little enough harm in the chase. I like to see the ladies after the hunt, with their cheeks whipped up to a colour by the wind and an appetite on them like a stableboy's.

'There's many a one of them would have married the Master, Indian baby or no Indian baby. He's a great head for business on him, not like some of the other gentlemen who've turned their rents into brandy casks and have them drunk while their houses are crumbling to bits around them. Himself thinks always of the improvements. He'll be bringing the railway as far as Ballynahinch one of these days, sending his salmon and his lamb back to England, where they'd go mad to have a taste of it. The food in England isn't fit to give a dying pig, they be telling me. The soot in the skies falls on to the fields and the rivers so everything tastes of it. You could be chewing on a piece of the finest beef and it would taste like ashes in your mouth.

'The Master met the Missus in Devon, where he'd been staying with some neighbours of hers. They brought your man down to the house one evening and she played on the piano and sang like an angel of the Lord. Not his parents, nor hers wanted the match, knowing the delicacy of her. The older folk thought the Master and his wild ways would be the end of her. She's as fragile as a rose in winter, the Missus is. Her skin is so sensitive on her, she has to wear her undergarments the inside out so that the seams don't chafe her. And sure, you'd hardly notice the seams if you held them in your hands, so soft and lacy they are and sent all the way from Paris on the steamer.

'As soon as he clapped eyes on her, he determined to bring her here and build Malina for the love of her. He's a hardy man; he hadn't a thought about what Connemara might do to her, with the rain hurling its wetness on her bedroom windows most mornings and the desperate sights you do be seeing still, even though the times are better. And our ways are not hers. When she'd hardly been here a month, he took her to Minnie Corrigan's wake to pay their respects and the keening nearly made her jump out of her skin, and when she saw the body sat up in its coffin, she looked more like death than the corpse. He got angry with her then and is angry with her still. She had been everything to him and then she was nothing, less than nothing. He is cruel to her in treacherous, teasing ways. He mocks her for her shyness, which worsens it, until she has reached the point where she can scarcely get a word out of her mouth when there's company. It's endured that she feels, she who was once loved like no woman had been loved. A pity for all women who bask in a man's love, for it can dry up as sudden as a puddle on a hot day.'

Binnie blinked and then stared at me hard. 'Mrs Trewin is the best woman who ever drew breath, Rose Erris. You have only to tell her that some poor soul is in want of thatch for her roof, and a stack of straw will be on the way before the words are out of your mouth. And there's many a bold girl caught in shame, whose parents would have put her in a convent and had the baby taken away from her if the Missus hadn't slipped the young man money enough to marry her, and these are people that she's never clapped eyes on, nor they on her. She is loved right enough by everyone except the one whose love would be life to her.'

What queer words these were, coming from Binnie, whose sturdy contempt of romantic love had been part of my childhood. I understood little of what she was saying, understanding would come later, and at a price, but I sensed that, in some way, a responsibility had come to me, that I must in no way aid Charles Trewin in tormenting his wife. As if reading my thoughts, Binnie said, 'Now don't you go making a show of yourself, Rose Erris, while you're in this house. You'll only be making matters worse.'

She got up to take our cups to the stone sink to be washed, and as she did so we heard, loud and startling, the angry thump of footsteps on the backstairs that led to the kitchen.

4

Did I claim to be without guile? Where little girls are concerned, this is a lie. We are born with the knowledge that we can empower and enslave men and then we put that knowledge to use. In my own house, my father never stood a chance against his daughters' wheedling. 'Ah, Da, Da, you will so, say you will, Da, darling,' the older girls, Anne and Betty and Vera, would croon expertly, when they wanted his permission to go to the dance at the crossroads at Maam Cross. They would bring him his tea and then blow solicitously on the steaming cup to cool it, they would rub their shining cheeks against his stubbly one, as he sat by the fire in the ancient armchair whose springs went blong, blong, blong as he shifted in it in pleased embarrassment to be attended to by his lovely girls with their shining eyes and lips parted theatrically in a show of anxiety. He could no more say no to them than he would have been able to take a favourite pony to the slaughterhouse. Meanwhile, my mother scoured pans grimly in the pantry and shouted over her shoulder to her noisy daughters that if she heard the smallest word about bold behaviour she would send them all off to the nuns. At which my father would give her a startled look, for it was the custom of the country then to whisk girls who were 'in trouble' into a convent, but my sisters would just nudge each other and giggle into their handkerchiefs.

Even two-year-old Geraldine had my father wound around her fat little finger. The very devil of a child, she would be sent to bed in the middle of the day for throwing Deirdre's new shoes into the fire, or for having taken one tiny bite out of every single apple that was laid out on the floor on the unused parlour as store for the winter, or for having fed our best missal to her pet goat, a page at a time. My father would hear her yelling, fit to flake the plaster off the wall, from as far as the hummocky field where he had been raking the hay. He would come rushing into the house, admonish my mother, who was trying to restore the singed shoes by rubbing them with dripping, with, 'Sure now, Nora, she's only a child, she knows no better,' and run up to Geraldine's locked bedroom. Geraldine, who, I felt sure, had been rehearsing for this moment for some time, would be standing up in her cot, dark ringlets lying damply on her flushed cheek, lashes spiky with tears, and her dimpled arms outstretched as she beamed yearningly and gurgled, 'Da, Da, Da.'

So, by the time I came to Malina that day, I knew how easily men could be charmed; what I did not know were the consequences that could result from charming them.

When Charles Trewin opened the kitchen door, he seemed to be gently steaming. Freshly bathed, his damp hair had darkened to the colour of treacle and lay flatly on his scalp. Without his streaming mane, he looked stripped of power, vulnerable and subdued. But when he addressed Binnie, there was anger in his voice, thick as smoke. He held out to her a reeking bundle of clothes: a pair of boots ribboned with strands of livid green seaweed, a tar-stained jersey, muddy cotton trousers.

'Dispose of these,' he ordered Binnie, whose face had suddenly lost its curves and mouldings and was as cold and smooth as a stone.

'The boat overturned near the quay. Such debris, such filth, I could scarcely credit it. And children swimming among the dead fish and sewage. There being so many of them, no doubt their parents don't mind losing a few to typhoid fever.'

Her eyes murderous, Binnie took the clothes. If she were to put them to the wash in the great copper that I had noticed in the scullery off the kitchen and were then to spread them on the fuchsia bushes to dry in the sun, they would lose their fishy smell and be decent enough working clothes for her younger brother, Roddy. But I knew that she would throw them away, even the boots. I thought she might even burn them.

'Hupla, hupla, hupla, hup,' said Charles Trewin. He had gone down on one knee, the other leg bent to make a platform of his thigh, which he slapped. I had never been to a circus but I had seen pictures of acrobats and knew exactly what to do. On tiptoes, my back arched like a dancer's, I ran towards him, jumped lightly on to his thigh, raised one leg behind me and flung my arms out sideways for balance. As I concentrated fiercely on not wobbling, I could hear Binnie open the yard door and throw out the clothes she held, heard the thump of the boots as they hit the cobbles and, inside my head, heard Binnie's voice of a few moments ago, warning me not to make a show of myself, a warning I had ignored. 'Whoopla, whoopla, whey-ya,' shouted Charles Trewin. He put his hands around my waist, I was a light-boned child and it was their exact span, and set me down on the ground.

'Time for you to see Malina, I think,' Charles said, and then to Binnie, who was leaning against the yard door, her arms folded and her breathing heavy. 'My wife is resting. Please see that she is not disturbed.'

What I remember most from that first time was the bleached paleness of white marble, washed silk carpets, curtains of a watery colourlessness looped and swagged and falling in cascades on to the shining beechwood floors. Even the pictures on the walls had a faded, lifeless quality within their great scrolled, gilt frames. Ladies with white, domed foreheads and tiny mouths rested their hands limply in their laps as though too tired to lift them; landscapes showed crumbling ruins poking broken towers towards stifling white clouds. Only the huge fire in the drawing-room breathed life and colour, its flames vital in the deadness of its marble surround. I ran towards it, glad for the familiar comfort of turf and sparks, and noticed the marble scroll set into the top of the manteltree, in which some letterwork, much looped and flourished, was carved. 'Antes muerto que mudado,' I read. The curlicued words swirled in a lively way on the stone although they made no sense to me.

'My family motto,' said Charles Trewin. 'Well, at least, I decided that it would be.' He slid off his signet ring and showed me the same words written around the inside of it. 'Sooner dead than changed, that's its meaning, Rose Erris. It's a Spanish notion but of universal application, I think. Your own country is the exception; if there is not change soon, death will be the winner. Now tell me, what is your opinion of my house?'

'It's grand,' I said. Then my child's honesty got the better of me. 'Only,' I muttered, bending low over the fire to hide my face, for I could not bear to meet the expectancy in those golden eyes, 'there's nothing there.' Startled, Malina's owner looked around the vast, high-ceilinged room. He saw a scattering of round footstools covered in faded embroideries and pale brocades, groupings of jade ornaments, pink and green, on tables inlaid with mother-of-pearl. He saw armchairs and sofas piled with cushions, breakfront cabinets with doors inset with pleated silk protected by brass latticework, bronze candlesticks from which crystal droplets shimmered; he saw the great Venetian chandelier, its ribbed glass branches holding rainbows of light, he saw great china jardiniéres, painted vases, five foot high, holding wild grasses, stiff arrangements of hydrangeas, pink, blue and pale lilac, splayed out on the deep windowsills.

'Nothing here? My dear child, if that is the case I have spent a fortune on a mirage. What do you mean?'

I meant that there was an absence of something that I could not name. The stillness of the big, beautiful room held life at bay, the care in its furnishings denied it substance. Your eyes could feast off its prettiness but your other senses were robbed. There was nothing to touch, hear or smell. I thought of my own home where the smell of turf clung to the shabby furniture, where the clock ticked and kittens purred and dogs yapped and where you could close your eyes and be comforted by the sound of the lid rattling on a pan as it boiled, or the squeak of Deirdre's chalk on her slate as she sat at the table trying to learn her tables, the soft clanking of the spinning wheel. Sometimes the noise was too much for my mother, who suffered from searing headaches. 'My head's in a vice,' she would shout into the household din. 'I'm off for a walk to escape this hullabaloo.'

'Hullabaloo,' I said to Charles Trewin. 'There's no hullabaloo.' His eyes flickered over the room again. 'No more there is,' he said. 'You have put your finger on it, wise child that you are. Hullabaloo is what's needed here, and I mean to have it.'

He crouched down beside me, as he had done the first time we met. 'Rose Erris, I seem to be always asking you favours and now I am about to ask you another. I have not the slightest idea as to how hullabaloo may be created. I must rely on your help. And now I shall attend to my poor wife. Harriet, I fear, is not in a mood for hullabaloo. I think you will find that young Roddy has the trap ready in the stable yard, so off you go. I will send word to your parents soon as to when I may borrow you to breathe some life into my cold house. Now, were you to look in the pocket of your dress you might find something to your advantage.'

I put my hand in my pocket and drew out six sugared almonds, coated in dazzling pink. 'Astonishing,' sa‸

Charles Trewin. 'A reward from the little people, I've no doubt.' He took me round the back of the house by a route that avoided the kitchen stairs and watched me as I skipped towards the waiting Roddy. Then he went back inside. I shared the sugared almonds with Roddy before I fell asleep, leaning against his shoulder, the coarse cotton of his smock cool against my cheek and smelling of bacon grease and horses and stale porter, the comforting smells of my childhood that Charles Trewin would soon teach me to despise.

'Mr Trewin has taken your girleen well in hand,' people said to my mother as we shopped in the village or mixed with the crowd on fair days. There was mockery in their voices and my mother's neck flushed, the skin rough and mottled as she turned her face away in the way she had. My visits to Malina had begun to be very frequent by then. Harriet no longer came for me in the governess cart for now I had a pony of my own, Murrough, a young mare that my father had been planning to sell in Clifden until Charles Trewin paid him his full asking price there in our own back meadow. It is a tradition that after a deal has been made, the seller must give the buyer a proportion of the price he has just paid; 'luck money' it is called and, by tradition also, the sum should be generous so that good luck will attend all those who are party to the purchase. But when Charles Trewin handed over a bag of sovereigns, my father did not open it and hand one of them back, but felt in his pocket for the few coins that were there and thrust them into Charles Trewin's hand in a surly way. Murrough was my favourite of all the ponies, a beautiful pinky-beige in colour like the inside of a shell, docile and loving. I was glad that she would be going to Malina rather than sold to a stranger in Clifden, but I still wept to see her go. I was snivelling as I handed her lead rein to Charles Trewin but, instead of taking it, he wound the rein around my wrist and said that Murrough was mine, the only stipulation being that I rode her to Malina whenever I could. My father began to make stupid little mutterings of protest but Charles Trewin gave him a challenging look and he was silenced.

I had great times at Malina. Charles Trewin let me choose a dog for the Big House; up till then there were only the gun dogs, kept in the outside kennels, and, at a breeder in Oughterard, I picked out a coppery spaniel with a tail so feathery that I called her Plume. Jumps were set up in the paddock and I learnt to clear them, first on Murrough and then on a disdainful thoroughbred that Charles Trewin brought over from England.

I learnt other things too, to say 'you' rather than 'ye', 'anyway' and not 'anyways'.

'As long as you are using the Queen's English, you may as well use it correctly,' Charles Trewin told me, smiling. 'There's talk that you people wish to revert to your native language, although I don't know how you will cope with words like journal or waltz or telegraph if you do. A real test of Irish ingenuity, I should have thought.'

And what of Harriet all this time? As the house grew noisier with Plume's barking and my chattering, she grew quieter, keeping to the veranda room on the first floor, where she made her finicky shell pictures, her only outings being to Horam's Cove on fine days. Occasionally, Binnie would be waiting for me outside the stable block as I arrived at the house, riding Murrough. As I dismounted she would grab me, quite painfully, by the shoulder. 'I'll not have you skeetering through the house with that dog today, or it's murdered you'll be, do you hear me?' she hissed. 'It's a divil of a time I'm having with the mistress, the poor troubled soul that she is, and your shouting and hollering goes through her like a knife. If it's himself who wants to get up to some lunacy, you tell him you'd rather be sitting in the library room looking at his fine books. He'll do whatever you say and well you know it, you little jade.'

In years to come I would ask myself why Charles Trewin devoted so much time to me. In the days when I went to Malina whenever I could, to ride through the woods with him or play raucous games of hide-and-seek all over the house or to row on the lake, he never touched me, not until it was right and proper for him to do so. But it seems to me now that almost from the day we met, a young girl and a man already entering middle age, he had marked me out for the future mistress of Malina. My youth and Harriet's existence were the obstacles that stood in his way. Nature would see that I would grow older and his own behaviour would ensure Harriet's destruction, a destruction that I, unwittingly (but is anything really done unwittingly?) helped to bring about.

5

Long shot. A gambling term as well as a racing one, and my husband is both a racing man and a gambler of sorts, people's lives being the chips he plays with. Harriet did not suit him, that much is clear. Perhaps her fragility indicated to him that she was not a long-living woman and that a replacement would eventually be needed. And then again he had in his mind a vision of the illustrious life he wished to lead, a public life, prestigious and showy. Did he have something else in mind too, a glitteringly conspicuous consort who would help him in his aspiration to be one of the architects who would drag Ireland into the new century that would soon be upon us?

My husband is a shaper of houses, railways and people. A woman already moulded would be of little use to him. But a child now, whom he could design to his purpose, snip and cut and pattern as she grew up, so that, by the time she reached womanhood, she was his creature entirely. A long shot indeed, but as gambles go, a challenging one. As other men examine the spindly fetlocks of a foal and see, inside their heads, a three-year-old thundering past the winning post, so must Charles Trewin have looked at me, a twelve-year-old girl showing signs of future beauty, bold, vital and sharp-witted, and imagined me a few years hence, mistress of Malina, full of energetic, enchanting gossip, a fearless huntswoman, an ensnarer of powerful allies. For the sake of this strange gamble, poor, fastidious Harriet had to put up with my unruly presence in her cold, magnificent house.

Not long after Charles's purchase of Murrough, Harriet's sister, Miss Florence Wingrave from Plympton, in Devon, came to Malina for a visit. She was tall like Harriet and almost as slender but had none of her younger sister's pale, gilded gentleness. Florence was all swishing skirts and querulous demands, mainly for heat and sunshine, orders which Malina and its demesne could not always meet.

By that time, I was back in Binnie McMahon's good graces. The reason why she no longer called me, jeeringly, 'yer brazen strap' was not because she had begun to approve of my behaviour but because she needed my help. Binnie was increasingly wracked by arthritis, her fingers bent painfully into claws, her wide feet turned inwards, her face looking flayed and yellow with pain. And, fearful of losing her attic room, she wanted her condition kept secret, although, most nights now, she could not heave her crooked body up the back stairs and slept in a straw-mattressed box-bed at the back of the kitchen. She bullied the other maids as she always had done – it was rumoured that Binnie had 'droic h'uil', the bad eye, and that it would be unwise to cross her, but the other maids were drifty, flittery girls and at times when Florence would be demanding jugfuls of hot water, they could be relied upon to be out of earshot, sitting in the hayloft mending their stockings or dozing in the linen press, comfy as kittens on the warm, folded sheets.

So it was me who Binnie called to feed the kitchen range with kindling to heat the great copper pans filled with spring water, which I would then carry up to the little room where Florence made her toilette. 'That one will wash herself away entirely, one of these days,' said Binnie darkly, 'and it's few would be sorry.' Her loyalty was to Harriet. In the kitchen that was limp and hazy with steam from the heating pans, she told me as much, told me how she feared Charles Trewin's discovery of her useless hands, lest he should put her out. 'And then what would become of my poor lady?' Binnie mourned, 'she, whose own kin has turned against her?'

It was Florence she meant. Binnie had no word of good to say of her, since the time, soon after her arrival, when Florence, who had planned a picnic by the lake, had spent a thundery afternoon glaring out of the streaky windows and had been heard to ask Harriet angrily why she put up with this land of micks and mackerel snappers. Florence shared her sister's nervosity but in her it took the shape of petulance and restlessness. The day she was to leave Malina, a day nobody in the household seemed to regret, her trunks were already strapped into the small sidecar which was to take them to Oughterard when, carrying a final jug of hot water up the stairs to Florence's dressing-room, I heard the voices of both sisters, Harriet's thin and edgy, Florence's loud and exasperated, from the guest bedroom which Florence was preparing to leave.

'If it's as bad as you say, Hattie, why for heaven'

sake don't you leave with me this very minute?'

'I would merely be taking my failure to another place.'

'Oh, Hattie, how you do *droop* so. No wonder that squireen of yours is frightened to let you have children.'

Crouched on the broad wooden stair, carpeted lushly with a deep crimson runner held in place with golden rods, my hands shook so that I spilled some of the hot water on my wrist, painfully.

Florence continued. 'It's hard to believe you were such an accomplished girl, *such* a sweet singing voice, *such* a talented artist. Although, I admit such gifts are wasted on this assembly of huntsmen and horse-copers that your husband forces on you. They even boast about their Irishness, though their forefathers came over with Cromwell and they are the descendants of thieves and knaves. And the state of their houses makes me shudder. You will scarcely believe this, Hattie, but when we dined at Lord and Lady Offerlane's last week I heard a strange whining behind the library door and my curiosity led me to open it a crack. There were books on the shelves well enough, but I doubt if any have been lifted off them these thirty years. The room had been turned into a dog-kennel; the entire pack of Offaly's hounds were there, waiting for their dinner and chewing the Persian carpet to bits the meanwhile. And during dinner, Offaly talked of nothing but his new hunters, while water dripped from the ceiling down the back of my dress.'

Florence's carping English drawl went on at some ·ngth about the deficiencies of my country and its people, but I was no longer listening. The words, 'No wonder that squireen of yours is frightened to let you have children,' had lodged in my head and took up all the space.

I had heard differently from the squireen himself. His visits to Shanvally were quite frequent now. His interest in horses, racing fillies and bay colts, geldings and brood-mares, had increased and he flattered my father by asking his advice about studs and racing stables, although he must have known that my father knew little enough about thoroughbreds and that the races at Galway were the grandest enterprises in which he had taken part. While he talked, he never minded my little sisters, Eithne, Deirdre and Geraldine, climbing all over him, rootling in his pockets for barley-sugar, or perching on his beautiful hand-made shoes and jiggling up and down until he lifted and lowered his long legs to give them a ride. My mother seemed resigned to these visits, although her shoulders slumped when Charles Trewin came through the doorway, like a blaze in human form, his hair streaming back from his wide brow in a golden circlet, his eyes vivid as a furze bush in bloom. There was something about his very robustness that seemed to exhaust her and make her surly.

'It's a wonder you wouldn't be having children of your own, Mr Trewin, seeing it's how fond of them you are,' she had said to him one day, as he sat in our most comfortable chair with Geraldine on his shoulders, happily nibbling the marzipan off a little iced cake which he had brought her and neither of them minding the shower of crumbs that were lodgin in his hair.

He had looked at my mother unflinchingly. 'Alas, Mrs McCalla, my wife can't abide children. She has often said as much. She finds their presence disturbing.'

My mother had returned his gaze boldly. 'Then she is fit to be a saint for allowing Rose Erris the run of the house, for that girleen could disturb the stillness out of a rock.'

'My wife is in your debt for allowing Rose Erris to keep our horses so mannerly, as indeed am I.' He had reached behind him and lifted Geraldine from his shoulders, settled her on his knee and wiped the squishy, sugary mess from between her fingers with a purple silk handkerchief, the colour of the pendulous centre of a fuchsia, the flower known here as *deora dia,* tears of Christ.

Florence's voice had grown louder, more insistent. The water cooled in the copper pan and the pain in my wrist lessened as I remained crouched on the stair, the image of the purple handkerchief dimming in my mind as I listened to her. 'If you are to stay here, Hattie, you must make some kind of life of your own, else you will go mad, or die of boredom or both: I know I should.' Then silence for a while, then the sound of ugly, desperate little squeaks, which I took to be Harriet crying while struggling not to. Then Florence again, more gently this time, striving to comfort, although a less comforting presence than that harsh Englishwoman would be hard to imagine. 'I always said so. Charles is too turbulent for you, he's lusty, gaudy, not quite the thing. Still, he'd have more respect for you, my dear, you were to bestir yourself a bit.'

Another silence, although I thought I could hear the

nervous swishing of Florence's travelling skirt, as she walked up and down the room, hoping to trap some idea that would end Harriet's desolation. She had it. The swishing stopped. 'The child,' she said. 'Why don't you draw the child? She's such a pretty thing in that wild, messy way. There's something clever to be done about the way those tangled curls catch the light, like the bloom on black grapes.' She warmed to her theme. 'Imagine how it would look, a sketch: the child barefoot, on a rock, looking out to sea. You wouldn't have to draw the sea, it's too difficult for a woman artist. Perhaps one of those plaid shawls that you see around here, artfully draped, of course. And then a fine oval frame . . . *How* you would make us all so proud.'

Harriet started to make silly bleats of protest, to the effect that the McCalla girls were all decently shod and the father was as proud as an emperor, and, besides, Rose Erris could not be still for five minutes at a time, perched barefoot on a rock, or anywhere else. Her slightly frenzied voice made her sound like a parody of herself, the Harriet that my sister Deirdre mimicked so perfectly, a study in startled agitation.

I stood up, walked carefully to the room where the two sisters were, knocked lightly on the door and opened it before I had been bidden enter. I could tell by the way they slid their eyes downwards that they knew I had overheard them. Anger made me want to embarrass Harriet. So I played the wild, peasant child that would have shamed my parents. 'Yer wath ma'am,' I said, dropping a crude curtsy which m the water slurp in the pan and splatter on to Flore glossy boots.

Florence, I knew, itched to box my ears. Harriet's embarrassment had turned to rage, a rare state for her to be in. 'Stop that at once, Rose Erris,' she almost shrieked. I flicked my curls and turned to leave the room. Harriet called me back, calm now, as though she had taken several deep breaths.

'I was wondering, Rose Erris. I was thinking of taking up drawing again. Would you sit for me, or rather stand, for I should prefer to be outdoors?' She made a scrabbling, ineffectual attempt at intimacy. 'After all, you're growing up so fast. Your parents might like to have a lasting record of your girlhood before you grow as tall as I am.'

She was appealing to me to laugh at her frail joke but I refused to. I was furious with her for having let herself be deceived by Charles. Did she know that he told people that the fault for their childlessness lay with her? How merciless I was (am I still?) to wish to punish the victim of Charles's cruelty, rather than Charles himself, a wish that was to stay with me until Harriet's death. And after that? Why, I railed at her poor, defenceless ghost and took my revenge on it.

I remember Florence Wingrave's parting words as she paused on the step of the sidecar that was to take her to the mail-train. She ignored Horty's hand, courteously extended to help her into the conveyance, nd frowned ferociously at the brooding mountains. was a sullen, spiteful day; the clouds rested clum- on the mountain peaks, hiding them unevenly hat they looked crumbled and broken. Beneath slopes, the black boats on the lake were sad as . Florence gave Harriet the merest of pecks and, loud enough for me to hear as I adjusted the reins of the harnessed bay, hissed, 'Thank God, we have no Irish blood in our veins.'

I remember something else about that day. It was the first and only time that Harriet caressed me. It must have cost her some effort, for she shrank from physical contact, jerking her shoulder away from the nuzzling, velvety mouth of the newly affectionate Pepper, withdrawing her hand when Plume put her damp nose in her palm in a show of love. Perhaps in apology for her sister's viciousness, perhaps to make amends for her own outburst of temper, Harriet put her arm around my shoulders and stooped low enough to press her cheek to mine. Her touch was like ice. I could feel her thin body shivering wildly although it was hardly the end of summer, the days only just beginning to shorten. Despair can draw the warmth out of you; I would find that out in time, huddled by the fire, my bones rattling as my tears fell on the fender, but, that day, I listed Harriet's freezing embrace as another irritant, a further sign of the spiritless lack of energy that annoyed me so. Harriet wore wanness like a badge of suffering. That's what I couldn't abide.

I owe my distaste of cloying self-sacrifice to Miss Gwynn. She had taught the girls of our village since she had been little more than a girl herself. She had seen them die from the exhaustion of annual childbirth, seen them lie uncomplainingly on the altar of some comfortless convent as the shears were taken to their bright hair before they took their final vows. Yet still she sought to save us from the life of wasted submission that lay in wait for most of us, was urged upon even, by priest and God-fearing parent. While we crookedly hemstitched grubby squares of flannel in Miss Gwynn's musty schoolroom, she would read us stories of Ireland's dead heroines: the Milesian Macha, the woman of red tresses, who disguised herself as a leper, bound her opponents in fetters and took them in slavery; Medbh, the warrior Queen of Connaught, who made war over the ownership of a single bullock; Granuaile, the pirate, who tied her ships to her bedpost with a rope snaked through the window before she slept at night. Dangerous, intrepid women whose slithery minds disdained obedience, duty, gratitude. While my dirty fingers poked the rusting needle through the limp cloth, I absorbed the message these ancient troublemakers sent out from the grave: be bold, be shameless, keep hope about you like a cloak, so that you are not worn down.

Harriet would have benefited from such teaching. But in Devon she had been educated privately by a series of governesses, genteel gentlewomen who sought to turn her into a more fortunate version of themselves. I suspect that the alarming, the blood-curdling, was omitted from their history syllabus, for had it not been, Harriet would surely not have been so frightened at the mention of Land Leaguers and Fenians, boycotting and burning, as she undoubtedly was. The history she learnt must have been as sunny as her own untroubled childhood, the green and pleasant land recorded in her story books and confirmed by the view of mild, cushiony downland and bloated, white sheep feeding on fatty meadows which she could see from her nursery window. Brought up to be the angel of the house, her misfortune was to be swept off her feet by a man who soon tired of her virtuous reticence. The devil's daughter herself would have been a fitting helpmeet for Charles Trewin, and in marrying me he probably thought that he had found her.

We went too far. And yet, until Harriet's soaked body was found on the freshly rinsed sand at Horam's Cove, we would have denied it. We drove her to her death by subtle, insidious stages, reduced her to a state of terror that she could not explain, even to herself. We were not in league, were ignorant of the other's ploys and motives. It is possible that I was no worse than what my mother called 'an unholy tease'. In the same spirit of mischief that led me to hide under the kitchen table and tie my older sisters' bootlaces together for the fun of seeing them stumble and fume, I would repeat to Harriet gory stories of Whiteboys and Rockites, perpetrators of agrarian violence in the early part of the century, stories I had heard from befuddled farmers as they sat drinking whiskey and water of an evening, after a fair day, with my father. With savage relish, I exaggerated tales of threat and mutilation that had perhaps never been true, even in their original version. Sent by Binnie to the veranda room to bring Harriet her mid-morning pot of China tea, a pale beverage with a musty fragrance I found repellent, I would stay, ostensibly to help her grade her shells, but, more enjoyably, to talk of tongues torn out of traitorous throats, human fingers found in the cooking pot along with the crubeens, and the flayed skin of a valuable horse greeting a householder as he stumbled into the stable one early morning.

I don't deny it. I told her of the upsetting things that had happened round about, not so very long ago, to make her squawk and tremble. It gave me power over her, a power that overrode all her advantages of wealth and position and the ownership of Malina itself. I felt as though I held Harriet in the palm of my hand, as I might have held a terrified fledgling that had been tipped out of its nest. Was Charles merely out to tease too? If so, he was even more expert than I. He was one of the first to subscribe to the new nationalist newspaper, *United Ireland,* and read aloud its glorifying of Mr Charles Stewart Parnell in mock alarm when he came to share his wife's pot of almost colourless tea. 'Well now, I understand from this interesting journal that what I took to be the gentleman's abject performance in the Commons yesterday was the perfect tactic to "baffle and baulk Ireland's enemies". Among whom we are undoubtedly counted, my dear. I wonder whether it isn't time to think of putting locks on the doors.'

It was ridiculous to think that the idle, good-humoured men of the neighbourhood would ever take to midnight marauding; there was no-one within miles who would have wished Harriet harm. Yet she paled. A few days later, while I was absently humming 'God Save Ireland' to myself, sitting on a sun-warmed stone bench in the stable yard and watching Murrough's folded nostrils snuffle the ground for dropped handfuls of oats, I got a stinging slap on the cheek and turned to see Binnie, hot with anger, that day's *United Ireland* crumpled into a ball in her hand. 'There'll be no more of that song, not in this house!' she shouted at me. 'The poor mistress is as feared as a hen that's smelt a fox. You're to go to Horam's Cove with her so, she's set on drawing you while there's a bit of sun in it. She thinks the drive will be settling.'

6

Harriet's stomach was as flat and immaculate as a Communion wafer. Although I knew her to belong to the ranks of the reluctantly unchilded, she did not comport herself like the barren women of the neighbourhood, those women who were to be seen at Mass, their white lips mouthing silent prayers for the signs of a baby quickening inside them, those women who were often to be found huddled on a pallet in our kitchen, while my mother piled bolsters under their feet and fed them carrageen jellies until something inside their bodies told them that this nurturing was useless; they would groan as if from some terrible hunger, and my mother would turn uselessly away.

In time, these women would accept their childlessness as God's will and their groaning would give way to a quiet mournfulness. God had little to do with Harriet's situation; it was her husband who had imposed this condition on her, as I had recently learnt. I was angry at her compliance, but such was her lack of sensuality – her icy flesh, the cold gleam of her knuckles – I did not think that the absence of babies with their sweet, yeasty smells and softly throbbing heads would be like a loss to her. But, of course, the loss was of her own self-esteem. She wanted a child so that she might present it as a gift to her husband. His cruelty in not allowing her to make that gift was to prove, literally, deadly.

Outings with Harriet were invariably exasperating. With her, it was never a question of backing Pepper between the shafts of the governess cart and setting off with a decisive shake to the reins. The vagaries of the Connemara climate had to be kept in mind, so Horty would make several journeys from the house to the stable yard, carrying cashmere rugs, umbrellas, parasols, stone bottles of lemonade, a spirit stove and its attendant tin kettle and tea caddy, a wicker hamper containing milk in a screwtop bottle, spoons and biscuits, a pair of Harriet's narrow walking boots, towels, cushions and a folding wooden chair with a woven leather seat. All this for a journey of three Irish miles, along a sea road rimmed with whitewashed cabins whose inhabitants would give any soul shelter from the rain and a cup of cool well water. Where the sun-baked rocks made accommodating seats, good enough even for an English lady who treated the natural world with reserve, if not suspicion.

Today, room had to be found for her sketching materials, a pad of thick creamy paper with soft, slightly fluffy edges and a tin box of charcoal crayons. 'Agnes could have a house furnished for the two of us with less than you're taking to the strand,' Horty said wistfully as he helped me tuck Plume, quivering with excitement and impatience, under my skirt, and handed me the reins. Plume, like so much else, was a source of concern to Harriet. She worried that, released from Malina and its demesne, the dog would worry sheep and kill chickens; it was best to keep Plume's presence secret until we arrived at the cove. Once there, free to chase the flapping waves that neatly folded themselves over beneath her frantic, scrabbling paws, Plume would be too far from home to be sent back, and I could ignore Harriet's ineffectual bleatings.

On that early September day the cove gleamed with a blond golden light that suppressed the shadows. Harriet shielded her eyes against the sun as I untethered Pepper, and decided that we might leave the rugs, umbrella and spare boots in the trap. Even so, we were heavily laden as we set out along the track. Cushions and towels stacked awkwardly under my arm, I stumbled once or twice as I trudged through clumps of rough grass that ensnared my ankles. Ahead of me, Harriet seemed to glide along the path, holding the hamper in one hand, chair and sketching pad in the other as though they were weightless. I had never seen her step so light, so sure; she might have been a bride floating towards the altar, woozy with rapture. Nothing disturbed her delighted progress, not even Plume's yapping investigation of one of John-Jo Doolan's straying billy-goats who was butting futilely against the dry stone wall that bordered the path, trying to find a short cut home.

The sand was firm and glittering as Harriet arranged her belongings in the shelter of lichen-crusted boulders, then began to arrange me. I had already removed my boots and knitted stockings and was skimming stones on to the calmly pleating water, to Plume's yelping joy. Harriet produced safety-pins and looped up the skirt of my gingham dress to show my legs. She removed her own lace fichu and tied it lightly around my shoulders, pronounced the effect charming and bade me stand on a low rock around which seaweed clung, glistening and shiny brown like toffee. Harriet took up several of the wet strands and set them down again in different positions as though she were arranging ornaments on a mantelpiece. Her face had a look of happy concentration and the tip of her tongue curled against her top lip, like a schoolgirl's.

It seemed as though hours passed, as I stood reluctantly on the rock, chin slightly tilted, one hand clasped against the knotted ends of the fichu as Harriet had commanded, although the sketch took only thirty minutes or thereabouts. Keeping still is not in my nature, neither now nor then. I am possessed of a wilful energy and need to move as much as I need to breathe. Even reading a book, I will not sit but pace Malina's great hallway, circling the fine rosewood table with its gilded undercarriage as the chill from the marble floor seeps through to the soles of my impatient feet.

'Enough,' Harriet called to me finally. 'Come and look, Rose Erris. You will see that you are a very gift to amateur artists. The sketch practically drew itself.' I kicked up sand as I ran towards the proffered sketchpad. Harriet had managed to reduce the tossed beauty of sand, rock and standing figure to a studied triteness. The girl whose chubby feet were planted artfully on the curling seaweed looked cutely bonny, a picturebook Miss Muffet who had clambered off her tuffet for a breath of sea air. The long-ago presence of some mincing drawing teacher lingered in the strokes of Harriet's charcoal stick, over-scheduled, over-schooled. She had learnt nothing from our ravishing, mouldering landscape; she did not *see* it even. I think it was at that moment that I started to hate her.

She reached for the chain of her pretty watch and announced the time shown on its face. 'Eleven o'clock. Shall we have some tea?' How English she was. Had her tongue been hanging out of her head with thirst, and had it been ten minutes short of the hour, she would have waited out those minutes with parched lips rather than alter her self-imposed timetable. I do not care for a clocked-in life, waiting with growling stomach for the dinner gong, the tea bell, the punctual summons to luncheon. Although my appetite is ravenous, forced to eat at appointed times makes it fade, makes me pick at my food like the pseudo-Englishwoman that I am in danger of becoming.

Almost crackling with the pleasures of achievement, Harriet set out cups and plates, coaxed a fervid blue flame out of the spirit stove, upon which the kettle presently set up a busy rattle. The tide was going out and the brown, bony fingers of seaweed-covered rock seemed to order the sea away into a greater vastness. Harriet arranged her belongings in the shelter of a dune so that the effect was one of odious, cramped cosiness. Her mood was bright and uncensorious as she sipped and nibbled. She said nothing when Plume and I ate of the same biscuit, or when I wiped the back of a spoon on Plume's back to dry it. She sat straight-backed on her folding chair while the dog and I sprawled and lolled on the sand. 'I feel happy here,' she said, her eyes, a candid washed-out blue, for once untroubled. 'This is the one place I feel at home.'

Home. She pronounced the word almost hungrily. I could see that nestled among the cushions and crockery, she felt safe, undamaged. I resented this. I resented her appropriation of the cove, *my* cove. One of my earliest memories was of stumbling after groups of women, some on foot, some riding asses, all with deep wicker baskets and all barefoot. They came to the cove to perform a vital labour: to collect the seaweed which was gently popping in the sun. I came with them to listen to the songs they always sang as they stepped like goats from rock to rock, their toes curved and muscular, like the toes of some strange female beast, their fingers icy from the sea water. They filled the baskets with seaweed, they heaved the baskets on to their backs and they returned along the narrow white path to strew the brown ribbons on the reluctant earth, to encourage the potatoes to grow on their patches of thin, villainous soil, each field barely the size of one of Harriet's silk-washed carpets.

I remembered the women now, their scratched legs showing thin threads of blood that matched the scarlet of their hitched-up flannel petticoats, their songs of yearning and remorse.

Harriet had closed her eyes blissfully, tilting her face to the sun as though she could never have enough of its heat. A slight breeze had begun to lift and dip the pleated ruffles that banded her grey silk skirt but she was reluctant to leave. Here, she was not the stranger in a strange land that I required her to be. But it was ignorance that shaped her happiness and I knew something about Horam's Cove that would shatter her contentment to smithers.

She opened her eyes and gave a little, theatrical shiver. The watch was retrieved from between silken breasts to confirm that it was yet one hour and thirty-five minutes before the luncheon gong would be struck. She wished to linger, but not to sit. 'Shall we walk on the dunes?' I suggested. 'There is an easy path up so that you wouldn't be ruining your shoes.' Her shoes were grey kid, criss-crossed with narrow straps. I tried to imagine her feet within them, and thought they would be thin, white and smooth as a pebble, slithery as a fish; feet that could no more cling to a rock than walk on water.

On the dunes I ran ahead of her while Plume thrust herself at the sandy entrances of burrows, her tail a stiff, excited feather. Harriet lingered, her step light and slow, watching the smeary walls of the nearby cottages brighten as the sun passed over them, listening to the pukka-puk of the cottagers' hens, their soothing natter carried towards us by the soft breeze, sniffing the combined smells of turf-smoke and sea, an intoxicating smell that eases the heart.

As I approached the grassy tip of the headland, I slowed my pace. Wild flowers were few in this place and at this late season but I managed to gather a few stalks of milkwort, pimpernel and bindweed, a spray of red goosefoot and a tough clump of sea beet. By this time, Harriet had caught up with me and followed me to the land's edge, a place where the grass was lined with an untidy row of small, flinty stones, their topmost edges pointed like the teeth of an old dog. I laid my wispy bouquet beside the first stone.

'Why are you doing that?' Harriet asked.

'Do you not know the way they are calling this place?' My voice was doleful. Harriet looked about her, puzzled that such an insignificant little patch of nothingness should be dignified by a name.

'It is known as Clochar na bPáisti,' I went on.

'What does that mean?'

'The stony mound of the children.'

'Why?'

'It was during the time of the agitation. The women were starving. But the babies kept on coming to them; they couldn't stop having them. They were born, and born, only to die of the great hunger. There wasn't the time to baptize all those dead babbies, no time to call the priest. And the graveyard yonder is for baptized souls only, those who will go to heaven. So they put the babbies here, under the small, little stones, although their souls go to a strange place that is neither God's nor the Devil's. I've forgotten the name of it.'

'Limbo,' said Harriet curtly. The sparkling day had suddenly become hueless, a limp colourlessness had overtaken sand and sky. Silently, we gathered up the picnic things and took the narrow path back to where Pepper, his head down, made a pale triangle in front of the clouded outline of Errisbeg. Harriet's step was no longer light. She seemed to whip through the air with long, shaken strides. As I guided the pony along the thin road that tricked its way between the deep ditches at either side, Harriet did not once look back.

'I shall not go there again,' she said. I did not reply but began quietly to sing the song the women sang when they hauled the heavy baskets on to their sore shoulders. 'What can't be cured, love, Must be endured, love,' I sang and although I sang almost under my breath, I knew that Harriet could hear the words. It was my intention that she should.

7

Harriet did return to Horam's Cove. In the two years that remained to her she took the trap whenever the day allowed, as though compelled to do so by some malign spirit. Always alone. Her fear of manoeuvring the pony, though great, was less than her dread of my spiteful company. Better to be flung from the twisted road into the rank ditch than listen to savage disclosures of a deadly time in my country's past, disclosures that rattled her nerves, forced her to acknowledge the tiny, rotting bones buried so near the sweet, smooth curve of the sand, the shining sea whose surface glittered with jumpy light, as though scattered with new pins.

She made no mention of her visits but left strange clues behind her. Often, when taking Murrough for a canter along the wispily grassed dunes, I would notice a thread of brightness among the sharp stones of the children's graveyard and know that the Englishwoman had been there that day. Up close, the brightness took shape: a satin ribbon binding a posy, which bore no resemblance to the straggly bouquet I had once left on the stones. The ribbon encircled flowers from Malina's well-mulched garden: peonies and tea-roses, delicately arranged. The effect of their formal pinks and mauves among the headland's wildness was disturbing.

Touching the glossy petals, I felt a sinner's unease. Increasingly, I wished that I had spared Harriet the story of the dead, unsanctified children.

Throughout the moist, drizzly autumn, Binnie's arthritis worsened. On a damp, dark afternoon, as soon as Miss Gwynn released her senior class from the tedium of a geography lesson, taught from a cracked, faint map, flaking away from its thin canvas backing, I walked along the lakeside road to Malina. In the kitchen, under the oil lamp's clammy light, Binnie sat at the table, her useless hands poking at torn and crumpled scraps of paper, trying to fit them together. I smoothed out two of the scraps and saw that they contained my own likeness, or rather, Harriet's sugary version of it. Before I could ask who had destroyed the sketch (but, of course, I already knew) Binnie pointed a crooked finger at a sack beside the yard door, crammed with what seemed to be rubble. I opened its neck wider and came upon the shattered fragments of Harriet's shell pictures, the shells smashed to brittle, pearly crumbs among the small pebbles and snippets of dried seaweed.

Slack, grey cushions of skin beneath Binnie's eyes told of sleepless nights. 'Why must you hate her so?' she asked me tiredly. 'What harm has she ever done you that you take everything from her, every last little pleasure that she had?' She expected no answer and I had none to give. My resentment of Harriet was set somewhere beyond the edge of reason. I could not acknowledge or explain what was almost a lust in me to make Harriet unhappy, or why, where she was concerned, I was as taunting and unscrupulous as any playground bully.

Harriet could not sleep, so Binnie sat out the nights with her, reassuring her that all was as it should be: that the tapping on the window was made by the dry, curling leaves of the creeper, the creak on the stair nothing but the settling of the wood, and that the sudden bang that made the horses whinny only the wind from the lake slapping against a barn door. Night after night, Binnie, fuddled and weepy from lack of sleep, her joints as stiff as Harriet's carved bedposts, urged her mistress to go back to England and avoid the worst of the coming winter.

But Harriet would not leave Charles. 'I've said it before and I'll say it again,' Binnie muttered, as she let me rub oil and crushed herbs into her ravaged, veiny calves. 'Loving a man is like a disease and women have yet to find a cure for it. There is the poor Missus pining away for him that does nothing but cast her low, now that he's away for a week or longer getting new roofs put on the cottages before the winter sets in. He wants proper chimneys so the room below doesn't have the eyes out of your head with the turf-smoke, but we've lived in smoky cabins as long as we can remember and never asked for anything different. Not that I'd wish for him back home, there's some men's absence is good company. Maybe himself being gone will have her the less lonely, for there's no loneliness like the aloneness of a woman living side by side with a loveless man. Never forget that, Rose Erris, for you are a good child in all ways but one, and it would crack your mother's heart to see the bold likes of you end up a poor wisp of a thing on account of one who's a very tyrant.'

I knew that Charles had gone away. The day before, he had given me a big, white dressmaker's box which held, between crisp sheets of tissue paper, a black riding habit. 'Hat and horse to follow on my return,' he had said to me before he went. He had taken my hand, pulled it so that my arm rose in the air, and produced a packet of tortoiseshell hairpins from my armpit. 'Well now, there's a useful thing,' he said. 'Perhaps you could practise putting up your hair with them while I'm away.'

Without him, the house seemed to have stopped breathing. Without his swooping energy, his shouted commands scudding and bouncing off the walls, the vast rooms and hallways were grave and unsunned in the shortening days. For some time now, I had been spending the whole of Saturday at Malina, exercising the horses and helping Binnie below stairs. On the first Saturday that Charles was away, I went, as usual, directly to the kitchen to scoop Plume out of her fireside basket and take her to the stables. The kitchen door was locked, an unheard-of thing throughout the west of Ireland, where the back of the house is a miniature market-place: women come to sell fish, geese and eggs and tinkers make regular visits for alms and left-over food. Nor could I hear Plume, alert to the sound of my step, barking her hysterical welcome. I knocked on the door and it was opened immediately by Agnes MacReion. In spite of her vigorous copulations in the coachhouse, Agnes always looked under-exercised, soft and white with colourless hair and lashes fringing fat eyelids which reminded me of dead slugs. She gave me a thin little smile that had something triumphant in it.

'Where's Binnie?' I asked.

'Away to her bed. The poor creature's almost killed with the rheumatics.'

'I'll go up and rub her legs.' I made to push past Agnes. She planted her flabby body in my path. 'You will not so, Rose Erris. You are no part of this house and never will be if I have any say in the matter. The mistress has me in charge now and I am to make sure that everything stays as quiet and decent as the grave itself.'

I looked past her into the shadowy kitchen. No Plume. 'Where's my dog?'

'*Your* dog, indeed. I'd say it was the master's dog, since it was he that paid for it. And nothing but trouble has that animal brought. She had me driven mad with her yelping this morning and then she lifted a cutlet from the table that I had all nice for Horty's dinner so I have her locked in the cellar and if the rats make a feast of her it will be too good an ending for her.'

I pushed Agnes hard against the half-open door and ran through the kitchen and down the cellar steps. In its mouldy darkness, Plume had already lost lustre. She lay shuddering in the furthermost corner, too frightened even to whimper. I held her to me, ran to the stables with the dog in my arms, concocted a sling for her out of a meal-sack, slung sack and dog around my neck, led Murrough from her stall and rode her home along the dark, puddled road.

'If it weren't that you lead a charmed life, you could be arrested for horse-stealing,' my sister Betty said, later that night, as she helped me settle Murrough into her old stall at Shanvally. Murrough looked disobliging and

cramped, like a grand lady down on her luck. She gave
me a cruel little nip on my shoulder as I bolted the
half-door. I, too, was beginning to feel disobliging
and cramped. I had had the run of fine rooms and
fancy horses for so long that Shanvally, in its shabby,
Saturday-night comfort, seemed small and mean. It was
as though Malina's soaring ceilings and the high trees
of its woodlands had encouraged me to grow. Already,
I was taller than my three older sisters, my body aching
for space to stretch and pace. While my sisters sewed
and chattered in the stuffy kitchen, I stood at the
window, rubbing a clear patch in its mist of steam until
I could see the pale outline of Malina, my magician's
castle, pressed against the darkness of the night.

I decided to try on the new riding habit, to make
my mind swerve away from thoughts of Charles's cool,
shelved library with its gilding, and carved doors and
rows of books with ridged spines, where I had been
drawn to on Saturday evenings such as this one, lapped
in tranquil privacy, reading leather-bound issues of a
story-magazine called *All the Year Round,* Plume sleeping on my lap and a plate of bread spread with unsalted
butter and sprinkled with sugar within reach.

I went upstairs and pushed the dressmaker's box
from under my bed. The habit formed a waist on
me, its strictly seamed bodice pushed my small breasts
upwards so that they jutted provocatively. Standing
on tiptoe to see as much of myself as possible in
the streaked and bruised mirror that hung over the
small mantelpiece, I saw, in its dim glass, a childish
face on a constrained and womanly body, a queer,
enticing mixture, I would soon come to realize. I

called down the stairs for Vera to come and coil my hair.

'Well, aren't you a picture,' she said, when the tortoiseshell pins were in place and the tightness of the coiled plait drew my eyebrows higher in my forehead. I did not think myself as pretty as she was with her translucent skin that was as fine as an eggshell and her smooth, silky mass of red-gold hair that, when released from its plait, fell like a shining curtain down to her waist, but I liked myself well enough that evening and skittered down the stairs as fast as my heavy skirts would allow to show myself off to the assembled household.

What did I expect from my parents? Admiration? Joy? Pride? Yes, all those things. In the black habit that nipped my body into new curves and my restrained hair, I felt, for the first time, the excitement of being a woman, a state of feeling that called for celebration. Instead, my mother's mouth thinned at the sight of me, my father's shoulders sagged. Geraldine started to toddle towards me on her fat, ruddy legs but then stopped, pointed to my upswept hair. 'You're all growed,' she said disgustedly and refused to say another word to me until I bribed her with a chain of paper dolls that I cut out from the smooth sheets of tissue in the dressmaker's box. After that, she consented to sit on my knee and count the round, covered buttons that marched from my neck to my waist. All my mother said was, 'You'd best take yourself out of that garment, Rose Erris, before it gets the smell of turf and rashers on it.' Her voice gave me a sense of shame and disgrace, as it so often did when her thoughts were on Charles Trewin. Her eyes glittered with angry tears but she held them in check as I went sulkily up the stairs to undress.

There would be another time, another dress paid for by Malina's squire, another staircase. A time when my mother would be unable to stop the tears that dripped from her pale cheeks on to her own finery. A time that lay only a few years away: my wedding day. I would descend the sweep of Malina's great staircase, my gloved hand trailing along the top of its marble balustrade, the train of my Worth gown disturbing the carpet's plush. As I reached the bottom stair, my mother's weeping would become harsher, turn into a keening, as though I were to be joined not to a husband but to death itself, and the embroidered satin of my dress was, in her eyes, the coarse linen of a shroud.

I folded the new riding habit and returned it to its box. That night, I could not sleep. On either side of me, in our sloping room, Vera and Betty snuffled soothingly. I heard the sounds of the house being put to rest until morning: the hiss of water as the fire was damped down, the click of the latch being fastened and, finally, the squeaky protest of the stairs as my parents went to the bedroom that adjoined ours. They were talking in half-throttled whispers but I could hear the words through the thin dividing wall of painted boards.

'She's too young, Nora,' my father said brokenly.

My mother's voice was exhausted, grimly resigned. 'For God's sake, Garrold, put it away from your mind. You know the way things are with us. There is nothing to be done.'

8

The night that Harriet died, Charles was again away. Increasingly drawn towards an elaborate life of ceremony and grandeur, he spent much time in Dublin and, during that summer, was assisting Lord Ardilaun and the Commissioners of Public Works in turning St Stephen's Green into a public park. Malina made him restless now. A dull, weighted stillness had taken the house over, changing it into a place of secrets and whispers. Even Agnes lowered her raucous voice to a bitter hiss as she fought with Binnie over the running of the household, and Plume slunk dispiritedly about the silent rooms, the click of her claws on the polished floors hardly disturbing the silence.

Sometimes, during one of his rare returnings, I would see a look on Charles's face as we rode our horses alongside, a look that was both beseeching and impatient, as though he were desperate for some gift that only I could give him.

On my thirteenth birthday, I had flung my schoolbag into the harbour at full tide and refused to return to Miss Gwynn's confining schoolroom. By then, I was so much help with the horses at both Malina and Shanvally that no-one, except the schoolmistress, objected. Charles had given me a horse to match my riding habit, a black mare called Emer, glossy as liquorice. Together, we enlivened the hunt, leaping the most treacherous stone walls to land neatly on the bank, as though horse and rider were one. I was sought after during the hunting season, admired not just for my fearlessness but because I could staunch a wound with cobwebs when barbed wire had scraped a horse's taut belly so that the flesh hung down in tatters, and could pluck a tick from a maddened hound. People said I had 'the cure', and from as far away as Ballinasloe they brought me their mangy dogs and broken-winded horses to grow well under my care. I have a natural understanding of what ails animals. This gift does not apply to my fellow human beings.

It was I who was at Malina the night Harriet died. Murrough was due to foal, and Horty O'Goole and I sat out the night with her, drinking strong, sweet tea with a nip of poitín in it. When Murrough's time was near, I took a pair of scissors from my apron pocket, snipped a thick clump of Horty's pale hair, and sprinkled it on the mare's straw. 'It will ensure that the foal is light-coloured,' I said. 'I want to look at the mountainside and see Murrough's firstborn grazing there, gleaming as whitely as the quartz standing stones.'

'You're a queer girl,' Horty said, fingering the shorn place on his head, 'and I'm not the only one to say it. Another time, now, and they would have had you burnt for a witch.'

But, when the foal was born, he glistened ivory white in the dusk of the stable, so beautiful that Horty ran back to the house to fetch Agnes to admire him, and, when she came, the rest of the household was with her. More drink was fetched and we drank toasts to the new mother and became lively through relief in the safe birth. Which is, perhaps, why none of us heard Harriet go from the house in the thick darkness. How quietly she must have passed on the drive, not causing one clink of gravel, or drawing a sound from the stalled horses who had always frightened her.

It is a long walk from Malina's gates to the cove, but in those days before we had gas lighting we kept the same waking hours as the sun, and on that moonless night Harriet would have known that, apart from her cavorting servants in the stable, the rest of the world was asleep and she would not meet a soul on the road. How fearful she must have been without a lantern to guide her, she who had always sought out the light.

It was in full sunlight that her body was discovered on the shore, beside the pretty shells that she used to gather. Grimly, Mr Graves, the rector, sent word to the Shelbourne Hotel in Dublin to bring the widower home, and grimly an exhausted Agnes hauled me out of Murrough's stable, where I had spent what remained of the night on a blanket, to ask for help in pressing and airing the bedlinen that would be needed for the mourners from England. The sheets with their crusty lace borders smelt musty and camphorous, stale with disuse, for there had been no house-guests at Malina for nearly three years. The death of its mistress brought the Big House back to life; noise fluttered from every quarter, murmurous sound vibrated like swarming bees. In the kitchen, where women from the village washed china and rubbed the tarnish from vast silver trays with their roughened thumbs, Agnes's mother, Maeve MacReion sat on a big sod of turf by the fire, her feet, in rotting, unlaced boots, stretched on the fender. It was she who had found Harriet's body. She had been out stranding, searching for driftwood for her fire, her sharp, watery eyes alert for other treasures too: rusted anchors, dislodged lobster-pots, glass bottles. The ghastly discovery had sent her racing up the path to John-Jo Doolan's cottage, the tongues of her disgraceful boots flapping, and her greasy hair streaming behind her. For a while, she had been so incoherent that John-Jo had understood her to say that she had found a mermaid on the shore, and had put her blether down to too much porter the night before, for Maeve had the reputation of having taken to the drop. But slowly he began to understand.

He had seen the bodies of drowned men often enough. He had held a lantern over the bloodied, bloated face of a fisherman, the body long in the water and dashed against the rockface so many times that it could not be recognized except by the pattern of the sodden, knitted stockings on the cold feet. But that had been after winter storms, when the herrings had blown through the air like birds, and the fishing boats had cracked and strained vainly against the iron seas. Sometimes it had been days before the ocean had flattened to a rumbling calm again and thrown its victims on the shore, sodden, and heavy as grain sacks.

Harriet's body, lying in slanted sunlight, terrified John-Jo as no other corpse had ever done. 'She looked alive still,' he said that evening, his meaty hands not quite steady around the glass of rum he held in

Meehan's snug. 'Not a fleck of blood on her, and her hair spread out in the sun, the sand on it making it glitter like sugar on the top of a cake. And her eyes wide open, staring at me and through me at something that is beyond all knowing. My knees softened under me and it was a long while before I found the strength to pick her up and carry her to the road, light though she was, like a thistle in the wind.'

In Malina's kitchen, Maeve was sobriety itself, mournfully crooning Harriet's praises, almost congratulating her for taking her own life. How we Irish relish death. Our heroes are men who have leapt gaily on to the scaffold, spouting pretty words about the thrill of dying; we value those who have died for Ireland far more than those determined to live for her. Harriet hadn't died for Ireland, a country she loathed and distrusted, but from an overwhelming grief that sucked out of her all desire for living. As I listened to the voices in the kitchen, I knew that they sympathized with her self-destruction, the melodramatic act always taking on a tinge of the heroic with them.

'For the one day that went with her, six went against her,' Maeve crooned over and over, holding the corners of her rank, black shawl and rocking her body in the sad rhythm of the bereaved. 'She couldn't seem to win for losing,' Binnie murmured in agreement.

Of all that company of women, picking over the details of Harriet's death with a grief that held a note of triumph in it, I alone, plucking hot sods from the fire and flinging them in the box-iron, seemed horrified. I alone seemed to be aware that suicide – and not one of us there doubted that Harriet died by her own hand – was a mortal sin. Not so far back, suicides were denied a Christian burial and laid to uncertain rest at the crossroads, a stake through their chest, since it was the belief that they had given themselves to the devil. I said nothing, since I knew that to talk of sin with regard to Harriet would elicit only scorn. It would be the opinion of those shawled women, scuttling about Harriet's kitchen in preparation for her funeral, that Harriet had suffered from living with the devil for too long here on earth to be asked to endure his presence in the life to come. 'Isn't he the devil himself,' Binnie had cried once, on a day when Charles Trewin had stumped crossly from the house, having been heard to call his wife 'a pathetic milksop' for taking fright during a winter gale that flung the roof slates into the flowerbeds and pushed the smoke from the drawing-room fire back down the chimney with a threatening whoosh.

Mr and Mrs Charles Trewin, as seen by their sentimental and tender-hearted tenantry, were haunter and haunted, villain and victim hopelessly entwined. To Binnie, Maeve and their like, Harriet's death, in spite of its ghastly circumstances, was a blessed relief, freeing her from her tormentor. Having witnessed her increasing terror of life over the last years, they were, perhaps, not entirely surprised when she decided to put an end to it. They understood her dread of Malina too, shared it themselves during dark and silent wintry days when its cold, smooth surfaces of silk and marble could make you break out in a fit of shivering. They preferred the smoky intimacy of the mud cabin to Malina's chilly elegance, looked on its monumental façade as a hated symbol of an alien power. But to me, the Big House was there to be conquered, like a dangerous-eyed colt that must be forced to the snaffle. Between Harriet's death and my marriage to her widower, there was not one corner of the house that I hadn't scrutinized, not one ornament that I hadn't repositioned to my own liking. I was convinced that, in days to come, Malina would be in my charge, although hazy as to how this might come about. I was the first to notice a loose floorboard or a splintered pane, the first to insist on its immediate repair if Charles were away. On his return, Charles and I would tour the house and he would thank me for bringing to his notice a flooded guttering or a chipped mantel, and show his small, dingy teeth in a smile that I had always found irresistible in its acknowledged complicity.

It had been decided that, in spite of an acquaintance with her husband, no member of the McCalla family would attend Harriet's funeral. Our religion forbade us entry to the service to be held at Mr Graves's Church of Ireland church in the nearby town of Clifden, and my father insisted that none of us should follow the carriages to the burial ground either. He knew that our absence would be taken as disrespectful, but would not be shifted. 'There'll be talk enough about us, whether we go or whether we stay,' he said, 'and I'm telling you that we shall stay, going about our business here and praying for the soul of the good woman that she was.'

Religion is a muzzy thing with us. Over the centuries there has been much toing and froing between Catholics and Protestants, not from any change of conviction, but because of a desire to intermarry, hold on to property, take part in the professions and public life. Between them, the Penal Laws of two hundred years ago, and the Great Famine had created a good many jumpers and hoppers – those families who thought it timely to abandon the Church of Rome. But among those new converts who primly attended Protestant services on a Sunday there were many who were hiding a Catholic priest in their cellar or had sent their sons to France to be brought up by the monks.

Had my own family failed to prosper during the great hunger, we too might have succumbed to the Protestant missions that were opportunely set up in the starving townships, and yielded up our true faith for a bowl of turnip soup.

Subterfuge and lies have always been part of the religious life of our battered, conquered nation. The sanctification of Harriet's death was another part of that lie. The coroner and the Resident Magistrate had pronounced that her death had been by misadventure, that the most likely cause of this tragic event was that Mrs Trewin, while taking a late walk in the place she was known to have loved well, had slipped from the crumbling dune into the pitchy sea. This blameless verdict permitted her Mr Graves's lengthy sermon on her modest nature and unstinting generosity towards the needy, as well as a coffin draped in velvet on which was embroidered in golden thread a vast cross, and six black-plumed horses to draw it in slow, proud progress to the cemetery that lay on a hill behind the town.

The weather continued to be as kind on the day of Harriet's burial as it had been on the day of her death. From the high pasture where I was setting up some low jumps for the show-ponies, I could see every kind of vehicle make its way to Clifden by the coast road. Closed carriages with crested sides and liveried drivers wearing mourning ribbons on their tall hats, phaetons carrying two or three black-clad passengers, traps burdened down with black-shawled women, more of whom were on asses, a small, sleeping child in each of the two creels that hung from the saddle.

The purposeful traffic with its dark-clothed cargo made me feel abandoned and resentful, a vague resentment whose cause was beyond my fathoming. In the afternoon, the funeral service long since over, my mother took pity on my black mood and said that I might ride to the village for a screw of tea and a box of kitchen candles. But when I got there, Fergus Keane had shut his shop and pulled the blind down over the window, as a mark of respect towards his best customer. Apart from some small boys playing on the quay, there was nobody about. The boys were shoving each other and kicking a rusted tin in a sullen, disconsolate way as though their jumpers were itching them. I wondered if their mothers had warned them not to make a noise, told them that their usual whoops and hollers would be unseemly on this day. The village street seemed steeped in remorse, but I felt none, believing with the harsh unclouded conviction of the very young that Harriet had been responsible for everything that had happened to her and that her own weakness and fear had, alone, resulted in her body, under its embroidered pall, making its last journey to the Ascendancy church at Clifden, a church under whose thin, brittle steeple I would, to my family's grief, be married. I hitched my placid little mare to a stump beside the schoolmistress's house and saw movement within. Miss Gwynn would give me the lend of both tea and candles. I knocked on her window.

Miss Gwynn was an ugly sight that day. Grief and outrage had brought out her skin in a flaky rash and the slack bulges under her eyes were mottled and sore looking.

'What brings you here, Rose Erris?' she said sharply. 'Repentance?' My heart jumped. 'Repentance,' she went on, 'for leaving my schoolroom before I had done with you? I could have made a fine, scholarly woman out of you, Miss, had you given as much attention to the words of wise men as you do to stricken animals.'

She was in the act of pulling on a dreadful squeezed black bonnet, and now tied its greasy ribbons under her chin. 'I'm back from the funeral and on my way to the Big House, although I've no more stomach for the bright, guilty world that resides in it than poor Harriet had,' she said angrily. 'How Mr Graves's oration would have amused her, his oily words about her love for what he dared to call "the country she chose to make her home". Little the choice that she had. The rector would have had more truth in him had he quoted the late Lord Orrery, who said, "All I entreat of fate is not to fix my dwelling here." It's a hard thing for me to go now and offer sympathy to those who have little need of it. The propriety of those there would have you quake in your shoes. Such order, such control. Even as the clods thundered on the coffin, not a snitch of a tear on their faces. I know how they'll be greeting me. Miss

Florence Wingrave will flaunt her faultless manners in my face and her voice will be so thin and removed that I shall shrink into something invisible. As for Mr Trewin, why, he'll give me that sleek nod of the head that he has, as though the world is his due.

'I should have known that Harriet was in a dreadful way,' she went on, settling a brackish alpaca cape over her shapeless shoulders. 'Only the day before she died, she gave me back the copy of Mr Yeats's *Poems and Ballads of Young Ireland* which I had lent her. It was no doubt men like her husband that he was thinking of when he wrote in his preface of the leisure classes who "read little about any country and nothing about Ireland".'

The schoolmistress looked at me narrowly out of her swollen eyes. 'Too busy making a show of themselves at the meet and the races to read a poet who has the measure of the very heartbeat of this nation of ours. But it's not just the return of the book. Harriet urged upon me some of her own notebooks. For safe keeping, she said, as though Malina itself was a place of danger for her.' Miss Gwynn pointed to a neat package on one of her faded chairs. 'There's been no chance to look at them, as yet,' she said, 'nor do I look forward to seeing all her sadness spread out on the page. But it's owed to her, and I shall brace myself for it before too long. Now here are your tea and candles, Rose Erris, and tell your parents I was asking after them, good souls that they are.'

We could hear the jingling of Miss Gwynn's hired trap outside the door. It was driven by a doleful, mountainy boy, a former pupil, who looked as though it were no treat for him to convey this particular passenger. He shook the reins and they left on a waft of the faint, stale scent that Miss Gwynn wore on special occasions: attar of roses, a spinsterish scent.

I pushed the tea and candles into my pockets, untied my horse and rode the long way home, over the headland from which Horam's Cove was brightly visible. But, as we passed, I turned my eyes inland, towards the mountains and away from the sea.

A widower has a dignity that is lacking in a husband. The stiff, black suits of mourning that Charles Trewin now wore became him gravely. Their dark fabric emphasized the gloss of his tawny hair, the ruddiness of his cheeks, yet muted both by constraining his powerful body in well-stitched sombreness. Increasingly, I gladdened at the sight of him.

During the year's mourning that was required of him, he travelled less frequently. Freed from Harriet's doleful, suffering presence, Malina began to buzz and hum again with its owner's hectoring energy. Parties of gentlemen came to the Big House now, to dine on Malina's salmon and game birds and rest for the night in the tapestried bedrooms where fires roared in ornate grates, yet failed to remove a fuzzy chill from the thick draperies. The visitors came from the northern counties. Many of them were English by birth and had come to Ireland to found great industries: graving docks and shipyards, seagoing vessels made from Irish oak, mechanized flax spinning. They came without their wives, arrived without guns, fishing-rods or riding boots. Hardly putting their noses out of doors, they spent long hours in Mr Trewin's study; the sound of loud, hacking laughter and the shuffling of papers reached my ears as I came round the east side of the house, guiding a horse towards its stable.

I, too, spent more time at Malina. Charles Trewin lured me (how willing I was to be lured) with gifts that, it was silently understood between us, were never to be taken home to Shanvally. His latest present to me was a harp, scrolled and gilded with a Greek key border of inlaid mother-of-pearl worked into its frame. He had it set up beside one of the tall, south-facing windows in the drawing-room and sent for blind Hogan, the minstrel from Galway, to show me how to pluck its wires into plaintive chords and trills. The harp, even more than the fiddle and the tin whistle, sets Ireland to music. Its wistful twanging suits the songs that every Irish child has known from the cradle: Tom Moore's *Irish Melodies*, laments of love and longing with silly, slushy words that crack your heart. When I sang to my own playing, my voice seemed something apart from me, soaring and dipping of its own accord, turning words to sound, as if by magic.

I was practising 'Love Thee, Dearest, Love Thee?' one grey afternoon when the lake had turned to a sheet of dulled pewter, hardly to be seen for the mist that tumbled from it, when Charles Trewin entered the room.

'Who is this Lovety of whom you sing?' he asked.

'What do you mean?'

For answer he took the point of my chin between his thumb and forefinger.

'Thee, thy, those, thine,' he said. 'Master that confounded *th* and you shall play for the gentlemen before they dine. Perhaps old Tom's haunting music will shift the columns of figures that fill their heads and inspire them to talk of something other than the contents of their account books.'

And so, when there were guests at the Big House, I sang for them. A pretence was kept up of asking my parents' consent. Letters in Mr Trewin's forceful hand, written on thick, slightly ribbed, white paper, were delivered to Shanvally: 'I beg your permission to allow your gifted daughter to play for my guests. They are men much troubled by affairs of state and would welcome such soothing distraction. She shall be returned to you in my carriage while it is still light.'

'He'd put sugar to shame for sweetness when he wants something,' my mother said sourly, tucking the first of such letters behind the rusting clock on the kitchen mantel. 'I don't suppose his visitors are so troubled that they won't notice what you have on your back. We'll go to the town tomorrow and look at patterns.'

But there was no need. Charles Trewin had already summoned Aideen the Pin and her Singer sewing-machine. From a trunk he brought out a length of dark pink velvet and some grey taffeta ribbon. 'The design I leave entirely to you, Miss O'Malley,' he said, giving poor Aideen, who had gone to Paris and found work in the couture house of Worth, until dragged home to tend her crippled father, one of his glinting, conspiratorial smiles.

Aideen held out the fabric in arms criss-crossed in thin, red scratches where the pins had scraped them. 'The colours of a rose growing by the flank of the mountain,' she said dreamily. 'You're all mush, Aideen,' I said. 'Don't be making it too tight; I need room to breathe when I'm singing.'

A week later, a group of Dublin brewers was being put up at Malina, to be coaxed into setting up a local cooperage. In my new dress with its soft, cloudy skirts and ruffled sleeves, I was to sing, at Mr Trewin's request, 'The Last Rose of Summer'. Given my name and the colour I wore, there could have been no more obvious choice.

I arranged myself on the low seat by the harp and looked at the visitors: six or seven men with dull, indoor faces, pasty, drawn cheeks and overworked eyes blinking behind spectacles as they reluctantly put down the ledgers they were studying. I sang:

'I'll not leave thee, thou lone one! to pine on the
     stem:
Since the lovely are sleeping, go, sleep thou with
     them,
Thus kindly I scatter thy leaves o'er the bed.
Where thy mates of the garden lie scentless and
     dead.'

The tired eyes behind the spectacles grew misty. Hard men grow sloppy towards the sentimental Ireland of the shamrock and the harp, the simpering disguise under which is hidden the turbulent, threatening Ireland of peasant violence and demands for liberty.

One of the brewers, who throughout my performance had continually rubbed his belly as though it were a favourite pet of his, demanded an encore. For answer, Charles Trewin led me from the room. 'Always leave them longing for something else, Rose Erris,' he whispered, as he handed me into the phaeton. A clue to his philosophy that I would have done well to have noted with suspicion. But I was too young, too excited by the way the brewers had clapped their plump hands to be suspicious or wary.

There was company at Shanvally that night, too. As the coach turned into the borheen, I could hear the chirpy notes of an accordion. It signalled that Finbar Kavanagh was at the house, perhaps others too, laughing as Finbar danced in a little circle as he played, his huge backside stuck out like a duck's. My father's friends were not sleek and doughy like the Dublin brewers. Horse-breeders, sea-captains, boat-builders, their faces spoke of lives spent tussling with wind and water: punished, weathered faces, stringy necks with throbbing, clotted veins, eyes squinting and watery from the blustery outdoors. They were good men but I did not like their gruff, stupid, masculine world, and would have gone straight to bed had Finbar not shot out an arm as I passed him, and seized mine.

'Now that's a dress and a half you have on you, Rose Erris,' he said, holding me fast. 'You have the rest of them beat to tatters and that's the truth of it.' His eyes flitted around the stuffy kitchen. 'Was it not last summer that Mrs Trewin was taken?' he asked nobody in particular, then supplied the answer himself. 'Indeed it was. And now the days are stretching again, each one more than the one that went before it, thanks be to God.'

His wandering eyes came to rest on my father, who was shifting from haunch to haunch on the uncomfortable settle. 'I'm telling you now that the year of mourning will soon be over.' His voice grew rough, accusing. 'And I'm telling you more than that.' He let me go, crossed the room to where my father was almost cowering and shook him by the shoulder. 'I'm telling you that your man will be saying the hard word.'

I ran upstairs without wishing any of them goodnight. There was no doubt as to who or what Finbar had been referring. In our part of the country, 'the hard word' is what we call a proposal of marriage.

9

My husband threw off his blue silk robe and, naked, came towards our bed. Below the beefy, barrelled torso, his legs were surprisingly slender. I smiled at him encouragingly, eager and curious for the experience that would change me for ever. I wasn't afraid; I had spent my life with rutting animals and knew what bodily union was: the stiffened rod of the male making its magnetized way towards the soft, receptive, hidden places of the female. What I had not known until now was the flushed intimacy of flesh sliding into damp flesh, the joy of it. My husband groaned and moved inside me and a fire's heat slid through the marrow of my bones. From somewhere far away, I heard my own rapturous screams. All that night, we nuzzled each other, not a hair's breadth between our hot bodies. Our tongues and hands stroked, sucked, licked, clung. Towards the morning, my husband, rubbing his flattened, velvety nose up and down my spine, whispered, 'I can't be gentle with you. Your combative grey eyes make me fierce. I am sorry.' For answer, I turned around and clamped my thighs to his sides until I felt him hardening against my belly.

We spent our honeymoon in Paris but saw so little of it that I can remember nothing of the city that spread outside our over-heated hotel room except for a peaceful thread of river, some self-consciously beautiful buildings along its banks with intricately carved windowsills on which pigeons wobbled. Inside the room all was clutter: a trunk spilled out evening dresses which I never wore, our underthings trailed along the carpet towards the vulgar brass bed, empty champagne bottles bobbed against the sides of ice-buckets in which the ice had melted into thin lozenges, guidebooks were opened at pages in which we had marked places of interest to visit – the Louvre, Versailles, the Tuileries – but failed to.

The city beckoned beneath our high balcony, but we chose to explore only each other, and our explorings were a celebration, a gloating triumph, freedom from the constraints of custom and religion. 'My jewel,' my husband whispered, rummaging with warm, experienced fingers through every fold of my body, 'my pearl, my priceless one, my treasure.' And we shrieked with laughter as we reflected that I had indeed cost him dear. Before our wedding, he had smoothed outraged feelings by covering them over with money. Malina's servants were to have regular wages – an unheard-of arrangement – instead of just their keep, to soften them towards a new mistress. Father Casey, the parish priest, whose church, as Charles's wife, I could no longer attend, was compensated for the loss of his most trilling choirgirl by the provision of new altarcloths and the building of a community hall where dances might be held under the priest's supervision: polite, tame affairs, unlike the wild, abandoned crossroads dances he splutteringly deplored. Thus mollified, the flustered priest attended my wedding party, shook my hand, fascinated by the merciless sparkle of the diamond on my finger, and wished me every happiness with a sincerity I had no reason to doubt.

It was not my husband's money that made my marriage to him acceptable to my parents; it was his power over them, a power whose extent my mother had sobbingly revealed to me the night before my wedding, when a heavy conscience forced her to speak.

The rickety structure of a series of Land Acts were as much to blame for Charles's hold over my family as his own need to dominate and bully. Over the centuries, laws made in England had been eased and fudged to fit more comfortably the realities of Irish life. Since 1829, under the terms of the Catholic Emancipation Act, thrifty husbandmen like the McCallas — 'strong farmers' was the legal definition of our kind — were able to buy land, and, since then, softened attitudes towards the native Irish and a rash of further Land Acts had taken whole tracts of the seeping boglands away from the large estate owners.

But our deeds of ownership were slapdash documents, as Charles Trewin, mapping out his own lands for valuation, had discovered. The McCalla title deeds applied to the homestead of Shanvally and the tumbled, rocky pasturage in which house and outbuildings were set. The better part of our grasslands, fields wrested from the rock, thickened by the strewing of seaweed that exhausted men and women had dragged from the sea's fringe, those fields that fattened our horses and provided the hay that rose in spiky bricks from the floor of the tin-roofed barn, these, our very livelihood, by some quirk in the laws relating to outright possession, were ours only on leasehold. Their borders, where shining blades of grass meshed and tangled after a fall of rain, belonged within the confines of Malina's boundaries.

My parents knew this well, had always known, but had hoped, since legalities were so rarely acted upon, or even examined, in our lax country, that they had an age-old right to the fields they tended and enriched. But seven years ago, at the pony show in Clifden, Charles Trewin had shown his hand, hinted that he had every right to hack deep grooves in the land where the spangled grass waved, so that a railway might run from Galway to Clifden. His lips shaped formal, clipped words in which there was the merest suggestion of a sneer, and my parents felt a helplessness becloud them, born of the seven-hundred-year-old domination of their race by his. Over those centuries, both races had come to a crafty accommodation with each other, as Charles Trewin and my father and mother were to do that show-day while, just out of earshot, I coaxed the tired horses into their boxes.

A furtive deal was struck. My father needed the grazing land, the estate owner wanted me at the Big House, in order, he told them, 'to help my wife overcome her fear of animals and then, who knows, her fear of life itself. An irrational terror which transmits itself to the horses, making them as nervy as she is. It's a vexing situation. Do say, Mr McCalla, that I may count on your daughter's help in improving it?'

There was no need for Charles Trewin to mention that, should his request be granted, the threat to our land would vanish. Wordlessly, this was understood, as so much is understood in transactions between English and Irish: adaptations, inveiglements, compromises made between our subversive allure and the conqueror's funless severity. We come to necessitous agreements but they are smeared with distrust.

As they shook hands on the deal among the drunken breeders and rootling horses, my mother and father felt as though they were pushing me into harm's way. Gossip caracoles around our small community. Lives are scoured for their minutest detail and not the smallest shame can be hidden. It had not gone unnoticed that beneath the gauzy sleeves of Harriet's rustling summer dresses two oval bruises, like thumbprints, could be seen, impressed on her freckled arms just above the elbow, where the flesh is soft. The two Casey girls, Connie and Honoria, sent to Malina as maids, were back home in a fortnight, frightened by the tyrannical atmosphere of the Big House, something that made the scentless air foul and unbreathable. They told of how one evening, Harriet, two queer spots of colour high on her cheeks, had come running from the drawing-room, holding in each hand one half of an exquisitely worked piece of *petit point* she had all but completed when Charles had snatched it from her and ripped it apart, so that the shredded silk threads were left dangling. As Connie went to help her retrieve the scattered needle and the tiny embroidery scissors shaped like a stork, they could both hear Charles's voice thundering into the hallway: 'Was ever a woman as small-minded as you? You think ou can solve this country's ills with a bale of hay to mend a washerwoman's roof or a sack of flour given to a hungry family, and that then you have earned the right to sit by the fire with your confounded sewing. Why was I not granted a wife to face the storm with me, one who realizes that Ireland's accursed traditions are bleaching the life out of her? God damn your kindness, Harriet, when it's courage that's needed, courage that you flinch from! Here, in this place, your gentleness is a crime. You sin, my sweet gentlewoman, you sin.'

Honoria and Connie said that they would rather salt herrings on the quay, with the rain pelting down their necks, than listen to that terrible, hoarse ranting. That night they clung to each other, weeping futilely, in the cloudy featherbed in Malina's attic, and before daybreak they sacrificed its softness for the straw pallet in their mother's reeking cottage, to which they returned like two startled, bedraggled chicks who have had a close encounter with the fox. There was tattle about Mr Trewin's meanness, too. He kept half a dozen hunters but let Murchin, the deaf-mute cobbler, wait a year for his money, kept count of the kitchen candles, while the chandeliers upstairs blazed with light.

'If he shook your hand, it would be with two fingers only,' Fergus Keane complained, as he made ready to present his bill to Malina for the third time. 'If it weren't for herself, the darlin', I'd tell him to shop elsewhere.' My father, examining clay pipes heaped in a basket, laughed appreciatively, knowing both that there was no other shop this side of twenty mil and that without Malina's account Fergus would out of business. Landowner and shopkeeper lived a state of mutual dependence, a state common in our wronged, haphazard country.

My mother hated the thought of her boisterous daughter entering the Trewins' unhappy household, where silent screams, barely withheld, seemed to echo in the pale, cold rooms.

'I looked into those taunting yellow eyes of his on that show day,' she told me, the night before I was to marry, 'and I felt the power that was in him. He looked above every law made by God or man; if he chose to snap my neck from my head and walk away, there wouldn't be one who would dare stop him.'

We were embroidering my new initials, R.E.T., in silk thread on some linen handkerchiefs, in the same room where Harriet had once worked her *petit point*, sometimes looking up from her tapestry to stare sadly to where the wind scoured the iron surface of the lake. Charles had given us the use of Malina that night, while he himself slept at Lisnagreve with his friends, Lord and Lady Fitzhaven, so that I would have space enough to hang up my wedding clothes, and servants to help me bathe and dress the next morning.

I moved closer to my mother on the glazed chintz of the sofa and put my arm around her soft shoulders. 'The fuss of all this has made you cranky,' I said. 'You and Da should have a wedding trip the same as myself, to Dublin, maybe or some such place where you might see sights. I shall have my own allowance ᷓom tomorrow on, so I can send you and keep the ᷓnies in my own stables; there's all the grazing you ᷓld wish for.' I flung out my arm towards the win-
demonstrating the reach of my new kingdom,

but my mother snatched my wrist and held it. Her mouth twisted like a crooked pin and her face had a liverish sheen like coarse porcelain.

'I have dreams at night,' she said. 'I'm walking along the edge of the strand at Horam's Cove, cooling my feet in the little waves. Something is lying in the sand; a bundle of cloth it looks like, some thin, light stuff lifted by the wind. As I come closer, I recognize the cloth. It's a muslin dress of Harriet's, one she favoured when the day was pleasant. Now I start to run, my heart against my side, for I'm thinking that she has fallen or fainted. But when I reach her it is not Harriet's light hair that I see but your black curls, Rose Erris, dredged in sand, and the great, grey eyes of you, lustreless as a pebble dimmed by the mist although the sky is bright and pitiless above you. And then you speak, but it is Harriet's voice I hear, that thin, startled voice of hers. Water and blood slip from her mouth as she speaks but I can make out the words. "You knew," she says. "All of you knew, yet you did nothing." Night in, night out, the sleep is chased out of me so.'

My mother let go of my wrist and pulled her skirt up to cover her face in the old gesture of grieving. Although the sun had gone down and night was dropping over day, I felt the air in the pretty room heat and thicken. I felt afraid, although I would have torn my head from my shoulders rather than show my fear to her. 'It's only the old indigestion that makes you dream,' I said. 'You should not have so much strong tea taken late at night, it unsettles you.' My mother uncovered her face and showed hectic e and a mottled neck. 'There's no blame on yo said soothingly. 'There was a good lump of land in it. Anyone would have done the same as you and Da.'

'He had her terrified,' she said, 'cowering under his shadow. He dragged her towards her death and shrouded her in the bitter smoke of self-contempt. May all be desert up to his door.'

'That's a queer sort of welcome for a new son-in-law,' I said, still trying to calm her. 'I give you that they weren't suited, Harriet being so wistful and strained and not having it in her nature to be thrilled by life. But it's a different thing entirely when it comes to myself. Didn't he make me into the woman I am now? A woman who greets challenge and change like dearest friends.'

'My sorrow that he did,'· my mother said. She sounded as though she had swallowed something that was dissolving her very bones. 'The way he spoke to your Da and myself that day at the pony show.' She stood up suddenly, stroked her nose in the way that Charles sometimes did and arranged her features into an expression of contempt. When she spoke it was in imitation of the Englishman. 'Ay've a notion that something could be done with yaw-er dawr-ter. I desire to be her benefactor.' My mother sat down again, falling heavily on the plump cushions. 'Benefactor is it? The way the English think they can be of benefit to the Irish is to pluck all the Irishness out of us and make us feel shamed by our race.'

She clutched my hand with its betrothal diamond. 's not too late, my dote,' she wheedled. 'My sorrow I didn't say to him long years ago that he could back from us every pick of a blade of grass, and we'd sell the ponies and go to America like many before us. But we can do it yet. You can never marry him, knowing what I've told you.'

I smiled at her. 'Leave Shanvally?' I said. 'Da would die first, and well you know it, Mammy. And how could I be marrying any man but Charles?' (I let the intimate, private sound of 'Charles' roll around my tongue.) 'He has made me into what I am, given me all I have. And you know that I'm mad for him, and for him only, and always have been, since he first came into the yard below and juggled with the eggs. There's nothing changed since then except that I'm old enough now to know how I feel for him. It's soul mates that we are, the two of us.'

My mother made her old, troubled gesture of seeking out loose pins in her coiled hair. 'Soul mates, is it, when there's a chasm there should be between you and him? You think yourself so swoony in love,' she said bitterly, 'but I wonder whether it's Charles Trewin you've fallen for or this great house of his. I'd say that these stone walls beside the lake have you enchanted. And if you put what the man has above what the man is it's a crooked kind of happiness ye'll be getting.'

I was nettled. 'I know you would rather I was marrying a raw brute of a farmer,' I said. 'But I'm used to Malina's ways. How could I ever be living in a snug little cabin where my harp would scrape against the bacon hooks on the ceiling and Eme would fret for want of decent stabling?'

I slammed the door behind me and left my mo to fold the handkerchiefs we had embroidered a pack them in a silk-lined case, initialled, like in shining lettering. When I unpacked them later, in a Paris hotel room, I could make out the dried marks of her salt tears on the linen.

My mother was not the only one to think that I was in love with Malina rather than its owner. Some months beforehand, I had taken Miss Gwynn some English magazines I had found in a wastepaper box in Malina's library. The schoolmistress came close to me and cupped in her palm, lined and shiny from the strong soap she used, the end of the string of small, fine pearls that Charles had given me for my sixteenth birthday. 'From Mr Trewin?' she asked. 'From himself,' I answered, and looked defiantly into her drooped eyes. 'Then he means to marry you,' she said, decisively. 'Pearls are what Englishmen give to their future wives. They are a symbol of purity, you see. To other kinds of women they give diamond brooches, as recompense for using up their lives while refusing to legalize the situation.' She looked at me steadily. 'To be mistress of Malina might be something,' she said. She opened her mouth, as though to say more. Her eyes flicked to the bookshelf over the flimsy mantel and then turned away from it. She decided to remain silent.

Since the evening at Shanvally when Finbar Kavanagh had voiced what the whole neighbourhood was thinking, mingled feelings of expectation and uncertainty had made me bashful in Charles Trewin's company, unable to look boldly into the marvellously ...ed amber eyes that had always reminded me of ...e gems that I itched to own.

He remained as he had always been, rumbustious, companionable, quick to smile, although, once, as I came into his drawing-room to practise a new song, I found him there alone, his fingers tracing the Greek key inlay of the harp's frame, his expression brooding and watchful.

And all the while the summer days lengthened, endless and airy. The shivering reflections of the mountains shone on the silken surface of the sea until late in the evening; then you could see the moon balanced on the water, its light glowing on hawthorn blossom, crusted and clotted on the bough.

To escape the heat of an August afternoon, Charles suggested sailing the pookawn around the bay, reported to be seething with mackerel. The boat was one my great-grandfather had built, its curves so true that it peeled back the waves effortlessly. We let down baited ropes for the fish, but indeed they were so plentiful that we could have leant over the side and scooped them up in our hands. Ensnaring what was so easily caught soon palled. We let the pookawn drift, shilly-shallying on the water. Charles, in a clumsy movement that was unlike him, took my wet hand in his and kept it there. Now it was his eyes, with their jewel-like fleckings, that refused to meet mine. He studied my hand, which was reeking of fish, the fingernails clogged with mackerel scales and shreds of bait, and raised it to his warm, dry lips.

'I am tired of pretending, Rose Erris,' he said, beginning to pick the fish scales from my dirty fingers. 'There are so many differences between us, yet what unites us is stronger. We share a rhythm. Can yo not feel its beat as we lead the horses down t' mountainside or follow a line of hounds? There is a defiance in you that matches my own; neither of us can bear to be thwarted in anything.' He lifted my captured hand to his downy cheek. 'I am blathering like a drunken tinker,' he said. 'What I mean is that I love you and would marry you if you'd have me. Will you?' 'I'll have you,' I said, and leant forward to kiss his flattened lion's nose, making the pookawn bob.

How fine he looked, my future husband, dappled with the sunshine that bounced off the scarcely ruffled sea, his shoulders broad and beefy and his ribcage, under the shrunken jersey of oiled wool that he wore for fishing, curving forward mightily, like that of a well-bred horse. Beside him, all other men seemed clumpish, unknowing.

'Without delay?' The order was veiled as a question.

'Without delay.'

'There'll be talk,' he said, as we guided the boat between the two stone piers and into the harbour where currachs and ropes were slopping about. 'But they can hardly accuse us of marrying in haste. I have known you since there was hardly anything to know except the blue-black shine of a curl and a pair of scratched knees.'

'I must insist that the wedding is in the church of my faith, or rather the faith I must profess to have.' Charles Trewin sat on one of the faded, lumpy chairs in Shanvally's stale, unused parlour. He no longer made n effort to charm my parents, now that he had all that e wanted from them. I loved the calm, harsh way he ued orders, felt myself carried gently along in his wake. My father and mother agreed to his every plan, wearily, dumbly. Only at the last minute did my mother reveal her breaking heart, a desperate, useless revelation that I tossed aside.

Dispensation was sought and given from the Archbishop of Tuam for my family to attend the church service. Aideen the Pin was put up at Shanvally, the arid parlour turned into a sewing-room where she stitched bridesmaids' dresses in misty blue chiffon for my sisters, to set off the chased silver bracelets that Charles Trewin had given each of them. A dressmaker's dummy in my measurements had been sent to Paris, to the seamstresses at the House of Worth. They sent back a dress with huge, moving skirts, over which vines of seed pearls trailed. After Mr Douglas Hyde founded the Gaelic League in 1893, it became the fashion for Irish brides to be married in our homespun linen. I am glad that in 1890 this had yet to be thought of. Linen, however flounced and embroidered, has an unassuming, modest look, more suited to the convent than the wedding dance. The heavy French satin, whose glossy shimmer had the same blue-whiteness as Murrough's firstborn foal, was more to my liking. In the dank parlour, Aideen the Pin made some fiddly adjustments to its swooshing train and led me towards the sideboard's greening mirror. Facing my glimmering reflection, I felt as though the birthday of my life had come.

My mother's tortured confessions that same nigh the grieving sounds she made as I came down Malin staircase on my wedding morning, left me c momentarily shaken. By the time my foot wa the bottom stair I was as unconcerned as a marble statue encased in my gleaming gown. No revelation of past treachery could dint my radiance. Beneath the skinny, needling spire of the invader's church, I walked down the aisle on my father's arm, past my mother, whose tears were barely dry on her cheeks, towards the sleek back of my waiting bridegroom. I held out my finger towards the proffered ring. The delicate circlet bound me to Malina, made me the queen of all its intricate passages.

10

Our fevered honeymoon over, we arrived at Cobh harbour for the homeward stage of the journey (how glorious it was to say the word 'home' to myself knowing that it meant Malina) after a day and a night spent in hushed compartments that were furred and plushy like the inside of jewel-boxes: first the luxurious carriage of the French train where I marvelled at the bed that flopped down from the wall at the touch of a porcelain knob. I have a lasting memory of that night – my husband, flung on top of me by a sudden lurch of the speeding train, with a ready-to-burst look on his face, and on his body too, if bodies can be said to wear expressions.

'Never before, never like this,' he whispered into my ear, the words like a chant whose rhythm thumped along with the train's motion, while outside the carriage window with its tasselled blind, a hunter's moon streaked behind the dark trees, whose leaves were already hardening, curling, ready to fall.

Our steamer cabin was another velvety confinemer where we tossed and rolled in time with the rollin the sea's gravelly surface. I, who had always ne space as much as I needed air to breathe, was to be coddled in the stuffy, luxurious room, le only when the southern coast of Ireland rose from the water. On deck, the cold, sparkling air was delicious, the spray hair-white as it flung itself against the hull. Charles gave orders regarding our luggage and I listened to his arrangement of things dreamily, delighting in the novelty of having a man take charge of me, making authoritative decisions while I leant on the rail watching the sure, green world of the Irish countryside form itself behind the scummy walls of the pierhead.

The homeward train smelt of hot dust, although the compartment was damply cold. There were frequent, unexplained stops at wayside stations, all the way between Cork and Ballynahinch, when we could overhear baffled and unconcerned conversations between stationmaster and guard. Three countrywomen in traditional dark blue cloaks nudged themselves into our carriage, murmuring 'Begging yer honour's pardon but every inch of a place else is taken up', and settled around us with their baskets of eggs, rush hampers that emitted the frail chirpings of new chicks, and embarked on long singsong commentaries on their every second cousin and aunt by marriage who lived along the route. Soon we settled into the soothy, inconsequential, seamless talk of rain and harvest and laying ducks that I found comforting and familiar after the long, strange journey. Charles did not join in the conversation but withdrew behind a copy of *Punch* and a Turkish cigarette whose fragrance seemed exotic in the stuffed compartment that, by now, smelt of chicken and soot and salty bodies as well as heated dust. Once or twice he lowered the magazine and gave me an amused smile because I was sitting the way the women were, leaning forward with my palms on my outstretched knees. When the women got out at Athenry, having given me a day-old chick to be kept warm in my cashmere muff, he raised a tawny eyebrow and wiped a speck of soot from my forehead with a corner of his silk handkerchief. Then, hand in hand, we looked out of the dirty window at the discontented cattle munching the cold, autumnal fields, the high, blank walls of convents, the persisting little rivers.

I know what happiness is. It is having everything you ever wanted right then, in the living moment. Father Casey would disagree. He would argue that happiness comes with the knowledge that our sufferings on earth will bring a heavenly reward. Yet the heaven he urges on his flock is a dull, sugary place that would bore me and make me long for the bad, enticing company of demons, such as I enjoyed in this mortal life. My own version of hell (although I doubt its actual existence in any form as much as I doubt that of its angelic alternative) is somewhere where I could not indulge my taste for the rare and racy.

I was in a private heaven on earth as the vague, sluggish train hastened us fitfully towards Malina. We arrived late at night, under a sky of spiky, arching stars. Horty O'Goole handed me down from the phaeton in a detached way, touched his cap haphazardly, as though his hand moved of its own accord, and led the carriage towards the coachhouse. A rich, yellow light streamed from the tall windows and splashed on the gravel chips of the drive, turning them to polished gems. Bringing a wife to Malina for the second time in his life, Charles did not repeat his performance of carrying his bride over the threshold and up the sweeping rise of the staircase. Instead, he pushed open the massive door, let it swing back against the wall, and had me pass before him into the glare of the marble hall. 'Mrs Trewin,' he said, mimicking a brogue, 'a hundred, thousand welcomes.'

The servants were in bed, except for Agnes MacReion, who had stayed up to mind the fires. There is something kittenish and vulgar about Agnes. She rolls her eyes when she talks and gives you vampish looks over one of her plump shoulders as she takes your coat and hat. Even as a little girl, performing poorly in Miss Gwynn's schoolroom, she exasperated the schoolteacher by passing notes to the boys and biting her lips to redden them when she should have been learning her tables.

She was oily to me now, as she went ahead of me up the stairs, holding the pink-globed lamp and leading me to the principal bedroom on the first landing, Harriet's bedroom, now mine. 'There's two stone bottles scorching hot in the bed for yeez,' she said, adding impudently, 'not that ye'd be in want of them.'

She wished for a sticky intimacy with me that I refused her − perhaps that led to my future undoing. I dismissed her with a muttered goodnight and did not turn my eyes towards the wonderfully curtained bed until she had left the room. Then I looked and was still marvelling at the way ice-blue silk had been swirled and tented and caught up in a gilt wreath on the carved ceiling, so that the bed seemed suspended in the air, when Charles came in, my small, urgent dog in his arms yapping uncontrollable welcomes. Together in that swirling blue silk, Charles and I were like two swimmers grappling together underneath the waters of a shining lake. At some point we became fluid ourselves, dissolving into each other, little puffs of warmth rising on our breath, although the stone bottles we had kicked to the foot of the bed had long since gone cold and the fire was crumbling into fine, silvery ash. Then my husband slept, his legs flung across my damp, musky body, trapping it. I lay awake, looking at the taut pleating of the draperies above my head as they darkened in the dying firelight. I imagined Harriet's disdainful limbs stretched out where mine were now becoming heavy with tiredness and wondered sleepily if her cold, drooping shade haunted the dreams of the passionate man who lay beside me.

Ruddily awake the next morning, Charles gave no sign of being ghost-shadowed. What I loved about him was his total, blinkered absorption in the thing in hand, reducing the rest of the world to something shadowy and dismissed. What absorbed him then were our private rituals: the shamelessly early dinners we gulped down so that we might retire early to a shared bath and hours of erotic, playful love-making. When he lifted my nightgown and parted with his tongue the petals of what he called 'my rose within my Rose', I felt myself idolized, turned into a religion that was fervently worshipped.

For the whole of that autumn, we practised our rapturous rituals undisturbed. It is the custom among the Anglo-Irish gentry that a newly married pair are given a short season of privacy before the calling-cards start to flutter in scurries on the silver tray in the hall and the couple are summoned to dinner parties where the recent bride is expected to wear her wedding dress until the date of her first anniversary has passed.

It was during this time, when tradition permitted us our intimate isolation, that we put in train what Binnie called 'thim improvings' to Malina. A glossy black patent stove with a square, ravenous mouth was installed in the kitchen to heat water and cook food and devour creel after creel of axed wood. 'Ye'd have the woods around destroyed entirely before ye'd get a lick of warmth out of *him*.' Wrathful against the incursion, Binnie reduced the stove to the level of a useless, cranky male, and continued to bake soda bread in the seed of the fire. Upstairs, a dressing-room was converted into a tiled bathroom, where water pipes knocked and juddered strangely and towel rails, fed by 'him' alternately burned your fingers or left the towels cold and soggy. Charles relished these domestic malfunctions, spent whole mornings in the cellars with wrench and hammer, oblivious of the cobwebs in his glorious hair. But, once the winter began, I sensed that, although he gave himself unstintingly to me and to Malina, he itched to recommence a public life. There was in him, as in all showy men, a quest for a state of self-reference, a need to be endlessly embroiled in negotiations with the social world.

I, hardly more than a boisterous, larky child, responded to it, understanding my husband's need to flaunt and fascinate, since it was a need I shared. Lord and Lady Fitzhaven of Lisnagreve Manor were the first of the Ascendancy families to lead us back into the social world. It is said in Ireland that because wave after wave of conquering armies dispossessed the current ruling nobility and pulled the aristocrats down into the mass of the people, even the roughest peasant may claim to have the blood of a prince ripping through his veins. If this is true, then so is its opposite. Look at some of our upstart nobles such as Lord Fitzhaven. Take away the expensive bay rum that makes the thin waves of his silver hair look stiff and engraved, remove the swagged and looped watch-chain that courts his prosperous belly, put a greasy cloth cap on his head, and his prickly, high-coloured face would be that of a corner boy. Two and a half thousand years of governance, of high-walled estates and hunting lodges, a town house and a title, sons sent to Eton and Cambridge and daughters married into the flightiest royal families of Eastern Europe had managed to put only a thin scraping of polish over peasant features: purply cheeks threaded with fine, dark broken veins, splayed, crooked teeth.

Lady Fitzhaven was flushed and blonde and attractively disarrayed. Her plump, pink arms in black lace gloves looked like netted salmon. She greeted Charles by rounding her mouth and blowing little O shapes into the air, then settled her lips into their own firm, squarish set and gave me a quick, unaffected hug as though she had known me all my life. 'My dear,' she said, her voice supple, tender and slurping, 'they tell me you sing. I shall call upon you the moment the gentlemen have rejoined us after dinner otherwise there'll be talk of nothing but Leaguers and railways all night.' She lowered her lovely voice and whispered to me intimately, 'My mother always insisted that three topics were forbidden at the dinner table: religion, politics and sex. Well everyone, including the rector, prattles away on the first two these days and I wouldn't be surprised if the third isn't given an airing before our days are done.' She raised her voice and gave me the briefest of winks. 'Come through, Mrs Trewin; we're all dying to hear about *everything* you did in Paris.'

She lowered her thrilling voice again, well aware of its spellbinding musicality. 'An edgy evening in store, I'm afraid. Thesper insisted on inviting some Home-Ruler from County Tyrone and the poor man keeps on giving me terrified looks as though he thinks I've plans to serve him up for dinner with the parsley sauce instead of the boiled beef.'

Lady Fitzhaven led me blithely into a well-heated and rather fussily decorated drawing-room much in the manner of one parading a particularly fine pedigree pup around a show ring. She frowned theatrically at the group of people in pampered-looking evening clothes who stood around the fireplace. 'See here, my dears,' she said. 'Here is Mrs Trewin at her very first dinner party and I forbid you to talk to her about anything that's the least bit improving. She is only just married and gasping to be amused.'

Her guests laughed dutifully and fanned themselves out into a wider, more hospitable half-circle. The Home-Ruler had been newly elected to the House of Commons, his electorate for the first time refusing to vote for their landlord's candidate. (The landlord had since gone to live mournfully in France.) In homage to his leader, Mr Parnell, Mr Damian Dashwood had grown his whiskers to a fine oratorial length and parted his hair severely in the centre. On Mr Parnell, the uncrowned king of Ireland, the effect of both was awe-inspiring. On his acolyte the effect was touchingly comical. For above Mr Dashwood's lustrous whiskers were not Parnell's dark, fascinating eyes but a pair of baby-blue ones, shining as though rinsed under a pump and as innocent and good-natured as a spring sky, arranged under fine, downy, surprised-looking eyebrows. He had the meaty hands of a ploughboy and winced at Lady Fitzhaven's twinkly banter, jerking back when she tapped him on the arm with her folded fan and said, 'Don't be deceived by Mr Dashwood's boyishness, Mrs Trewin. He would have us put out of Lisnagreve tomorrow and some desperate co-operative of turnip-growers digging up my azaleas and keeping pigs in the gazebo. But I shall let him take you into dinner nonetheless, to show there's not a speck of ill-feeling between us.' Her teeth appeared brilliantly, then scuttled away as she began a drifting organization into the dining-room.

A young man with a clipped, precise profile like a paper silhouette solicitously held my chair back for me. He was Busho O'Cleary; I knew his name well because it had often been told me that his grandfather, who had spent most of his wife's fortune landscaping his estate in the English manner, had evicted a tenant family and knocked down their straw-roofed cabin with a battering ram for no other reason but that it marred the view from his back windows. Yet, during the hungry years, this same man had mortgaged his sumptuously rolling acres, sold his wife's diamonds to keep his tenants alive, paid for their sons' and daughters' tickets to America and funded a workhouse where, after visiting it, he caught famine fever and died. Now Busho, his grandson, whose evening clothes were worn thin at elbow and knee and had the bronzy-green sheen of age, said, 'How delightful to find myself seated beside you, Mrs Trewin.'

'How delightful to find myself seated at all,' I said. 'My feet are flattened on me from standing in new shoes for so long.' The crisp profile folded itself into dozens of amused creases and its owner began to talk to me in that loud, lavish way the upper classes have in Ireland, as though it would be unthinkable for them to ever run out of words.

Opposite me, Busho's wife, Emmeline, was twittering across the furious glitter of the crystal to the young woman seated beside the still-subdued Mr Dashwood. The two women might have been related; both had thin, nervous collarbones, jangly overactive faces in which beautiful hazel eyes flickered expectantly. Handsomely dressed, their hair rolled and fringed in an assured way, they had the creamy manners of those whose lives are lived entirely in public. They bobbed about on a sea of sociability, engaged effortlessly in twinkly conversations. You had only to hold a smile on your face, till you felt you would never have it picked from your lips if you lived to be a hundred, and they would drown you politely in warm, steamy waves of babble.

I kept a sappy grin in place and looked at the marvels of the Fitzhavens' table, listened to the soft, extractive sound of pulled corks. Six glasses were ranged beside my place, and round their bases white, etched deer chased each other in a never-ending circle. Steaming courses followed one upon the other: a clear soup, a wild-eyed salmon, a boiled joint, a pale, shuddering pudding that tasted vaguely of cloves, all rather bland and washed out. Our faces grew flushed with wine while, under the table, our feet grew numb with cold: it was always so at dinner parties in Ireland, as I would soon discover. At some point, as the tasteless fish gave place to the insipid meat, Charles raised a tawny eyebrow, a signal that I was to turn away from Busho's fizzing chatter and address the gentleman seated at my left. This was a man in his early thirties with a thin, downward-curving mouth like that of a freshly caught fish. His long fingers picked fussily at a pappy white bread roll as he looked at me beadily.

When he spoke, it was as though he had knives in his mouth. 'I beg of you, do not mention the Leaguers, they are my *noirest bêtes*.'

Since our views on the Land League were bound to be contrary, I too was eager to avoid politics. 'What would you like to talk about?' I asked silkily. Above the unfortunate and ugly mouth there was a narrow nose, fatly lidded eyes and a balding crown that rose to a bony point. Among the frazzling energy that vibrated around Lady Fitzhaven's table there was something attractive about this balding man's weariness. I slid my company smile in place. 'Myself,' he said surprisingly. 'In particular, my ailments. The rattle in my chest would awaken the dead; I'm surprised it hasn't put you down with a headache.' He eyed me slittily from beneath his smooth eyelids. 'I see you are too young to know about headaches. We have not been introduced

– my name is Myles Lavelle, if that means anything to you – but *your* fame has spread before you. It's said that you can look at a dying horse and it will rise to its feet and come in first at the races.' Myles Lavelle gave a flickering little cough and closed his eyes in distaste at the sound. 'Pretend I'm a horse and effect a cure, there's a dear woman. Only please don't recommend exercise. Turning the pages of dear Mr Trollope is as much as I can manage.'

I took his hand. It was as limp as a rag and the bones seemed to swim under the thin, slightly moist flesh like a swarm of little, lost creatures. I remembered that the *cailleach,* the healing woman who lived in Clifden, said that the first sign of the TB is when the bones start to feel loose under the skin. I remembered other things she had said. 'You'd need goat's milk,' I said, laying Mr Lavelle's floppy hand gently on the shining tablecloth. 'And be sure that when the lad milks the goat, he dips his finger in the pail and makes a cross on the goat's rump. And when it's the chest that's troubling you, goose-grease is your only man. You'd be rubbing it in thick and then putting brown paper round the top of it.'

I faltered as I noticed that the room had gone quiet around us. Sweat trickled from my armpits and down the boned seams of my bodice as I considered whether age-old Irish cures were on my hostess's list of forbidden table-talk. While I was wondering whether the unwelcome silence indicated appalled politeness or gripped fascination, Myles Lavelle took my hot hand and raised it to his drooping, greyish lips. 'Oh my, Trewin,' he called across the table. 'This is no mortal woman you have here. Admit it, you bought her from the Banshee. What bargain did you strike, I wonder? Did you sell your soul to them in return?' He pressed his unpleasant lips again to my hand. 'I know I should have done,' he said feverishly, 'had I such a thing as a soul to exchange, instead of a pathetic rag-bag of attitudes and prejudices.'

Lady Fitzhaven recovered something of her indolent, drawling manner. 'Emotion always makes Myles reckless,' she said mildly, as the reckless one crumbled into a series of harsh little coughs. 'Resist the temptation to let him put you on a pedestal, Mrs Trewin. It would only be because he wants a better view of your ankles.'

The dinner table was restored to spangly good humour, the pattern of relentlessly animated nattering re-established. Soon afterwards, Lady Fitzhaven led the ladies back to the drawing-room. *Papier poudre* was fished out of reticules and applied to shiny, hawkish noses. Emmeline O'Cleary hoiked up the back of her lavender moiré dress and leaned against the fireguard to warm her legs. Her friend, Julia Gibbons, declared that a much-regretted second helping of pudding was making her stays twang against her ribs in complaint. But, in spite of all this female intimacy, their voices did not soften. Everything was discussed in brittle, cheery voices full of a cold energy. Even when they mentioned their small sons, sent away to hellish English boarding-schools like the one Charles had so hated, their voices remained spiky, amused. They lived in a country that was bubbling with revolt against their tolerant, lazy ownership; they despatched four-year-old boys, howling at being torn away from their Irish nurseries and teddy bears, to an alien England, tame and orderly, which regarded these odd, wild, delightful children as misfits. Lady Fitzhaven, Emmeline, Julia and their like refused to crack. On they went, proud, horsy women, mindless of discomfort and danger, dedicated to reducing life to ritualized fun. Admirable, disturbing women, as different from the native Irish mothers with their scared, baleful devoutness and sweet, soft hearts as whey is from thick cream. It was pleasant to listen to the brazen, flimsy talk in Lady Fitzhaven's house. It soothed me, turned the new, strange world I had entered into something harmless and inconsequential.

When the gentlemen joined us, flushed and unsteady after port and political argument, Mr Dashwood came immediately to my side. There was an angry sheen on his babyish face with its scarcely visible eyebrows. 'You should never have talked so,' he said balefully, his rosy mouth pettish. 'You pandered to the picture they have of us all, all quaint tilted fields and old, useless ways. You make it hard for the likes of me to persuade them that we're grown enough to manage our own country, and indeed we have a right to do so, when you play the barefoot girleen with your cures and fallals. God save Ireland from those who would hold her back.' He gave me another admonishing look, set down his lacquered coffee cup with a shaking hand then strode towards the window and glared out at the shrubs.

My husband was quickly at my side. 'Pay no mind to that young desperado if he has been upsetting you,' he said gently. 'Like all Irishmen, alluring women frighten the hide off him. He has a notion that they turn men's minds away from the important things in life, such as making speeches and clamouring for further land reforms. I think our hostess is about to ask you to sing. Juliet and Emmeline are looking particularly catty tonight, which means they are jealous of your Paris gown or your grasp of medicine, or both. Go to it, my love, the world is ripening to your harvest' – he mimicked a brogue in the teasing way he had, a way that I had not yet found hurtful – 'as they do be saying in these parts.'

I crossed to the rosewood piano as Lady Fitzhaven made a to-do of arranging her guests on spindly gilt-backed chairs, where they sat, poker-backed, with rather mettlesome expressions on their well-bred faces, except for Myles, who looked at me slobberingly. These Ascendancy families would not be as easily ensnared by my singing as the sentimental businessmen who snuffled into their big, clean handkerchiefs when I struck the opening chords of 'Carrickfergus' or 'My Lagan Love' during cloying musical evenings at Malina. Busho and his kind had an ancestry that was fierce and unyielding, giving their menfolk up to valorous exploit in battle for Strongbow, Cromwell, King William, England's honour, Ireland's glory, heedless of pain or death. Yet, throughout the stern centuries, they had been readily ensnared by a quality in the Irish peasantry that they felt lacking in themselves: a lazy charm, a catchy, seductive way of speaking, a rueful, unregretting way of coming to terms with life. That's what makes them stay here, selling up their fine town houses in Belgravia and Park Lane so as to have the money to lay a damp-proofing course in the stable block of some ruinous, rambling Irish estate. They are terrible for coddling their horses and neglecting their children.

So, in spite of pretended indifference, they were grudgingly ensnared by my siren songs. Busho's crisp profile softened, even haughty Julia sighed and relaxed her lovely shoulders against the fragile chairback. I did not insult them by singing about abandoned girls and dead babies and tragic, yearning mothers, all the mushy, squelchy emotional ballads that might bring a sneer to well-bred lips. I chose a lighter repertoire: songs of the sea and ships, fields and cows, set to jaunty, jingly tunes.

I was succeeded at the piano by two other ladies and an elderly gentleman, who bent his neck low over his music, revealing the back of it to have the thick, pitted texture of boiled tongue.

How ridiculous they sounded, their voices thin and pained, the words of their stifled, self-conscious songs – 'Come into the Garden, Maud', 'After the Ball is Over' – silly enough to have made me giggle if Charles had not placed a warm, controlling hand over mine.

'Well, you were the hit of the evening, Mrs Trewin,' Lady Fitzhaven acknowledged pleasantly, as we climbed into our waiting carriage. 'You will have all the gentlemen round to Malina, begging you to rub them well with goose-grease and wrap them in brown paper.'

We nestled inside the carriage, dappled with success, warmed in a conspiracy of love. 'I'm thinking of trying to get government funding to plant conifers in the far valley,' Charles murmured into my hair. 'I'll have the Viceroy himself to stay. You'll serve him boiled crubeens and drisheen and sing to him that air about the herring boats sailing out into the blue and I'll guarantee he'll have his life signed away to you before you can say Brian Boru. What say you to that, my mountain Rose?'

'Soopar, soopar fun,' I said drowsily, giving an imitation of Emmeline O'Cleary's whinnying drawl that wouldn't have disgraced my sister Deirdre.

11

That year, we refused to let the winter tighten our lives. At the time of the Viceroy's visit, it was perfect hunting weather, the sun shining on a cold, clear world that seemed made of glass. Our hounds streamed over fields where each blade of grass, each dew-coated pebble glimmered tautly in a sharp light. The clouds were white and crisp as meringues, the lake water barely skimmed in the windless air and took on the mysterious mottled silver of a tarnished mirror, reflecting the small, inky birds that flew overhead, V-shaped scraps in a blithe sky.

The Viceroy sighed deeply with pleasure as, the hunt over, we let our horses amble back through the borheens, towards Malina's vast fires and cups of hot buttered claret. He was a countryman whose family estates were in Derbyshire, and he loathed the confinement of life in Dublin, the forced, tamed city life that made him feel numbed and stilted.

He warmed to Connemara, to the scrambled, disarranged earth and scarred, grey rock shouldering its way through the thin soil. 'There's a lot to be said for you Irish, my dear,' he said cheerfully, 'for you never founded a town in your lives. Dublin is Danish, Kilkenny Norman. Your people have a horror of towns: if you took one in battle, you burnt it to the ground. Shows your good sense.' He looked appreciatively at the mountains linked heavily around the motionless lake. 'How good are you at local names, Mrs Trewin?' he asked, pointing his whip at a toughened ridge of hillside in the far distance. 'What is that perilous-looking hillside called, for instance?'

'Magaire an Deamhain,' I answered.

'Meaning? '

'The devil's balls,' I shouted over my shoulder as I urged Emer into a trot.

At dinner that night, the Viceroy, red in the face and spluttering with laughter, declared that he'd never suspected the native tongue to have such richness in it. I served him snipe, cutting off the small, neat heads myself. Holding them by their long bills on a toasting-fork, I cooked them over the fire until they were soft enough to split open, then spread the creamy brains on sippets of toast for our guest. Before he left us, a grant to start forestation on the mountain slopes had been promised. That winter, in spite of the cold that sprang up in your face every morning, Malina's oak front door stood open under its stone arch to welcome the meet. The round hall crackled with noise as the hunt breakfasted at trestle tables, while outside the hounds yelped and horses, shiny in the sunlight, reared and snickered, sending the gravel skidding and dropping steaming rounds of dung.

Here was hullabaloo at last and Harriet would have had none of it. The disarray would have terrified her: the wild expectancy of the animals and of the huntsmen themselves as they prepared for the chase

147

with that intense mingling of terror and pleasure that makes hearts thump beneath scarlet coats.

Malina's back door, a more modest affair of nailed, white-painted timbers, always rather chewed and softened at the edges by the salt sea air no matter how often replaced, stood open too. The back of the house now swarmed with unofficial retainers who bartered produce for our frequent supper parties or entreated my help, as I flitted between kitchen and drawing-room, in curing a goat that wouldn't milk or a gimmer that wouldn't thrive, or who just came to observe the excited bustle of the humming, vibrant house, sitting on a warmed sod of turf by the kitchen fire, oblivious of the snagging wind that blew through the open door.

In spite of her charitable nature, Harriet would not have welcomed these visitors, smudgy and dirty as they were, to her fireside. She would have sent kindling to their rotting cabins rather than have them finger her china while their scabby dogs licked a cut-glass bowl for the leavings of a rich trifle that clung to its sides.

I kept the back-door visitors a secret from Charles for, although it was Binnie's pride that, as she herself boasted, 'As much is thrown away in this house of a day as is used,' I sensed a pinched English parsimony only partly hidden behind my husband's showy extravagance (the village tattle regarding the counted kitchen candles lingered in my mind). I urged my uninvited guests to hide the ham bones and crocks of broth I gave them under their cloaks as they stole from the house like lumpy shadows as dark fell.

My mother and sisters visited but rarely, my mother never passing the rent table in the hall, with its indexed drawers that narrowed towards the centre like slices of cake, without throwing a throttled curse at it. She came to the Big House for one purpose only: to stealthily install bowls of holy water on shadowy shelves in parts of the house where she knew Charles never ventured. Sometimes, mounting Emer to join the hunt, I would see a curtain twitch at a window and know that behind it, my mother was crossing herself for my safe return.

I started to notice a change in her. Always hard-working, she now had an aura of saintly drudgery. She sighed when once she would have laughed, had fallen prey to a religious melancholy that withered everything it touched. Had I not been so occupied with my own rollicking life, I should have been more suspicious of a strange new look of stoic powerlessness that began to appear on her face. I was told the reason for her annoyingly virtuous expression on a rainy morning at Shanvally, where I was visiting the father who refused ever to visit me in my own house. Even in the place where he was master he had lost the shifty charm of the horse-dealer and now had a squinty look, like a beaten dog. Mastered by Charles Trewin, he felt shamed before the world and did not even try to keep reproach from his voice as he reluctantly answered my questions about horses and dogs.

'Vera will be taking her vows,' my mother interrupted our muted conversation as she brought us both steaming cups of tea. She sounded so smugly martyred that I flung my cup against the hearthstone in a fury.

'Is the girl's mind turned to mush?' I shouted. 'What about Declan Coady – has she forgotten that she's promised to him, and he having made the farm ready for her with new delft and a painted press for it?'

'You are a fierce one for possessions, Rose Erris,' my mother chided me, sounding wronged and tearful. 'Declan has taken the news like the good man he is; he understands that Vera feels called and is proud of her, as all of us here are the same.'

My mother sat back in her chair, brimming with self-sacrifice, mindful of the respect due to a nun's mother. I blamed her own church-terrified devoutness for my lovely older sister's madness. 'You'd have her twisted into a nun if it killed her,' I yelled. 'Just for a bit of swank in the village.'

My mother looked at me levelly, at my crimson gabardine dress with its embroidered sleeves, my diamond earrings, my coiled and teased hair. 'Swank is it?' she asked. 'I'd say you'd be the one who could be giving us all lessons in that department.'

I left the house angrily and stomped through the yard to the stables across cobbles which were dismally veiled by eddies of rank, muddied water. Vera was mucking out the stalls, her bright hair plaited and tied up with a suspect rag. She had on half-wellingtons with rotted toecaps and her old brown skirt was tucked into her bloomers. She whistled the air of a jig as she raked the soiled straw. My thunderous face sent her into snickers of laughter. 'If you are able to climb the ladder to the grain-loft in your silly old dress, let's go and have a talk there,' she said.

The grain-loft was our childhood plotting place, where the seven of us clambered to prick eggshells and then blow out the dribbling insides so that we could paint them for presents, our little pointed tongues curled against our top lips in concentration. Or we would rehearse the plays that Deirdre had written and which relied heavily on impersonations of people known to us. They were chucklingly received by our friends and neighbours when we performed them in the paddock. The one I remember best had Deirdre, dressed as Harriet in a white dress made from a length of the muslin we used for straining the curds, urging 'the feenest walnuts sent eespecially from Larndon' on a toothless tinkerwoman, acted by me with a mouthful of blacking and a moth-holed horseblanket for a cloak.

Grown up now, Vera and I climbed the rust-flaked ladder and sat on two sacks of oats which gave spongily under our weight. I leaned forward and caught Vera's upper arms, my thumbs pressing the soft flesh. 'How *could* you, Vee, you who had to be dragged to Mass roaring crying and then falling asleep in the pew and giving cheek to the chapel-women? Are they offering you up to compensate for what they think of as *my* bad ways? Are you to be shown up as the good daughter to make up for me being the evil one?'

'Do you give me no credit for having a mind of my own, Rosie?' Vera asked with no rancour in her soft voice.

I let go of her arms, helpless before the glint of her purpose. 'But why you, Vee, you who can dance the night out and who loves to be with children, why would you want such a terrible smother on your life?'

Vera turned my angry face towards her and flicked one of my gold-looped earrings so that the diamond swung against my cheek. 'It wouldn't be right for God to have only the gloomy ones,' she said. 'I want to do good, Rosie, and that's the truth of it. It's hard for our kind of people to do good; we stumble on so many obstacles – the centuries of backwardness, our colonial past, our pride, our powerlessness. I think that's why I need to renounce the distractions of life in the outside world, so that I do not dwell on the pain of history but give myself fully to God.'

I felt broken. 'I know well what you mean by distractions,' I said bitterly. 'Haven't I heard Father Casey drone on about the distractions of the flesh, all down the length of his nose as though he's having to force himself to pick up a maggoty crow that's fallen down the chimney. But now that I've sampled these distractions, I know that they are the centre of life itself. Father Casey makes the whole blind delight of it sound paltry and shameful, but what is it except the showing of love, love that fills your heart and makes you hold out your arms to welcome the world as well as the man whose flesh is as your flesh?'

'Love of man is your calling, Rosie, love of God is mine.' Vera spoke quietly although her cheeks scorched. 'Come and help me feed the ponies before you go back to the fleshly pleasures of Malina. You've no more chance of making me change my mind than I would have had in urging you not to marry a man who smacks of danger and intrigue.'

A sombre travesty of the bustle that attends a wedding now took over the house where I was born. Aideen the Pin returned to the seeping-walled parlour with her sewing-machine, but now the floor was strewn not with bolts of satin, whose icy sheen caught the light, but with the lengths of coarse, scratchy cotton that my golden-haired sister would be required to wear at all times, even when she bathed.

Once again, the driver of Bianconi's long car drove his vehicle through the snaky borheen to deliver presents from its hold. But for Vera there were no enticing packing-cases from London department stores in which cut glass and fine china nestled in straw beds, but lumpy parcels tied with old, greasy, much-knotted bits of string. They held rosary beads, holy pictures and biblical texts in burnt pokerwork. ''Tis well that all your possessions will be held in common at the convent,' I told Vera savagely, as I helped her stuff a pile of smudgily printed prayer books in a canvas case, 'for nobody of any taste would want sole ownership of such morbid slop.'

Vera looked at me forgivingly. 'Ah, Rosie, even when you were a little girl, you loved to hoard "treasures" — scraps of silk that Aideen had over, or pieces of smoothed glass from the strand. You're a treasure-seeker still and can't get it into your head that I'm not. You have your treasure now, Malina, and all the shiny wealth that is in it, and I have mine, the daub cell with the cruci-fix above my bed that will give me peace and refuge. Let us pray for each other that we are both worthy of our chosen lives.'

I would not go to Vera's novitiate. I did not trust myself not to scream as the shears closed crisply on her lustrous hair, nor could I have borne the sight of the starched wimple cutting cruelly across the silky wings of her eyebrows. I pictured my parents simpering before the priest and the reverend mother, puffed up with the martyred pride of 'giving up' a daughter, and I determined to do something to shame them.

I chose the day that Vera entered the convent to give a ball at Malina. Outside the Big House, a bitter wind wailed over the shelter of the wood, blew over the lake, clattering the pebbles at its shoreline. But, inside, Malina's great, high rooms fluttered with skittishness. Blind Hogan sat at the new piano and played slurpy waltzes all through the bright night until the gentlemen's silk coats were splattered with candle grease from the brimming chandeliers and the ladies sank down languidly on the puffy sofas and lifted up their swollen feet to show that the undersides of their dancing slippers were worn to threads.

Damian Dashwood was there that night, although Charles knew that the baleful glance of the member of parliament's baby-blue eyes made me feel tainted and troubled.

'The man's a fanatic, I know that,' Charles had said earlier in the evening. 'But men like him represent the future of this crippled country and we must accommodate them. His grandfather was old Fitzhaven's grandfather's gardener. The old scoundrel stole enough cabbages to set his son up in a grocer's shop in Claregalway and now our man is well enough set up to go into politics although it would be unwise to enquire into his source of funding. You can't blame him for his ambition, the Ireland of his steely vision won't come about by building boats and breeding ponies' – I fancied I could detect something malicious in Charles's voice – 'A republic fit for grocers is Mr Dashwood's dream and I dare say it's an improvement on the cringing, wronged nation he grew up in.'

He looked at the smooth, gold disc of his watch. 'Eight o'clock and no sign of anybody. If you people had as much respect for time as you do for fairy forts and holy wells, you might be a bit further on than you are. Mr Dashwood would agree with me there.'

I patted my piled-up hair in the high mirror over the drawing-room manteltree and glanced at the marble scroll below it with its motto *Antes muerto que mudado:* sooner dead than changed. Unlike the Norman conquerors of Ireland, many of whose descendants would be attending my ball that evening, traces of their ancestry still evident in their heavy, squarish heads and drooping eyelids, our most recent invaders, English entrepreneurs like Charles, were unlikely to become *Hiberniores Hibernicis ipsis* – more Irish than the Irish themselves.

'You and your old punctuality,' I mocked. 'I've never understood why you left England, with all its clocks dinging on the hour and everyone as prompt as cuckoos.'

Behind me in the mirror, Charles's reflection darkened, there was a slight tightening of his lips. But he answered composedly, 'You wouldn't ask that, my darling, if you knew the barren monotony of English life, its cold beef and drab, dispirited women.'

He came up behind me and rubbed his warm, flattened nose in the hollow of my exposed nape. A moment later, we heard the thick trundle of a carriage in the drive, whooping, excited laughter of people out to snatch every crumb of gaiety from the night. In the mirror, Charles and I smiled conniving smiles at each other. He took my arm and, together, we stepped through the lighted hall to begin our honeyed welcomes.

It was well after supper before Damian Dashwood walked awkwardly towards me, around clots of well-nourished people, and asked me for a dance. By then, the triumphs of the evening had been duly applauded: the swan sculpted in ice that held out-of-season raspberries, the cutlets coated in nutty crumbs, the vanilla soufflé with its high, foaming crust. I felt woozy with success and longed to sit down and rub my feet. Mr Dashwood agreed to sit out; we settled in the library with a brandy apiece and I whistled for Plume, who rushed into the room and began to lick my sore toes.

'I hear that your sister was taken to the convent today,' said Mr Dashwood diffidently. 'Aren't you proud?'

'So proud that I couldn't bear to go with her. So proud—' I flicked my hand towards the open door through which we could hear Hogan's bleary playing and the determined thump of dancers, 'that I had to distract myself from my misery with all this.'

'I'm planning on kidnapping Vera,' I went on wildly, for I had drunk a lot of champagne. 'I'll lure her out with one of Binnie's best sponge-cakes. Oh God, Mr Dashwood, Vera will never survive on what they give them there, unsalted broth and watered gruel. She who always stuffed herself in spite of being as slender as a willow branch, so we used to say she had a tapeworm coiled around her gut. I was raising a pedigree sow to give her and Declan Coady for a wedding present, that way they would always have a flitch curing once the piglets were grown enough.' I burst into noisy tears.

Mr Dashwood spoke gently, as though to a child who has grazed its knees. 'Rashers are no substitute for religion to those like Vera. She is one of those who have no taste for wrestling with the thrill of evil. Religion takes away the weight of life from her. She will find it easy to be good in her convent because she will not be allowed to taste the choice between good and evil.' He patted my shuddering shoulder as though it were a dog of uncertain temper. 'Come now, Mrs Trewin, leave the girl to the fate she insists on having and, rather than planning kidnap, think of what else you could do for our immaculate, wronged nation. You are a powerful woman now that the Lord-Lieutenant himself has sworn that he'd cover the mountaintops with rose bushes were you to ask him to.'

'I thought you didn't like me,' I muttered into my handkerchief.

'I don't like the way you manipulate people, it will lead you into harm's way before too long. But I like your defiant spirit. If your dog has refreshed your feet, put on your shoes and we'll get Hogan to stamp out a polka loud enough to incense a bishop.'

At dawn, as Charles and I climbed into our tented bed, I sleepily repeated some of Damian Dashwood's thoughts on religion.

'The thrill of evil, eh?' he said, his hand reaching under my nightgown. 'To say no to evil but to say no knowing what it would mean to say yes. A battle in the mind that your beautiful sister was not willing to face or try to understand. But you, beloved huntress, you, I think, will treat evil with more respect.'

He began to make love to me and I melted mindlessly away from everything that was not connected with our two rapturous bodies. When we drew apart, I thought once more of Vera and the cold convent bed that denied night-time pleasures, then I resolved never to think of her again.

12

Almost a year after Charles had ushered me through Malina's great door as the new mistress of the house, a photograph of Harriet in a narrow silver frame appeared one day on the leather-topped desk in Charles's study. It had not been there the day before. I disliked the study. It was a cramped, octagonal box of a room at the back of the house and faced directly on to the end wall of the stable block, so that my husband could read the results of the surveys he had initiated on the development of transport, food distribution, education and training without the distraction of the lake, that watery enchantment that drew the eye to its changing surface, sometimes gravelly, sometimes stretched as smoothly as ironed silk. To aid his concentration further, Charles insisted on the musty velvet draperies being drawn, even on the most sunlit day. With its feebly flickering oil lamps, the study was airless and eerily silent, but for the weak wing-beat of moths, neatly folded triangles at rest on the pelmet, and the fizzing noise of trapped flies.

I entered this unpleasant room every day, but only for the time it took to read the newspapers, or rather the parts of them that Charles had underlined in ink for me, so that I might be well informed about the ways of the world and able to respond intelligently to the talk of the public men with whom we increasingly mingled.

The day that Harriet's photograph was put on display was 7 October 1891, and the subject that filled the newspaper columns was the death of Charles Stewart Parnell, which had taken place in Brighton the day before. Articles had been heavily underlined and the left-hand margins filled with comments in my husband's vigorous handwriting. A whole morning's reading before me, when I would rather have been riding in the autumn sunshine along the woodland path, gulping lungfuls of the crisp, singed October air.

But I knew I must stay in the musty room and read the news of Parnell's death. My husband was an admirer of the tragic statesman and often repeated his statement, 'What I am, I am, what I am not I cannot be', words which echoed the sentiment of Charles's own, unyielding family motto, carved into Malina's stone mantel. Parnell, like Charles a Protestant landowner, had demonstrated that men of his class could still exercise political authority in Ireland and need not fear disestablishment.

I had met Parnell, the 'Uncrowned King of Ireland', at a subscription supper held after he had addressed a public meeting at Westport. I had watched as men dislodged the horses from his carriage and pulled it themselves through the cheering crowds towards the platform where he was to speak. It was possible that among those who cheered themselves hoarse were men and women who, but a year later, would fling quick-lime in his eyes though they knew him to be dying.

Parnell had been courteous to me, yet remote with a withdrawnness I could not melt. From his speeches I knew that he loved Ireland in his way, but with a love that had something of horror in it. When he had married Katherine O'Shea in the June of the summer that had just passed, I had wondered how such a solitary-seeming man could have inspired so much passion in a woman that she had deceived her first husband, abandoned her children and faced the scalding fury of all those in Ireland to whom my husband referred contemptuously as 'the roaring machine of ignorance'.

The topic of Parnell made Charles flustered and contradictory. At times he would insist that the man had not a drop of Irish blood in him, at others that his arrogant, fiery pride represented all that was best in Ireland.

For myself, I thought it hypocritical of the clergy to rant against Parnell's unlawful marriage, since you could hop over any workhouse wall and see children who looked the very spit of prominent citizens who had no lawful business being their fathers.

'The pusillanimity of the Catholic middle class is an outrage,' Charles had thundered at hearing of some new treachery against the toppled, heartbroken statesman. A very predictable outrage, I considered it, since so many of Ireland's finest lived in terror of upsetting their tyrannical old mammy or the narrow-minded priest, but I did not wish to fuel my husband's rage, and kept silent.

Now, I settled myself in the study's most comfortable chair and picked up the *Irish Independent* and the *Evening Herald* with reluctance. Both papers derided

Parnell in thrilling, palpitating language that seemed washed thin beside the scorn of Charles's margin notes. 'You crushed him to death,' he had scrawled accusingly, 'you netted his soul and kept it from flight. You devoured his heart.'

As I read his words, I began to feel that they were addressed to me, rather than my turncoat country. I looked up, away from the fury of Charles's pen and my eye came to rest on the photograph of Harriet on his desk. A pale splinter of sun eased through a gap in the heavy curtains and settled on the silver frame. Within it, Harriet in profile, her long chin tilted, looked stainless and untouched. Studying her, I felt suddenly opaque with shame and misery; a vision of the future clouding before me in which the hopeless horror of incompatibility would be part of my daily life.

I slunk from the sunless room, too dispirited now to ride in the woods. Instead, I crept into my tented bed, the first time I had ever lain in it alone, and fell into an unsound, whimpering sleep. When I woke in the early evening, my heart ached with the silent clamour of resentment that, in the rosiness of Charles's memory, Harriet, the ghost-wife, had been resurrected as perfection itself, docile, meek and mannerly. I feared the role that this resurrection would cast me in. What other role could there be except that of the usurping strumpet, irresistible and false? I started to dress for the evening ahead, with no appetite for the company talk that would be bound to fritter into chatter. The glass of the frame that housed Harriet's photograph expanded in my troubled mind until it formed a solid sheet of ice that stood between me and the social world I now precariously inhabited.

Charles entered my dressing-room as I stood at the triple mirror, smoothing against my body a new dress in black georgette with a tracing of silver stripes, thin as wire. A day spent indoors had made me blowsy. I was newly conscious that my hips were set too close to my waist and that, although tall, I was not shaped in the languid, lanky, narrow-loined way that is the stamp of good breeding.

'Why the frown?' my husband asked. He folded me into his arms. 'You look as luscious as a peach, or perhaps a ripe plum.' He began to fondle my breasts through the gauzy bodice. The gesture was coarse and lustful; it was unimaginable to think that he had ever touched Harriet so disrespectfully. As he painfully tweaked my nipples, I reflected that I had absorbed the negative image of a seductress.

I need not have dreaded frivolity that evening; the talk was all of death. The company was subdued, all minds concentrated on the frail, austere body of Parnell that was being borne back on the Holyhead mailboat to the country that betrayed him.

High-born guests sat at my table that night, tall, white-skinned aristocrats like Parnell himself and, like him, uncomfortable and estranged in dull, prim England, bored and irritated by the orderly English who were startled by Anglo-Irish eccentricity and waywardness.

'What of us now?' asked Myles Lavelle in his high, dramatic voice. 'We are certain to be the Jonahs thrown to the whales, banished from Ireland to the prisons of red-brick villas in Surrey.' He paused for effect. 'Yet what is life for Anglo-Irishmen, our uncomfortable breed, except a living death suspended between a buried past and a buried future?' He made a sound somewhere between a groan and a cough and hid his ravaged face in trembling hands.

'Don't create so, Myles,' said Leonora Fitzhaven. She struggled to retrieve the indolent sensuality that was the basis of her social self, but I sensed something pale and torn behind the vivid mouth and sauntering gestures. 'Ireland has always accommodated our sort,' she insisted. 'It's a place that's as responding and congenial as the limestone that allows itself to be crinkled and shaped by the sea. There is nothing, nobody that isn't accepted here.' She laughed her lovely, gurgling laugh. 'Do you remember how the new curate at Lisnagreve got a girl into trouble and how her father and brothers threatened to kill him unless he renounced the cloth and gave the child a name? And do you remember the to-do there was when he left the priesthood suddenly, with his mother screaming blue murder and the bishop trying to cram a lid on the whole seething trouble and the pair of sinners running off to Roscommon, where Thesper (she smiled fondly at her husband) found him a place at the jute mill? Well, your man came back last week for his mother's funeral – she'd finally screamed herself to death – and didn't I see one of the girl's brothers, who'd been vowing to kill him just a year since, go up to him and lay an arm on his sleeve and say to him, as soft and pious as you like, "How are ye, Father, and how's the family?"'

Leonora laughed again, drained her glass, and said, comfortingly, to dispel the tense mood in the dining-room, 'So you see, my dears, what with the new class of landlords like Charles here' – she smiled fondly at *my* husband – 'men of business who come to settle and get our lazy bones rattling and the old, neglected estates working again and extending the railways, we will all be welcome to stay, I'm sure of it.'

It appeared that none of my dinner guests would be attending Parnell's funeral. Although they had admired him, had known his family in the tight, exclusive world of balls and hunts and regimental dinners that enclosed Ascendancy families in uneasy privilege, they would not put on a public show of sympathy. They viewed death as a kind of failure, it made them evasive; it was the point at which their courage failed. They think it queer that we native Irish honour the dead by picnicking in the cemetery, keep fresh corpses company by playing ribald games beside the coffin to shoo away the terrors of that long, clouded journey out of this mortal life, let our children play beside the newly dug grave with its wormy sides. Charles derided these customs that evening, called them barbaric, papish habits. At once I became all rebellion and spite.

'Barbaric is it?' I said. 'Barbaric to allow children near to death so that they lose their fear of it?' I glared at Charles who was unconcernedly pouring a glowing ribbon of wine from decanter to glass. 'Barbaric to hush their fear of death, so that it does not haunt them all their lives?'

I scrabbled angrily for more words but was silenced by an outbreak of pointlessly smooth conversation by those around me. They sensed some tingling annoyance in the air and sought to calm it with silken sentences and clattery jokes, to which they responded with false, bright laughter.

After dinner, when we had assembled in the drawing-room, Thesper Fitzhaven, with unusual insistence, urged us to play a favourite parlour game, in which points were scored for correctly identifying a quotation. But even while my guests searched their memories, they could not loosen their minds from the question of Ireland, their country that could never be their nation. Every saying that they flourished before each other for attribution brought reminders of Ireland's terrible geography and pleasurable ways.

'A land flowing with fun and whiskey in which irregularity was the rule of life,' Thesper quoted.

'Sweet Tony Trollope,' guessed Myles correctly. 'How he would have appreciated Rose Erris; irregularity should have been her middle name.' He pulled one of my irregularly descending curls lovingly.

My husband's mood was dark that night. 'That fruitful source of constantly recurring and painful discussion.' Charles snapped Sir Robert Peel's verdict on Ireland with growling hate in his voice, a hate that remained when he quoted Edmund Ludlow, Cromwell's iron-hearted lieutenant in west Clare: 'Savage land, yielding neither water enough to drown a man, nor a tree to hang him, nor soil enough to bury him.'

'I say, steady on, old man.' Thesper Fitzhaven was on his feet, signalling to his wife with rheumy, distressed eyes that it was time to go. I realized that my husband had overstepped some moral and social boundary with his reference to Cromwell's soldiery, embarrassing the raffish, good-natured nobleman, even though, or perhaps because, the Fitzhaven fortunes had been enriched by some scoundrelly settler-adventurer rewarded by the infamous Lord Protector more than two centuries ago.

'Stay a while,' I said, not rising from my chair. 'I haven't had a turn yet.' My guests struggled to keep surprise from their faces for I had not much reputation for book learning. I began to recite; my voice was steady, although my heart lurched:

> 'My love for that man from another land
> beyond all living men
> has drained my colour till I've little left
> and will not let me sleep.
> I was modest as a child
> and unused to sins of desire.
> Now I have reached unsettled age
> I am confused by lust.'

Silence greeted my recitation. 'You cannot surmise the author?' I asked. ''Tis no shame to you, for these lines were written by one of my ancestors who went by the name of Anonymous, Anon for short. They form part of Créide's Lament for Dínertech, written in the ninth century. It was after the battle of Aidne that Créide grieved so, for couldn't she see that Dínertech had seventeen wounds in the breast of his tunic. I'm thinking that Mr Parnell is not the first man to be mortally wounded on Ireland's account, nor will he be the last.'

167

Uneasily, but with portly politeness, Lord Fitzhaven took his leave. Myles went reluctantly, his ugly, drooping mouth leadened by sadness. 'We each bear a cemetery within us,' he said bleakly as I walked him to his carriage in the sharp, delicious air. So much talk of death had left him bloodless. He shivered as I tucked a rug round his thin knees. Like Parnell before him, he was terrified that he might die in that stiff, alien land over the water.

He forced his drooping lips into a smile. 'Goodnight, Rose of my heart,' he said. 'How fortunate you are to be native to your own country. I, alas, am like a lamprey in the riverbed, half fish, half eel, neither one thing nor the other. My isolation is innate, an affair of origin. Be grateful that *you* will never know such a state of unsettledness.' Myles sank back among the carriage's several cushions, white with nervous exhaustion.

'I think my state is unsettled enough,' I said, looking back at the house, where I had left Charles stalking the drawing-room, drawing angrily on his Turkish cigarette.

'Pah,' Myles said. 'You descend from the great Anonymous, that most feared and glorious of ancestors. Your race is sanctioned to be all flair and outcry from now on.' He gave another ghastly smile. 'There's nobody I would rather have dance on my grave than you, Rose Erris. Pity I won't be able to see your quick, brown ankles when you do.' Suddenly racked by a fit of coughing, he motioned to the coachman to take him home.

I returned to the drawing-room to find Charles smiling, his anger gone. He held out his arms to me and whirled me round in a dizzying waltz, singing the silly words of 'After the Ball is Over' so tunelessly that it made me laugh. Running his hand down my leg he said mildly, 'What a meaty girl you are, my love. I wonder if you're not getting a little heavy for Emer these days.' He looked thoughtful. 'Harriet now, she was weightless, might have been fed on flowers.'

Growing up with six sisters, I had learnt not to respond to teasing, so I smiled at my husband as we danced, thinking all the while how satisfying it would be to rip the picture of the weightless Harriet out of its frame and snip it into tiny pieces with her own embroidery scissors with their crane's-head handles.

Charles spun me round in a final flourish and then, while I rested giddily in his arms, unclasped my long pearl necklace and, throwing back his head, fed the glinting string down his throat, like a fire-eater swallowing a flaming torch. He pushed me lightly on to a sofa, pulled down my drawers, spread my legs wide and then drew out the necklace from between them. 'Still up to my tricks, you see,' he said, fixing me with an amber gaze. 'Time for bed now, I think.'

From that night on, my husband began to diminish me, in subtle, damaging ways that I could not give shape or words to. At night, with all his lover's skills, he still aroused me to fiery climax. But afterwards, instead of holding me gently against his breast and stroking my hair as he had always done, he turned from me quickly, as though my passionate response disgusted him, as though the desire that he himself had brought into being, had conjured up as once he had conjured sweets from my ear, was something soiled and perverse.

His grabbing shows of affection, no longer accompanied by milky words of love, made me feel voluptuous and unwholesome, a glamorous, suspect and outlandish woman who had no place among Malina's gilded refinements. I craved his old, conspiratorial smile, to encourage me as I flirted mechanically with men from whom he craved favour. Denied it, I was torn from my sense of self and my identity started to become a hazy thing.

I escaped to Shanvally from time to time but knew my mother and younger sisters were embarrassed by my too-frequent presence. They blushed with shame when the goose waddled out of its coop below the dresser and excreted on the flagged floor, knowing that Charles thought the Irish habit of keeping geese and pigs in the house dirty and backward-looking.

Yet it was torture to stay at Malina with all its graceful formalities when I was no longer sustained in my role of chatelaine by my husband's conniving love. I felt unworthy and crumpled, heard in my voice, as I strove to make sparkling gossip, a note that was bitter and insolent.

Every so often, as I laughed and talked across a dinner table, I would turn to look at the man I had married, longing to meet his tawny gaze that was half quizzical, half amused. But his eyes never met mine; they were focused on something beyond me, so that I was not just excluded but annihilated. By the time the paddock had begun to brighten, after a long winter, with the hopeful-looking grass of early spring, I had become dull and muted, passing my days in some borderland of disconnection, isolation, unease and hopelessness. How subtly Charles tortured me, how impossible it was to accuse him of betrayal when he still paid me so much attention, bringing me jewels and fine clothes and underthings: the attention a pimp bestows on his whore.

Myles came to visit one morning when the flickering of weak but determined sunshine picked out the swoops and whirls and the pale gold marquetry in the deeper gold of a tapered side-table and flicked sudden warmth on door handles set in gilded discs.

'I have always found Malina to be at its most beautiful in early spring,' he said.

'I like it best in winter. This sunshine glitters so ferociously it's overpowering, makes me feel like an intruder.'

'The first Mrs Trewin loved the sun, I seem to recall.'

'I can't remember,' I lied.

'*You* used to love Malina in all weathers,' Myles accused. 'You and this house seemed to have a shared, secret life, so that one always thought of you and Malina as some mingled thing of beauty.' He sniffed the scentless air. 'Something's missing from Malina now,' he said. 'Some hopeless emptiness has returned to it, the emptiness that you dispelled when you came here. Before that time, this house always used to remind me of Mr Dickens's description of the Dedlock mansion in *Bleak House*. How does it go? "Fairyland to visit, but a desert to live in." Can you not trust me, Rose Erris? Can you not tell me what has happened to make you and Malina so changed?'

Without speaking, I took Myles's moist, weak hand and led him through the house to Charles's study. The sun had not reached this back part of the house yet and the room retained a clammy morning twilight. I lit the oil lamp on the desk and pushed it forward so that the photograph of Harriet became the sole focus of brightness in the room.

'Ah,' Myles sighed pensively. 'This is what ails you, as well it might. There's something strange about your husband, Rose Erris, a kind of platonic hatred one might term it, that is, a hatred that is empty of emotion. I've never known what was the cause of it. Perhaps it's frustrated ambition; he tears around this sleepy country, trying to knock it into shape, and most of the time he must feel as though he's beating the air. But I've an idea that there's more to it than that. Charles seems to relish cruelty for cruelty's sake; he's as remote, capricious and faithless as a troubadour's unattainable lady. I believe he has set out to make you suffer, just as he made this poor, dead woman suffer.'

Myles moved the lamp away, so that Harriet's photograph was no more than an oval blur on the desk. 'The worst thing is, that I won't be here to help you battle against him.' He noticed that I gave a start. 'I came here, Rose Erris, to tell you that I am going to a sanatorium in Switzerland. It seems that I am beyond goose-fat and brown paper cures now, my dear, for I am coughing up blood until I am bored by the sight of it. I feel like a portable abattoir, not at all pleasant. But do you not think me mad to travel so far, so that I might be made well for just long enough to come back and die in Ireland? Ah, I've made you laugh, finally. You took your time about it. Let us leave this vile room before I'm tempted to splatter blood over that neat pile of surveys.'

When we had returned to the front part of the house, Myles said, 'I will give you some advice: go and see that schoolteacher of yours. I once heard a terrible argument she had here in the house with Charles, the day of Harriet's funeral. I couldn't hear everything they said for they were hissing at each other like a couple of maddened geese, but I suspect that she has something belonging to Harriet that she refused to return and, as you well know, your husband hates to be thwarted, it makes him behave like a destructive baby.'

Myles laid his loose, cold lips on my forehead. 'Be brave, be strong,' he told me, 'and remember our arrangement. You mean you've forgotten it? What a feckless girl you are, to be sure.' He looked at me with eyes made watery by so much coughing. 'The arrangement I proposed, the evening after Parnell died, was that *you* should dance on *my* grave, not I on yours.'

13

It must have been the stubborn pride of my race that stopped me from shaking Harriet's secrets out of Miss Gwynn, as Myles had suggested. That same pride made me press my lips together rather than beg my husband to tell me why he had created a bond of emptiness between us.

I tried to toss off the feeling of being entirely unmoored by spending even more time with my horses, teaching them with a determined harshness not to funk high walls or greasy landings. With Leonora Fitzhaven, I devised a cross-country course towards Moycullen, over swerving pastureland, with obstacles to be cleared along its way, likc a steeplechase. 'Our reputations as hoydens of the finest order are now unmatchable,' Leonora said as, panting with exhaustion, we limped back to Lisnagreve after an afternoon in the saddle and often out of it, our habits daubed with mud and our hats crushed like old tins. She leant back against a tilted wall and fished a round cardboard box of Bourjois face powder from a pocket, together with a tired-looking puff attached to a square of chiffon. As she blotted the shine from her chin, she asked, 'Will you be hunting again this winter?' There was something deceptively casual in her voice.

'What a question, Leonora,' I said. 'You know hunting gives me a roar of power.'

She shrugged her shoulders. 'Ah well, you're young yet, I suppose.'

'Young for what?'

Leonora's neck showed pink below her thickly powdered face. 'Well, they do say that if you glue yourself to a saddle, you'll not find it easy to conceive a child. Just old nonsense, but there might be a word of truth in it. Look at me and old Thesper. Fifteen years married and, mercifully, only the two brats to show for it. Thank God for horses if they've something to do with it. A large brood would have been intolerable.' Leonora shuddered as though recalling sticky fingers grasping her cool, plump arms, and the night-time clamour of the nursery. 'I detest children, including my own,' she admitted briskly. 'They gobble you up so.'

Emer had her head down in an unpromising patch of scrubland. I rubbed my lips against her sleek forehead and her ears went backwards and forwards in a gesture of love. I thought of Charles with my baby sister Geraldine on his shoulders, both of them unmindful of the cake crumbs she was snowing down on his hair; Charles giving a shrieking Eithne a ride on his outstretched leg; Charles, the first time I ever saw him, gently placing my finger on his strange, flattened nose. More memories unspooled: Florence Wingrave's scolding voice: 'Oh Hattie, how you do *droop* so. No wonder that squireen of yours is frightened to let you have children'; Charles, again at Shanvally, insisting to my sceptical mother that his wife could not abide children; Harriet's stricken, averted face as we drove back to Malina in the trap on the day I had told her about the tiny, rotted bodies that lay under the stones beside Horam's Cove; the bouquets with their bright ribbons that she left there afterwards.

Perhaps it was true that Charles denied Harriet a child of her own because he had feared the consequences of childbirth on her narrow body and overwrought mind. But he loved children himself, had loved me when I was a child. I must give him a child of his own as a gift, for which I asked only for the return of our lapsed intimacy.

Charles and I were dining alone at a small, round table set before the fire in the panelled library, two candles in porcelain holders between us. Charles took my left hand in his and scrutinized the bruises on it, the result of frequent tumbles from Emer's back on to stony ground. He pressed a small, round bruise on my palm, painfully enough to make me wince, and then kissed the place that he had pressed.

'Do you think it wise to spend the day falling off horses with Leonora Fitzhaven when the house is so loosely ordered?' he asked quietly.

Our surroundings were immaculate. Books ran in tight rows on the polished shelves, doors shone beneath their marble copings, the pale silk rug beneath our feet had been so recently scrubbed that it gave off a faint smell of damp cloth. 'Loosely ordered?' I asked, my voice as quiet as his had been.

Charles sighed; the sigh of a man who is sorely driven by the incompetence of others. He walked over to a long, carved chest beneath the window, raised its lid, and brought out a mottled, misshapen pear. The sickening odour of rotting fruit blew across the room. I had stored the pears in the chest to ripen, and then forgotten about them.

'I deny you nothing, my dear,' Charles said. I hated that 'my dear', heavy and cold as stone; the same words, the same voice in which he had always addressed Harriet. 'However, I loathe waste and neglect. Good husbandry is called for, unless you wish Malina encumbered and sold up.'

It was absurd to claim that a few pounds of wasted fruit could bring down a great estate, but I did not laugh. Forgotten pears were lying in drawers all over the house, and must be disposed of, secretly, before Charles had cause to say 'my dear' in that terrible, cold way again.

'I'm sorry,' I said meekly.

He gave a flinty smile. 'The matter is forgotten. What news of Lady Fitzhaven?'

'She was telling me that she did not like children.'

'How typical of her class. They feel it a duty to produce an heir to safeguard the title and then another son as a precaution against the death of the elder, and then hope that their family is complete. Not altogether unwise. Large broods, unless there is need of their labour are economic folly, as the half-starved brats around this unfurnished countryside testify.'

Under the table, Plume's tongue scraped against my fingers, giving me courage. 'Should you not like children, Charles?' My question was hardly louder than a whisper, yet my husband's tawny eyes darkened in fury to a purplish black, like damsons.

'Children? Yes, I think I should like children well enough, as long as they were not fathered by me nor mothered by you.'

I left my chair and, so that he could not see the astonished horror that must show on my face, began to busy myself at the fire, piling up the sods of turf with the brass tongs, whose gripping-ends were shaped like a pair of supplicating hands.

Charles went on eating. I could hear him swallowing wine, cracking fresh walnuts and then chewing them. He addressed my back as he chewed. 'It's a question of lineage. You, a breeder's daughter, know the importance of pedigree. I'm from bad stock, Rose Erris. There's a trail of bad blood behind me that I dare not allow to spread. Children are out of the question.'

I stood up to face him. 'What about my pedigree?' I asked, louder now, for I was shamed and angry. 'Does my coming from generations of decent people count for nothing with you?'

Charles's eyes had softened to amber again, but the look in them was full of disdainful patronage. 'Hardly thoroughbreds, even so. Do you think I haven't noticed those garish knick-knacks that your mother has set up in the darkened corners of this house, where she thinks they are hidden from me? *Nothing* is hidden from me, my dear.' There it was again, that icy 'my dear'. 'Suppose we were to bear a daughter who inherited her grandmother's moist piety? How intolerably Father Casey would gloat over us.'

Charles's voice turned suddenly soft and wheedling. 'Rose Erris,' he said, 'do you remember the day I gave ou Murrough? You knew that your father had sold her to me, and you led her towards me with your face as mucky as a tinker's, but for the two tracks that tears had traced on your cheeks. Since then, I have bought you a stableful of horses, and will buy you more, provided that you don't bring Malina to ruin with your Irish fecklessness. You are a superb horsewoman. Confine your ambitions to the hunt and forget about motherhood. I have yet to meet a woman who deserved to have children – you may take that any way you wish. Will you be so good as to ring for Agnes to clear?'

Among the new installations at Malina was a cat's cradle of cords that connected fluted, brass bellpushes in the main rooms to a row of tin clappers hung above the kitchen door, each labelled with the name of the room which had set off its jerky clatter. Binnie asserted that Charles had devised these mechanized summonses to torment her with their pounding noise, but I suspected he had installed them to keep me out of the kitchen quarters. Now that I could press a bell to demand fuel or food, I had little excuse to run down to the back part of the house with its soothing bustle and clandestine visitors.

'God be with the times for the good that was in them,' Binnie would mutter as she winced at the sudden shrillness of a bell. 'Wasn't it enough for you to be calling down the stairs for whatever at all you wanted, without our ears being torn from our heads with the racketing?'

Agnes came in now, looking overstuffed in her tight black dress and starched apron. Her manner veered between calculated, excessive obsequiousness and pointed insolence. Sensing something troubled between Charles and myself, she chose insolence. 'Why, you've hardly touched your dinner, Madam,' she said, prodding an untouched cutlet on my plate. She lowered her hateful voice as she bent close to pick up the dishes in front of me. 'And you that's always in need of energy later,' she smirked, greedy triumph in her small, hard eyes.

Charles went to the study to work on a new proposal to extend the railway. Did he retire there to commune with Harriet's vapid photograph as well? My mood was black as I walked to the stables with Plume to make sure that the horses were comfortably stalled, but I returned to the house soothed, as I always was by the way my handsome animals called out to me as they recognized my step in the dark.

I was halfway up the stairs on my way to bed when Binnie called me from the hall.

'Will ye come?' Her voice was hoarse with horror.

I ran downstairs, along the passage that led to the kitchen, Binnie hobbling behind me on her twisted legs, spitting out words I knew were curses although I did not understand them.

The kitchen was gorgeously hot after the draughty passage. The maids were nudging each other in a cluster around the big table that was marked with the brown circles left by hot pans. In the centre of the jostling group was Pegeen, a new scullery maid who had been at Malina for only a week. She was holding a tattered book that the other girls were gawping at. I came closer into the circle of light from the rusty, fly-splattered oil lamp hooked above the table and saw that Pegeen's mouth hung open. She had no teeth and the inside of her mouth was like a small, dark cave. Wordlessly, she gave me the book. A hole, singed all around its edges, went precisely through its middle. Binnie clawed my arm like a frantic animal. 'Do yer not see how it is?' she hissed. 'Isn't it himself who shot a hole through the Holy Bible and hung it in the maids' privy as wiping paper? Is there any manner of meanness your man hasn't learnt the measure of?'

I unlocked the cellar door and brought up a sup of brandy which I made Pegeen drink in a bowl of milk, until its warmth drove the outrage from her face. I threw the tattered bible in the fire and took from the store cupboard a packet of thin, paper squares which I pressed into Pegeen's grimy hand. I did all these things with gravity, yet all the while I could hardly suppress my laughter. Every time I thought of Charles carrying the old, disused bible into the woods to shoot at it, or of Pegeen, suddenly realizing what paper it was that swayed handily beside the privy, my shoulders started to shake.

I let my laughter loose when Charles came to bed that night. Almost choking with giggles, I scolded him for scandalizing the maids with his novel economies. He did not join in the laughter.

'You know as well as I do that Pegeen cannot read,' he said dismissively. 'There is but one way a bible can be of use to her. I wish you would not try to ingratiate yourself with the staff by siding with them. You have nothing to gain by it. No brandy and milk you can offer will ever win their respect. After all, you are not Harriet.'

14

Someone can take away your life without killing you. He can turn away from you in the night, roughly and determinedly, leaving a wide space between two sleeping bodies that once lay slotted one into the other like a pair of nesting spoons.

Even as the summer began to warm Malina's dove-grey walls, the space between Charles and me in the silk-swirled bed stayed icy, as though a bitter wind were tunnelling a divide between us. My liveliness repelled him as once Harriet's reticence had done. I had no wish to remain lively; I wanted only to give way to tears for there was no bottom to my sadness, it flowed all the way through me. But I was trapped in the social image that Charles had helped me construct: an image embroidered on, little by little, of a bold, laughing chit of a girl, to whom the beguiling, homely turf-reek still clung, vaguely discernible beneath the expensive French scent dabbed on her strong, horsewoman's wrists.

It was this supposed lightness of spirit that appealed to the Ascendancy people whom Charles sought to be-friend. My tumbling chatter made them forget, for the space of an evening or two, their doomed, half-hearted lives. There had been a time when Charles's amber eyes had glittered with love when I hitched up my skirts and taught Emmeline O'Cleary and Julia Gibbons the intricate, spring-heeled steps of a reel until their thin knees clicked and cracked like burning kindling and the polished floorboards of Malina's ballroom groaned and shifted. Now my husband's eyes hardened when the company called upon me to sing or demonstrate a jig.

'This air of festivity you have about you, my dear, lacks exility,' Charles told me coldly one evening in early summer after the guests had gone. Exility. I looked it up in the library dictionary. '*Exility*: slenderness, refinement,' I read, tears leaking into my eyes. I trailed the crammed columns of words. '*Evagatory*: a wandering from the prescribed path. *Exogamein*: to marry outside the tribe . . .' The mottled page leered at me. I was guilty of evagatory and exogamein and lacked exility, a quality my tribe had not troubled itself with. Unlike Harriet's tribe, a fragile, thin-skinned people who oozed exility fragrantly and were so wearied by life that they rested the afternoons away with the blinds drawn against the clamorous world.

During those dreadful days, when Harriet had taken to her bed, Charles had stormed about Malina, looking likely to smash his foot through a window or crunch a china ornament in his fist, while the Big House became an annexe to a sickroom, with pale, minced, pappy foods brought up from the kitchen and the maids tiptoeing along the hushed passages with startled eyes. Harriet had brought her heritage across the sea with her: the genteel English tradition of quietude and feverish chills, silk shawls and translucent teacups. When she died, Malina ceased to be a place of exhausted, faded silences, that much I had changed. But, as I yawned wretchedly over the dictionary, I knew that Charles would always be the same. *Antes muerto que mudado,* sooner dead than changed. What he held to, unyieldingly, for reasons that would be revealed to me in time, was a merciless desire to destroy any woman who loved him. I should have paid more heed to those unflinching words, carved in stone above the extravagant, inadequate fire, etched in the gold of the signet ring my husband wore always. Since my childhood, they had brought me a stark message that I had refused to read. I danced on a razor's edge, not knowing from one day to another which of my actions might bring a stinging rebuke. At night, Charles possessed me as a stranger might, his detached, mechanical lovemaking making me feel like damaged goods.

The summer was beautiful that year, mocking the crunching misery of my spirit. Sleeping poorly, I would saddle Emer at first light, cantering along damp, gold sands, or picking a way through the bogland where weaving lakes glimmered in the early sunlight like the roots of a silver tree. As the sun rose higher, it struck a glow on the stones that stretched across the little lakes, stones scratched with the paw marks of otters. The village was still sleeping as I passed the flat-faced houses with their thin, dark windows, narrowing my eyes against the dazzle of the whitewash. The day's clanging activity was yet to begin; there was no sound except for the cows bawling in the further fields, the startled scattering of chickens as Emer's hooves clattered on the baked earth and the light drip of the suspended oar as a lone fisherman returned to his bed after a night spent on the peacefully shifting water.

Such calm made me forget for a while the scornful blaze in my husband's eyes, so that, on my return to the Big House, I was able to arrange a smile of welcome on my face and greet the drifts of pleasure-seekers who came to Malina that glorious summer to picnic by the lakeside; bright, chattering groups among the wild iris and saxifrage, dipping careless, expectant hands into sally-rod baskets for fresh loaves wrapped in warm cloths, roast chickens with glazed, crinkled skins and bottles of pale gold wine.

Yet before that summer was over Emer had become nervy, jolted by the snapping of a twig or a broken reflection in a pool. More than once, she stopped dead on the crouching, homebound road, snickering with distress as I coaxed her to return to her stable. On a cloudless morning she tried to kill us both. Instead of turning towards the road, she lunged for the headland, making dreadful, maddened sounds as though the flames of hell were licking her flanks. I managed to jump from the saddle without releasing the reins, but was dragged along the ground for what seemed like hours before I could whistle her to a juddering stop. We were but a few feet away from the steep side of the dune, beneath which the sea rolled innocently. My mare's beautiful purple eyes were red-rimmed and her sides quivered. I did not remount her but walked her slowly home, stopping often to stroke her fear away. I avoided Malina's tall gates with their intricate filigree and led her through an unfamiliar path through the woods, coming upon the stables through a gap in the stone wall. She let me lead her docilely until we reached her stall, and then began to quiver again with terror. When I offered her another stall, she grew calm again, nuzzling my hair as I unsaddled her and whickering companionably as I wiped her streaming sides with a dry sack. My knees were bleeding from being scraped along stony ground but some impulse made me stop on my way back to a bath and bandages and enter Emer's usual stall. It was early yet and the stalls had not been emptied. My mare was a fastidious creature and dropped her dung in a corner, leaving most of the straw on the ground undisturbed. An empty feedbag on the straw made me stumble. I picked it up and a dribble of oats fell from its neck.

Never feed oats to a highly strung mare. My father had taught me that as a child and Malina's grooms had instructions that oats were forbidden to Emer. The feedbag in my hand explained the reddening at the rims of her eyes, the frantic whinnying, unpredictable behaviour and her rush for the headland that morning. As rattled as my poor horse, I leant against the stall's lumpy wall and took a deep breath. I drew deeply on the comforting smell of horses, rich, pronounced, a mixture of animal and dung, hay and woollen blankets, leather and saddle soap, as familiar to me as the smell of baking bread or gorse in flower.

I could smell something else though, something false and flowery, delicate yet cloying: the scent of carnations. I folded the feedbag thoughtfully and left the stall's dimness to enter a darkening world. The bright sky of early morning had filmed over with dusty grey. A racketing wind had got up and blew the lake backwards on to the bony ringing of the rocks around its shore.

An empty coachhouse showed that my husband had left for his day's business at Tuam. As I walked towards the house I met nobody except one of the grooms, stumbling to the stables, a bucket in each hand, blinking away the caked sleep from his eyes. I asked him to harness the trap, then I bathed my raw legs, put on fresh clothing, took a bottle of good malt from the cellar and stowed it in the trap. Through slackening rain I drove to the schoolteacher's house.

'Well, here's handsomeness,' said Miss Gwynn, holding the bottle to the light and admiring its honeyed glow. 'You look in more need of it than I do, Rose Erris. Your cheekbones are showing so pointy that a finch could land on them.'

'There's something I want in return that could maybe ease my mind more than a sup of whiskey.'

Miss Gwynn pursed her mouth, which deepened the pleating of the withered flesh around her lips. 'You wouldn't be a McCalla if you didn't look upon life as a deal to be struck. Though,' she looked at me sharply, ''tis clear you've struck one deal too many.'

'There is something of Harriet's you have here,' I persisted.

'It's Harriet's secrets I have. To reveal them would be to disgrace her memory and lay her poor soul bare.'

I sank into a bulgy armchair that smelt of cats, put my hands over my face and cried the frustrated tears of the defeated.

At once Miss Gwynn was by my side, splashing whiskey into a cracked and riveted cup, which she held out to me. 'It's as sad as life to see you bawling in that chair,' she said. 'Your tears sound like the poisoned echoes of Harriet's tears, when she sat where you sit now, looking as wasted as the ghost she would soon become. For you to be the same way, Rose Erris, you who were always the rowdy girl, makes a mush of my mind. Tell me your trouble, whatever it is, although the feeling is on me that it's a story that's been told to me before.'

'Charles,' I began, the word slicing into the air like a cry.

'Charles, is it? Your husband is as clever as sin, the way he has on him of smashing fine women to pulp. Now *there's* a man who assumes a closed gate doesn't apply to himself and tramples whatever he treads on.'

'He hates me and I don't know what I've done.'

'You've done nothing; less than nothing. He is using well-tried methods to baffle and unsettle you. To think that this terrible history is relentlessly repeating itself.' Miss Gwynn suddenly swept a pile of leather-bound books from a shelf with the flat of her hand and tossed them into my lap. 'There you are, these are what you came for. May Harriet forgive me for breaking my word but we owe something to the living as well as to the dead. Read them here now in this house, my poor girleen. If they were to be found at Malina Charles Trewin might be inspired to perform some strange conjuring tricks on us.'

She took up a patched umbrella with a stained ivory handle. 'My thoughts are murderous. I shall walk to the bay and watch the sails gather in perfect peace and marvel at the capricious colours of the sea. There's a bitter lesson to be learnt in those ravings of Harriet's.'

I did not open the notebooks until I heard the little rusted gate at the end of the crooked path clang angrily, then I arranged them in front of me according to the dates etched into their spine with some sharp instrument, perhaps a hat-pin.

Harriet began her diary soon after she came to Ireland in the 1860s. She wrote in notebooks whose pages were thick and rimmed with gold, protected with dark red leather bindings which closed with two brass clasps, stiff now and dulled by the dampness of the cottage walls. The first entries, written in a thin, quivering hand, described the young bride's nervous delight at so many unfamiliar sights: the bare countryside with its 'great want of trees', the funeral keening – 'my ears are dinged with the Irish howl' – a picnic feast of 'swilled mouton, that is a sheep roasted whole in its skin'. She was horrified that lavish mansions 'the hall of one is so large that while some visitors take breakfast, others may play battledore and shuttlecock or listen to someone play the harpsichord without any of these activities disturbing the others' were surrounded by wretched, filthy cabins 'where I have never seen so much misery. The Irish life is one of extremes, the people live with a great profusion of things or with nothing at all.'

Harriet listed her charitable undertakings with unconscious smugness. 'I took some fruit from the greenhouse to the Dohertys' cabin. Afterwards I washed my hair in white spirit and changed my clothes. I worry about fleas. Binnie assures me that were I to attract any she would put a pig for a night in my bed and it would drive the fleas away. I find this prospect more worrying than the possibility of fleas.'

In time, as she grew more alarmed by the customs of the country, Harriet stopped visiting the smoke-choked cabins with their foul open drains, but her charitable intentions endured. She read the books of Alexis Soyer, the famous chef who improved the diet and saved the lives of soldiers in the Crimea, and was inspired by *The Shilling Cooker for the People* to give Mrs Doherty a shilling and instruct her gently on the preparation of one of Mr Soyer's sustaining broths. But Mrs Doherty went to Meehan's public house with the shilling and a large tin pail, and returned with the pail brimming darkly with porter. 'When I remonstrated with her,' Harriet primly recorded, 'she said, "Sure, isn't there eatin' and drinkin' in that as much as any owld soup, and singin' and dancin' in it too". Charles laughed when I told him this and, for a week, whenever he raised a glass to his lips, he repeated, "Sure, isn't there eatin' and drinkin' in that".'

Charles laughed a lot in those days. Smiling and happy, he boasted that his wife was a Dresden figurine set down among common clay pots. He whooped with laughter as he helped her gather the pink and white and yellow shells that rimmed the shore, whisking her into his arms when the waves that fanned out in spreads of creamy foam threatened to soak her narrow, kid shoes. But, after some three notebooks had been filled with accounts of social visits and charitable missions and timid drawings of shells and flowers, the tone of the diaries grew more sombre. Increasingly, Harriet was ailed by headaches, stiffening limbs, throbbing chilblains in winter, dizzy spells in summer and, worse than these, crippling self-doubt. Her husband no longer picked her up and flung her effortlessly into the air, lovingly insisting that she was weightless and must feed on flowers. He hardly touched her now, flinched when she rested her cold hand on his. Harriet wrote wretchedly: 'If I am beautiful, as I have often been told I am, my beauty must be like that of the angels – which rather than inflames love, extinguishes it.'

The week after this entry, a twelve-year-old girl with tangled hair, the pony-breeder's daughter, came to Malina for the first time. Harriet wrote: 'Rose Erris McCalla is to be my newest torment. She has ridiculous eyelashes, long and straight like those of a horse and, despite her clumsy boots, is a most graceful child – she sings with her body. Charles encouraged her to make a clamour all over the house until my nerves were shredded. When, later, I mentioned a headache, he said, "We must be thankful, my dear, that you are childless, since you lack the stamina for motherhood." I said that any child of mine, had I been permitted to bear one, would not have been unkempt and unruly like the McCalla girl. Charles hinted, as he has done so often over the years, of something in his past which determined him never to father a child. Because of the pain in my temples, I could not swallow my anger as I usually did but shouted at him, "If you nurse some shameful secret, I, as your wife, have a right to be told." He replied that I knew nothing about genetics, "unlike Rose Erris, who already keeps an entire stud book in her curly head and can trace bloodlines back to when the Spanish steeds swam ashore from the wrecked

Armada". He slammed out and left me to a desperate silence that poured back into the room after him.'

Harriet filled three notebooks in 1885, the year of her sister Florence's visit. Reading them, I discovered that Miss Wingrave's arrival in Connemara had been caused by an anxiety for her younger sister. Since her marriage, Harriet had written regularly to her family in Devon: lively, detailed letters about the customs of the country in which she found herself. 'Florence has often told me that I should have made an excellent anthropologist,' an early diary entry boasts, 'such is my skill at observing and recording a primitive people.' But by 1885, 'Florence chides me for writing so rarely, and for letters that "are all bland evasions". She insists on stopping at Malina, although the thought of her arrival makes me uneasy. Florence is a fine woman, and a well-meaning one but her voice could rasp the dead and she is sure to complain about the backwardness of all we have here.'

And so it proved to be: 'Florence manages to turn every mealtime into a sad Sunday,' Harriet recorded. 'At luncheon, when Agnes brought in the pudding, Florence glanced at her plate and, while Agnes was still in the room, barked, "I've heard of a fly in the ointment but never in the blancmange", and laughed at her own joke. The "fly" was only a clove but Florence's close inspection revealed Agnes's thumbprint on the rim of the plate, a cue for Florence to rail against "the dirty, stupid Irish". How her voice carries. I suspect she raises it on purpose so that the servants might hear. Why? Does she think that her rudeness will improve the housekeeping, or has the bad weather put her out of sorts? It has not stopped raining since she arrived, a sharp, needling rain that hits the windows like flung handfuls of grit, provoking further outbursts from Florence. After one such, Binnie came into the breakfast-room, unsummoned and without knocking, and almost dragged me from my chair with her twisted hands. "Let you be getting some rest now, ma'am," she insisted, guiding me towards the stairs and, although Florence was in earshot, she said, "That one's temper could tear the skin off the sky; she thinks she's the whole push, so she does. Pay no heed to her now."

'Binnie knows how things are between Charles and myself and offers only comfort; Florence has guessed and offers me the cold clatter of fact. "There's darkness in his ways, Hattie," she announces, prodding the sods on the fire in a way that is certain to make them lose heat, "a sleek violence to him that was not there when I saw him in England. This country has got to him; he rejects it and feeds on it at the same time. He can exercise a power here that would be denied him at home, so he will stay. But I should advise you to return, rather than live for the edge of his smile in this sodden badland."

'One afternoon, she suddenly yanked back the sleeve of my tea-gown and saw the oval bruise on my arm. From the way she knitted her brows, I saw that I did not need to tell her how it came there. Earlier that day, Charles had wanted me to attend the funeral of one of the tenants, a young fisherman drowned the night before. It was raining again and I could not bear to stand in the graveyard, watching the men measure out the grave with bramble switches and throwing up the blackened boards of old coffins, pieces of bone, sometimes a skull, along with the clay as they dug the new grave. Death was already too much on my mind to stand such sights. I had sunk further into my pillows and pleaded a slight fever. Charles had seized me by the arms and pressed his thumbs into the silk of my peignoir. "Ah, you are in flamboyant ill-health yet again, my dear," he said. "Being married to you is like being forced to stand on one leg for the rest of my life. You hamper me in every aim I have." I could hear his step in the passage sounding like an army.

'Florence rolled down my sleeve. "This is shocking," she said, surprisingly quietly, and then, more quietly still: "Nobody would blame you for making changes in your life." Perhaps it was at that moment that I began to think of the greatest change that I could make. On the day she left Malina, Florence again urged me to return with her, but England offered insufficient change. There was but one welcome I could be sure of; I held out my hands towards death.'

But it was another three years before death took Harriet's outstretched hands and led her from one kind of darkness into another. Meanwhile the diary entries continued, sometimes dispirited, sometimes impassioned (when a splutter of ink-stains on the page showed that a nib had been pressed furiously to the paper and had snapped) up until the day before Harriet drowned. Bitterly, she noted my thirteenth birthday, the day Charles had given me Emer. 'From my bedroom window, to where I had retreated since I could hardly drag my limbs across the carpet – which Dr Parsloe says is due to a mild bout of rheumatic fever but which I know is caused by the lack of sunshine which would coax this clammy waxiness from my bones – I watched Charles bring the child here in the carriage. The fact of the carriage and Horty in his uncomfortable uniform on the box meant that it must be a special occasion of some kind.

'She stepped out of the carriage, leaping into Charles's outstretched arms without shame, although she is hardly a child still, being tall and comely, with something calculated and knowing in those astonishing grey eyes that have the metallic shine of sunwarmed flint within their screen of lashes. Charles took a red silk handkerchief from his pocket and blindfolded her with it, both laughing. Then he obviously bade her wait while he fetched something, which she did, swooshing circles on the gravel with the toe of her scruffy boot. Charles returned, leading a small, quick mare, coal black and self-consciously graceful. I watched Rose Erris as she heard first the click of hooves on the gravel and then the beast's snickering. She reached out and combed her dirty fingers through the long mane, traced the rims of the folded nostrils. From my high window, I could not hear her yell of delight but saw her mouth open, showing the full, red underlip that had become womanly and enticing. Charles took off her blindfold, and they stood facing each other. I thought that they might embrace – my mouth filled with bile – but he made no move to touch her. Instead, she took her hand from the horse's neck and pressed her forefinger along Charles's flattened nose, as though he were a beloved animal. I limped to my bed, spent with pain and misery.

'That evening, Charles brought me a glass of port, which he said would raise the level of my thin blood. I challenged him about Rose Erris: "Childhood hardly exists in this region – the children are put to work so young, girls grow into womanhood almost as soon as they have left babyhood behind. I was watching Rose Erris today; she has become so proud and shapely, no longer a ragamuffin with scratched knees. Almost an object of desire, would you not agree, Charles?"

'Charles seized my aching arms and held them in his punishing grip. "Desire, Harriet? What do you know of desire? Decorum is your province, my dear. Decorum, such a cool, clear English device for living. That, and urging some exhausted peasant woman to prepare a shank of mutton so that it might feed her family for a week, when she has neither the time nor energy to do so."'

I turned the remaining pages quickly, looking for some reference to my own vileness, some admission of how Harriet felt towards me after I had ruined the slender happiness she knew at Horam's Cove. But there was no mention of the jagged headstones or of the bright bouquets she laid beside them. Perhaps she could not admit to this morbid gesture even to her own diary.

A few weeks before her death, Harriet wrote, 'We don't really die of diseases, we die from what others do to us.' I reached the last entry, the words on the page spiralled jerkily in an uncontrolled hand. 'I wish I could think he will be haunted by me until his own death. But it will not be so. Although dead women bear so many tales, he will convince himself that what I am going to do has nothing to do with him.'

I wiped some patches of mould from the leather covers and put the books on the sagging shelf above Miss Gwynn's fireplace. I travelled home in the rinsed, pale twilight, unquieted by the clop of the pony's hooves or by the pearly mingling of sky and water. Malina's walls stared at me as I made the turn of the lakeside road, silent in their sources, throwing their louring reflections on the lake.

The door groaned on its hinges as I pushed it open, an unwelcoming sound. The love that I once felt for Malina had turned into a fear that ripped through me. The Big House was my enemy. And I had become another Harriet: jittery, uncertain and unsafe.

15

'You have fallen into a soggy trap of blarney, ballad and self-pity,' Miss Gwynn said crossly, banging down a fragile teacup on a spindly side table and causing both to wobble. She came often to Malina these days, on the pretext of consulting Charles's collection of botanical books, for she was compiling a companion guide to the wild flowers of Connemara for the growing number of summer visitors, but her real purpose was to urge me into vibrant life again.

It exasperated her to find me seated at my harpsichord on a scorching afternoon, singing old, mournful songs in a voice that had grown reedy and tremulous. 'These are loathsome airs you sing, seeping and treacly,' she complained. 'They would have you believe that being Irish is all a matter of torpid longing and frustrated desire.' She slurped the last dregs from the pretty cup and thumped it down again, where it righted itself uncertainly. 'Do you forget other songs of ours, Rose Erris? Songs which affirm that ancient kings without number are ancestors to all of us here, songs that allow the tinker in the sodden ditch to dream that his sires had towers and great names? Songs such as those should be your history books now.'

She looked at me closely out of eyes that were

bright and inquisitive within looping webs of wrinkles. 'People who lack a sense of their own history are vulnerable to takeover, and taken over is the way you look, wan and enslaved. It will not do. You are not Harriet, nor anything like her, so shake yourself free of this ridiculous morbidity.'

She pinched my cheeks angrily to put some of their old colour back in them. 'Not just you, but all our people are bent back like a twig, but, like a twig, if released, will lash the hand that restrained us the more furiously.'

'I cannot hope for such release,' I replied in a squelchy, hard-done-by voice which made me brim over with self-hatred but which I seemed powerless to change. 'My husband will have me killed before then.' I told Miss Gwynn about Emer's bolting, about the forbidden oats I had found in her stall and the cloudy trace there of the carnation-scented cologne that Charles wore.

'Such dramatic conclusions you come to,' the schoolteacher scoffed. 'What is this – a plot from one of the penny-dreadfuls that your maids read on wet afternoons? Killing you by poisoning your horse is not your man's way at all; he is too subtle and clever for that. There must be another explanation, perhaps another enemy. I have a way in my head to find out. I have a mind to call on that mucksavage Horty O'Goole. We might see sights.'

You couldn't hope to fasten your eyes on a less ruffianly sight than Malina's head groom as he sat in the tin-roofed harness-room that was tacked on to the end of the stable block, a row of small, stiff brushes laid out before him, with which he was slowly picking out hardened polish from the grooved embellishments of a dozen or so horse brasses.

Miss Gwynn gave him a freezing smile. 'How gratifying to see you so, Horty. You who were always as lazy as a toad at the bottom of a well. I hear that the way you keep the stables is something to boast about.' She looked at him in a way that made his fat cheeks redden, and settled her bony haunches on the bench beside him. She began to squeeze facts out of him, coaxing and bullying, as she had done years before in the sooty schoolroom, when she had demanded that Horty recite to her the names of capital cities and faraway rivers and mountains with strange names that made Horty halt and stumble, mumbling, eyes on the floor, while the rest of the class waved their hands in an eager forest, to show that they knew all the answers and could put the poor, fat stupid boy to shame whenever they chose to.

''Tis you that's in charge of hereabouts entirely?' Miss Gwynn flapped bony fingers in the direction of neighing and clattering and the rustle of hay being laid in mangers. The insistent questioning made Horty a mumbling schoolboy again, the swagger and dash knocked out of him by that hard, clear voice that dangled in front of him wretched memories of schooldays.

'I do be left in charge of the seeing to necessaries and the costing of them,' he said grudgingly, 'but himself wouldn't trust St Patrick to do a job of work without interference. He's in and out at all times, making a tally of the soft rags I've managed to save from the old blankets that have the moth to them and seeing that Agnes has them all herringboned round the edges and that not one scrap of a thread is wasted.'

'So Mr Trewin is often about the stables?'

'More than he's welcome to be,' said Horty, whiningly. 'It wouldn't be worth my while to flick a stale crust to a robin in the bush, for that he'd be on my neck demanding an invoice for it.' Horty looked at me, daring me to rebuke him for his insolence, but I turned away and began to pick flakes of rust from a horseshoe nailed on the wall.

'And Agnes,' Miss Gwynn persisted. 'Does she keep you company while she binds the edges of scrimped rags?'

Once more, the groom's face blazed. 'I have the little sewing-room set up for her where the stores are kept,' he muttered, as though this might be considered an immodest enterprise.

'I wish to see it.' Miss Gwynn's tone was imperious.

Reluctantly, Horty withdrew his thumbnail from a caked-up groove in one of the brasses and, shoulders slumped, led us to a door in the far corner which opened on to a neat little slice of a room, its shelves stacked with tins and boxes, piles of ledgers, cards of bias binding and a pincushion stuck with rusty needles.

Miss Gwynn, while inspecting the label on a box of Elliman's Universal Embrocation, shot out a thin, scaly elbow and knocked Agnes's calico apron from its peg. She shook out its folds before replacing it and a few rolled oats rained out of its round pocket. 'Thank you for your time, Horty,' she said calmly. 'Tell Agnes I was asking for her.'

She bristled and shone with triumph as we walked round the side of the house to where my trap was waiting to drive her home. My hands shook on the reins but Miss Gwynn stopped their trembling by rapping my knuckles with her dry palm.

'Agnes MacReion has a mind that is warped and clouded, and has had all along,' she said. 'Clotted with envy she used to be of all you McCalla girls and the grand company you had of each other, like young colts in a field. The stumpy, whey-faced child that she was, brought up by that disgrace of a slattern for a mother, you'd be sorry for her, really. Agnes should not be let stay the way she is. A wedding would do for her; husbanded, she might settle into herself less spitefully.'

She struck my knuckles again lightly. 'Aren't there the rooms above the coachhouse that she and Horty could have?' she asked.

Indeed there were. Rooms with strange slants and curves and creaky floors and thick, lumpy walls.

'They'll do well enough, as long as you furnish them with a bed where those two great puddingy creatures may make their night moves undisturbed,' Miss Gwynn said. 'There's a powerful attraction between the both of them. Like calling out to like, I suppose it is; both so fat and puffy-eyed like steamed potatoes, it's God's gift that they found each other.'

As I handed her down from the trap, she gave my shoulders a fierce shake. 'Whatever happens, live your life as though there were a blessing in it,' she commanded.

'But loss withers my heart, I feel so abandoned,' I

bleated, screwing up my eyes to stop shaming tears.

Miss Gwynn gave a sharp sigh of irritation. 'There you go again, clacketing on like a penny novelette. Do you not know that to be abandoned, in its old sense, means to be set free?' She began to clump up her front path, slashing at the yarrow flowers with her stained umbrella, unsettling the droning bees.

Inside my brain, a library had set itself up, its shelves crammed with Harriet's diaries. Her quaking words were always on my mind and made the Big House seem full of things that were not there: Harriet's weeping accusations, Charles's fury, the ghost of my childhood self tearing around the high-ceilinged rooms, while Plume flitted in circles around my running feet. But when I returned to Malina that afternoon, I could hear a voice that wasn't lodged inside my head, a privileged voice, high and dramatic, that streeled through the half-open door of the drawing-room. 'Myles,' I yelled delightedly and ran through the door. Ignoring Charles's scowl, I flung myself into Myles's arms.

'Have a care, dear heart, I'm still as delicate as a dewdrop,' Myles said, taking my hand and rubbing it against his loose lips as he had always used to do. The mountain air had turned him rosy; his dear, bald, bony head was peachy with health and his shoulders looked broader since they were no longer hunched protectingly around his chest. But the biggest change was in his style of dress. Instead of the silk-lined, close fitting, London-tailored jacket that he used to wear, he was dressed in a bainin, the traditional coat of west of Ireland men, an ill-fitting garment in slubby tweed, the colour of cooked oatmeal. He held out a book for me to take. It was called *Love Songs of Connacht* by Mr Douglas Hyde.

'Friend of my soul,' Myles said, in that ridiculous, over-excited, gasping way that always made me laugh. 'Here is this man who signs himself *An Craobhin Aoibhin* – do tell me what that means in the Queen's English – Ah, "the pleasant little branch", how self-mocking. He has founded the Irish Literary Society in London; it's very modish, William Morris sometimes attends. I can tell by your gormless expression, Rose Erris, that you haven't a notion who William Morris is. *Chintzes,* my sweetness, covered in the dearest marigolds and bunnies in such pleasing, *burnished* colours. You should have this silk ottoman recovered in one, the sofas too. Malina is acquiring a bleached-out, picked-over look, pale and neglected.' He looked from Charles to me. 'As indeed, Rose Erris, are you.'

I shook my head at him, a warning to change the subject, and he returned to the doings of the Irish Literary Society. 'The point is that Mr Hyde is about to launch the Gaelic League in Ireland and I mean to set up a branch in Connemara, a pleasant little branch, perhaps,' he added waggishly. 'You see, all the long months I was away I felt one word, and one word only, relentlessly slapping about in my head and that word was' – Myles dramatically drew in his breath so that his nostrils slitted – 'home. I would stand on a mountain peak and shout "Home!" and "Ireland!" into the snapping air, and hear the words echo and resound from every slope.'

Myles stroked the rough sleeve of his bainin self-consciously. 'There was time to think during that dull, lonely time in the sanatorium, and what I thought most about was my own puking ignorance of the country I love. I felt lower than a worm wriggling on the edge of a spade. And then, on the homeward journey, by happy chance I stopped in London for a few days. I met Mr Hyde and knew that fate had fastened its eye on me. What a teller of tales that gentleman is. There is a word for that in Irish, Rose Erris, but it's slipped my mind.'

'Sennachie,' I said. 'The sennachie, the storyteller, was the most honoured guest a house could welcome. He travelled the roads from place to place, bringing the news to those who had none, before there were newspapers or those that could read them, and handing down the old stories of love and war so that we would not forget the times when the skies were dark with arrows.'

'Indeed, the senna . . . senach . . . whatever you call the man, an exponent of the oral tradition,' Myles said loftily. 'And the love songs in Mr Hyde's book were part of that tradition. They originated here in the west, songs that have been passed from mouth to mouth since time began. I expect some of them are well known to you, Rose Erris.' There was a powdery trace of condescension in my friend's voice.

I fluttered the pages of Mr Hyde's collection and found the words on them dimly familiar, like an old dream. 'I was brought up on Moore's *Irish Melodies* and songs from the English music halls like everyone else hereabouts,' I said, sullenly. 'It's only Miss Gwynn who knows well about these old lays. Very few sing them now, or know the airs of them.'

Myles shuddered. 'Tragic that only one pithy old schoolteacher has a sense of this ancient idealism of fable, emotion, style. All the more reason why we must set up the Gaelic League here as soon as we can.'

As though remembering his presence, he turned to Charles, who had been sitting all the while in a fireside chair, his elegant legs encased in their golden tweeds, outstretched, his attention all on his lustrous red-brown boots that were flicked with the reflections of the pointed flames that wavered in the grate.

'Would you not agree, Trewin, that the Gaelic League will recover Ireland for itself?'

'The Gaelic League.' Charles repeated the words in a hushed, disgusted voice, as though they represented the symptoms of some unsavoury illness. 'An affected, effete primitivism' – he studied Myles's homespun jacket with such loathing in his glittering eyes that my friend folded his arms awkwardly across his chest, wanting to shrink from that deadly gaze – 'a dreamy, Celtic escapism full of morbid race memory. But,' he stood up and looked challengingly at the two of us, 'if this safe, literary Fenianism keeps my tenants' minds away from Home Rule, I am for it. I'll even provide funding enough to build a meeting hall, where you can spout your backwards-looking idiocy and learn to babble in a tongue that no decent, civilized man ever spoke to your hearts' fill.'

He took a step nearer me and put a hand possessively on my shoulder. 'As for you, my dear, why should you not improve on your Irish? There was a time when I had hoped that you might perfect your English but that is not to be; you mangle and maul the language of

Shakespeare and Milton like a cat toying with a dead mouse. Perhaps having to learn an ancient tongue will teach you to hold grammatical constructions in some regard so that you will not shame me in public by exclaiming, "It's after having come on to rain."'

My husband said these last words in a mock-winsome way, coy, simpering and hateful, a cruel mimicking of me that shredded my heart, as he knew it would do. 'By the way,' he sneered at Myles, while preparing to leave the room, 'that fellow Morris is a socialist. In spite of his marigolds and bunny rabbits, he would have your inheritance and estate off you and leave you with nothing but that absurd coat on your back.'

'The atmosphere at Malina seems to have worsened since I was last here,' Myles observed drily when the door had closed on my husband's powerful back.

We sank, exhausted, into soft, pale armchairs, both of us breathing heavily, until at last I found the energy to attend to the spirit-kettle by the fire, turning up the flame under the silver teapot and hoping that Myles might have a flask of gin in one of the creased pockets of his bainin, to settle our splattered nerves and demolished spirits. As I tended the fretted, fiddlesome knobs of the kettle, Myles started to cough, the racked, heaving, desperate coughs of a dying man.

16

'I seem to have lost every gift God gave me,' I said. A russet heifer, the hairs of its coat dulled and dampened into quivering scallops by fever, lay in the straw of my sister Anne's barn, regarding me balefully from filmed-over eyes. I had laid hands on it, firm brown hands that had once cured creatures of whatever ailed them, but which had become powerless. As I knelt uselessly beside it, the calf snorted, as though frustrated by the thought of living any longer, spurted a stream of yellow froth from its speckled lips, and died.

'Don't wrench your heart out over it,' Anne said, consolingly. 'What we won't get in milk, we'll make in selling the hide for shoes and book bindings. Come inside a while, Rosie, you look almost done. I should never have fetched you down, only for that, since you were a little girl, you were a great one with the cures.'

Anne had been married to Kyle Donovan for three years now. As we walked under a scudding sky towards their gaunt grey farmhouse, her steps dragged under the weight of her third pregnancy. A shawled baby, Sile, her tufted head poking out of the shawl like a hazelnut, slept in the crook of my sister's arm, while two-year-old Josie stumbled alongside, his fingers clutching a fold of the ugly smock Anne wore.

The Donovans were 'strong farmers' like the McCallas, and Kyle and Anne were well enough settled. The house, which generations of thrifty, cunning Donovans had kept up, was ringed by dark, sunken sheds, where milch cows yielded generously twice a day, making rumbling, unprotesting moans as their yield swished idly into tin pails. In the yard, the ground glinted with oyster shells, added to the feed of Anne's hens to toughen the shells of their eggs so that few were lost to breakage.

Kyle was a member of a farmers' co-operative. He and other local men pooled their profits to maintain horses and carts, which took their produce to the townlands where it was despatched to biscuit factories and cheese-makers. It was an idea begun by a fine Ascendancy gentleman called Horace Plunkett, who believed that great things might come to Ireland from creameries, pigs and potatoes. Kyle, believing him, had set up an office for himself off the kitchen with its tobacco-stained ceiling and reeking chairs, and would sit there of an evening, moving his lips as his stumpy fingers travelled the figures in his ledger. Kyle Donovan had thick wedges of eyebrows and a mild, slightly stunned expression in his clear blue eyes. I could not imagine him ever hurting anyone, or ever wanting to.

It was peaceful in my eldest sister's kitchen, listening to the hiss of water in the kettle over the fire and the thrumming of rain against the smeary windows. I shifted myself forwards and back, forwards and back, in the rush-seated chair, Sile, a yeasty-smelling warmth against my shoulder. 'You chose the right man for marrying,' I said.

A brooding look took over Anne's face as she folded sheets, tucking one side underneath her chin as she stretched the other. 'Chosen was it?' she said. 'Sure the match was arranged between us when we were no older than Sile. There was a *cleamhnas,* a matchmaking, when we came of age and all went as smooth as a knife through butter, for that Kyle had no brothers to want after a share in the farm. It was all a matter of arrangement. The Donovans came to Shanvally where they were fully expected and Dada started the proceedings. "Creud ta sibh ag iarraidh?" he asked, "What are you come for?" And so they went on, first one side then the other, until the dowry was agreed – a hundred pounds to be made up in cash and in kine – and the ceremonial heifer chosen. Then Mammy and I were called from the back of the house, and,' she patted her bulge proprietorially, 'the deed was done.'

'So,' I said. 'Had it been that I was the eldest, it's myself who would have been promised to Kyle.'

My sister shrieked with laughter, waking the baby, who gave a long, shuddering sigh before rootling into my shoulder again.

'Promised?' Anne spluttered, spittle bubbling on her lips. 'The Holy Father himself wouldn't make promises where the likes of Rose Erris Trewin are concerned. From the day you were born, with those great grey eyes on you, and lashes that nobody has a right to, there was always a disease of admiration for you, always the unspoken agreement in the house that you should be allowed your own way.' My sister spoke fondly, without bitterness, looking at me as though I were some exotic bird who could not be expected to peck at the same mash as the yard's humdrum hens.

'And then,' she went on, 'before you could hardly walk, you were up on a horse. There you were flying, the pony's hooves eating the ground up. Lord save us, but you had a brilliance, a promise. If there was a chance to be taken, you took it. If Dada and Mammy had tried to settle you as they did me, you'd have legged it over the wall, *cleamhnas* or no.'

Sile grew heavy on my shoulder; the clock ticked, the rhododendrons outside the house rattled in the wind. I said, 'It might have suited me well enough to be in your place.'

'Not you. You're drawn to all that's strange and interesting as a fox is drawn to a roosting-pole. It's no wonder to me that you up and married Charles Trewin, a came-from-away, a stranger. *You* would never let your ideas be pared down by Ireland's history and misfortune. There's defiance in that.' Of all my sisters, Anne was the proudest of my rebellion.

'Only it's that I sometimes think you have more than I do.' I kissed the top of the sleeping child's head, felt the steady throb inside it.

'Ah, that would gall you. You could never abide anyone having so much as a hair-ribbon that you had not. But all that I have, including that babe in your arms, is the result of expediency, and that brings sorrows of its own, though Kyle is as decent a man as you'd find in a day's walking. My life is all mapped out for me here until I'm laid out, even though I was born a McCalla, a tribe with ambition in its blood. Ambition is a thwarted thing with me; there's too much work to be done and,' Anne tapped her belly again, 'there'll soon be more of that. It was decided almost from when I was born that I'd be set down in this farmhouse and bear a fine brood of Donovans to carry on the work of their fathers, and that's the holy all of it.' My sister took Sile from me and unfastened her smock to feed her.

'But it doesn't have you tormented?' I probed.

'Yerra, you'd need time for that and I haven't it.' Sile woke up and started to make expectant, lip-smacking noises.

I walked across the yard to where my pony waited, picking my way through the braided rivulets that swirled into the gutters: alone, unchilded, denied the full of my life.

But Myles had started to have the full of his. Since returning to Connemara, the place he reverently referred to as 'home', he had tossed off his languid ways. The limpid afternoons no longer slipped by while Myles read novels ordered from the London Library, nesting listlessly among the sofa cushions like a beaky, fleshless bird. He forced himself into the flap and whirr of action, although, away from the crisp sunshine of Switzerland, his skin had regained its watery greyness and his shoulders hunched around his chest as he lurched with a spasm of coughing. When I begged him to return to the sanatorium, he said I was sentencing him to death by boredom, the dreariest kind of dying known to man. He had decided to leave his mark on the world by erecting little monuments of beauty, so that, he explained, 'those who look at them after my death may call me to mind fondly'.

One of these monuments was the meeting room set up for the Gaelic League. On a rocky promontory a half-mile away from the village Myles had designed a curious, flat-roofed building with walls of the local granite and a floor of Connemara marble which Charles said made him feel that he was walking on green slime but which I admired for its swirls and mottlings of light and dark. Sombre, uncomfortable chairs with narrow backs, inspired by the work of William Morris, were arranged in forbidding rows, and wall-hangings embroidered by the Misses Lily and Lollie Yeats, the artistic sisters of the young, flared-faced poet, were commissioned. The Misses Yeats were also much influenced by Morris and their embroideries were of bleak, melancholy women with egg-shaped faces and rigidly rippling hair like frayed wire. Myles, in his new mood of desperate activity, insisted, too, on taking charge of the restoration and redecoration of the rooms above the coachhouse which I was to give as a wedding present to Agnes and Horty.

I should not have let Myles have his way over those rooms. I knew well enough that Agnes longed for plush and fringes and tassels, sofas with bulbous legs and a fretted overmantel divided into fussy crannies on which to display the white and orange china dogs that old Maeve MacReion was giving the couple on their bridal day. 'Grocer's furniture,' was what Charles called the objects of Agnes's desire and it made no difference to him that Myles turned her first home into a shrine to his own refined taste, or that Agnes and Horty watched with sour, sullen faces as they saw the apartments take shape without ever being asked if the rooms were to their liking.

Myles had these strangely shaped rooms white-washed throughout so that sun and shadow played on their walls. The pieces of furniture he had made were few and austere. When Agnes sat down on a harsh settle and complained that it was uncomfortable, Myles told her sternly, 'If it's comfort you want, go to bed', and left her with her mouth slack and her eyes slitted with hatred.

Knowing my friend to be soon dying, I indulged him in everything, even allowed him to instruct Aideen the Pin to make me tea-gowns in a dull chartreuse yellow velvet in mediaevalist designs with ugly square necks and trailing sleeves that swept glasses off the table. The shade was at war with my wan face and the clothes made me feel shapeless and forlorn, although Myles thought that I looked like a Pre-Raphaelite fantasy, remote and mysterious. But I should not have let him treat Agnes's wedding gift as a toy to keep his mind off death. She did not forgive me for it and the consequences of my thoughtless behaviour were terrible indeed.

I was easily persuaded by Myles to attend meetings of the Gaelic League which he energetically chaired. Charles was seldom at Malina now. He had been elected to the Kildare Street Club, a mark of his acknowledged social status, for this was the heartland of Ascendancy grandeur; he sat on the Land Commission and his several enterprises took him often to England. Even when he was at the Big House, I hardly saw him.

He had removed himself from the principal bedroom and our silk-swirled bed, claiming that his late retiring and early rising would disturb me. Without his heated body beside me, the sheets on which I lay felt as smooth and cold as the swan made of moulded ice which graced our supper parties. A row of chilblains like scarlet buttons shone on my toes. For the first time in my life, I began to feel the cold, feared the first stiffening of the oak leaves that foretold the coming of winter, although winter could not chill me more than I was already chilled by the ice-palace that my bed had become. I did not think I would miss the lovemaking that had lately become a dull ritual, distasteful to us both, but, now that it had ceased, I found that I did. Rigid with loneliness, I whistled for Plume, who left the kitchen fire and snaked beneath the blankets to lick my numb toes. As I reached down to stroke her ears, I recalled the silkiness of Sile's hair, its trembling tufts like the *feohanagh,* the bog-cotton flower. I wept that I had no child, nor any promise of one, and Plume slithered up the cold sheet and chewed gently on my eyebrow in a show of sympathy.

It was to take my mind off myself that I went to the Gaelic League meetings, although what took place there had me collapsed with tedium. Schooled by my English husband, I always arrived punctually, to find an unwelcoming room, its rows of hostile chairs looking set out for nobody. But, an hour after the meeting was due to start, they were groaningly filled. Not by the people whom Charles called 'the rabblement'. They were too busy getting on with the real business of life – digging turf, minding children and animals, scraping a living from the thin, ungiving soil – to be able to indulge themselves by stewing in the poisoned juices of Ireland's past. Myles's audience was composed mainly of dingy young women with peaky, triangular faces, daughters of traders who had prospered and sent their girls away to good schools in Drogheda and Mayo. There were as many Protestants as Catholics, high-spirited Ascendancy ladies like Leonora Fitzhaven and Emmeline O'Cleary, and some academic young men whose stern faces were angular, plummet-measured. In a spirit of solemn fellowship, all these dedicated their Wednesday evenings to reassembling their fractured culture, each group, Gael and Gall, assuring the other of their Irishness, although none in that austere room had suffered the grievances and tatters of the dispossessed, which I felt to be the mark of the true Irishman. They professed an impatient rage to discover what they took to be their lost heritage: a troubling bequest of tragical story, ancient language and weeping music, which they had been persuaded to forget for more than a century.

Myles himself had been sent to Eton and taught nothing of the land where his people had been settled since 1649, the first of them a ruthless Ironside, rewarded by Cromwell with an Irish estate. Now he was intoxicated by Ireland's old, dangerous dreamland, delighting in the myths and legends of Tir na nOg, Land of the Ever Young. He regarded even the coarse bainin as too corrupted by modernity and cut an astonishing figure in the more ancient costume of tasselled stockings, saffron kilt and a woollen cloak fastened by a Tara brooch of handbeaten silver.

I thought the Gaelic League ridiculous, self-conscious and arch; its veneration of the old ways and the old language absurd in a bustling, bursting era of lengthening railways and rushing machinery. Mutinously, I studied the streaks in the marble floor and listened to the bleating idealism of the traders' daughters as they talked hotly of a de-Anglicized Ireland returned to its roots, a state I could imagine only as some barbarous utopia. To me, Ireland was a country whose past cannot be predicted. There is too much confusion in it, too much sleight of hand, too many jabs and asides for any one truth to emerge. Yet truth was what the Gaelic Leaguers demanded, every Wednesday evening from six until eight, with refreshments afterwards and some 'real' Irish music if Mrs Trewin from Malina would be so kind as to indulge us.

Their favourite Irish song had been written in English by Tom Moore. Moore was Irish-born but studied law at the Middle Temple in London. An Irish nationalist, he was Lord Byron's best friend and the toast of comfortable drawing-rooms on both sides of the dividing sea – a symbol of Ireland's churned, muddled and unsolvable past. The much-favoured song of his was 'The Song of Fionnuala'; it tells the story of Lir's daughter, who was changed into a swan and made to glide on the waters for thousands of years. One of the academic young men who attended the Gaelic League meetings had turned the English words into Irish ones, so that they no longer scanned and gave Moore's lovely song a tremulous mediocrity. The translator smiled smugly as he listened to his own version, as though he had put something over on the conqueror, whose language Moore had borrowed to tell an Irish tragedy.

'Stop by for a *deoc an doruis*,' Leonora Fitzhaven urged me, as I climbed into my trap and shook out a clanging from the buckled harness. A *deoc an doruis* is, literally, a door drink, the last drink of the evening, hardly a fit description for the flutes of champagne that would be served at Lisnagreve. Leonora was enchanted by the old language. Half-mockingly, she speckled her talk with Irish words instead of the French ones that had once enlivened her amused drawl. *Aperçu, ennui, tendresse* – all banished now. She called me *lambabaun* – lamb-child – instead of the familiar *ma chérie*, and said she would have a *smahan* – a taste – of champagne waiting for me at Lisnagreve.

'Although,' she said, her eyes flickering in her high-coloured face, 'I know you are laughing at me. There's a dance going on in the corners of your mouth.'

I would have liked to have loitered in the village which, in the lilac twilight, had a strange beauty, vivid and narrow. Its life was going on entirely in the here and now, harsh and warm, heedless of ancient ways and mythical heroes, owing them nothing.

Dosshie Cahill, the victualler, was staggering towards the doorway of his blood-smeared shop, wearing a dead sheep over his shoulder, its dainty, stiffening front leg grazing his cheek. In the street, eking out the last threads of light from the day, Dosshie's three little daughters turned a skipping rope, jumping easily to the same beat, their long plaits thumping between their shoulderblades as mine used to do. In the window of

Keane's store the light from a gas globe wobbled on square, rusting tins of musty biscuits; the squeak of a flailing fiddle came from Meehan's public house. A crow gawked on a thatched roof, wagtails lurched and skittered from one side of a borheen to the other. Framed in her kitchen window, a strong-chinned woman was flouring her bakeboard with a goose's wing, while the smoke from her chimney streeled towards the sea. Had I been other than who I was, the village's raucous innocence would have sheltered and sustained me. But I no longer belonged to it; married to my came-from-away, I was a stranger in my birthplace, an exile in a plumed hat and handstiched gloves. I set the pony's harness clanging a second time and set off on the road to Lisnagreve.

Among Leonora's elaborate furnishings, I would feel the prick of champagne bubbles on my tongue and a shallowing of myself in my soul. I was becoming exhausted by the weight of a false, bright self and the dazzling mask I never dared remove. But they were all I had to hide my anguish. For I knew that were I to reveal it, Charles would destroy me as surely as he had destroyed Harriet.

17

Grimly, insistently, I filled the days, a bustling, forth-coming woman, whose heart had died. Together with Busho O'Cleary I became the Joint Master of Fox-hounds of the Moycullen Hunt, smashing through puddles in a silk bowler hat and a riding habit made by a visiting tailor from the House of Messrs Doré of George Street, Hanover Square in London, who came to Malina in late spring to take fittings and catch brown trout before he returned to his grimy workplace.

'The divil makes work for idle hands,' my mother used to say when I was a child. She would yank me from the upturned bucket, where I sat dreamily watching the aweless birds tossed in the sky as carelessly as a handful of crumbs, and put me to work beating down sticky cobwebs from the ceiling with a twig broom. For idle minds too. To keep mine occupied I continued to attend the Gaelic League meetings, although I didn't share its members' fervour for a vanquished people's folklore. I didn't see the richness or significance of it or how the meaning of life could be revealed in old stories about fairies and fisherfolk. I had the *blas* — a fluency in Irish — but, like the poet William Butler Yeats, whose careless cravats and wire-framed spectacles would not have looked out of place at our Wednesday evening study groups, I said, with a conviction equal to his, 'Gaelic is my national language but it is not my mother tongue.'

I repeated the poet's words to Leonora Fitzhaven, who pulled huffily at the pearls beneath her chin and snapped, 'Well, it ought to be your mother tongue, even it is not your mother's.' Realizing how absurd this was, she gave a smoky laugh and collapsed mildly on to a tapestried sofa, her champagne glass held high like a flag.

As for Malina, there was a feel of absence there that made existence like doomed exile. When Charles was at the Big House, he dedicated himself to making me wilt and crumple. When I told him about a new planting in the woods or a way I had found of stacking turf so that the wind blew through the sods more thoroughly and dried them sooner, he raised a gleaming eyebrow in pretended boredom, or glared at me as though he would have liked to suck out my brain and feed it to the ravening heron who pierced the silk of the lake. Could there really have been a time, not so long past, when Charles, returning to Malina, had taken my small, dirty hand in his warm paw and let me lead him through his own house, showing him the pine-cones I had heaped in a fireplace, or a lightning-shaped crack in a wall that called for repair? Had he willed himself to forget those companionable, complicit wanderings, when he smiled tenderly at the seriousness with which I regarded Malina's maintenance? His wide, lazy smiles had enticed me into a state of being that left me, like him, by possessions possessed. With a trapper's cunning, he had encouraged in me an itch for ownership of fine marquetry and the fiery cascade of crystal droplets from high chandeliers. I still did not fully understand how he had turned me from one kind of woman into another kind, but my ignorance was not innocence but a sin.

Now, when Charles tired of trying to break a wife who was so wilfully defiant, he spent hours in his study. I took to skulking outside the door, stupidly hoping to make some discovery that would solve the mystery of why my husband now hated me as possessively as he once loved me, but all I heard was Charles rehearsing a speech. He spoke often to audiences of well-intentioned men, coming together to create a new, brisk, oiled Ireland. From the passage I could hear his voice, so hateful and biting as he had left me, now gentle and confiding: 'The old paths are slipping from us and our feet are not yet planted on the new,' I heard him say in a tone of sweet regret. Perhaps, as he practised his speech, he was addressing Harriet's photograph, looking at it with the golden light of his eyes, holding the silver frame in his strong fingers.

My defiance was a superficial thing, filmy as foam spreading over ridged sand. Alone at night, denied the passions of the flesh that I craved as ardently as once I had craved wreathed cornices and enamelled vases, my mind entwined itself around Harriet's shade and would not be dislodged. Sleepless, in the bed that was cold as steel beneath me, I accompanied her on her deadly journey to the cove, again and again, as I am certain Charles intended that I should.

Eventually, I slept a sleep of savage, swirling dreams,

and awoke to the needling sound of rain and the slip-slop of the maids' footsteps as they carried trays along cold corridors. On one such dismal morning, Agnes and Horty were married. I had said nothing to Agnes about her attempts to unnerve my horse, but kept a watchful eye on the feedstuff that went to the stables, glad for the occupation it gave me. By mid-morning, the rain had slackened to a soft, stifling wetness and the low sound of lake water grumbled in the clinging air. Besides the rooms above the coachhouse, I had given Agnes five guineas, clinking sturdily in a coiled silk purse with a tasselled drawstring – the sort of pretty, vulgar thing I thought she would like. But, when I gave it to her, she thanked me curtly, and when I held out my hand in a gesture of forgiveness and goodwill she turned away, pretending to hear the summons of the electric bell.

As she left the village church with Horty, her puffy hand on his arm, it was evident that Agnes had spent none of the five guineas on finery. She wore an ugly brown dress, gathered below her bulgy chest so that she looked like a badly wrapped parcel. Horty, at least, had made some effort to look festive; he wore a new celluloid collar, high and shiny, which cut horribly into his soft, melting chins, and a new pair of boots creaked on his feet. I had lent the bridal pair an outside car and the wall-eyed mare that was a favourite of Horty's. Since old Maeve was shrieking after her daughter as though she were leaving for America instead of for a week's lolloping at Salthill, I began to smooth the mare's mane to reassure her that Maeve's ravings wouldn't raise cats. Agnes bent over the rim of the car and hissed in my ear: 'Horsewhisperer, ye have always had the jinx and the bad power on ye. 'Tis well for ye to be up to the dodge.' I looked more closely at her bulk and saw that she was with child. I looked into her resentful eyes, pink-veined and raw, and realized that she had not wished to be. Her jealousy of me had convinced her that I had the power to remain childless on account of some sorcery of mine. The truth was such a different matter that I laughed in her face, causing her to frown blackly and Horty to click the mare on in a rush.

Binnie scuttled crabwise out of the crowd and put an arthritic arm around my shoulders, as though I were a spindly child threatened by the school bully. 'Get you home, you're chilled,' she said and, although the rain fell warm and moist on my face, my teeth were chattering. Inside the carriage I kept the rug around my knees, although it was slightly damp and carried the sweetish smell of Agnes's sweat where she had lain on it in the muffled darkness of the coachhouse.

I had a fire lit in the veranda room and tea brought there, as Harriet used to do when she had sorted and ranged her pretty shells at the table by the window. I started to read one of Mr Yeats's fairytales, but the crazed look of penetrating intelligence that I had seen on the poet's face made the story offputting; besides, its title was 'Flory Contillon's Funeral', an unsuitable read for a wedding day, even the wedding day of an old enemy. I put it down and stared aimlessly out of the window, across the lake to the sodden land beyond it, tigerishly striped in grass blasted yellow by salt winds, and dark ridges of peat.

My eyes fastened on a thorn bush, pushed sideways by the scouring wind which had failed to uproot it. Frosted with pale, flaked lichen, the tree clung to the soil in bitter triumph: rooted, tenacious and unyielding. It mocked me with its courage and I began to close the curtains, although an evening breeze was bundling away rolls of cloud that sudden sunshine had crusted with gold. But before I could blot out these marvels with folds of flower-splattered chintz, the view changed. Rounding the turn of the drive, heedless of the grandeur of mountain and water and dappled land, the shabby figure of Miss Gwynn appeared, moisture clinging to the hairs of her scabby, sealskin tippet. Catching sight of me, she waved her umbrella like a victorious general gloating over the count of enemy corpses, or an explorer sighting the misty verges of an undiscovered country. She brandished and twirled that umbrella as though she carried news that would change my life. I left the curtains open and ran down the stairs to let her in.

PART TWO

18

'Do not understand too much, or you will, perhaps, forgive too much,' Miss Gwynn said, clearing her throat to ready herself for disclosure. But how can you measure out understanding meanly, by the cup? It overflows boundaries, splashing clear, dazzling light on the murk of the past.

As the schoolmistress unfurled revelation after revelation, all the ragged threads of my days were drawn together into an undeniable shape. I understood two things now: that the thrilling bliss of my early life with Charles was the bliss of the deluded and that, empowered by what Miss Gwynn told me, I would be able to shake off the mournful, never-ending remembrance of Harriet and grasp the right to define myself in any way I wanted, resume any future that presented itself to me.

Miss Gwynn augmented her salary by receiving paying guests during the long summer holiday, when her students were freed from the classroom to help with preparations for the harvest. Many of these lodgers of hers were Englishmen with a dogged love of nature, bachelors with a poised, manageable loneliness, whose faces took on a dissociated look in the company of women. They indulged themselves with expensive, complicated binoculars, showy walking boots and mackintoshes of the most artful cut and design, everything they wore so crisp and new and studied that they looked somehow in disguise. That summer, a gentleman called Crispin Tyler had occupied the best bedroom of Miss Gwynn's cottage. He was a well-cared-for man in his fifties with a gristly nose and the Englishman's steady gaze and tender lower lip, as well as the Englishman's manner which manages to be both effusive and dreadfully shy. Mr Tyler lived in Norfolk, a flat, uninspired place, and on setting his expensively booted feet in Connemara became at once enraptured by the high, changing drama of the mountains, the way that in the space of a few minutes they transformed themselves from smoke made solid into dappled peaks that swooped and skimmed the sky. He marvelled at all that was there: the sweet, short sound of birds in the bush, the mooching cows swinging bright chains of spittle in the frail grass, the little crooked seaward paths where the orange flutes of montbretia flashed among the rain-pocked boulders strewn with fishing-nets, the picky steps of a cormorant beside a river that dimpled in the sun.

'Change comes late to the people of islands and high mountains,' he pronounced weightily to his hostess one evening, as both sat at ease at the fire, a pronouncement not entirely to her liking, since Miss Gwynn thought of herself as a progressive woman, studying the past only to apply its lessons to the future.

'Tell me,' Crispin Tyler had continued, 'does a man by the name of Charles Trewin live hereabouts?'

'Is he known to you?' Miss Gwynn had asked sharply, for Mr Tyler's mouth seemed full, suddenly, of guarded, uneasy laughter. 'It's a cold enough evening,' she said then, and went to fetch a corked jar of the purest, clearest poitín that ever emerged from a hidden still.

Then, as he studiously polished his binoculars, Crispin Tyler forgot both shyness and caution and told her how the troubling of my husband's life had begun, a troubling which he has never resolved but hides behind a mask of poise and certainty.

Crispin Tyler's father had been Charles's father's company accountant. 'The elder Trewin was a brilliant businessman but ruthless enough to throw both ends of the rope to a drowning man,' Mr Tyler said, the moonshine warming his guts and sharpening his polite manner. 'He cared for nothing except for spreading a network of smooth, black roads from one end of England to the other. Strangely, for so harsh a man, he married for love. Josephine had been the governess to one of his young sisters and was without fortune. Charles was their only child and his mother doted on him. She called him her little beau and gave him everything that her purse could provide. Does he still do conjuring tricks? He does? I am not surprised, for when he was a tiny child, Josephine hired the great Zapati himself to come to the house and teach her pet magical ways. Charles was the most amusing small boy in the world and his beguiling prattle compensated his mother for the frequent absences of her husband who, though he loved her, was too absorbed by fortune-making to remember to tell her so.

'Josephine was a pretty woman,' he continued. 'Even as a small boy myself, I noticed that. She had large, slanty, amber eyes, and usually wore clothes that brought out their colour; one fox cape of hers was particularly fine. She was convinced that her precious boy was exceptionally musical and that the local gentlewomen who taught the pianoforte were too limiting and provincial to inspire her darling. Nothing would do but to engage a tutor from the Royal Academy of Music. You wonder why such a man would give up a lively life in the capital to teach a spoilt child in a grim, sootwalled mansion in Huddersfield? As my own father told it, Josephine offered him thrice the salary. It did not take the tutor long to discover that the child had no musical gifts whatsoever. And there was another discovery he made in that ugly house: that he loved the golden-eyed woman who was so often alone.

'The tutor was of Italian origin, it seems, and the Italians are an impetuous and passionate race. In less than a year he had persuaded Josephine to flee with him to Verona. She left her husband a letter, asking him not to judge her too harshly and that the boy might be sent out to stay with her in Italy from time to time. A pointless request indeed, for, by leaving her husband and her home, she must have known that she would be forbidden by law to see her child again. And even if that had not been the case, her husband's nature was of the most unforgiving kind, as any man's might be were he to return home to find his wife gone and his son left in the care of the nursery governess who was quite hysterical because the amusing chatterbox had lost the power of speech. The shock of losing his mother had made him mute.

'A series of expensive doctors finally got him talking again, but, throughout what remained of his unhappy childhood, his father seemed to blame him for the mother's sin. He sent him away to school young and I myself met up with him again some years later when we were both at Rugby.'

Miss Gwynn told me that her paying guest had blushed at this point and tossed down another glass of poitín before continuing.

'I found Charles fascinating,' he said, at last, shame-facedly, his eyes on the lenses of the binoculars which he had rubbed to a glitter. 'Many of the boys there did. There is no place like an English public school to diminish the life in you; the mildest lark will serve to get you beaten to a pulp. The object in those places is conformity, and every classroom ritual is designed to wipe away originality and replace it with something wooden and dutiful. Charles Trewin rebelled against all that. Everything he did was taken to the limit. He drank, smoked, gambled, and went on doing so, no matter how many times he was beaten for his impudence. And beaten he was: the hiss of the cane must have become as familiar to him as his own scornful, mocking voice. But he went too far; like his mother he was over-fond of taking risks. Did I not mention this, Miss Gwynn? Things went badly for Josephine in Italy. Once her jewel-case had been emptied, her lover left her, and she died of drink and despair in a Roman tenement, wrapped up against the January cold in the golden fox cape that brought out the colour of her eyes.

'Of all Charles's magic tricks, the most deadly was to make other boys fall in love with him. You are shocked, Miss Gwynn? Nothing should surprise you when it comes to our public school system. There is so much hatred there that those within will turn anywhere for love, even if that love brings nothing but disgust and disgrace. Heartbreak was traded there as readily as marbles and conkers. And Charles Trewin was the cause of much of it, always the seducer, never the seduced, even of boys much older than himself. One of his conquests was a boy called Hubert Blessington, a high-born boy, his aunt is a lady-in-waiting to the Princess Royal. Blessington was a brilliant classicist, head of school, captain of sport; you would suppose that every badge of honour and achievement was embroidered solely that it might be sported by young Blessington. It was the time of the Cambridge entrance examination and a scholarship was expected of him. Instead of that, he was found hanging from the bed he had upended, in his hand a letter from Charles, coldly declining to take tea with him that day.

'I don't think it was Charles's expulsion from Rugby that made his father so angry, rather it was that by causing the death of someone as well connected as Blessington, Charles had ruined his father's chances of a knighthood. Think of it, Miss Gwynn, all that bubbling, heaving pitch spread on all those miles of road, all those guineas given to charitable causes dear to the heart of our reclusive Queen, and the chance to feel the ennobling sword against the shoulder lost entirely. The old man took his revenge by taking his son into the business and, though he was but a lad, putting him in charge of dubious ventures which my own father warned him were bound to fail. But of course the senior Trewin already knew this and embarked on them so as to besmear the young man in shame and failure.

'But shame is a weakness, and weakness had been flayed out of Charles at Rugby. Shame, like decency, was beyond him. He had met a young girl, Harriet Devereux, scarcely out of the schoolroom, and was determined to marry her and escape from forbidding, intolerant England. Both his father and Harriet's people forbade the match, since both were under age, but Charles did the one thing to ensure that permission for his marriage would be granted, a caddish, dishonourable thing, but entirely in character.

'I have seen or heard nothing from him for thirty years. How does he fare? Is he still a lawless desperado, or have Harriet and this place's desolate beauty smoothed his warring impulses?'

Miss Gwynn had again filled her visitor's glass before she told him of Harriet's death and Charles's marriage to a pony-breeder's daughter who had a great way with horses.

'So, he has wedded a flower of the mountains,' Crispin Tyler had responded grimly. 'I hope she is a hardy bloom.'

'I assured him that you were,' Miss Gwynn told me, looking at me closely out of exhausted eyes. 'I hope there was no word of a lie in that.'

I shook out the sleek cushions behind her head, lifted her poor feet in their cracked, wet boots on to a little footstool that Harriet had once morbidly worked in strands of her own glorious hair, and thin glass beads.

'It was not the truth then but it is now, or may I never stir from this spot,' I said, once I had her comfortably settled. 'You know that I first came to Malina when I was twelve years old. Not to this fine room with its scooped mouldings and bellied windows, but down below, in the kitchen. It was there that Binnie told me of the bad, low deeds done in this house, and since then I have seen so much wickedness at Malina that sometimes I felt that the bad time, the *drockshaol,* had drifted down on all of us here and muffled the goodness out of us. But Binnie had only half the story, as worthless as half a coin. I have the all of it now, thanks to the poitin you slipped down Crispin Tyler's throat. I had not dared to meet Harriet's eyes in my dreams; I shrank from her spirit, frozen into a state of tyrannical beauty and goodness, just as I shrank from Charles, the way he rumbles and threatens like the Italian volcano in an engraving he has. Little wonder that he does or that he's in the grip of hatreds that make him lash out at those who love him best. However could she do it, fling her child from her like an outworn coat? Could she not see that the poor, discarded boy would never forgive her, nor any woman who came after her?'

'There's an odd triumph in your voice,' Miss Gwynn said worriedly, pulling down her lower lip. 'Are you yourself, Rose Erris? Should I ring for Binnie to mind you?'

'No. I have no need of her, nor anyone else, now that I can let Harriet be dead and let myself live.'

But the grooves furrowed further on Miss Gwynn's face and her eyes searched for the bell that would bring Binnie, who might be persuaded to give me a valerian draught of the kind she had made for Harriet when her ravings had become desperate.

I flapped my hands in front of the old woman's face to shoo away the anxiety on it. 'This very day,' I said, 'Agnes said I was a horsewhisperer and cured sick animals through sorcery. But the gift of healing that I had was only a sharpened instinct, and the way I taught myself how to be watchful at all times. Sometimes some small thing, like the way a cow scratched her head on a boulder, or a horse stopped flicking away the fly on its nostril, told me that the end was nearing and none of my cures could alter what was certain to be. But with Charles, my senses were all asleep. What he did to Harriet, so that she couldn't live a life but only withstand it for a short while, and what he still does to me should have alerted me that he did wrong to amend a wrong done to him.'

'You are a sudden woman,' Miss Gwynn said. 'Did I waste my good poitin to have you melt and ooze with sympathy?' She kicked away the footstool and sent it skittering.

'Could I refuse sympathy to the drowned man's widow or the rabbit dragging its crunched leg from the toothed trap? Beneath the man with all his bold, bright power there's a jettisoned child who's as deserving as they. Charles was stretched across the whole world and I could not move a step without encountering him. But the pity I have for him has shrivelled him to the size of a withered apple. He can't shake the blood in my heart any more. I'll begin to live the way the Protestants ride their horses, as casually and unwatchfully as though they were sitting on a gate. If Mr Tyler's head does not pain him too much, tell him that the man he knew in England is not married to a flower of the mountains but to one of its thorn trees.'

19

There's freedom to be had when you lose the need to be loved. I was no longer frozen and adrift in my huge bed, but stretched my strong limbs delightedly, my own energy heating the smooth sheets as I planned a life of determined independence.

I did not blame Charles for hating me. His silly, indulged, tragic mother had killed the meaning and spirit of love for him and turned him into a moral cretin who lusted after domination and, where he had dominated, sought to destroy. But I refused to be the victim of his past or to allow him to force me to my knees any longer; I had arisen at last.

The wedding ring that I wore was the traditional one of the west of Ireland: the Claddagh ring which has a heart held by two hands and surmounted by a crown. The story goes that if a woman wears the ring with the point of the heart downwards, towards the wrist, she is spoken for and her heart already taken, but, should the heart's tip be pointed towards the fingers, she is waiting for life to come and lead her in the dance. The night that I realized that all that was sinister in my husband would always be so, shaped out of a terrible loss, I turned the ring around on my finger so that the point of its golden heart was directed at the world that faced me.

The first thing that the world offered me was death. It moved ghoulishly towards me through autumn's crackling grass, persistent as a cloud of midges. It took my father; hunched in the old, blowsy bed, he became more and more folded in on himself, his eyes dim with unreachable grief. His long yellow teeth hung down heavily from his gums, as though the weight of them was too much for him to bear, and his rough hands became slack and tapered, the hands of a corpse in which the rosary entwines itself. He died on All-Hallows' Eve, a decent Christian time now, but once, long ago, it went by the name of Samhain, and began a three-day feast of the dead which marked the end of summer, a time when folk shuddered as they felt the presence of the sidhe, the fairies, at the black margins of the woods.

His widow and daughters, all except Vera, who had been changed into a distant stranger called Sister Assumpta and was bringing God to those who had little need of him at a mission in Africa, heaped his grave under the high hill of Errisbeg, to the sound of cold grass being torn by the stooping cattle on its flanks and Father Casey's ready, empty words of comfort. My mother refused to be comforted; she seemed offended rather than saddened by bereavement and her ice-blue eyes whipped dementedly about her depleted house, as though she hated its ordinariness and the life of commonplace sacrifice she had led in it.

Half the neighbourhood had come to be dealt cakes and ale and whiskey after the funeral, and it was a long time before we had the house to ourselves. Then, tiredly drinking tea and chewing thick slices of barm brack with my sisters, I yearned for the intimacy of shared grief, to sit and talk of gentle things about my father and all the wasteful virtues that had kept him rooted to the uncongenial mountainside, as darkness sidled up the walls of the house and the sea flashed, laden with stars.

Yet when I started such talk, I could feel the sentimental words flop about unheeded like stranded fish. My mother and sisters rose from their chairs and threw themselves into a fierce bustle, or would talk only of sticky domestic things. My mother's large, scrubbed, restless hands fiddled with her coiled hair needlessly, or crumbled the faded leaves of the geraniums into brown dust, and, finally, although it was late by then, went to the hen-house to kill a chicken and came back with her hands greasy with blood.

'If you cannot be still, we should perhaps be planning how to keep up the ponies without Dada,' I suggested. My mother gave me a crucified smile and primmed up the corners of her mouth. ''Tis all brought about,' she said. 'Geraldine is to marry Murph Delancey, and he'll be living in this house and doing the dealing and breeding.' She sought to defend herself: 'What else could I do, and the way it is with us. There's no man here in all our seed or breed.' Her voice was cold, excited.

When St Patrick banished the snakes from Ireland, there was one he forgot and that one was Murph Delancey. Murph was a corner boy, a loafer with shifty, metallic eyes, who could be found on most afternoons leaning his belly on the harbour wall, turning a quid of tobacco with his tongue into a far corner of his mouth, his cap on the back of his head as he squinted out of sliding eyes at the clanking business on the pierhead. When he had nothing better to do, he was a good horse-dealer, full of knowing, wary charm. But, usually, he did find something better to do: cock-fighting, drinking, going after slatterns and dollymops in Galway city, a smile of alcoholic malice on his drained face. He sang an old song under his breath:

> 'And he that will to bed goe sober.
> Falls with the leafe still in October.'

'No wonder you waited until Dada was dead to fix up this match. It would have killed him before now,' I shrieked at my mother.

'Ah sure, my heart is scalded,' she said mockingly, 'As though your own arrangement didn't leave him for dead. There's no great choosing of a man to be had here, and it's time for Geraldine to be settled. Wilful, provoking girl that she is, and has been all along. It must be yourself that she favours.' She lowered her voice so that Geraldine, who was combing her wayward, jungly black hair in the scullery, couldn't hear her.

'Well, Murph Delancey will quiet her down, if he's ever around to do it,' I said.

'O, a love match is the only way for happiness when all the parties can afford it,' my mother said bitterly, beginning to pluck the slaughtered hen. 'And why is it that you have your wedding ring turned on your great lady's finger? What are you after now, the stench of the divorce courts?'

My mother could slide a martyred expression up her thin, narrow-winged nose as smoothly as she could pluck a fowl. Before one could claim her features, I was already on my horse, clopping along the darkening road beside the little lakes that flowed from the stones.

Myles died as November began to sharpen its bite on the rocks, and the raw, dark smell of newly harvested potatoes clung to the earth. He had been attended by a ruffled pack of eminent physicians from Dublin who could do nothing for him except scold him for his foolishness in giving up the sparkling dryness of the Swiss Alps for the wet wildness that is Connemara. The dankness in the wintry air fingered Myles's shuddering body as he lay dying; his bald head had a cloudy lustre like a mushroom and his slack skin looked steamy. Debonair but conflicted in plum-purple silk dressing-gowns, Myles considered it a duty to make his last days in this world agreeable to his friends, and gave bedside tea parties in a magnificent oval bedroom that smelt of pot-pourri, linctus and death. He liked to have me sit on his bed while he twisted my hair into hundreds of tiny braids which, when released, made it fan out in the rigid rows of waves that, he said, made me look like Ireland's very soul. 'Promise me,' Myles said, as he took up the ivory-backed hairbrush, 'that, you know, *afterwards*, you will be firm with Leonora, or she will have the whole thing turned into a romp. She sizzles at all those white-faced schoolmasters and I know that what she's after is to put on some political drivel of a drama so that she can play Cathleen ni Houlihan in something flimsy and indecent and command the

243

enchanted suitors to bare their miserable chests for a tease.'

'But there won't be a Gaelic League here without you, Myles,' I said, shaking out my hair over my face so that he wouldn't see me weeping, for both of us were as sick to death of tears as we were of stethoscopes and steel dishes in which bloody sputum floated. 'None of the rest of us has your fervour to be Irish. The young women come to make gloppy, smooshy sighs at the lads and the lads come to be exquisite and for Leonora to dissolve them into puddles of lust.'

Myles raked my hair with weak, groping fingers. 'You're not much cheer for a chap who has the measure of his coffin,' he said. 'Never mind that; I have ordered some inspiration from America. His name is Peadar Griffin, he will be here inside of a week and unless you splash your blotchy face in spring water he will be sure to think you the ugliest old hag in Connemara.'

Three days later, I was smoothing on my black gloves and carrying my pocket bible for the second time in a month. For a man of such jerky, compulsive passions, Myles's funeral was very decorous. The rector, in spite of his calling, was uncomfortable with mysterious, inexplicable things. He mentioned God once, death not at all, and spoke of Myles in a tolerant, amused way, as though the body in the brass-handled coffin was at a meeting and would be joining us shortly. He noted Myles's fine art collection but not his romantic, aesthetic brand of nationalism, the courage with which he had borne his illness but not his mastery of it through wicked wit and uneasy ideas. The sermon was no more than an unperturbed murmur of sympathy, a song you sing to a troubled cow. There was no wildness to it, nothing to call forth a man who was fey, sudden and unholy. Myles would have been disappointed in the weather too; the November wind had stopped its dramatic rumble and a blue sky held the slender beam of day.

I stayed at the graveside a while, after the stately black-caped mourners had started to make their way to their cold carriages. On the ground, a larger shadow blotted out mine and I looked up dully to see an absurdly tall man whose old black coat was worn in a shambolic way, refusing any thought of partnership with his gangly body.

'Mrs Trewin?' he asked, in an American accent. 'I recognized you from the photograph Myles showed me once. I am Peadar Griffin.'

The man's pale face was mild, open and dreamy. Behind thick-lensed spectacles his eyes looked milky and innocent, but when he took off the glasses, hunting unsuccessfully in a pocket for a handkerchief to wipe them on, I saw that, exposed, his eyes were the dull green of broken glass, the long, dark eyes of a wanderer. He stood framed by the little, lyrical fields that were glazed by a wintry sun, but the sight of him gave me no feeling that the birthday of my life had come, then, or for a long time to come. He told me that in his native Chicago he had been a poetry teacher, that his own verse had been published, and that a thin, limp volume of it had been bought by Myles, who had then written admiringly to its author.

'Do your poems have golden harps in them and wild swans and trembling veils?' I asked the tall stranger.

He turned his gentle, spreading gaze on me, startled by the weariness and lack of civility in my voice. 'They mention all those things by name.'

I noticed that he had a cleft chin and dimples crammed with a grey-blue stubble, like lichen in a rock's crevice.

'You write in Irish?' I knew the answer before he had given it.

'Always. I helped to set up the Irish Language League in Chicago.'

He had a city boy's pallor; a scholar's hunched shoulderblades poked triangles in the shoddy cloth of his coat. He did not know that the ewes nibbling the heather on the mountainside were splashed with a blue or red mark to show which ram had tupped them; he had never felt the sea through the currach's tarred skin.

For all the muzzy dreaminess in his face, he showed an unquenchable persistence. 'Would you not agree that to de-Anglicize themselves, the Irish must arrest the decay of their language? As things are, they have ceased to be Irish without becoming English.' His pleasant, unhurried voice grew quieter. 'Although, ultimately, some think, the language alone will not suffice.'

'There's all kinds of ways to be Irish,' I said. 'It's something that weathers all conditions, even in your own country where you do not rule. I am a Gael; the dear man in there' – I kicked a scatter of earth over the grave beside us – 'was one of the Gall. We are both different from each other but closer to each other than to the *Sasanaigh,* the Englishman.'

In the thin sunlight, we began to walk down the tree-lined path that led from the church to the sea wall. Without discussion we stopped there, leant our elbows on the wall's crusted granite and watched the rising tide veer around the moored fishing boats, outriding their curves.

'There's a sight you'd never want to take your eyes from,' I said. But the American poet would not be diverted.

'Yet you are married to an Englishman?' he probed.

'I am so. To an Englishman so concerned with my nation's future that he has no time to regret its past.'

'And what of your own regrets?' I looked at him sharply, wondering how much Myles, that dear, dead gossip, had told him about my marriage. 'Myles told me that your husband's first wife took her own life. An act of violence in its way.' His voice was not censorious but merely interested, and his guileless face looked clear as water.

'Something in the past led her to it, something she could not put right.' I spoke hurriedly, stretching my glove over my wrist to show that I was ready to depart.

'Well, your past is something you can't not have,' he said pleasantly. The strip of water where it met the farther shore was the same dark, glassy green as his explorer's eyes. This was something else he would never notice. 'The Irish need the freedom to achieve freedom,' he muttered vaguely, pressing his palms on the top of the wall, as though the weapons to achieve

247

freedom might be concealed under the cold, curved stone rim.

'You sound like my husband when he makes speeches to the boards of public companies, but he is talking about free trade, and I understand you to be talking about the freedom of the spirit.'

'Is that something you know about?'

'All I know are my own truths, the truths that are hard come by and worked out by myself. Those are the ones that will sustain me.'

'May I show you some of my poems, Mrs Trewin?'

'Surely. Just so long as too many of them don't start with lines like "Now stolen is the soul from Erin's breast."' I rolled my eyes and clawed at my furs as I said this and the serious-looking man in the smeared, tin-framed spectacles began to laugh. Not so much laugh as to become laughter. His knees sagged against the wall until he was forced to lean his head on it, his eyes brimming. His laugh was a deep, splashy rumbling like a far-off waterfall. It was as catching as a yawn and soon we were both slurping and spluttering, leaning helplessly over the wall, our shoulders touching companionably, aware that people in the village going about their business were tautening their mouths as they passed us in our funerary black, scandalously trying to shake tears of pleasure from our eyes. I thought: this is the part of the day that Myles would have approved of; it has a whiff of scandal to it.

Some days later, I was rubbing almond oil into Binnie's ulcerous legs with their wriggling blue worms of veins. Malachy O'Goole, Horty and Agnes's baby, lay in a rush crib on the kitchen settle. However did that lardy couple bear such a beautiful creature? Malachy had a high, delicate head, a sweet, heart-shaped face and wise, shimmering dark blue eyes. I rubbed some of the oil from my hands on to his feet and he curled his toes and gave me a smile like a gift.

'You're coming in handy enough for him now,' Binnie said, wincing as she tried to lift the iron kettle, and it was Charles, and not the wise-eyed child, that she meant.

At the age of sixty, my husband had been appointed by the Chief Secretary of State for Ireland to be the Commissioner of the Board of Works in the west of the country, responsible for bringing work and wealth to the area. He looked to Ulster, the contrary region in the north, to supply him with the help he needed to set up a lace-making school on the quay, to build a hotel for English tourists, to extract iodine from the kelp, which would be bottled in a new local factory and shipped out to heal a wounded world. The engineers and lace teachers and factory managers from Ulster whom Charles hired on short, fixed-term contracts to start his new ventures were energetic and dour. They complained that 'The Lord created this place last' when Connemara's capsized, muddy roads held up deliveries, but they left with some regret when the time came to go back to their angry, well-ordered province with its sooty shrubberies, tight prosperity, linen decay and dull, burdensome rituals.

I was, as Binnie said, a handy enough appendage for a man appointed to a post created and funded by a British government. When Charles had to deal with contractors of a Nationalist persuasion, he would manage to drop a reference to his Irish-born, Irish-speaking wife, even mouth the odd *Eire abu* (Ireland to victory) and *beannacht* (goodbye) when it suited his purpose. I alone noticed the mocking, amber glints in his eye as he did so; I alone knew how carefully he measured cordiality and correctness and that his impeccable public charm was a trap on which to snag all who encountered it. My husband's hair still streamed back from his forehead in a thick mane, no longer the tawny gold of a lion's, but a dense, glimmering silver, the only sign that he was growing old. The dark perversity within him had made him try to break my heart and spirit, but these days he seemed rather pleased to have failed, treating me with a cool respect, so that I felt kept behind a glass wall that I could not break.

So might the schoolmasters at Rugby, who beat Charles so savagely, have been pleased that the bold boy would not be broken by the lash. Yet although Charles appreciated the convenience of an Irish wife to soften the edges of his own lofty, unmistakable Englishness, it did not rekindle his love for me. My bedroom remained mine alone, and Harriet's photograph still stood in my husband's study.

On the handsome round rent-table in the hall, there was another photograph. It had been taken recently by a photographer from the *Connacht Clarion,* when Charles's appointment as Commissioner had been announced. It showed me seated on Milo, my Palomino pony, whose silver mane matched my husband's hair, although both showed as muddy grey in the grainy photograph. I am wearing my faultless riding clothes and the line of my heavy skirt is stiff and unrelenting.

Charles is standing beside the horse, his hand lightly on the rein. He is looking up at me, the expression on his face civil but distant. We could have been any high-born couple in Ireland, born to a life that was sociable and pleasure-seeking, made so by the land's short distances and definite places. Few would guess that we were something in disguise, that the smooth-browed man with the silken hair was distorted by an ancient hatred, or that the handsome woman with the sweeping eyelashes and a mouth that looked like a bruised plum was empty and barren, worthless as a husk. The truth about our household would never be revealed by that charming, formal portrait. It resided in that other likeness, the one of a woman dead by her own hand, in the room that was the real, hidden heart of the Big House, the dark, sullied, airless room, guardian of all Malina's terrible secrets.

20

'I'm going to stop going to the Gaelic League and I advise you to do the same,' said Leonora, easing off her boots. She released her blond curls from the restraining net she wore when riding and scratched her head vigorously.

'I'm surprised at you, Leonora,' I said, making my voice grave. 'Whatever happened to "When ign'rance enters, folly is at hand; learning is better far than house and land"?' I quoted from the preface of Oliver Goldsmith's play, *She Stoops to Conquer*, to bait her, and succeeded too.

'Well, it's getting stuffed full of bowsies and hillsiders who demand the end of empire and bloodied heads. Do you know what one of those fellows said to me last night, Christy, I think it was, the one with the scattered, black moustache. He said Ireland must welcome war as she would welcome the sight of the angel of God. And when I told him that I didn't think Father Casey would agree, he gave me a punishing smile out of rotted teeth and said that he'd put it on the long finger for now but that the ebbing tide was with me and the flowing tide with him. Charles would be horrified to hear such things,' Leonora concluded primly.

'It's likely that Charles would agree with him. Only

he thinks he can hold back the tide a while by killing Home Rule by kindness. That's why he's building houses for the tenantry at Aillenacally. He thinks they'll be in a swamp of gratitude and won't listen to the out-and-outers.'

'There is one mistake your husband keeps on making.' Leonora yawned fastidiously, like a cat. 'He *will* go on giving the Irish things they have not asked for and do not want. Do you think good will come of this or will he be seen to be throwing red herrings across the path of Home Rule?'

'You can no more predict what is going to happen in Ireland than tell if lightning will seize the knife box. Still, I am restless in the Gaelic League. Everything taught there is thrilling but useless.'

'Peadar Griffin is interesting enough, though,' Leonora said, enskeined as usual in her own haphazard thoughts. 'There's something of beauty in his white face; remote, spiritual and ideal.' She paused shudderingly after each word before tearing laughter rattled wickedly in her throat like knives and forks.

Remote, spiritual and ideal. These qualities did not seem to appeal to the rough, frantic men, the 'bowsies' who came to the League's meetings. They stood at the back of the room, not trusting their bulk to the narrow-backed chairs, in the same way that they loafed at the back of the church on Sundays, watching the sad-eyed women making the stations of the Cross. Peadar Griffin's dark eyes smiled peace at them as he recited in Irish an account of the Gaelic seers, the *fili*, our storytellers, who brushed all the hearts of the people into one strong, towering pile of belief. The men met the poet's gentle smile with scowls, and disrupted his readings by leaving before the end, their damp, wretched coats hitched up over one ear to protect them from the rain. They retired to Meehan's public house to thicken the air with cigarette smoke and failure.

I did not find them as repellent as Leonora did. I had shared a schoolroom with them. I had shared their indifference when Miss Gwynn told of the vital importance of our ancient ways, and shared it now when Peadar Griffin gave his scrupulous renditions of Ireland's mournful folklore. And there was something else I sensed sharing with these shabby, stricken men: a keen desire for something to happen to all of us. I was the tinder awaiting the match; a tension I couldn't explain nagged and fumbled inside my head. My celebrated instinct, or perhaps the recognition of a reckless despair in the bowsies' reddened eyes, made me certain that they had to be taken into account, that it would be dangerous to dismiss them.

I needed time to concentrate, time to decide how best to resolve a problem that, as yet, had no name. That was reason enough to slink away from the Gaelic League. It would be courteous to tell Peadar Griffin that I was leaving, so, on a shining July evening, so warm that its heat dissolved the harshness from the land and covered its starved skin with light, I took the sandy road to Foyle harbour where Peadar lodged with an old fisherman called Marty Kenneally.

The sun slapped against the lumpy white walls of the cottage and Marty sat outside it mending the frayed brown squares of his nets, an upturned currach beside him like a watchful pet. He wore a beret the shape and colour of a cowpat and he was crouched against the wind out of custom and habit, for the air was stone still. The smell of fish on him could have knocked you down.

'Well, shite and onions.' Marty stuck his netting needle into a clump of red-hot pokers, spat on his filthy hand and grasped my own in it. I had long been a favourite of his, ever since I had strengthened his sick cat by discovering that it had no tolerance for cows' milk.

'You're as handsome as the day that is in it and have the walk of a queen,' Marty said, approving my frothing muslin and the diamonded sea behind me. 'Is it the big fella you're wanting? You'd need to be quick, for it's an American wake we'll be having soon enough.'

When someone is to emigrate on the following day, families and neighbours hold 'an American wake' to make him too drunk and weary to be crazed with grief at the parting. 'The house will be dark without him so,' Marty said sadly. 'Never a day that he didn't tell me a small little poem of his own making, myself not having the reading of it. Such gentle ways he has on him; for all the size of him, you wouldn't see him raise so much as an arm to a soused herring.'

'Ah, the light of poetry he is, sure enough,' I said lightly, and then faltered. I had always told myself that Peadar Griffin was a big, milky thing who trembled with tenderness towards the rough world. Yet to think of him strapping his books and nailing the lids of packing cases had me tormented. I had made silly jokes in his company to hide from him deeper needs of mine; I had listened to the verses that streamed from his mouth and had not admitted to myself that what I most wanted was to squeeze kisses on his lips. I had willed myself away from the lure of his gentleness, but at the thought of him climbing into Bianconi's long car and arranging his suitcase on his sharp knees, beyond my will my heart was lost. There are two ways of it and the pity is that you cannot be at the choice of them. I hesitated for a moment in the sunlight, and then my truant nature convinced me that if I let Peadar Griffin leave, my life would become a makeshift thing, cobbled around his disastrous absence.

I ran into Marty's cottage as though the soles of my feet were scorched; ran into the smoky darkness that blinded me, batted at it with outflung hands, as though it were an impeding curtain, dazed by it as I was dazed by the shock of love.

I pushed the plank door at the back of the house and my heart crumbled at the sight of the back of Peadar's head and its disarrayed curls, pale brown like winter barley. The sound of my rasped breath made him turn round in his chair. The mossy dimples in his cheeks deepened as he smiled; his dangling wrists looked so insecure I thought they might drop from his arms. I held my breath in the unattended moment.

Peadar Griffin tilted back his chair perilously and looked at me with his wanderer's eyes. 'I'm writing a farewell speech for next Wednesday's meeting, which will be my last.' He gave a sigh which he unsuccessfully tried to turn into a yawn. 'I'm afraid it's all a bit long in the sleeve, as usual,' he said.

I raked my mind for a mocking joke that would

make his long body unravel into laughter in that absurd way of his, but every joke I knew had fallen out of it. I heard myself say, 'Don't go, please don't go.' Then, excited, lost and untroubled, I stepped inside the dim room.

Peadar raked his scarecrow hands through his hair, helpless and baffled. 'I have failed in this place,' he said harshly. 'I felt that I was brought here on the currents of life but I do not understand the way things are merged in this place, this combination of high society and warring notions.' His hand took another swipe at his untidy curls. 'Sometimes, I think that Marty out there lives more complexly than the most devious hoodlum in Chicago. That old man knows how to negotiate life in a way that I don't. I love the people here more deeply than any I have known but I am stupidly unworldly among them. I lack the necessary craftiness to survive in these hushed fields and lovely, uneasy light.'

I wanted to hold him in the hollow of my hand. Instead, I moved a teetering pile of papers from a rush-seated chair and sat on it. 'But you love the Irish language and teaching the old ways.'

'More than all else.'

'You are like my old schoolteacher, Miss Gwynn. She is convinced that Ireland's past will solve the secret of its future.'

His eyes smoked over with rapt dreaminess. 'The past cannot be thought away,' he sighed. 'But how to dispel it while learning from its lessons? This is where I have failed. With you too, Rose Erris,' he reproved me. 'Sometimes, while I told the most beautiful stories, you broke their spell by squirming in your chair like an eel.'

'Oh, that would have been when you were spouting Lady Gregory of the Golden Mouth and all her misty blather.' Muzzy with love, I still clung to mockery.

Peadar looked stung. 'Does your history mean nothing to you then?' he asked quietly.

'Love means more,' I said and slid off the chair. I stood over him, put my hands on his wide, thin shoulders, felt them tremble as he looked into my commanding eyes. The pages of his speech fell from his hand on to the rough floorboards, unheeded and unnecessary.

'History was then, we are now,' I murmured into his troubled brow. Peadar nodded thoughtfully, his eyes closed. Then he opened them, two glinting shards of bottle green in his tired face. They burned my flesh away as we stared at each other in the monumental stillness of the moment. I knew then that he would stay. We came to each other on the eve of *Lunasad* at the end of a blazing July: a woman unhusbanded in all but name and a poet with dimpled cheeks who had crossed an ocean to make a delicate appointment with her heart. The season itself made deception effortless, for deceivers we were, made such by love. In the gentle evenings Marty was out with the fishing boats, scooping the catch from a mackerel-crowded sea until daybreak. And, once the old man was away, I would leave my mare cropping the grass in a daisy-scattered field and wind my way, unseen, unheard, hidden by the thorn bushes arched over the ditches and the thickness of waxy fuchsia, clambering over the rocks splashed with pale blue lichen, until I came in sight of the oil lamp in Peadar's window. And all my thoughts were as bright as its steady flame.

I had married a man packed tight with fierce certainties, a man who, as Miss Gwynn had said, assumed that a closed gate didn't apply to him. I took as a lover a man as gentle and tentative as a newborn foal. On the straw mattress of his narrow bed, he touched me with a wary wonder, traced the curves of my buttocks with awed delight, as though it were a miracle for him to have discovered their shape. And, again reminding me of a shaky, newborn animal, he took little, nuzzling bites of me, to make sure that I was really there, really his. His cramped, scholarly life had left him innocent of the fleshly world, and I took advantage of that innocence, drawing him to me through the old, skilled ways that women such as I are born with. I put my soft lips to his organ. It was smooth, cool, buttery, like a rose petal. My touch made him electric, taut as a humming wire.

Peadar. The sound of his name was like a summons to my blood, which swooped up to the top of my head where it prickled furiously. At times such was our shared desire that there seemed to be one skin between us, doubled and twinned. Our joyful discovery of each other was like something we had both known before and had always been waiting for. But desire was only a part of all we had. We had, too, a nearness of spirit that allowed us, after passionate moments, to each take up a book and read together as though we were old, well-established friends, or to argue about the merits of restoring the old language — that most of all — and to laugh and tease each other until I got the hiccups and Peadar's long body pleated up with laughter.

He would put on a show of pedagoguery for my amusement, pushing his spectacles down to the end of his large nose that had a diamond-shaped bump in its slope. 'Narration is the customary form of customary knowledge,' he would drone. 'All that remains of the mystery of the past is the tale and the fable.'

'All them stories,' I said dismissively, wiggling my bare feet to warm them. My chilblains had smoothed themselves off my toes, banished by love, as loneliness had been. 'People should be free to make their own stories,' I insisted, pulling the old flannel quilt around my lover's shoulders, for we had neglected the small fire in the grate.

'As you did, Rose Erris?'

'As I am doing,' I said, and rubbed my hands up and down his long, bony flanks to warm them and excite him.

But on the Irish language our quarrel was serious. After some years now of studying the tongue of my forefathers, I had come to hate its mournful glamour of sacrifice and martyrdom. It spoke in a voice that, for all its beautiful cadences, stank of the centuries disfigured by distress. One of its grammatical constructions was called the dative of disadvantage. With what sad relish, I wondered, had some ancient grammarian worked out a way of conveying misfortune through the ending of a word. I connected the Irish tongue with despair and defeat; no language for an insurgent people, strung out on drink and disappointment. It was English we needed, the conqueror's own words, to steal and use as a weapon of ridicule against our long-time invader. I put this thought to Peadar as we picked blackberries together at the foot of Errisbeg, filling his tweed cap with the fruit, fat, firm and purple.

Our expedition would cause no shocked talk in the neighbourhood. In his shapeless, flapping clothes, Peadar did not seem to occupy his body in any way, or to have any connection with physical life. Besides, he was that unexpected combination, an American who was poor, and it was a widely held view that I noticed no man but a wealthy one, who would put hunters in my stables and trick me out in trinkets. A spiteful view, but it suited my purpose now.

Peadar sat down clumsily on a rock and set the cap of blackberries on his sharp knees. 'What an unmemorious woman you are,' he said. 'Do you think that you have invented ridicule as a weapon? Can you not remember our own Gaelic seers, our *fili,* who were feared for their satire which could raise blisters on the faces of its victims?'

I sat beside him and we set about emptying his cap of its contents for a while, thinking on these things while our fingers blotched to a juicy crimson.

'If the *fili* were here today, they would be speaking in English,' I said stubbornly, after some minutes.

'Ah, but speaking English in bad faith, knowing it was not theirs.'

'Not at all. They would have fashioned it in their own way and made it theirs. The English that we Irish speak is of our own devising. I should know; my husband corrects mine often enough,' I said, urging Condy, the Labrador puppy who had succeeded Plume, to sit up and beg for a blackberry.

'What is it exactly that you want, Rose Erris?'

I considered Peadar's question as I rubbed the puppy's satin ears between my thumb and forefinger. 'You, above all things, and ourselves in love. And, besides that, for something to happen, something that will stop us feeling on suffrance in our own country. The reason that I resist the old ways that you honour so much is that they dwell so much on sorrow. I would rather we had words to sing that had larks and scoffing to them, songs that made the English out as the blundering bullies that they are.'

Surprise at myself made me stand up suddenly so that the blackberries tumbled from Peadar's cap. My words sped; I was an engine of eagerness now. 'And I shall write them,' I said, sure, at last, of my calling. 'I have always been applauded for my musical gifts because I can twang a pretty air from a harp. It is time to write my own airs, for my own race, as it is now, this day, and for its reality.'

'And these songs of yours will be in English?' Peadar questioned me sadly.

I sat down again and wrapped my arms about him. 'My love and my delight, my love and my calf, my love and my darling, my love and my sweetness, my love and my treasure, my love and my secret,' I murmured as I rocked our clinging bodies together on the wide rock. 'It is through you that I have been able to grasp the past so that I may let go of it. But the songs I want to write need resources which the old language sets its face against, for I mean to insist that the English will fall on powerless days.'

All ideas excited Peadar, even those he disagreed with, and moved him to gentle discussion. He took off his spectacles and fished a handkerchief edged in Guipure lace out of the pocket of my skirt on which to wipe them. 'There was a brief time,' he said quietly, 'just over a hundred years ago, when Ireland and England were in a natural, cheerful alliance, in spite of all the bloodshed that had gone before, and there was a new constitution that established Irish independence peacefully. Everything went on smack smooth for a while then, until the revolution in France spawned a new revolt and a new comedy of terrors began. But that peaceful time cannot be talked away, you know.'

'Neither can it be talked back. You are homesick for a distant past of fairies and beauty. But it is the day before yesterday that needs to be avenged, the days when our whole race came close to vanishing from this world, men, women and childer dying on the roadside, their mouths stuffed with nettles that they had tried to keep alive on when the English refused them corn.'

I had stood up again, too excited by my plan to remain still. Peadar's bottle-green eyes blinked at me, anxiety shimmered off him, and I knew that my cheeks blazed in spite of the evening chill that had begun to mist over the blackberry bushes. 'I have never come across a woman as bold or as vulnerable as you,' he said, 'or one so fearsomely at large with the world. You are all pneuma. Do you know what that is?' I shook my head. 'The spark of your soul,' he said. 'Its dazzle is greater than that great clump of diamonds at your throat and I am besotted by it. Now I know how a man who can be a rock to all the world is like a bit of wax in the hands of a woman.'

On our way back we passed a rock that marked the

end of the path where it joined the crossroad. It was called the Rock of the Weeping of Tears and there is one like it in every place in the west of Ireland, the sad spot where families mourn, as a son or daughter leaves them there, to begin the voyage to America. The rock we passed was dust-pearl with silver eyes, the granite that covers Connemara and makes its people feel that they live on the very bones of the earth.

I touched the silvery surface. 'On me will be the grief if I ever have to weep for the leaving of you at this rock,' I said.

'Put away all thoughts of that day, woman,' Peadar said, his voice strange for the grimness and loving in it. 'If you are serious about those songs of yours, I must stay here to keep you from harm.'

21

Everything is moonshine compared to the education of the heart. I, a horse-trader's daughter, who had viewed life as a transaction, giving nothing unless sure of a return on my investment, had learnt how to squander myself, to give and give and ask for nothing in return.

Peadar, blinking and stringy and prone to stomach disorders, was made for coddling. I put him to bed at the first sign of upset and made him drink burnt whiskey out of an eggshell to drive the cold from his guts. He fretted to be away from his classes, shifting his untidy length on the bed in a dislocated way like a huge rag doll, looking at me owlishly over his spectacles as I stood over him to make sure that he supped every drop of the whiskey whose taste he hated, saying it was the taste of sin.

I had lived so long with a man who clawed his way upwards by a fatal blend of calculation and charm that I marvelled at Peadar's lack of tricksiness. Peadar had a weak stomach but no moral sickness tainted him. Perhaps his upbringing in America, the land of the free, had saved him from that: our Irish sickness of an occupied people who have learnt to say one thing while thinking another, or the English sickness which is to lie and lie and swear that truth is in their lies. This is the wormy disease which makes the English such bland and excellent public men with ivory manners. Badness is in the best of them, in the strutting names of the gentry and the smiling way they refuse to remember what we Irish cannot forget.

Peadar was as clear as a pane of glass. He said only what he thought in his heart to be right, never wheedled his ideas into other men's minds but set his arguments before them in his mild, open way, convinced that with the facts before them, they would judge his reasons to be sound. Only in love did he dissemble and it troubled him deeply. 'How is it that you lose no sleep at night over this sin we commit time after time?' he asked me miserably, twisting my wedding ring around on my finger. 'Is it that a strong woman, such as yourself, has no need of morality?'

I was unmoved by his wretchedness. 'Morality, is it?' I said. 'Come down out of that. Father Casey always told me that being moral is doing what you know to be right. What wrong can there be in what we do when I, who was as empty as a soap bubble, am now slapped into hope, and the grass on which I stand soughs with life? If there was any wrong done, it was to live the crammed, shapeless life that I led before.' I took off his spectacles and smoothed his eyelids. 'Peadar, I am an Irishwoman, with the Irishwoman's careful heed of fate. It leans me towards doing what I want to do and then being prepared to pay the price; that is the only bargain that fate understands. Have I not suffered enough from Charles's cruelty without having to bear the pain of regret for a love not loved out?'

The nights had grown too cold for Marty to be out with the fishing boats but I had found a secret place where Peadar and I could meet and love. It was a deserted house beside loch Áinín Rua, the lake of the red-haired woman who was said to have drowned in it. The stone house, broken and weed-choked, still testified to the lives it once contained. Some way up the chimney a nail hung to receive the iron pot, although that vessel was now rusting blackly in the long grass beyond, and on the earth floor with its bitter smell I sometimes found fragments of blue and white delft which had gleamed on a dresser's rack.

Nobody came here; they were too fearful of the thin rustle of the wheat-coloured grasses that pricked through the lake water and which they took to be the cackling of poor Áinín's ghost. But I had lived too long with the clamouring shade of one drowned woman to be disturbed by others of her kind. Strewing clean, dry straw over the floor's thrusting nettles, I offered thanks to the spirit of the red-headed woman for dying in such a way as to offer me love's hiding-place. Little by little, I made the house my own, making surreptitious journeys there under the glassy, star-pricked November sky, sods of turf hidden under a blanket in the back of the governess cart, along with some mice-nibbled cushions that would never be missed and Harriet's old spirit kettle, which once accompanied her on her expeditions to Horam's Cove. The old stone walls held warmth easily, shielded by a few tall, curving trees that hid the dangerous curl of fire from the eyes of the world. In this place Peadar and I reached out hungrily for each other on days when the sun was low at the edge of the world and we could be as shadows, anonymous as blades of grass.

'We should marry,' he said, 'go to America where scandals are soon forgotten, not even recognized as scandals at all.'

I shook my head. 'I have things I must do here.' I felt in a pocket for the notebook and pencil which I always carried with me now to write down ideas for songs as they came to me. 'I will never leave Connemara; its mountains are my protection. Without them I would be a shrivelled, lost thing. But I have no right to hold *you* here, I know that.'

'You know also that I cannot live away from you.'

I shrugged my shoulders. ''Tis no use taking it to the fair then.'

It was a wonder to me that Peadar and I could argue and disagree without speaking in sharp, hunting voices that sought to make of each other a quarry to stalk and wound; a wonder that we could inhabit each other's ideas as easily as we came to inhabit the old, hidden house, so that it took on the rainy smell of our clothes and the strong metallic smell of the beef tea we drank there, while we, in turn, had its turf-smoke always in our hair, the dusty smell of dry straw on our flesh.

I breathed deeply of this odorous world, greedy for it after Malina's spacious, chilly rooms, scentless except when Charles was in residence, when a faint trace of carnation-scented cologne, a suave, supple scent as prosperous and foxy as Charles himself, glazed the air and set it shimmering on pale, silken surfaces.

I had told Peadar about my husband's torn child-hood, and how it had left him merciless, whapped him into a cold, vigorous hatred of the two women, myself and Harriet, who had loved him. Peadar let me have my dark say, the marine light of his eyes fixed on my face in tender concern until I had finished.

'And isn't that the great pity,' he said then, pulling me into the shelter of his chest. 'And that it should have torn the heart out of you, my darling, for all those long years. I would not have had you so troubled by those evil, deadly things for all the world.' He cleared his throat and the sound seemed to travel a great distance down his long neck. 'The naming of names can make devilry less black,' he said. 'There is a name for the way your husband is that you could add to the collection of words I see you scribbling in your notebook. It is indehiscent, which means not opening at maturity. You see, fear and sorrow closed your man into a tight bud that could never bloom, so his life has become a distortion instead of a destiny. Poor fellow; I should pity him, were it not for the harm that might have come to you.'

Potatoes in their skins were baking on a trivet. I set them in two cracked bowls that I had stolen from my own kitchen, and poured buttermilk around them. We ate with our fingers, wiping them sometimes on the crackling straw on which we lolled. This was the dish that fed and strengthened the might of the High Kings of Ireland, to whom the potato skins were a great delicacy to be saved until last as a treat. The taste of the savage, broken earth in them was sweeter to me than the oysters packed in seaweed which were sent from Charles's new fishery to the King of England.

'Turma de tierra,' Peadar said incomprehensibly.

'Have you a flick of potato skin stuck in your throat?'

'No, that's the Spanish for potato. It means earth testicle.'

It seemed a good name to me, for the potato gives life, just as a man's two swinging pouches of seed give life. I held my lover's testicles in my hand, liking the grainy weight of them on my palm, and licked the buttermilk that had spilled down his chin out of the stubbly cleft. For a long time I had told myself that the moment I would become happy was always just ahead. Now it had arrived.

I was rich in love, rollicking in it. But I had more than love to sustain me. All my little abilities had dropped away from me, to reveal a savage, narrow gift. Out of my notebooks' scrawls and scribbles songs emerged, songs that came not from the smug centre of the mind but from the ragged edges of the soul, songs with plain, unvarnished words that could be understood by all who heard them. They were powerful words that sounded as though they had fallen out of silence, and I set them to a lilt that would make you tap the shoe leather off your foot. I wrote them out of some need in myself to outwit history, to bring Ireland's crown from out of the deeps of time, to resolve a quarrel I was having with myself. I sought to reconcile the perilous magic of the past with my dangerous dreams of a future that would be destructive and beautiful, wild and rhythmic. Old rages that I thought had died in me now spurred me into creativity. Memories of Miss Florence Wingrave floated upwards through the years and settled inside my head with a bitter brilliance. That shuddering recoil of hers at the sight of Malina's sodden azalea shrubs tottering in the wind became as intense as though it had happened that same morning rather than two decades ago. Only when my songs began to take shape did I realize how much I hated not the English so much as Englishness, the punctuality, pettiness and condescension of it that glinted thin and cruel, like the edge of a knife.

I had turned Harriet's veranda room into an office in which to plan the season's meets. A map of the hunting country to the south of Connemara was tacked on the wall, stuck all over with small paper flags in different colours to represent coverts and gates and places where riders were to be collected. The room was disgracefully rumpled: letters stacked in crumpled piles, drawers jammed by an overflow of calendars and lists, everywhere drifts and blizzards of paper. This was a deliberate sloppiness, for there was another business I attended to in this room, the business of composing subversive songs, and it was easier to hide the evidence of this in a disordered atmosphere. Charles's hatred of the disorganized would stop him probing more effectively than a locked door, which would arouse his suspicion.

On the rare occasions when Charles needed to discuss something with me while I was at work, a work which I pretended was all to do with kennels and compensation to farmers whose land had taken a battering by the hunt, he would stand in the doorway, a crusty smile of reproach on his face. The smile indicated that my working methods were a disgrace but that time had taught him to expect nothing better from me. 'You're becoming lazy, my dear,' he said once, eyeing the teetering stacks of bills which covered the pretty carpet with its silky wreaths and swirls. 'Laziness is the vice of the contented,' I replied levelly and turned away from the door to jab another flag in the map behind me.

Through my songs I was biting into life. Words flowed out of me; perhaps they had always been there, like the dark, secret stone under the fountain's froth. But Peadar read what I had written despairingly, his face haggard. 'I suppose I might as well put my fist around smoke as ask you to stop all this,' he said, his voice hopeless and given up to fate. I nodded miserably, hating to see his beloved face so stricken. But I was possessed by a dark, rending energy which would not let me move to someone else's rhythm, not even Peadar's, even though, when we loved and nestled in our bare pelts on the warmed straw of the old house where the trees made a haze around us, I felt unbolted with happiness.

'You should not be writing these songs unless you are prepared for men to go out and shoot or be shot,' Peadar said, in a stern, miserable voice that I had never heard before then. 'You are hurling the little streets against the great with them. It's a pitiful jaunt you are on, my darling girl. Is this what you want Ireland to come to? A nation of handgrips and passwords, a secret swarming in the hillsides, a glint of a rifle in the cleft rock? Do you not see the danger your songs may bring about?'

The marine light of his eyes had dulled with grief and worry, but I could no more stop what I was doing than stop the wind sifting through the leaves.

'I see only that the people feel diminished,' I said. 'The past will not help them; only a vision of the future will. They need songs that insist that there is no place for the English in Ireland and that their disappearance is a matter of time only. There must be change, Peadar, and the old lays you moon over are not enough to bring it about. Lookit, my darling, what is it that Keane's does the fiercest trade in? You know well it is in those wretched cardboard suitcases, every last one of them taken in the grip of some farmboy's raw hand, as he pitches and trips over the cobwebbed grass with teary eyes to scratch out a life in America; for all that is here for him would leave him a rickle of bone and emptiness. It's for such as he that I write.'

I had begun to shiver. Peadar wrapped his long, knobbly body around mine, submissive and comforting. 'Let us skid and lurch our way towards freedom then,' he murmured into my hair. 'Let us wander into the unknown and wait for history to utter a kind word. I cannot disapprove of you for long, Rose Erris. You make the air around you your own, lay claim to it, somehow. I would go on loving you if you were to take the bite from my mouth.'

He made love to me then, intensely, ardently and frowning, as though he were trying to commit every inch of my body to memory, like a poem. I fed him the fatal feast of myself and knew that because I did, he could refuse me nothing. We lay together in the abandoned house, where ivies thickened on the crumbling walls, listening to a badger squealing in its sett. Love put a boldness on us. A thousand ghosts might people the dark around us for all we cared.

We did not mention my songs again; their cruelty and jibes scalded his heart. Even so, I meant to have them published so that all those who had had their dreams bleached out of them by hopelessness might heed them. Accordingly, on a fine May morning I set out to visit Mr Damian Dashwood at the house where he had recently settled on a remote headland a few miles west of the village of Cleggan. Mr Dashwood was greatly changed since the time I had first met him at Lisnagreve, a young man with baby-blue eyes above an unsuccessful beard, who had scolded me for acting like a winsome colleen to charm Ascendancy aristocrats, a charge that had a mile of truth in it.

He had stomped out of the Irish Party soon after the death of his hero, Mr Parnell, and had lately joined a group of men who called themselves Sinn Féin ('Ourselves alone') which, he had admitted to me was 'more of a sentiment than a party'. He had shaved off his beard to reveal a scabby jut of chin, and fatigue had faded his eyes to the limp paleness of dying bluebells. In spite of the exhaustion that greyed his face, there was a crackle and spit to him, something jaunty and devious that made me uncomfortable.

When he saw me making my way along the seaward path, the day's warmth pressed on my face, he gave me a tired, wary smile and slid the binoculars with which he had been scanning the shoreline of the island of Inishboffin, behind a rock.

'Well, aren't you the welcome woman,' he greeted me, although there was no welcome in his voice. 'Have you come to convert me to the Gaelic League's literary politics?'

'A frittery way to pass a morning *that* would be, ' I said, knowing that the Gaelic League's rootling around in forgotten folklore annoyed him like a hair on his tongue. 'I came to show you these.'

I had made fair copies of my songs and wrapped them in an oilcloth folder that I had found in the balcony room, recognizing it as the one Harriet had used to protect her flimsy sketches from the damp.

I sat beside Mr Dashwood on the headland's spongy grass as he read the folder's contents. I listened to the hoo-hoo of the cuckoo, the pluck and knock of the tide, the sound the shingle made as it scrambled after the sucking surf and, every so often, the sharp intake of breath of the man beside me, whose wide, white forehead had begun to gleam and flash light like an opal. I sat stock-still but my mind was as restless as the wingbeats of memory.

'You're a contrary piece,' Mr Dashwood said eventually, putting the sheets back in the folder. 'These here are a far cry from all that smooshy old glop you used to sing. What happened to make you take on so? Has the tempest that devastates the cabin swept over the Big House at last, or are you picking a quarrel with that land-grabber of a husband of yours? And to think that he plucked you from out of the crowd and set you up as fleet and flashing as any Ascendancy viscountess. Well now he'll recognize that this is a place where no good deed goes unpunished.'

I ignored his taunting. 'Do you think these songs could ever be published?' I asked.

'Published is it? They could be sung in every place in the country where men and women gather to face up to the coming storm. You'll be putting your name to them, so you will,' he said with stony irony.

'They are to go under the name of Áinín Rua,' I said.

'And there will be the devil to pay if it's discovered that the red-headed songwriter has curls that are as black as pitch and is hung about with an Englishman's gold bracelets. What madness am I talking of? That is all the way of things now. Did you hear of a lady called Maud Gonne? She's as contradictious as yourself; half-English, beloved by an Irish Protestant who pours out poems and plays for love of her, while she fans a rebellion that would make her class and his shrivel into extinction. Well, no matter to that. We had best be talking about your royalties.'

I scrambled up from the slippery grass and straightened my skirt huffily. 'Money is not in this,' I said. 'I wrote these songs for Ireland.'

'And Ireland is in your debt entirely.' Mr Dashwood's sarcasm was relentless. 'That is, spiritually but not financially. Money is in everything, even in patriotism. I have friends in what might be considered low places who'll circulate these songs for you and see that you're paid the right whack.'

I was astonished. 'Is it enough people you have to organize suchlike?'

Mr Dashwood looked at me angrily out of his faded eyes. There was something grimy about him, a staleness as though he had gone without sleep for endless nights. His hair was dull and floury. 'You think we are a gang of fanatical patriots mashing around in cloaks and brooches like your departed friend Myles Lavelle? That's not the way of it, at all. We are everywhere, Mrs Trewin. In the cabin and the suburban villa, among the peasants and the professors, the lawless and those who make the law. As your own song has it, "We Are All Ireland".' He looked at his watch and seemed agitated. 'Will you come on into the house now for a drop?'

I said that the day that was in it being so fine, I should like to have some tea, there, on the tussocky grass. He gave me a sharp look which I returned with one of those artless smiles that I had perfected over many years, and he made his way to his house, his back bowed with fatigue. I strolled a little way and began to pick daisies, knowing that he was watching me from a window. I directed my steps behind the rock where Mr Dashwood had left his binoculars, picked them up and trained them on the island. I could see a small figure, ant-sized, with an ant's frantic scuttle, moving towards a cave near the harbour mouth, something in his hand that could have been a spade, or a gun. I replaced the binoculars and was childishly absorbed in making slits in daisy-stalks with my thumbnail when Mr Dashwood returned with a tray of tea and slices of a certain kind of barm brack with cloves and shredded lemon peel in it, which I knew to be a recipe of Binnie's, one that she jealously guarded.

That glimmering morning turned out to be a weather god's tease. The rest of the summer dripped and drizzled, the roads became long puddles linked together in a darkly shining chain. On St Macdara's Day, halfway through July, I went with Charles and a large gathering of people to Carna, to watch the hookers set out in celebration of the fisherman's saint. He was a stickler for courtesy, this saint of ours, whooshing stormy winds down on any boat whose sails weren't dipped in respect when passing his rocky island. The hookers had hardly left the harbour, fleet and stately as dark swans, when a shower of round white hailstones was flung out of the sky and settled at our feet like stone blossoms. Leonora, anxious for the silk roses on her hat, shooed our elegant party into a nearby shebeen, a poor squat cabin with an earth floor and a feeble, mutinous fire. A group of packmen moved themselves and their sacks of needles and threads and bales of shoddy cloth away from the fire's inadequate warmth to make room for us. Charles repaid this kindness by buying them tots of a dark, sticky rum, served by a slattern with her skirt hitched over a filthy scarlet petticoat. Warmed by drink, the packmen became expansive. They complimented the gentlemen on the comeliness of the ladies, so charmingly that Leonora, who in a spirit of fellowship was drinking the same treacly rum, thinned down with hot water, became as splendorously creamy as the silk roses in her hat.

The unseasonal hail bounced off the whitewashed window-ledges of the shebeen, and the bottles of rum on the scarred wooden counter began to empty at a faster rate. One of the packmen brought out a harmonica, another found a tin whistle. 'Oh lovely,' said Leonora, whose glow by then was greater than the fire's. 'They're going to sing.'

It was the first time I had heard my songs sung. The familiar (though to me alone) words of 'We Are

All Ireland', 'The Torn Heart' and 'Free to Dream'
spun on the air, insouciant and defiant. I watched my
husband's face. It was as impassive as a boulder but his
strong fingers were clenched around his blackthorn
stick. When the men had done, the hailstorm had been
scattered by a watery sunshine and we all blundered
unsteadily into the bright day, Leonora insisted on
shaking each of the packmen by the hand. 'Those
were great songs,' she said. 'I don't believe I've heard
them before.'

'Them ones is spanking new and all the rage in the
towns,' said one of the men, who was having some
difficulty tucking his trousers into his boots before
getting on his bicycle. 'It's happy I am that you found
them agreeable, my lady. Sure now, I was kilt with
thinking that it might have curdled the drop in your
mouth to listen to things of that nature.'

Leonora looked confused. The songs to her were just
agreeable tunes and words that she didn't understand,
sung out as they were in the packmen's drink-clotted
brogue. She recovered herself. 'They're only songs,'
she insisted and turned to my husband. 'What did you
think of them, Charles?'

'Randoliering trinkets,' my husband answered, his
voice thundery. After curt farewells, he walked me
quickly to the sodden trap and, when we were settled
on the damp cushions, whipped the pony with such
anger that it had the trap clattering over the rutted
road so dangerously that I could feel the bones in
my spine scrape against each other.

22

'Don't give it to them to say about it,' Binnie implored me. She stood in the doorway of my disordered work-room, holding in her crooked hands the painted papier mâché salver in which calling-cards were placed. It contained several cards now, put there by the ladies of the neighbourhood, who had driven out for a visit in their carriages and jaunting cars to be told by a reddening, awkward maid that Mrs Trewin was not receiving that day.

'The sight of you,' Binnie went on. 'You whose looks could drive a man demented. What's happened to you at all, that there's ink on your chin and your hair is fit for a nesting rook?'

Writing songs had me gripped. Impossible for me to make tinkly talk over the teacups while my mind was on deep-down things, so I had invented a list of vague indispositions which sent the carriages, many of them of the new, open type, appropriately called a sociable, rumbling down the drive again, their owners denied the gossip and silly laughter they had sought at Malina, and left to wonder whether the second Mrs Trewin was becoming as strangely reclusive as the first.

I decided to distract Binnie with something more troubling than my lack of hospitality.

'I was meaning to tell you,' I said. 'I was calling on Mr Dashwood a while back, and didn't he only serve me a slice of your own barm brack. I was asking myself how would he have got hold of it.'

The effect was more than I had bargained for. Binnie sank to her knees in the doorway, her face turned the colour of dirty ashes. 'Is it Festy?' She croaked out the question in a voice so frail and woebegone that I ran to put my arms around her humpy shoulders.

Festy was her nephew, a handsome, lazy streel of a fellow with quick, darting eyes. She doted on him, encouraged the idleness that came naturally to him by letting him hang around the kitchen, eating the leavings from our table and warming himself at our fire. I had a liking for him myself. There was something of grace in the easy way he took Malina's food and shelter as something due to him, greeting me with a side-to-side flick of his head, as though he were shaking water out of his ears, when I came upon him taking his ease on a stone windowsill, chewing the roasted leg of a duck that my husband had shot.

'It is only to Festy that I gave the brack, the way he wouldn't go hungry,' Binnie moaned. 'Why would he be giving it to Mr Dashwood, the ould heister?' We knelt beside each other in a doomy silence, as we pondered the implications of Festy's association with the Sinn Féiner, who was, in Binnie's opinion, a man of violent purpose and had always been so. She crossed herself distractedly. 'It's hanging about with all them gobshites in the village has brought Festy to this,' she said. 'Christy, Packy and them other bowsies, going on the batter and cattle-driving and putting decent people in the halfpenny places.' Binnie's wretchedness made her sound unshapely, wronged. She uttered an old curse against Mr Dashwood, accused him of turning her nephew's head and giving him dangerous notions.

'Croch ard gaoithe,' she muttered, 'a high, windy gallows to him', and made a crabbed, painful progress down the stairs to put the salver of cards on the hall table. When I heard the kitchen door bang behind her I followed her down the stairs, scooped up all the cards and threw them in the drawing-room fire, so that, were Charles to return from London unexpectedly, he would not find evidence of neglected social duties.

The afternoon had lightened. The shadows of branches swung in the bright grass and the whirling song of the wren kept me company as I rode to the deserted house by the lake. Peadar was reading beside a glassless window. Seeing him there turned all my thoughts to honey. Just to look at his huge, knobbed wrists and the way the light brown curls whirled out from the crown of his head would make you think that the creation of the human race had been a good idea.

I ran to him through rustling straw. 'My most chosen darling of my heart,' I said and took the book from his hands. How I loved to have him near me. His skin covered him so sparsely that as he moved inside me his whole being seemed exposed. His heart knocked against my breast and the blood in his stiffened member made a hard heat, warming me into desire. He was so gentle, it was like a giftedness he had. Stroked inside by his searching organ and outside by his ardent hands, I became moving silk, sleek, limpid, turned almost to liquid. This was a love intense and grave, yet it left us high-hearted, knowing that our tender closeness was a measure of the growth of our lives.

I hated leaving Peadar that day; it tore my heart to see him walk away and then disappear behind a curl of the grassed-over track. There was pain and peace in him and a nature of such sweetness that I accused him of having treacle in his blood.

But my lover's capacious goodwill made him kindly and compromising; for all that he loved me, my commitment to the coming times appalled him. He accused me of nonchalant cruelty, a ferocious way of looking at the world that was flawed and compelling. It saddened him that I could not be content to remain in the unreal estate of memory as he did, and that my songs strove to disinvent all the traditions he clung to. He told me, only half-teasingly, that, like Connemara's legendary pirate queen, Granuaile, I was set to become 'the nurse of all the rebellions in the province for forty years'.

As though mourning his departure, the sun sank behind some smudgy clouds. As the day darkened, the mountains turned into their own ghosts, fleeting, pale and adrift on a cold sea. A mournful wind got up, howling like an old woman at a wake, the hazel scrub whitened against the dusk and shook like rattling bones and the ditch water moved too fast, a twisted stream of brown glass. As I turned the horse towards Malina, an ashen sense of awfulness began to hum behind my temples. When I came within sight of the house, it stood out against the sky, threatening and melodramatic, the higher windows cupped in the curved fastnesses of cut stone like windows on the painted backcloth of a stage, the light that seeped out of them a hideous, stinging yellow.

Horty rushed out to me, as though he had been listening for the sound of my pony's hooves but, instead of stabling her, he grabbed my hand and dragged me towards the kitchen. Agnes sat there with terrible cried-out eyes, raving with grief. She held her beautiful little boy to her chest and, when I approached her, shrank back in the chair. But I came closer, terrified to see that his face was as white as the Irish hare in wintertime. I touched the child's feet. The little oval heels were stone cold; he was dead.

Binnie's rocky hands were kneading the table. She looked at me distrustfully. 'I sent the gossoon,' – Fintan, her little kitchen boy – 'hereabouts and thereabouts to seek you out, the way you might have saved the child with the touch that you have on you, but there was no finding you.'

Useless to suggest that they might have sent out for the doctor. Dr Parsloe of Clifden was a Protestant, a man whose views were considered enlightened by people of his own kind but dangerously newfangled to those who sat in Malina's kitchen, sorrowing over the dead child in Agnes's arms. The doctor's reliance on sterile bandages and patent medicines was loftily out of keeping with their lives. Agnes, Horty and Binnie believed in the old *pishorogues* and sorceries, charms and prayers. They believed that all manner of ailments could be lightened by tying cloths to the bushes around a holy well or by worship at the old mass rocks. They believed that good fortune would attend those who planted their first potatoes by Good Friday and that a horsehair that falls into a well will grow a little head and become an eel. Superstition was the soft, peaty basis of their lives; pagan, stubborn, hardly hidden by the religion that had been spread over it.

'I'll ride out for Father Casey,' I said, and, with hands that had only an hour since been stroking my lover's thin loins, I closed Malachy's white eyelids over his wise, blue eyes.

'May heaven be his bed,' Binnie said quietly, and as she did so we heard the rattle of gravel shifted by hooves and wheels, the slam of the front door and Charles's loud voice complaining that nobody had seen fit to light the candles in the sconces and the hall was black as porter.

When it came to children, my husband was the cream of the earth. He had been as devoted to Malachy O'Goole as any one of us, bringing him toys from England, giving him rides on his leg, and finding fat, golden humbugs behind the child's ears, in his pockets, behind his neck. Plucking them from all these unlikely places with a practised deftness he would say, 'Malachy, tell me the truth now, you're not a boy at all, you're a humbug tree', making the child shout boisterous denials, crowing with delight.

Now he wanted to give the boy the finest funeral to be had. 'Tell Agnes and Horty to have whatever they want and not to stint themselves of anything,' he told me brokenly. For the moment, we had both forgotten the quiet hatred between us, a hatred we had settled for, so familiar with it that we hardly noticed the way it simmered as the years went by. Grief united us briefly; at one point Charles wiped a tear from my cheek with his finger and comforted, 'There will be other children,' as though we were mourning our own child. For the first time in years he took my hand. He looked quickly at my wedding ring with its outward pointing heart and then at the signet ring on his own finger, the words *Antes muerto que mudado* inscribed in the heavy gold. He released my hand as though it had become slimy under his touch.

In spite of Charles's intentions, Agnes and Horty were to be denied the healing comfort of pomp and ceremony. There would be no funeral carriage drawn by black horses leading the procession to the sanctified burial ground, no elaborate tombstone cut from the rosy pink Italian marble that Agnes had a fondness for. Malachy, the little love of all our lives, had died unbaptized.

At first I could not understand what Horty was trying to tell me. 'Three shillings and fourpence,' were the only words I could make out as he stuttered and yammered at me in the room above the coachhouse which Agnes hated so much. Horty's breath was rank with whiskey and grief and his words were slurred. Exasperated by my lack of comprehension, he pushed me into the bedroom and lifted the edge of the bed's slippery coverlet so that I could see the half-dozen cardboard suitcases stacked beneath it.

Then I had it. Malachy had not been baptized since the occasion would have had to coincide with Agnes being churched after her confinement, at a cost of three shillings and fourpence, which she was reluctant to spend. 'It is the way she do be a bit stingy,' Horty mumbled, 'but we were saving the price of a passage to America, herself and me and the babby.' He flung himself on the bed and beat the grubby pillow with his fat hands. I left him and walked back to the house, ready to choke Agnes for her troublesome economies.

My ill-temper was tame stuff besides old Maeve MacReion's goings-on. In the kitchen where all her kin was gathered, Maeve pointed a filthy finger at her daughter. 'Didn't I see her give the child *troander*' – whey made with buttermilk and sweet milk – 'from the cow that was sick and her gloating at the cheap price she paid for the cow on account of its queer eyes. Now here it is where her mingin', stingin' ways have brought her, to the side of her own child's grave.'

Maeve saw me in the doorway and her finger scraped through the air until it faced me directly, like a gun. 'Look at the cut of that one,' she jeered, savage in her heartbreak. 'Only for herself and the divil she's wedded to, the Missus would be alive yet. It was that which had the heart scalded inside her, seeing this jade thick with yer man. Wasn't it I who found her torn corpse on the strand, the life crushed out of her? By her own hand it was, but them ones have the blame of it, as surely as though they'd pitched her into the sea themselves.'

Binnie made a lunge for her, her crooked hand ready to rake Maeve's cheek, but Maeve stepped out of her way and made for the back door. From the step, she shrieked back into the room. 'A godless house this is entirely, and no example set by those who have no nature.' Then she disappeared into the darkness, where the wind had begun to throw thunder on the stones.

'Take no heed of her,' said Binnie, 'the lying, thieving hag that she is.' The maids shuffled and nodded in a way that was meant to reassure me of their sympathy but my hands shook as I bolted the yard door against Maeve's reappearance.

Charles had sent a closed carriage to Father Casey with a letter asking him to come to the Big House as soon as he could. The priest came within the hour, looking mouselike and wary, as though he would have liked to scuttle behind the curtains. He brought with him a whiff of rancid loneliness and boiled cabbage. He sat stiffly on the edge of a chair, reluctant to surrender his back to the wicked comfort of its cushions, and held the crystal glass in which Charles had poured him a full measure of whiskey as though it might break in his fingers out of spite.

Charles nodded at me to explain the situation. I spoke to the priest submissively, my eyes on the carpet. I took the blame for not ensuring that Malachy had been baptized, said that I would have paid the three and fourpence out of my own pocket and gladly, but that being so occupied with arranging the next season's hunt I had not known about the matter. I explained about the cases under the bed and Agnes's wish to be gone to a new life. I asked that Malachy might not be refused a Christian burial.

Father Casey looked at me with scandalized eyes and all the stubbornness of a born coward. 'It cannot be done,' he said. 'If I do it for one, others will expect the same and sins will multiply as one bruised apple transmits its sores to another. It's not that I'm not sorry for Agnes, but if there were more ones like her, Ireland would be a place of empty churches and empty souls.' He gave me a dark look, reproaching me for my own defection of years before, and for the compromises which, beguiled by Charles's power and money, he had made then. Years had passed, but he blamed me still for having walked defiantly to the edge of society, beyond his reach: an outsider, someone special, someone with notions.

The situation might yet have been saved. A promise of funds, a lavish sympathy demonstrated for Father Casey's difficult situation, and the priest might have found a smudged way to allow Malachy's tiny body a sanctified repose. But all Charles's practised wiles deserted him that dreadful evening. He would not slide and ease the way into a solution but harangued and hectored the old man, accused him of fettering his own faith with his intractableness and of holding back Ireland's progress in the modern world by refusing to shift or budge, a stance typical of the least adaptable people on earth, the race from which he had sprung.

Father Casey looked at him with a tired dignity. For a moment he struggled with the desire that all Irishmen have, to tell the stranger among them that which he most wishes to hear. But his better, sterner nature prevailed. 'Now hear to me, will you, Sir,' he said. 'Progress is not my concern; the law of God is.' He left the house and all its godless riches to return to his own joyless home and its sulky housekeeper, whose face was as pale and grainy as the sago puddings she dished up in the draughty, austere dining-room.

Charles splashed more whiskey in his glass. Rage seemed to stiffen his silver hair, turn his golden eyes to dark flint. 'Religion is an abomination,' he said. 'A crushing weight that keeps mankind in a drugged servitude.' He raised his glass in a toast. 'May the shining advances of this young century put an end to the cringing faith in a God that cannot be proved to exist.'

I thought of my sister Vera, sweltering in the dark and dangerous continent, sustained by her faith. 'There are those who need God to quell their fear of the unknown,' I said.

'And are you among them, my dear?' An upward wiggle of his eyebrow was like a sneer.

In all the years we had lived together, we had never talked about religion. Charles was a freethinker, a rationalist who thought that the Church, any Church, was something outmoded, quaint and purposeless. As for myself, the religion in which I was brought up belonged to my old life, the one I had thrown off to become Malina's chatelaine. During my childhood, Mass-going had been a matter of tiresome obligation. For all my mother's devoutness, every one of her daughters had chafed at the restrictions imposed on us by the God she worshipped; his laws embarrassed us, the soupy pieties of the Mass a-chatter with unanswered prayers went against our wild grain. That is what made Vera's later defection so hard for me to bear.

Maeve MacReion had been right in her bitter ranting of an hour before, when she had accused me of being godless. I could no more believe in the doleful, wispy man painted on my mother's wall-plates, all bleeding heart and martyred, supplicating fingers, than I could believe in horsehairs turning into eels. My belief was in some hazy, undefined evil, and in a goodness, equally undefined; an absent good that could not be brought near. 'No, I am not among them,' I gave Charles my answer. 'The unknown holds no peril for me. Even so . . .' I faltered.

'Go on, my dear.' Charles looked at me with a concentrated interest, the way he examined a horse he was considering buying.

'Even so, if God does not exist, responsibility for good lies within ourselves. There being no God, the more important to behave as though there were.'

'And do you behave so, Rose Erris?'

'Perhaps no worse than those who sink to their knees at Mass and church.'

The long, dreadful day had drained me. I turned to leave, longing for my own room where I could howl with grief for Malachy unrestrainedly. Charles opened the door to let me pass. 'Perhaps no better from some accounts,' he said, his voice bland as Father Casey's sago pudding. 'We will not discuss such metaphysical matters again. You fall too easily into a peasant priggishness that, as would any civilized man, I find repulsive.'

Agnes had always had leanings towards the dramatic and outrageous. Now she insisted that her child must be buried at Clochar na bPáisti, in the old way, wrapped in a linen shroud and without a coffin. When the time came to take the tiny corpse to that pitiful graveyard, she was too feverish with guilt and heartbreak to make the forlorn journey to the edge of the land. Horty set out alone, on a windless day clammy with drizzle. By the time he came in sight of the village with its thin-faced houses, the wetness in the air had sharpened into a slicing rain. Either out of despair or to keep the linen-wrapped remains beside him from getting soaked, Horty took shelter in Meehan's, sitting on a splintery plank propped on wooden barrels, his child's body against his huge thigh. The few men who were in the place showed their compassion by urging whiskey and porter on him, so several hours passed before he stumbled out of the public house and turned the trap towards Horam's Cove. He left the pony to ramble and took the spade out of the trap. Drink had numbed his misery; he was so drunk that he could hardly stand as he dug a shallow hole at the rim of the headland, oblivious to the sound of tearing grass or the drooling waves that babbled and flapped on the shore beneath him. Only when a foot of poor, sandy soil had been crookedly exposed did a realization break through the murk of his drunkenness to shame him, then and ever after. He had left the shrouded body of his child on the rough bench of the public house.

The bench is there still. Every visitor to Meehan's has it pointed out to him and the story of Horty's forgetfulness is rolled out before him, already part of the folklore of the place and, like many folktales, bringing gasps of horror or shrill, shocked laughter, or both. The scandal was the finish of Agnes. Always unstable, she went queer in the head, confined herself to the unloved rooms above the coachhouse, except when she knew her mother to be around Malina; then she hid in the wood until Maeve was sure to have left.

Horty took to the drop. You could find him any evening in the soothing, obliterating fug of Meehan's back bar, where he drank in the committed, morose way of a man who asks for nothing but to forget who he is or what his life has become.

Charles saw the whole tragic episode as being typical of something he referred to as 'the Irish problem', a demonstration of how backward and savage we were; how lacking in the civility and courage necessary in those who sought to have charge of their own nation and their own destiny.

23

The dreamy music of the waltz. That, decided Emmeline O'Cleary, was what all of us needed to make us forget for a few hours the bad taste in our mouths which flavoured our lives with unease. On New Year's Eve, 1913, the O'Clearys gave a ball, removing the buckets from the ballroom floor which were evidence of their decaying roof but not bothering to sweep away the dog hairs from the sofas or darn the frayed table linen, so that the occasion had a patchy, improvised air.

During the supper interval, Leonora and I, as we often did at parties when the warm, posh splutter of small talk began to pall, sneaked up a back staircase and into a spare bedroom, where we took off our shoes, lit cigarettes and rearranged the pins in our hair, while we settled down to what Leonora still called 'roaring girls' talk', though both of us had turned forty. The room was harshly lit by gas globes which threw our reflections onto the dressing-table's big triple mirror. Leonora looked at our mirrored images with critical, screwed-up eyes while taking long, greedy puffs on her cigarette.

'You are wintering well, dear girl,' she said. 'Lucky for you never to have had that frilly fairness that gives out after a while. Your type just grows more honed and chiselled, sharpened up to meet whatever it is that is going to happen to you.' She powdered her cheeks recklessly. 'With me it's a different story,' she said.

My voluptuous friend had aged; the gently tumbling allure of her creamy flesh was becoming overblown and frowsty, the undersides of her plump, bare, generous arms were slack. That evening I noticed that the pearls she wore to emphasize her blond peachiness were short of three strands, a sign of her family's slippage in the world. The Fitzhavens of Lisnagreve had been chilled by exposure to change. A persistent application of Land Acts had seen them begin a downward slither into penury; the house in London had been sold as well as part of the Irish estate, and Thesper had shrunk into a quieter, sadder version of himself, the victim of a disappointed pessimism and purposelessness that exasperated his wife. Leonora herself was in an unbridled state, caught in an agony hour between the pleasurable past and a coming carnage that seemed as certain as tomorrow's sunrise. Her children, now grown, seemed to have inherited their mother's energetic disarray. Her son, Garret, was in the Irish Guards, running up spectacular mess bills which, I suspected, were the cause of the pearl choker missing some of its strands. His sister, Daisy, was a suffragette, one of the first to realize the propaganda value of the hunger strike. She was argumentative, indignant and treated all men from the Secretary of State to the lowliest crofter with a con-descending heartlessness that made them smitten and lustful. Once, I would have charged Leonora with a dismissive, loveless tolerance of her children that was typical of her class but the years had taught me that her art was in the seeming. She might peck Garret's cheek lightly when his leave was over or tease Daisy about the vulgarity of the banners she carried on marches, but I knew that her idling, indifferent manner hid a love that was almost demented in its fierceness and pride, a love kept hidden so that her children might step blithely into the treacherous world without feeling the guilty weight of motherlove upon them.

Leonora pursed her lips at her reflection. 'Cripes, growing old is the very devil, Rose Erris,' she said. 'I feel as though my life has been bottled and put away in the cellar before I've done with it. Maybe I should keep away from looking-glasses, then perhaps I'll be able to believe that I'm still insanely desirable. It's clinging to that belief that makes one so, of course.' She lifted the lid of a small pot of face cream on the dressing-table, sniffed dubiously at the contents and began to work some of it into her roughened hands. 'I have always had friendly thighs, you see. Some women count their money to send them to sleep at night, but I count my lovers; well, at any rate, the ones whose names I can remember. Sex is the loveliest little thing in the world. Your church is very misguided to make a sin of it.'

We laughed together in the unmannerly and ribald way of women who are intimate with each other's failings, as we rewound our padded chignons. Leonora started to sing a song softly as she twiddled with her bangs and the sound of it clogged the laugh in my throat. The song was one that I had written and delivered to Damian Dashwood a few days before but which had not yet been published. I knew there could be only one way that my friend could have come by it.

'Talking of friendly thighs,' I addressed her reflection in the mirror, 'how *is* Mr Dashwood?'

Leonora's recently powdered chest reddened; her chin almost sank on to it. 'How on earth . . . ?' she began.

'You are singing the words of a song that only he knows about.'

'But you know about it too?' Her face clouded with confusion, then almost immediately cleared. 'It's you,' she said. 'Áinín Rua is you. Can you really be so hungry for the future as to write those songs of incitement?'

'I write them because I must, not because I can, Leonora. Do you have the same compulsion where Mr Dashwood is concerned?'

Leonora tried to look chastened but her eyes were bright with shameless fun. 'My standards of behaviour are insufficient, I know,' she said, resting her cheek on mine for a moment. 'It's only that without sexual escapades I seem to walk on a pathless path that leads only to extinction and silence. Damian Dashwood makes me forget my troubles for a while. The thing he calls "the cause"' – Leonora paused dramatically and rolled her shining eyes – 'is the only thing that matters to him. He doesn't notice that my knees creak and that my breasts hang down like empty purses. He gives me his body as though he doesn't notice what he's doing. Ah, but *I* notice, Rose Erris, *I* notice. It gives me something to look forward to. Without him, life would be quite hopeless.'

I thought of the Shinner's grimy cuffs and dazed, deadened eyes and looked at her reprovingly. Leonora met the look with a gurgle of delighted mirth. 'Oh, he's hardly a prince on a white horse, I know; in fact, he's a blackness ten times black in many ways. Still, the man has a feral potency that stops me feeling ragged and sad.' She linked arms as we made to go downstairs. 'We are fortunate women,' she said. 'We have a gift for survival.'

'Unlike Harriet,' I said.

We paused at the top of the staircase. Below us, dancers swam in and out of circles of candlelight, tense and expectant, for it was only some minutes to midnight. Leonora put her hands on my shoulders, her dancing eyes serious now. 'Harriet had the lure of the graveyard,' she said. 'She gloried in her own vulnerability; that is why she put up with Charles's sadistic teasing. Love was a terminal illness of hers; she wilfully refused to understand, as we women must, that the love object can never be commensurate with the love we insist on giving. You know I have a poor opinion of your husband, the way he stakes out his own importance and talks like a collection of mannerisms, but I could understand the way Harriet grated on him so that he struck her down into the mud. She was *mal dans sa peau* – bad in her skin.' (Leonora had stopped sprinkling her conversation with Gaelic words and returned to French ones.) 'There was a subtle insanity about her; she lived all her life in death's antechamber.'

Leonora shivered and gave herself a little, impatient shake.

As we stood there in the shadows, drunk with shared confidences, I wanted to tell her about Peadar, the joys of his thin body and the way I loved and nourished the deep wound of doubt in his soul, but I kept silent. If I told her of these things, Leonora would warn me of the danger I was in, remind me that Charles was not like Thesper Fitzhaven, tolerant, accepting, decent and resigned, but a man who went about the business of destruction, secretly, meanly, craftily. I did not want her to wave in front of me the fear that I kept in the back of my mind, that, were I to anger him, my husband could strip me of any significance as carelessly as he would strip an orange of its rind.

My friend looked at me closely, then patted my arm. 'Shall we join the gentlemen, Rose Erris, and pretend for a while that marriage is something other than trying not to hate the man you were once set on loving?'

We reached the last stair as the chimes of midnight broke the edgy silence. My husband stepped forward into a pool of light and handed me a glass, his face expressionless. Glasses flew to lips like birds. 'To peace, peace . . .' The murmur rose like a prayer towards the dripping candles of the chandelier. The women stretched their white arms upwards, a forest of pale fronds reaching towards the ceiling; the men's hands were startling at the ends of their impeccable black sleeves. I too raised my glass, so that my diamond bracelets clattered on my wrist. But my toast was silent, unheard. The words I did not mouth were the words of Henry Grattan, that frosty foe of the Union between England and Ireland in 1800: 'Live Ireland – perish the Empire.'

But the pleas of those supplicating arms went un-answered. On 3 August 1914 the lights went out all over Europe and all its citizens stumbled into the fog of war. John Redmond, the leader of the Irish Party, pledged Nationalist Catholics to defend the British Empire, a move applauded by Charles for its canny pragmatism. The ghastly exhilaration that war brings had entered my husband's soul and made his black heart as young as a whistling boy's, ready to chase the clouds. He relished Redmond's willingness to throw his people into a murder machine, saw the gesture as grown-up and worldly, likely to bring about the kind of Home Rule for Ireland that Charles himself could admire and be part of, a Home Rule that was windy and statesmanlike, English in everything except its own postage stamp.

How the times suited Charles, filled him up like a sail cupped by the wind. Other men of his age wore spec-tacles, had weak bladders, leaned heavily on walking sticks with stricken, liver-spotted hands. Charles stood out among them, a lord of life with strong, meaty shoulders and glittering eyes that were watchful and impatient, bringing with him a sense of overpowering tumult whenever he walked into a room.

It was Peadar who had aged. As the wind of bluster began to blow, his thin shoulders became stooped and his long stride slowed, became cautious as though he walked on a raft of bones. Only rarely now did the mossy dimples in his cheeks flicker into smiles. He had been put in charge of the newly opened public library in the village, two rooms of a seafront cottage, where he sat confusedly among books and catalogues and little square boxes of indexed cards, stamping the dates on flyleaves with an inked rubber pad, and a sad, dreamy reverence. The children came to him after school was over and sat cross-legged on the dusty floor, looking up at the worn-down poet with their little, unfinished faces, while he told them stories. He had taken on the Irish way of storytelling, which is to mourn aloud the things that can never come back. In his flat, American voice that still had the sound of the big, brisk city in it, he told of Devorgilla and Diarmuid, of Niall Noígiallach (Niall of the Nine Hostages), Cuchulain, who defended the gap of the North, all those dangerous, eternal things that had exasperated me always. But Peadar had the gift of making complicated things transparent; he talked of our ancient troublemakers as though they might charge into the room in a moment, shrieking for blood-justice. The children listened to him in wonderment, gnawing their thumbs with neglected, greenish teeth.

Sometimes, when they had left to run wild in the raving autumn, he and I drank tea in the innermost room, sitting thigh to thigh on an ugly sofa covered with mildewed carpeting, which had been provided by public subscription. We never made love in that library; the seriousness of the bound volumes of Gibbon and Macaulay inhibited us; we felt the disapproval of all those stately words that fell dead from the page as you read them. Those blue spines with their tin-coloured lettering banished passionate impulses and drew us towards a bloody crossroads where literature and politics meet. Among those shelves, packed with Englishmen's rhetoric, we found that we could talk only of violent things.

Peadar was horrified by Ireland's involvement in England's war. 'War corrupts even the most honourable of causes,' he said bitterly. 'For Irishmen to join the English army is to murder the past. What an amazing kaleidoscope of contradictions this country is. One minute we are all for wild autonomy, the next we have become the soul of the crowd marching towards the trenches to be slaughtered on England's behalf. The chime of freedom will never be heard through the unavailing cries of the battlefield. This war is an outrage against simple men.'

I must have been only half listening, for Peadar knocked his fist very gently against my chin and said with no blame or reproach in his voice, 'I can see boredom banging in your face, sweetheart; I'll not go on.'

And indeed it was pointless for him to rage against reality. Irishmen were joining the British army as fast as the winded fox was flying. They saw the war as a route to a life that was not broken-backed, the means to boots on their feet, food in their stomachs and a separation allowance for their families. For others, like Horty, the first man in the village to volunteer himself as cannon fodder, the war was a way out of the mess of their lives, a means of escape from drink and black rage and wordlessness. Such men as these looked to soldiering to cock them up.

Peadar did not understand the dishonourable desires of other men. This noble lack in him made him seem as unreal as a doleful, wayside statue, something other than a man — a presence, a regret, a light, an ache. To make him flesh again, I began to kiss him with hot, demanding kisses, mindful of the dry English histories shuddering distastefully in their bindings above my head.

His lips had begun to burn against mine when there was a knock at the door. Daisy Fitzhaven stood in the smothering rain. Without speaking we got into the waiting carriage and I held her hand in mine and said not one word all the way to Lisnagreve, knowing why she had come without being told. When we arrived at her home, Doctor Parsloe was already there, trying to persuade Leonora to take some laudanum so that she might sleep for a while and have a few hours unhaunted by the death of her son. But Lady Fitzhaven had as little need of the doctor's solicitousness as poor, wretched Agnes had when she had held her dead child in her arms. Garret's uniform had been sent back to Lisnagreve, a neat, round bullet hole on the tunic's chest, from which the daubed, dried blood spread out in smeary rays. Leonora, notebook and pencil in hand, stepped round it where it had been unwrapped on the hall floor. She walked in purposeful circles, skirt swishing, her chin jutted in a dreadful show of bravery, making arrangements. A wire must be sent to Thesper in London, a memorial meeting got up, letters must be written to the mothers of the men in the regiment who had joined Garret in a fellowship of the dead.

Leonora's brittle, dry-eyed courage brought out the old, buried Englishness in her, that part of her that could summon pluck and grit at will and would not be absorbed by the country she claimed as home: Ireland, a country where her restraint in the face of death would be thought grotesque and indecent.

As I set about helping her accomplish the series of comfortless tasks demanded by death I realized that willpower alone was keeping her from collapse and that this steeliness would finish her as a woman. All that had formed our friendship would be lost: her dinner table always in a roar, her aristocratic unconcern for respectability and the opinion of others, her fine, old, shameless, gleeful ways and crows of laughter, her lures and velvet smiles. She would leave off the clamorous sexual distractions that had once been a joy to her and turn into somebody reliable and worthy, whose life would dwindle into fusty gloom. I sensed all this as I banished the servants to their own quarters, knowing how much their snivelling was grating on their mistress's nerves, and that the sight of one of the maids mourning Garret's wildness and gaiety and telling her beads with her dustmop beside her would have unhinged Leonora entirely.

I stayed at Lisnagreve for a week, after which time Doctor Parsloe urged Leonora to join Thesper in England, where they had been invited to stay with some Shropshire cousins, whose sons were army officers. I saw her on to the train at Ballynahinch, her delicious fullness restrained in a severe mourning dress, her hair scraped under the brim of a velvet hat on which the gleaming corpse of a small, black bird peacefully slept, a symbol of greater slaughter. She kissed me goodbye, not in her usual way of clasping me close so that I felt drowned in her rich, warm fragrance, but pecking the air beside my cheek with cold lips, as though she had already forgotten the hunting and the parties, when she had been a wild piece of goods, and I with her. She waved to me from the train, someone already mysterious and marginal, belonging to the past.

In the station yard, Damian Dashwood was loitering, something displaced and guilty in the way he fingered my horse's reins. 'What way is she?' he asked, wistful with unvoiced love.

'What way could she be, everything she had being taken from her? But Leonora knows well how to cover a heart of loneliness with a veneer of hardness.'

'More than anyone could say of yourself,' Mr Dashwood said. He gave me his handkerchief to wipe my dripping cheeks; it smelt of the Rangoon oil that you use to clean revolvers. We two were marking an anniversary of sorts: more than two decades had gone by since the first time I had howled into his handkerchief, roaring crying because my sister Vera had been put in a convent. I reminded him of the occasion.

'You did well to cry at that time,' he said. 'To such a one as yourself, the spiritual tyranny of the convent would seem as black a place as hell.'

'We talked of evil,' I recalled, 'the thrill of wrestling with it.'

'Aye, that too,' Mr Dashwood agreed grimly, handing me the reins and leaning his elbows on the glossy wood of the trap. The pungent smell of his handkerchief was still in my nostrils. 'Do you believe still that men must wrestle with evil to understand what is good?' I asked.

He gave me a splintery smile with no warmth in it. 'We are many years on from that night, as you say.

And you are something other than the child-bride who loved to coax the blarney and the begorrah from the harp-strings to amuse your new Ascendancy friends. With the songs you bring to me now, like a thief in the night, I'm reminded of a lace-edged handkerchief dipped in blood. Small blame to you for that; our chilling inheritance demands to be warmed by songs such as yours.' He ran his finger along the little horsewhip that lay on the seat beside me. 'I was raised in a stockwhip culture like yourself, Mrs Trewin. Neither of us was brought up to subtle and intricate ways of thinking; it comes hard with us to turn a hard moral glare on life and examine the silence in the sources, the beauties and severities around us. You ask me about evil? I know only this: that a man will not do wrong unless he is in the grip of a passion he cannot help, that comes upon him as irresponsibly as a storm settles on the sea.' He looked at me keenly out of bright, terrifying eyes. 'Remember that in the coming times,' he said.

I longed for Leonora to tease away this fearsome talk with her amused drawl. 'Do you think Leonora will ever come back to Ireland?' I asked.

The fanatic light in her lover's eyes dimmed at the mention of her name. It struck me that the Shinner was a man who both desired intimacy and sought to evade it, that he found in love both fulfilment and the violation of himself, and that these things might explain the revolver he carried. He shook his head angrily. 'No, she has not it in her to see it out here. Like all her kind, she will come to look on Ireland only as a source of embarrassment and humiliation. She'll be easier in her bed at nights in the fatty English grasslands, sliding around on the edges of life, crimped by etiquette, although the thin English ways and the perched English smiles won't suit Leonora at all.' His voice grew thick, frightening. 'And we'll do without her, Ainín Rua; we'll do without all the spoilt energies of her kind. We've had enough of the stranger in our house. Only the likes of us will fight for Ireland. Ourselves alone.'

He seemed reluctant to leave but stood still, like a horse being put in harness, breathing heavily. 'But for all that,' he said, 'Leonora knew how to love a man, as though he *were* a man, and not a half-grown lad.' He looked at me keenly and then said, not with spite as Leonora herself might have done, but with the small amount of sympathy he was capable of: ''Tis a gift denied *you*. You write songs as dangerous as shards of glass but you want a man to be a child to you.'

I shook the reins and made the sound – Tpr, tpr – which was the signal for the pony to pull me away from this awkward conversation, but Mr Dashwood gripped the side of the trap again. 'Don't worry yourself,' he said. 'I'm the only man on earth who knows your fancy for that shuffling drip of a poet. I was about some business on the island one autumn day and my binoculars caught the both of you picking blackberries, when all I was hoping to see was Festy giving the sign that he had the ammunition landed safe. You reminded me of my own mammy, the way you cradled his head in your arms that day.'

'What has you cracked on that goose-face?' he persisted needlingly, 'and you a woman who despised delicacy in others before him.' It was Harriet he meant.

Losing Leonora made him want to wound me, since my own lover had not run away.

'You wouldn't understand,' I said coldly. 'You are all push and heat and would not know the way of a man like Peadar who is so wide open to things, like the city he was raised in: Chicago, the gem of the prairies, where the buildings have their heads in the sky, like poets.'

'Poets,' he mocked. 'As the man said, a poet is someone who constantly thinks of something else. What does he think of those songs of yours that urge one thing only, and that to drive the English out?'

'He thinks they are harangues. It saddens him that they are so strident and might lead men into actions they do not fully understand. I accused him of slinking out of things once with his romancing of the old language, but with all that's happened since, all of Europe a slaughterhouse, I feel shamed by the songs I wrote. The flag my songs honoured, the orange and the green, is only a coloured rag on a stick, not worth dying for.' I lashed the pony the merest flick, and left Mr Dashwood looking after me, his face looking pierced with surprise.

24

To live in those days was like watching a stream of blood come from beneath a closed door. The cardboard suitcases in Fergus Keane's shop stayed put on the top shelf, yellowed and dusty, but the black crape ribbon he sold for mourning bands rolled off their bobbins. Nearly every family in the townland needed a length of it: for a cousin from Dublin who had joined the 10th Division of the Irish Brigade and had been cut to pieces in the rocks at Suvla Bay, or for a son in the National Volunteers, whose head had been blown off among the trampled poppies of northern France.

I dreamt of horses, their flanks in tatters, sinking into gulping trenches, buried alive in the blood and mud that bubbled and foamed over them. Waking at dawn from a tossing sleep, I would stumble to the stables for the comfort of my own horses' satiny flanks and bright, battering hooves, their warm necks and the veins that pulsed under their shins. One such dawn, in that cloudy, brown confusion between sleep and consciousness, I heard the ring of hooves striking cobblestones, the trundling of horseboxes and the coaxing noises that grooms make to frightened animals. I threw on a flannel gown and ran barefoot to the stable yard.

Charles was supervising the despatch of all twelve horses; he stood in the middle of the yard in his shirt-sleeves, his face full of vigour and brutality, a damp, dark line of sweat tracing his spine.

'Sorry about the disturbance, my dear,' he said. 'The French War Ministry made me an offer for the horses. It would be foolish to refuse, the times being how they are.'

'The French eat horses.' My voice was like a mouse squeak in the snap of the morning, hysterical and ridiculous.

'True. If an army marches on its belly, that belly must be kept full.' Charles approached a little Palomino mare, Morrígan, who was trembling and bucking at the sight of the horsebox, and began to joggle his whip in a show of magnificent impatience.

'I'll pay you whatever they will, only to keep the horses.' Now I sounded like a desperate, wheedling gawk.

Charles's gleaming eyebrows quivered. 'You can always be relied upon to rise to the small occasion, my dear. But if you have it in mind to raise the money by selling your jewellery, I must tell you that there is no market for such trifles in wartime.' He cracked his whip on the dewy cobbles. 'Whoopla, whoopla, whey-ya!' he shouted, like a circus ringmaster. That same cry of urging encouragement had made me leap onto his thigh on the first day I came to Malina.

I walked towards him, the cold ground gnawing at my bare soles. 'I have other money,' I said.

My husband looked at me narrowly. Something satisfied about the set of his mouth told me that he had expected me to say this. 'My father left me some money, so,' I lied, convinced that Charles could look inside my head and must know about the stash of coins earned from the sale of my songs and buried in a corner of the earth floor of the house where I met my lover.

'Ah, indeed, your *father*, that fine, high character,' Charles said. 'How could I take money from you that he earned from the moil of his life?' His eyes were watchful now. I knew that I had fallen into some trap and that the whole operation of emptying the stables was a ploy to make me reveal my secret income. I met his eyes boldly, rubbing the sole of one freezing foot against my calf in a casual way, as though I hardly noticed the cold.

'We'll make a deal,' he said. 'I'll keep the horses if you will come to Dublin with me. In my position it would be helpful for my wife to be seen to take part in the war effort instead of roaming the mountainside like a goat girl. You could be photographed rolling bandages and reading to blinded soldiers and all those other charming little ministrations and folderols that fall to women.'

He motioned to the grooms to lead the horses back to their stalls. Then he spat on his hand like a horse-dealer and held out his palm. I laid mine against it, my icy fingers against his warm ones. Cold never touched his body; it merely froze the abandoned temple of his soul.

I knew him well enough to be sure that for every two words he spoke he told three lies, knew him to the very core of his ignoble heart. When he slapped his palm on mine there was an open, honest look on his face that was not to be trusted and made me sick with unease. Why should he want me to go to Dublin with him unless it was to make me suffer in some way?

Peadar thought that I was too much alarmed. 'It's reason enough for him to want you there when he knows you would rather be here. To have you inconvenienced in a strange city is motive enough for him.'

It was a windy day and the waters of Loch Áinín Rua were in delirium. Peadar and I cycled past a sea that tipped furiously against the shore, where the seaweed lay in wilted whips and the thinned-out croppings of grey rock looked to be dissolved by the constant scouring of white-haired waves. But the old stone house was warm enough with the fire lit and the broken windows stuffed with cushions. 'Stretch out your limbs and sleep, my love,' Peadar urged me, drawing a rug before the fire. 'If the lake's ghost were to see the cut of you, she'd pity you for cheeks that are whiter than her own.'

How could I sleep? When I lay beside Peadar I was like a cat with a saucer of cream in the room. Time out of mind we had hurled our two bodies into a world of love, and though after so many years love was a habit with us, each time our flesh met it was to the naked thrill of the first time.

I had shattered my youth against Charles Trewin; had I only met Peadar first, perhaps I could have learnt to seek after things that were good and necessary in themselves, and to turn my back on the world that Malina represented, a life that was seductive, enchanting and pernicious.

'I wish that I were a better woman, only for your sake,' I whispered into my lover's neck. 'I wish that

I were severe and perfect. As it is there are too many desperate evasions in my nature, too much to ask you to forgive me for.'

He tucked my hair behind my ears and began to stroke me, as though he were ironing me smooth of every crease of worry. His huge, awkward hands moved over me and he murmured love, so that, at last, I closed my eyes and listened to him in that state of soothed muzziness in which a child hears a lullaby, convinced by the soft words that it is in a safe place, beyond all harm.

'My love for you is unconditional, Rose Erris,' were the words I heard. 'Your eyes are my climate; you take the shine out of everything else in the world and there's nothing in it to touch you. Together we will live on work and hope and strain like light against darkness, led by our dreams. Listen to an English poet for once:

> And throughout all Eternity
> I forgive you, you forgive me.

William Blake's words, ours too.'

His fingers found the inside of my thighs, strayed higher. I pressed them inside me and was wetted, slithery, transformed into an ache of acceptance as we began on that familiar quest of each other which started in wonder and ended in a tender, private happiness that was like coming into bloom.

'We are like characters in a fairytale,' he said afterwards, 'you and me and that monster you were odd enough to marry. He's not your everyday kind of ogre though, more like the Minotaur in the old myth who kept his women lavishly but under a reign of terror. Now see here, honey, when you're crushed by the snaky desperadoes of Dublin city, remember that you have to battle your way back through the murk to rescue your ould sweetheart from his brooding loneliness beside the ocean-whittled, wind-scoured mountains. It's a bit of an arsy-tippy fairytale but you are better able to slash through the thickets than I am; your nature has been strengthened by glimpses of the dark.'

I left Malina in November. The village children had been sewn into their flannel underwear for the winter as I had once been. The tired and twisted leaves on the stunted trees made Malina's woods desiccated and the wind smashed to pulp the few remaining flowers in the garden. The high interiors of the sea seemed so desolate that you saw why the Irish word for west is *iar,* which has other meanings: the end, everything last, after, backwards, blank, and dusty. Defeated words, all of them.

I was travelling reluctantly eastwards, dull and miserable as I saw the bleak land speed away from me through the train window. East – in Irish *airech,* which means first. Charles sat facing the engine, his glowing face keen and expectant; strong, fluid-looking magician's fingers tapping his knee. His whole body was tense, ready to snap with excitement.

From the moment I stepped onto the streets of Dublin, under a mean, low, lacquered sky, I could feel some cushy, crawling corruption there. We put up in a suite at the Courtland Hotel, a place of showy opulence where the gilded ceiling of the vestibule rested on fat pillars of oxblood marble veined in creamy-white, like rolled-up slices of raw beefsteak.

Charles showed me into the larger of the two bedrooms. 'I have a meeting in twenty minutes on the other side of the city, so will you find your own amusement for this evening? There might be something interesting on at the Abbey theatre if all the peasant clerics in the country haven't got it banned. Whatever you decide, don't loiter on the quays; some scrawny-necked bowsie would tear the earrings from your lobes.'

He left in the brisk, bustling way of a man energized by his own self-regard and I dropped, wilted, onto the bolstered bed. I already missed Peadar as though I were suffering from a wound that wouldn't heal. The way his trousers dragged untidily over his big feet, the way he could catch all my approaching thoughts and understand and forgive them. The way his talk left a gleam in my mind and his body brought a shock of joy to my blood. Although I missed our shared landscape of Connemara, the turf-smoke that hung over the cabins and the wild tossed skies, I did not miss Malina.

Lying in the tawdry comfort of the hotel, I wondered how the grey stone house rising from the lake could have been the focus of my life, all its pale beauty a condition of things, the source of all enchantments, a magic inhalation. I lolled on the bed, patting my future life into shape. Once the war ended, Home Rule for Ireland would come peacefully about, the gift from a grateful England for all the blood-ripe Irish lives we had given her to send to the slaughterhouse that had once been Europe. I had heard about a squint-eyed, half-English master at St Enda's school at Rathfarnham. His name was Padraic Pearse and his gory imagination never left him alone. He shook out the nightmare of history in front of his schoolboys' astonished faces and rewarded them with prizes of revolvers rather than books. Men like Pearse and Damian Dashwood had caused Douglas Hyde to resign from the Gaelic League he had founded. Hyde's dream had been for an Irish-speaking Ireland; more dangerous infiltrations demanded a free one, bought with blood.

When Irish troops were so appreciated for gallantry, Home Rule would come about at the point of a pen not at gunpoint, in spite of Pearse's notions of redemption and sacrifice. And when my country belonged to itself, so should I. I would leave my songs behind as remembrancers, their savage words reminders of how the English had been shamed and disconcerted and more inclined to back away from their wayward colony. Pearse and Dashwood had had their day, they and their dream-led followers, innocent men whose minds had been sent reeling by their mad masters. They were out of touch with the times. The war had changed everything; when the lights came on again in Europe, Ireland would have her own beacon blazing.

I would leave others to decide whether Ireland was a nation, a culture, a people or a religion and go with Peadar to America, to a country that was none of those things but a great, open space where all men and women could turn themselves into what they wanted to be, tossing the past aside like an old newspaper.

Exile had always been a glorious thing to the Irish, it would be so for me. I should have left with Peadar long before, instead of being as stubbornly rooted as the impermeable granite which is Connemara's earth. I could be reborn as a poet's wife, shabby and decent, making fair copies of Peadar's verses and living on cabbage and bacon. My heart humming with desire for every impossible thing, I stepped out into the night-time city and made my way to the quays, since Charles had forbidden me to.

Slow, unsteady, almost opaque raindrops fell listlessly on the city from a sky that was a sulphurous pall. In spite of the rain, the air was poisonous, an acrid haze in the sooty streets. Water makes its presence known, long before you can see it. I sniffed to get the direction of the river Liffey and made my way towards it, following its greasy, winding ribbon to the poor, stunted houses on the quays.

Dublin: from Dubh Linn, dark pool. The place was well named. It swarmed with people: drunken men with caps sliding on the backs of their heads, pale-faced lawyers in dinged silk hats, truculent jossers and mean, perky women. There was a bizarre, irresponsible gaiety about the cut-price crowds parading in the close, stale air, yet the city was a centre of paralysis. Here was everybody, but nobody could move. Under the livid street lights, faces were sly, expectant, waiting to see what the sky would drop in the way of a dubious opportunity. The city's motto was *Obentia civium urbis felicitas* (the obedience of the citizens, the happiness of the city) but it had not been heeded. I leaned on a grimy wall looking out from Burgh Quay to the ships and docks, for inland there was nothing to see but streets. Behind me was an unceasing rumpus as men were thrown out of public houses and women screamed encouragement. Music spilled out from the open door of a dark brick building called the Scotch House. My music. I had written it for people such as these, whose greedy mouths were halfway down thick tumblers, written it to put fire in their souls, fuse them into a nation. It seemed to me that night that I had just added another jarred note to the city's ugly commotion.

'I love them songs, they're the eel's eyebrows.' A woman leaned beside me on the wall, her back to the river, nursing a baby on a fat breast. Her hair was black as porter and she had no teeth.

'Do you think the men in there think of Ireland when they sing them?' I rootled in my pocket for some coins to give her.

'Them ones, is it?' She shifted the baby competently to the other breast. 'Oh rocks. Them fingerlings and gripers that would be thinking only how soon they would be seeing the bottom of the glass.'

'I wrote those songs,' I said.

She gave me a pitying, disbelieving look. 'Arrah, why wouldn't ye?' she said kindly and held out her hand for the coins. 'Mind yerself, now,' she called after me as though I were a child, or an idiot. Perhaps I was both.

No light showed under the door of the adjoining bedroom. The brass doorknob didn't turn in my hand, locked from the other side. Throughout the night, I listened out for sounds of Charles's return: water splashed into a glass, a match struck, a mattress creaking. There were none.

He appeared as I was breakfasting in my room; dressed in a silver-grey frock coat he was sleek as a pigeon. He had arranged for me to work in an auxiliary hospital for the rest of the month. It had been established in a house called the Laurels on St Stephen's Green and the nursing staff included many women of high birth, who worked on a voluntary basis, reading to the wounded soldiers and preparing their meals. 'Some of the wounded men are rather coarse,' Charles said, steering me into the frosty sunlight, 'but I have never found that a worry with you.'

As he hustled me along the pavement I felt that I was in a different place to the night-time city of a few hours ago. I could feel the sting of the sea on my cheek and a sharp wind that blew off distant, hazy hills. I shook off Charles's elbow to stop to admire Nelson's Pillar in Sackville Street, a statue that was partly funded by the merchants and shippers of Dublin, grateful to the adulterous admiral who had kept open the seas for them in troubled times. We walked along terraces of speckled brick with high flights of steps in front of them, tilted outwards to drain off the rain. We stopped in front of a house whose fanlight was like half of a daisy made from clear glass. Inside, in a long hallway, a fat English colonel was giving orders to a young Irish nurse. Her pleated, starched cap quivered respectfully as she listened but I caught her eye, that disconcerting blue Irish eye with a round-the-house-and-mind-the-dresser spirit of the jig in it and sensed that the orders stood no chance of being carried out.

Charles led me into a room where plaster Muses gleamed plumply on the walls and a painted, naked

Juno stretched her limbs on the ceiling. Admiring these, it was some while before I noticed the woman standing at the far end of the room, in front of a noticeboard divided into sections by narrow red ribbon held by brass drawing-pins. The woman had her back to us. There was a shocking familiarity in the way sleek, golden hair was coiled above a long neck, in the sloping shoulders and the narrow back down which a line of grey silk buttons met a line of rolled loops until they reached a small waist. Was it Harriet again, that eternal revenant, who was dead but wouldn't lie down? The sight of that tapering waist made me feel as though I were spinning headlong down a hole, and only Charles's hard grip on my elbow kept me from falling. The woman turned to face us and, as she did so, Charles said, with a low, mysterious tenderness in his voice, 'This is Marianne Pennington, my dear. Miss Pennington, I should like to present my wife.'

Her face was nothing like Harriet's. Her beauty was of a more ruthless kind: a broad, forceful forehead, wide, squarish mouth and eyes of a colour that had dazzled me once – lion-gold, flicked with tawny lights. The look in them was as venomous as a snake bite. I flinched and turned away, and saw that Charles's face blazed with bliss. It was obvious they were lovers and I thought how entirely in character it was for Charles to be so brutally without scruple. He gloried in another woman in front of my eyes, ripping the scabs off all my wounds, and enjoying it.

Marianne Pennington explained to me how the volunteer system at the Laurels worked, while Charles growled approval at her at all times. He boasted proudly of the remorseless way she raised funds for bedlinen and bandages, took on fallen women to cook and launder for just the cost of their keep, and persuaded the biscuit factory to provide broken biscuits free of charge. For a long while, they discussed financial matters in that assumed way English people have, and then Miss Pennington turned her glittering glance on me and said, 'I'm told that you sing, Mrs Trewin.'

My mind swooped down all the long years, until it heard Leonora, young and flushed then, plump arms straining against her black, lace gloves, say the same words. I sighed and nodded my head. 'Frightfully useful,' Miss Pennington said. 'Music distracts so nicely, and some of the boys have nothing but wasting and dying before them.'

Charles looked at her as though she were a goddess who could hold back the tides of death at whim. 'I must leave,' he said reluctantly. Although he and the goddess stood six feet apart, they might have been glued together, so inseparable were their golden glances. 'I shall send a carriage for you later, my dear. You will want to rest at the hotel this evening for Miss Pennington will not let you stay idle today, and besides I have another committee meeting.' His eyes slipped off Marianne's and I knew they had an appointment that evening.

Fate always uses a blunt instrument, I thought sourly, as I followed Marianne's narrow back up a flight of broad stairs. It was a very well-bred back, the kind that could come to grief only by drowning in luxury. I now knew why Charles had made me come to Dublin: to humiliate me by flaunting his amber-eyed mistress in front of me in a place where I did not belong. I longed for the look of love in Peadar's smoky green eyes and the smile on his seamed cheeks as we undressed each other by our secret fireside. Away from his hands that smoothed my flesh, I felt awkwardly-angled, unlovely and unchosen. I gave no thought to where I was and what went on there until Marianne stopped at an upper landing and opened a panelled door.

Two rows of iron cots seemed to go on for ever, and not one of them held a whole man. Everywhere I looked I saw evidence of something missing: an empty eye socket, a legless torso, a stump of a hand that had no fingers on it. In the great rumble of bibble-babble, grunts of pain could hardly be heard for the loud, mindless hilarity that dispelled fear and pity and disgust. It followed my progress down the ward. 'Begob, Missus, come and give us one. I've lost me legs but I've still got me ould parnell' . . . 'There's divil a much to eat in this place. I'm starved enough to bite the arse of a reverend mother through the seat of a cane-bottomed chair' . . . 'Who's the ould bollocks I seen you come in with when I was looking outta the windy?'

When she reached the end of the ward, Marianne folded her arms across her pretty bosom, stuck out her chin in a way that was openly contemptuous and waited for the silence that came almost immediately. In such a situation, Harriet would have twisted her knuckly hands in anguished pity while her face showed fastidious, flustered disdain. How could I have imagined Marianne to be her ghost? There are no ghosts: we haunt ourselves.

Marianne said, 'This is Mrs Trewin. She will serve you your luncheon' – she emphasized the word heartlessly – 'and then she will entertain you for the afternoon.' She stopped the weak attempt at a snigger with another tilt of her chin. Then, her golden hair lit by the sunshine that poked through the high, dirty windows, she walked back along the narrow passage between the iron beds, her eyes reeling in the men's desire as though it were a hooked fish. Even the sightless men turned their heads towards her as she passed. As she reached the door, she turned back and gave one of her snaky, sidelong looks at a soiled patch on one man's pyjamas, a cigarette butt smouldering on a block of parquet. A collective sigh of relief followed the thump of the door closing behind her.

How many blood-soaked bandages do you have to scrape off a seeping wound before you are sickened by the slaughter that caused it? How many times do you have to stroke back the sticky hair from a dying man's brow before you understand the gift of life? By the end of one day's nursing I was a convert to peace at any price, with a red line of blood under my fingernails and a blouse that stank of death where I had cradled the head of a seventeen-year-old boy as life fled from his gangrenous limbs.

A year or so since, Damian Dashwood, reading my latest song, had told me that I seemed to be inspired by hatred, a long-buried hatred that had forced its way out in a cascade of fury which glorified his own violent conspiracies. How I wished now that I could snatch back the words of every song I had written, tormented by the thought that they might yet provoke murdering deeds, even though Ireland seemed to have moved on to respectful, constitutional beliefs.

People streamed in and out of the Laurels all day; society ladies making some dabbling little war effort by spooning raspberry jelly down the throat of a weak soldier, officers come to raise their wounded out of their invalid sloth, Dublin's men of commerce to discuss jobs for those who could not be returned to the battlefield. Marianne had an Englishwoman's frantic detestation and distrust of everything and everyone Irish. She wriggled her shoulders in annoyance at the businessmen's sentimental assurances that they would 'see right by the boys' and by the blather of the boys themselves, disputatious and dreamy as they smoked cigarettes in the short evenings, accepting the applauseless life that lay ahead of them without shame or bitterness.

Armless, legless, eyeless, witless. As soon as any one of them showed signs of recovery Marianne pulled every string that a young, beautiful woman of high birth can pull to get her charges housed and in work. When they thanked her, in tumbling words full of gratitude and blessings, her tawny eyes kindled so dangerously that I thought she might slap a scarred face or kick the crutch from under a cripple. Only when bouquets of flowers arrived for her, bunches that seemed to gather up the whole golden autumn in their colours and smells – sprays of chrysanthemums, dahlias, some late roses, every bloom matched to the gilded glints in her eyes – did her face soften. Then she would give the flowers a venomous look and dump them in a pail that had recently been used for soaking gory cloths. She would carry it into the ward, where the raw outdoor scent of the flowers would be forced out by the stronger odour of young men's bodies growing stale.

The hectic atmosphere of the Laurels made the men jittery. I soothed their nerves by telling them about my childhood, dragging their beds into a half-circle around the fire, while I sat on a low stool like the storytellers in the old, lost days, the sennachie.

I told them of the marble quarries and the streaked, green beauty of their stone, said to be five hundred million years old. I told them how I walked to Miss Gwynn's schoolroom, carrying, as all the children did, a sod of turf among my schoolbooks that kept my hands as warm as though it were an ermine muff during the journey and was then added to the schoolroom fire. I told them how I raced back to Shanvally as soon as school was over, past the thorn bushes where sheep's wool hung like grey threads, to look after my ponies who were of that same stock that a French visitor to Connemara, in the fourteenth century, had written: 'They are small, hairy, unkempt little creatures who scout the hills and valleys and they are fleeter than deer.' I told them of the warm chimney corners of the smoky cabins and the swirling tips of the grasses, pale with light, of the seal-shooting by the harbour and the strange light of the west of Ireland that makes the sea gleam silver and strikes the mountain clefts an intense, almost transparent yellow. And although their wounded bodies were heavy on their beds, their minds became chainless, adrift in the luminous landscape that my stories shaped for them.

One evening, Marianne stood in the doorway listening. She had been about to leave and was wearing a cape of fox fur which I felt sure Charles had given her, driven to the purchase by some heartbreaking memory of his own golden-haired mother wearing such a fur. She looked at me with a watchful restraint, her eyes empty of their customary harshness. 'You are not what I expected,' she said.

'And what did you expect?'

'Someone with less poetry in her, someone not as rich and rare as you are.' She raised one fine, gold eyebrow, the shape of a tick upside down. This unconscious imitation of one of Charles's habitual gestures seemed shockingly, obscenely intimate and I felt bile rise behind my teeth. Her lovely face looked troubled as she left, snuggled into her furs. Charles had no doubt painted a picture of me as some country-cute horsewoman, whose talk was dreary and false so that boredom sat heavily on her husband's soul. I could imagine his patient, self-sacrificing sighs, hints that he had been gulled into marriage with a wild, Irish beauty who was socially beneath him and whom he had come to see as full of sordid purposes, beyond his civilizing influences, coming, as she did, from a race that had not long since been jingling brass money and stomping about in wooden shoes.

Marianne might have been touched that a man so creamy with success and power had been trapped into a lifelong union with someone brash, ignorant and unmannerly. Besides, she loved him; that had been clear from the swarming glances between them. Had there been other gifts besides the sumptuous cape? A high-ceilinged flat with a lacy iron balcony in Merrion Square or Dawson Street, with a warm, hushed bedroom? I looked out of the window and saw Marianne being helped into a motor car by a tall, stiff-legged British army officer. His hair gleamed brilliantly, like polished coal, his profile was grave, and his mouth seemed to twitch at the corners. Then I knew that Charles's love for Marianne was something insanely willed. He must know that one day she would leave him, for this man with bright, metallic hair or for some other, near to her in age and without the complication of a living wife. And by leaving Charles, she would fit into the intricate, fated and destructive pattern of his life. The sound of the car's engine had hardly faded when I discovered that my teeth were chattering and that my nails had made dark crescents in the heels of my hands. What might Charles do when Marianne slid out of his life? Butcher the horses? Burn down Malina?

That evening, Charles and I were to dine together for the first time since he had brought me to Dublin. Our hosts were an English couple with identical long, passive faces, who had invited us to their house in Mount Street to thank us for our valued work on behalf of the army. Mr Colthurst was in munitions and the war had left him and his wife uneasily stranded in the foreign place that was Dublin, trying to co-ordinate the passage of guns and ships.

It was a sombre evening. Mr Colthurst had a quiet, bitter temper that made him attack the city in which he was so miserably marooned: the dirt, the poverty, the porter that swilled from the barrel to make men rowdy and dangerous – standard attacks on my country which I knew from backside to breakfast-time. His wife let him splutter on disagreeably until coffee was served and then took over the conversation. She wagged a roguish finger at me. 'You are a great success at the Laurels,' she said, as though I were attending parties there rather than caring for men who had waded through blood. 'The poor boys love your little stories about the immiserated west. We are all so lucky,' she continued quickly, noticing that she had fanned a fury into my face, 'that dear Marianne decided to join us in our beleaguerment. She could have had France, you know. Lord Kitchener begged her to take charge of the VADs there. But, no, she insisted on Ireland; she said that was where the need would be greatest, since the people had no notion of how to organize themselves in wartime, and Lord Kitchener understood, perhaps because he is an Irishman himself.'

Again, Mrs Colthurst realized that she had caused offence. Kitchener was indeed an Irishman, but had allowed an Ulster division to fight, sporting the Red Hand as its emblem, while refusing the southern counties their own division or to display the Irish Harp. Mrs Colthurst changed tack, giving us a litany of Marianne's antecedents – the duke on the mother's side of the family, the former Viceroy on the father's. Marianne had studied the Classics at Oxford University, although naturally, Mrs Colthurst said, lowering her voice as though the subject were the slightest bit indelicate, as a woman she had not been allowed to take her degree. As the silly creature continued her rattly recital, Charles listened to her, smoothing his waistcoat over his chest from time to time, as though he kept the gorgeous, golden-eyed girl he loved close to his heart.

I tried to forget the way Marianne had tucked her skirt around her long legs as she had swung herself gracefully into the motor car. Suppose she were to tear herself away from all her clever, cultured friends, leave London's theatres and concert halls, Oxford's literary salons. Suppose she were to come and live with Charles in Connemara, a second Harriet, as golden-haired and elegant as the first, but bolder and more worldly. How easy it would be for me then to run away from Malina, as easy as it was for women under our old Irish laws who, when they left their marriage homes, were not punished and could take with them their lap-dogs, cats, looking-glass and spinning wheel and start their lives all over again as though the past had never been.

The young officer's quivering mouth and rigid back forced themselves into my mind and I knew that Marianne would not give me the chance to escape from Malina. I would find my chance some other way. Whatever happened, I would escape from the beautiful house I had come to hate. I would follow Peadar to the other edge of the Atlantic. I would listen to my heart before my time ran out on me, before I became as dried out as an old boiling hen.

25

'Baby's breath and tiny yellow rosebuds, I think, don't you?' one of the society ladies spoke dreamily as we rolled bandages in the corner of the ward at the Laurels the following morning.

I blinked at her stupidly, wondering if the sight of so many broken bodies had made her take leave of her senses. She fluffed herself out and patted my hand. 'You don't know? Marianne has become engaged. It was quite sudden. He's a catch, the youngest major in the British army, mentioned in despatches and nothing between him and a rather good title except for a failing old bachelor of a cousin.' Her eyes began to swim again and she let the bandage she was holding grow slack in her fat little hands, which wore too many rings. 'And a gold lace overlay on the bodice to emphasize the eyes . . .' She lowered her voice in the way people do when they are about to tell you something to somebody else's disadvantage. 'I've heard that combat has left him slightly unhinged. He's the sensitive type; before the war, he was studying at the Royal Academy to become a professional pianist.'

She was interrupted by a scullion with a dripping nose bringing me a message, one of the disgraced girls engaged by Marianne at a bargain rate to clean the house and riddle the cranky boiler. 'Please return to hotel immediately,' Charles's decisive handwriting instructed me. 'We are leaving for Malina as soon as you arrive. Your packing has been undertaken. There is no need to make your goodbyes to Miss Pennington.'

I turned the sheet of hotel writing paper over, scribbled a note on the back and pinned it on the noticeboard in the salon with the beautiful plasterwork where I had first seen Marianne. 'To all my friends here: a long life and a wet mouth. *Dia dhuit* – God be with you. R.E.T.'

The skin around his lips was as white as paper and his glittering, rakehell eyes seemed dulled over with soot. Had I not been so frightened of what he might do to avenge this second abandonment, I might have wept for him. He paced up and down on the pavement in front of the hotel, beside the long, black hooded motor car he had hired with its uniformed chauffeur to drive through the night across the whole waist of the country to see us home. He explained this to me in harsh, broken words, which emerged raggedly from his throat as though after unbearable effort. Crouched in the back of the car, he became silent, his breathing heavy in his chest, and I wondered if this second loss of a golden-eyed woman would affect him the way his mother's desertion had and whether, his life wrenched out of shape all over again, he would be struck dumb.

The clotted silence inside the car was broken by the driver's brogue, sweet and comforting as buttermilk. The backs of his ears were the colour of raw bacon, rimmed with pale hairs, and his head shot straight up from his thick neck without a curve. He picked up speed as we passed through Chapelizod on the road running west and said, a countryman's relief in his voice, 'It's not sorry I am to be out of that.'

He voiced my own feelings. Dublin, named for a dark pool, was a foul cesspit. I had hated the incessant twanging of the wires that shunted the jolting trams around the streets, the pitiless glare of the street lights, the stewing tenements, the stink of the sluggish river, the creaking hackneys drawn by scabby, ill-used horses who shuddered under the whips of jarveys whose noses were clogged lumps of red sponge. A place where no bird sang – you could scatter crumbs on a sill for them in the evening and find the crumbs still there in the morning.

Charles spoke at last. 'Yes,' he said, 'it was time to leave. The city is good for nothing except as a place to dump your illusions.' He made a sound in his throat, something between a sour chuckle and a sob. Then he put his hand on my knee. 'It was unsettling for you too, my dear. I should not have taken you away from your mountains and lakes. You did not look well in the city; women are like clover, the closer to home you find them, the sweeter they are.'

I was relieved by the quiet tenderness in his voice. Would I never learn? How many years would I need to get the correct contour of a man who spurted with hatred for me, since only by hating could he shake his fist at a world that had allowed his mother to desert him?

The tenderness drained away from his voice and he said in the familiar, contemptuous way, 'Soon we'll be in Connemara again, and you will be queen of all you survey, all the dirt and ignorance.' As if on cue, the driver began to hum the air of a song called 'One Step Nearer Home' as we drove full into the black fall of night until the grey humps of mountains curved against the sky and the waterlogged land looked like something you would measure by the gallon instead of the acre, bare but for the few deformed, wind-shorn trees leaning inwards, away from the salt-laden winds.

We came back to Malina so early in the morning that we could see the mist fizzing above the silver lake by the lamplights flickering in the tall windows. I went straight to the kitchen to be coddled by Binnie with tea and boxty pancakes which I ate hot from the griddle with the new churning of unsalted butter.

'Tell me more, tell me all.' I made the age-old request to the old woman, letting the kitchen dog lick the grease from my fingers.

'There'll be trouble, I can smell it coming,' she said, her back hooped over the smoking griddle.

'Festy?' I asked.

'Aren't I kilt all over, only for him and the whole howling pack of them with their drilling and their rifles and their sniggery. They will be out in their marching orders given the word, the pig's cheek of them.'

'It's just their strutting, Binnie. If they had seen the sights I saw in Dublin, boys younger than themselves without a foot to stand on nor an eye to wink with, they would leave off their fighting ways soon enough. They are marching to the wrong tune, anyways. Not one drop of blood needs spilling for Ireland's sake. Freedom's put on the long finger so long as this war goes on but Home Rule will follow. Tell that to Festy, the ignorant bostoon.'

'Tell him to put away his saltpetre and his bullets is it? Them's words that would go as unheard as a whisper in the ear of death. Festy swears he'll die for Ireland, not that the Good Lord is so desperate that he'd make a snatch for the likes of that caffler.'

The hands of my diamond-framed wristwatch showed ten o'clock. Peadar would be opening the library now, holding a newspaper to the fire to make a draught, rolling the rubber stamp to show the new day's date. As I opened the yard door, a hen wandered in, flew onto the table and knocked to the floor the cup that I had just set down. Binnie looked at the shattered fragments with a knowing eye. 'A sure sign of a leaving that is,' she said, reaching for the broom. 'When a chicken comes in the door and knocks something over, there's always some kind of a parting.'

'You're a miserable ould hairpin,' I said. 'I'm going out to find a warmer welcome.'

'And little blame to you to leave this place where no child plays and there is no promise of a child nor respect for the smalls of life. There's neither luck nor grace in this house.' She banged the warped door after me.

I believed in the old superstitions and, riding to the village, a borrowed and unread copy of *Childe Harold* in my saddle bag the excuse for visiting the library, I wondered if the shattered cup on the stone floor foretold my own leaving, along with Peadar's.

The man I loved was an unlikely object of passion on that raw, cold morning. His eyelids were sticky and his nostrils red and sore. 'You're a sorry picture,'

I said, flipping Lord Byron onto his desk, but his gaunt face was sunshiny to my eyes.

'Come into the back room and I'll tell you how I caught cold in more ways than one.' His voice was tired and grim.

While I had been away, he had cycled over to Loch Áinín Rua many times: 'I missed you so; I needed to be at the place where I could feel you all around me, to put my head on the cushion where your head had been and smell the smell of your hair on it.' A few days since, he had been about to leave the reedy lakeside when he noticed something glinting in the winter sunlight. It was a tin tea caddy, one of a pile half-hidden under a blackthorn bush. He took the tin in his hand – it showed harshly tinted likenesses of King George V and his queen in coronation robes – perplexed as to why it should be so far from any kitchen. He heard the grasses rustle behind him and turned to see Festy, wearing the dark green uniform of the Volunteer army, a slouched hat on his handsome head.

'It's a grand place for hiding what you don't want the world to know about,' Festy had said, grinning. 'You and I both know that, teacher.'

'For a moment,' Peadar told me now, 'I thought he was threatening to blackmail me. But I underestimated him. He had no interest in our hiding-place; he minded nothing except for Ireland's freedom, told me fantastic tales about the number of Volunteers who were on permanent alert, awaiting the chance of armed rebellion, along with James Connolly's Citizen Army and some daughter of the Ascendancy with a Polish name who's been drilling women and children to capture Dublin Castle. At least, I thought his stories fantastic until he led me to a little hillock, thrust some binoculars into my hand and asked me whether I could see anything unusual out in the bay?'

'A hump-backed whale?' I suggested hopefully, although my heart curdled.

Peadar shook his head. 'Not a bit of it. It was a sloop. Festy said that he and his men had been promised a consignment of guns from Germany and the British navy must have got word of it and was on the prowl, but it was of no matter because there had been some muddle over a coded telegram and the guns were to be landed further down the coast. The tea canisters were to be the casings of home-made bombs, by the way. I wouldn't have given it to Festy to be so ingenious. Tobacco tins serve the same purpose, he told me.'

'Did you ever hear the beat of that.' I kept my voice mild. Then I took two handfuls of Peadar's soft curls and yanked at them until his eyes watered. 'The clearest water that ever slid down a mountain stream is thick soup compared to the transparency of you,' I yelled at him. 'Not one flicker of your soul goes unrecorded on your face and I can read you more easily than I can follow Lord Byron's bookful of guff. And now, the way your eyes are skimming the floor and the dimples in your cheeks are drooping with guilt tell me that more went on between you and Festy than you're letting on.' I tugged at his hair again so that he yelped. Then he sneezed and felt in my pocket for a handkerchief in the old, familiar way that broke my heart.

'Festy was after telling me that the President of the Executive Committee and Chief of Staff of the Irish

Volunteers is a man called Eoin MacNeill.' Peadar paused to allow the words he said next their fair share of significance. 'He's a Professor of Archaic Gaelic at the National University of Ireland.' I let go of his hair, put my head in my hands and groaned. 'Heavens save us, Peadar, don't tell me that on the strength of that you let Festy persuade you to join that gang of gowks. All they are are over-excited fools with violent urges. Every time the feeling is on them to smash in a few heads they declare their anxiety to spill blood for Ireland.'

Peadar took my hands in his and looked at me sadly out of his red-rimmed eyes. 'It was I who started them on this business when I persuaded them to spend their Wednesday evenings at meetings of the Gaelic League. All the stories I told them of Ireland's mythic past: who knows but that it was myself who inspired them to this. I can't hold myself back from them now.'

'You know that Douglas Hyde never intended that the Gaelic League should be political and he resigned when it was taken over by cranky visionaries like Padraic Pearse and dangerous louts like Festy.'

'Douglas Hyde tried to make the people Irish without allowing them an Ireland of their own. I think, now, that his was a muddled vision.'

'And yours isn't?' I spat the words at him.

He pressed me into his arms, although the curtains were drawn back and the gaslight blazed and anyone passing in the laneway could have seen us through the window, swaying sorrowfully together like two windblown flowers. 'My life has been all blundering chaos,' he said, 'every minute of it except for those I spent with you, when passion put a wonderful order

337

in everything. These self-styled rebels are a laughable rabble, but I'm no better than any of them and I owe it to them to see things out alongside them. They look to me to help them keep faith with the past.'

He found my handkerchief again and blew his nose; his face was as limp as a flag on a windless day. 'You said to me once, Rose Erris, that you would understand if I left you. The way things have turned about, now I must be the one to say those same words to you. Believe me, my darling, I will understand and never blame you.'

I remembered another day long ago. We had picked blackberries until our fingertips had purple caps on them and, sitting beside Peadar on a slabby rock, talking of language and love and history, I had suddenly decided that my calling in life was to write songs that would ridicule the English out of Ireland. And Peadar had put aside any dreams of leaving that he might have had and promised to stay beside me and keep me from harm. I rumpled the hair that I had pulled. 'Leave you, is it, when you could be in danger? Aren't you my ould sweetheart, and isn't it on me to watch over you for all the days of your life?' My heart seemed hurt with lead but I smiled into his green eyes. 'All the days of your life, my love, and I'm hoping that there will be too many of them to count.'

Shuddering behind veils of rain, brief cold days followed one upon the other, days without colour apart from the uncountable shades of grey that hardly divided the mountains from the sea. In the wintry silence, every sound seemed harsh and remote; church bells clinked like tin spoons, an ass's bray would make you think it was probing your tooth.

Rain pelted against my back as I cycled to Loch Áinín Rua on a darkening January afternoon. A wisp of smoke trailing into the clouds told me that Peadar was already there. We still came to this place whenever chance allowed, to make love with an intense tenderness, nuzzling against one another's shoulders, nosing one another's throats like two affectionate horses in a field. But, since Peadar's discovery of the pile of tin caddies, we always felt a faint uneasiness, a sense of trespass, like outside dogs who sneak into the house on a wet day.

Peadar was smoking an old clay pipe mended with twine, his tin spectacles on the end of his nose as he read a letter by the light of the fire. He looked pale and dwindled and I went to put my arms around him and rub my cheek against his. As I did so, he threw the letter he was holding into the flames and looked up at me with hopeless eyes. 'It's to begin,' he said, 'the bloody protest for a glorious thing or' – he smiled at my furious face – 'as you might prefer to call it, the nonsensical rebellion. It's nothing but vague talk as yet but what's being scorched in the fire is an order from the Director of Organization of Irish Volunteers. We are to prepare for special manoeuvres at Easter.'

He stood up, loosened my hair, then smoothed it behind my ears and blew on my neck as though I were a nervous foal he was asking to trust him. 'Now here is something to make you laugh,' he said, and sank down on the cushions, pulling me onto his lap. 'The boys have given up the tea caddies for a bad job. They've the real doings now, a consignment of Lee Metfords. Wait till I tell you how they came by them and stop looking at me with those angry eyes or you'll burn me to a crisp with crossness. Well, didn't that husband of yours order some blocks of Carrara marble from Italy to refurbish the railway station and didn't some Italian fellows, thrilled at the thought of bloodshed, hide the guns between the blocks for us like the good men they are.'

I did laugh then, although I could hear my laughter emerging as a sort of mad howl. Charles had a low opinion of the Volunteers. A ceremonial obscenity was how he had described one of their uniformed marches through the village, although the march had consisted of twenty boys, chaotically out of step with the piper who was leading them to the tune of 'Wrap the Green Flag Round Me', to the delight of several small children who hopped and skipped around the marchers and tugged at the bright buttons on their sleeves, and to the fury of their mothers who flapped their shawled arms like ragged wings and bawled, 'The sight of yiz would sicken an ass; it's at home saying yer prayers yiz should be', which made the boys grow red in the face and their feet to flounder on the broken road.

As the green uniforms had faded into the drizzle, Charles looked about him at the barefooted children, the shawled women, the men sitting on the upturned currachs scratching their legs and at the bog-mantled granite moorland behind him. In a foully civil voice, he had told me, 'Most certainly you are a race, my dear. Whether you are a nation remains to be seen.' There was some tragic pleasure to be taken in the knowledge that the guns destined to make Ireland a nation once again had been smuggled in with the Englishman's marble.

I related Charles's disapproving remarks to Peadar as we sat by the fire, arms wrapped around each other, laughing more easily now and beginning to fall into the mood of familiar, coupled solitude that came on us when we were alone together.

Some hours later we stepped into a night where a thin, pared crescent of a moon cast a cold light on the sedge. Peadar held out the sides of his scuffed frieze jacket and I lit a cigarette in the shelter of his chest. 'Safe home.' I kissed him goodbye and waved to the shape of his crouched back as he rode clumsily away.

I had finished my cigarette and was about to mount my bicycle when I heard an aggressive *kraa-kraa* near the mossy step of the house. In the moonlight I could make out the black head and grey belly of the hooded crow, a sight to put my breath in my fist and my heart in my mouth. *Corvus corone cornix,* the hooded crow, was the war goddess, Badb, in one of her many disguises. There was a time when the sight of her ungainly hop on the ground and her ugly croak drove strong men from the fields and into the safety of their cabins, for her appearance signalled slaughter or misfortune and her favoured flight was over the corpses on a battlefield, eyeing her most chosen carrion with a greedy eye.

I rode quickly away from the sound of that terrifying croak until the only thing I could hear was the soft kneading of the cinder track under my bicycle tyres. I thought of many things on that homeward journey: of how there wasn't the like of Peadar Griffin in the whole world and how his easily entreated heart would draw him away from me into the old nightmare that was riding Ireland again. I knew that I would have to give love away since it would flee from me whether I did or not and that there was little chance of following Peadar across the ocean, little chance that the world would pause to wonder at my happiness. All that would be left to me would be the memory of dark green eyes and loving, searching hands; poor faded souvenirs of passionate moments.

I must have more than that. I hesitated for a moment, then turned down the moonlit borheen and pedalled towards the light that showed in the kitchen window at Shanvally. I wheeled my bicycle over the iron cattle-grid and scrabbled softly on the back door, waiting for my sister Geraldine to let me into the house where I was born.

26

'You would need to wait until *Lughnasa,* the way I did myself,' Geraldine said. The mother of seven grey-eyed, black-haired daughters, my sister had once been embittered by her barrenness. Like many childless women before her, on the eve of the harvest quarter-day she had made her pilgrimage to Croagh Patrick, the conical mountain tipped with white quartz. She had slept on its summit where the ancient goddess of the mountain had given birth, before the holy saint drove her out and put to rest the stories of Cruachán Aigle, the mountain's old, unsaintly name, on whose peak the pot of harvest milk used to come to the boil.

'I can't wait until *Lughnasa,*' I said. The Friday of Crom Dubh, the harvest god, was in July, a world away. Peadar would be long gone by then. Geraldine began to scrabble with her hairpins at the back of her neck in the same way that our mother used to. Her brown skin had whitened from a life spent too much indoors, spinning and cooking in the house, kneeling and praying in the church. She had lost her skill with the ponies, leaving their upkeep to her daughters. So competent were they that their father, Murph Delancey, was free to travel to all the big fair days, eyeing the horses and the women, smug and greasy, with the crafty, merry face of a man who knows his business well. His wife had changed from a reckless girl to a soft-voiced, sombre woman who moved around the house slackly, in a faint cloud of martyrdom.

'And it already January.' She smiled rather anxiously. 'Is it yourself, and you having waited half a lifetime already and your man with you? I always wondered why you wouldn't be childed, him having always had such a liking for children.' Her eyes became gentle as she remembered the rides she had had on Charles's burly shoulders, the sweets and cakes he had magically discovered in unlikely places – the teapot, the turf stack, the hen coop.

'You've left it late enough but you've had your own way in everything else the way I ever knew you, so why not in this? There'd be a bit of a scandal to it but there's many a woman far gone in years who birthed for the first time, doesn't the Bible give name to them?'

She settled herself in her chair the better to remember all the men and women in her own lifetime who had astonished the neighbourhood by carrying a cradle into the house when all had thought the time was near for them to be seasoning wood for their coffins. She was put in mind of an old mountainy man who, left a bit of money by a nephew in America, married and became a father within the year, and a faded, dutiful woman in the townland who had not been allowed to marry while her foul-tempered mother lived but, after that, had done so and had become finally, joyfully, a mother of twin boys.

'It's oysters you have to rely on,' Geraldine said, 'as many as you can swallow and a good wallop of

344

porter with them.' Her voice was teasing; she knew I hated the taste and feel of oystery slime in my mouth. 'Ah, go on,' she urged, more kindly. 'It's worth the trouble for the way a child of your own rises your heart.' We both lifted our heads towards the ceiling to listen to the giggles and soft, pleased cries and fleet, scrabbling steps of girls trying on clothes and combing their hair into new ways and turning the short, winter days into their private secret.

'Murph now, he's no more use to me than a feather, only for our girleens, the treasures,' Geraldine said, affection in her voice for the husband she had never pretended to love. 'He would drink the eye out of a cat, only for his daughters. If he has the humour on him to get into his old, bad ways I give him the baby to mind. She has the same slate grey eyes as yourself, the way they had our own Dada fixated, may God be good to his soul.' My sister squinted out of the window towards the unseen mountain. 'Named after Errisbeg, you were. Dada used to say that he could never look at it but that he would be reminded of something steady and remorseless and that he would get that same reminder when you looked at him. May the good Lord see fit to give you a baby girl with those same eyes,' she smiled at me generously. 'It's great company she'd be for you in the rainy days.'

She stood leaning against the kitchen door as I got on my bike, a soft, white-skinned woman with dark, untidy hair. 'Remember the oysters now,' she called after me, 'and all the other bits of business you have to be going through to get a baby for your two arms to hold.'

I imagined my baby as I drew nearer to Malina along the dark road by the lake. It would be a girl with hair as black as my own but her eyes would not be the grey of Errisbeg's crags or the glinting topaz of Malina's squire. When she watched the currachs dance over the waves like corks it would be out of eyes that were the dark, shining green of glass bottles. The mountain that had named me lay ahead, its sleeping outline a hard, clear black against the softer black of the answering sky.

Caterpillars couldn't have tasted worse than the oysters I slid down my throat night after night in a shadowy corner of the kitchen, slitting their ridgy shells with a lethal knife, not bothering with the niceties of crushed ice and lemon juice and hot pepper, as they would only prolong the time it took to get the wet, rubbery bivalves from the shell to my protesting stomach.

I began to feel limp and queasy and my listlessness transferred itself to the animals. The under-exercised horses looked seedy and snorted distressfully when they saw that I was too droopy and leaden to canter away the cold morning, the cats lay in moody coils, turning their backs to me as I took the oyster knife from the long, wooden box that hung from a nail through its heart-shaped hole. The latest Labrador gave me a reproachful worn-down look from damp, chocolate eyes when I whistled to her to come for a walk, and slunk under a sofa's pleated flounce. Even the foxes that slipped over the stone walls looked mangy. It seemed, as I stumbled tiredly around the stables, that the animals' cuts refused to heal and their scratches festered and that the whole world was wounded in some way.

A detachment of troops was to embark from the station with its new Italian marble platform, on the first stage of a journey that would take them to the Somme. Charles made a festivity of it. To enliven the drizzling morning, he had some local men form an archway of fire by holding sticks with lighted sods on them. The company commander led his men through the blazing arch and onto the freezing platform. He was pitifully young with the high-bridged Ascendancy nose and backward-leaning teeth. The years spent in an English military academy had flattened the lilt from his voice and turned it into something overbred, full of fishbones. He made a vapid, embarrassed speech about being able to count on the loyalty of every true Irishman, unaware that he stood on a block of marble that had aided the transport of rebel guns. As he stepped inside the train, Orla, one of Geraldine's daughters, lovely in a dark blue dress and a matching ribbon which failed to restrain her loosening, glittering plait, presented him with a creamy winter rose for his buttonhole. He waved it to the crowds as the train pulled out of the station.

Geraldine looked at me admiringly. I was wearing a grey velvet tailormade edged with a band of silver fox around the skirt to match the fur collar. 'Oyster grey, is it?' she asked, her lips brimming into a smile. 'Your man's in a high frump, are you tiring him out?'

Charles was scowling as he talked to the men who had held the fiery archway. There was some dispute over payment since the men claimed that they had lost a morning's work, although none of them had ever been seen working of a morning. Charles took a handful of

347

guineas from his pocket and flung them on the muddy ground, where they landed with a soft chink.

Later that week, we were at the station again. Charles, always a tireless intervener in the market-place, was needed urgently in Kerry to advise on the building of a new coastguard lookout, for the crinkled coastline further south was said to be favoured as a place to bring ashore German arms safely. The British Embassy in Washington had intercepted a coded message from the German military to the Volunteer headquarters to that effect and Charles was peevish at the lack of response from Dublin Castle. 'Arrest the ringleaders and have done with it,' he said crossly, as I drove him to the station in the trap. He pulled at his strong thumbs, massaging their rosy tips, gloveless even though frost glittered on the thorn bushes. 'The Castle crowd have spines made of dough; they think that Ireland is too amusing to be taken seriously, with the pig in the parlour alongside the priest like a *Punch* cartoon.'

In Ireland it has often been that the conqueror falls into the habits of the conquered, but this had never been the way with Charles. After years of living at Malina, he spluttered with an energetic lack of sympathy that was triumphally English. 'You people,' he called us. 'One comes along and tries to do something with you people but . . .' Then he would shake his head in a show of sorrow.

When I set him down, he kissed my forehead chastely then wiped his lips on his handkerchief. 'Your brow is clammy, my dear; in fact, you look damp and ill. Rest when you get home. Your tediously lengthy girlhood seems over at last, although, until now, I would have agreed with those who claimed that you tricked time.' He climbed into the carriage of the waiting train as nimbly as a boy.

The oysters having conspicuously failed to make me fertile, I had begun to drink hot water poured over dried tansy leaves, remembering that in my childhood the *cailleach,* the healing woman, had said that this was a cure for barrenness. In long-ago summers I had always picked a bunch of the bright yellow tansy flowers with their ferny leaves from the hedgerow; my mother liked to keep them in a jar in the kitchen to rub on joints of meat to keep off the flies. In the scattered cabins on the mountainside, people laid sprigs of tansy over corpses to stop them decaying until the coffin was made. Trying to keep my thoughts on life rather than death, always difficult at Malina, I took the steaming potion to my upstairs workroom where a fire had been laid. I set a match to it and sank into a chair, sipping the drink which smelt, not unpleasantly, of camphor.

I was in a bloated, dozy state but suddenly the room seemed to bloom with terror. Harriet was staring at me from the flames. I could see her clear brow and slightly downcast eye nestling among the crackling twigs and smoking sods of turf. She lay on the flames, gently tossed and lifted on them as though floating on a yellow sea.

I must have screamed because suddenly Binnie was in the room. She followed to where my shaking finger pointed and fished about in the fire with the tongs until she brought out Harriet's photograph, its edges smoking and mottled with black. It was the likeness that had stood, silver-framed, on the desk in Charles's study for most of the years I had lived at Malina. Still holding it in the long tongs, Binnie opened the window and shook the tongs into the cold air to cool what they grasped. But it was too late for salvage. The heat of the fire had made the old paper brittle and the photograph crumbled into ashy flakes which drifted down into the bare shrubbery. Before they reached the ground, I had run downstairs to the back of the house and was rattling the knob of the locked door of the study.

'Festy, you dirty little caffler, come you here.' Binnie's shout echoed down the long corridor. She lowered her voice. 'There's nothing you could teach that one about slipping through iron bars the way they might be cobwebs.' She had come to terms with her nephew's dubious associations. Though her voice was tinny and tormented when she spoke of him, she had decided that 'his only sin is in being so witless that he'd go a bit of the road with anyone who asked him, and sure if there were no wild boys there would be no great men.'

Festy sauntered down the passage, chewing the ham sandwich he had been enjoying in the kitchen. As he bent to the lock, I could see the light through his thinning hair and the pink curve of his head. He too had lost the knack of tricking time. He bent the lock back with one of my hairpins and we all three entered the room, walking into air that was thick and close in spite of the cold weather.

'Now that's a gorgeous piece of goods entirely.' Festy gave a low whistle of appreciation. There was another likeness of a woman in the study now: a portrait in oils in an elaborately scrolled gold frame. The picture was crudely painted and the hair and eyes of the sultry beauty it displayed were a strange orange-brown. But I knew that, in life, the hair had been a rich lion gold and the eyes amber, sparkling with gilded flecks. It was Josephine Trewin, born in Huddersfield, died in Rome.

'Anyone you know?' Festy asked.

'Better than I know myself,' I said.

'Is it some scut he's leading into the dance?' Binnie continued the questions, sucking in her cheeks, drawn to the bright, false colours of the painting and the flaunting beauty of its subject.

'No. It was she who led him – into a dance of death.'

I pushed them out of the room and watched over Festy as he straightened the lock and made it fast again. An old uneasiness, a frost of cares, settled over me and I felt a fear that reached the bone. I dreaded Charles's return and hoped that the whole involved business of coded messages and meetings with men who became excited schoolboys when the talk turned to traitors and bullets would keep him away from Malina until I could manage a show of composure.

The weather turned strangely, dangerously unseasonal, hot and clear, as though winter had become summer without going through the tremulous process of spring. At the beginning of Holy Week, I walked to Ainín Rua, the dead grass crackling under my feet like tinder, the wild grasses murmuring like a swarm of bees in the soft breeze. It was early morning and I passed Volunteers scattering back to their homes after an all-night exercise, the backs of their jackets daubed with flour so as not to lose sight of each other in the dark. They were homely men who had sung the songs I had written in their small, tight tenor voices in Meehan's of an evening and were unclear about the exact place where heroism ended and folly began. As they trudged home to scolding wives and hot breakfasts, pensive sheep with lustrous black faces shaped like thin hearts moved out of their path and then resumed their nibbling of the heather.

More than his dreamy, disjointed walk or his awkward, tender, sexual fingers, Peadar's long, naked throat took the sight out of my eyes. He was asleep on a pile of cushions, dressed in his Volunteer's uniform, his enormous boots on the floor beside him next to a one-volume *Collected Works of Shakespeare* and a notebook. It was the English playwright's approaching tercentenary and Peadar, in the intervals between rifle practice, was writing an article on Shakespeare and nationalism for the *Connacht Tribune*.

I lit the fire and set the iron poker in it to mull a jug of porter for Peadar's breakfast. Then I stretched myself out beside him, as comforted by his breathing as though it were the birdsong you might hear on the soft, dark walks through the woods. Peadar was the thing in my life I would never regret, for even if passion is an unhappiness, you cannot go against it and not be in error.

I saw him wake, the shimmering delicacy of his eyes

quickly shadowed by despair, and I noticed the canvas haversack leaning against the window. 'The time is on us, my honey,' he said. 'I have my orders to leave for Dublin.'

'You're a fool,' I said bitterly, my heart like a hot stone. 'If you die it will be for a people who don't exist, a people you imagine as awake only for Ireland, whereas, if you were to look about you, you would see that their hearts and souls aren't with you and all they want is a pint and a pipe and a British army pension if they can wangle one.'

'I know it, Rose Erris. Still, our wisdom arises from defeat, and to every generation its deed.'

'You talk like Pearse and those other morbid dreamers. Killed is the great thing to be with them.'

'I care not if I live but a day and a night, so long as my deeds live after me.' Peadar quoted the words of Cuchulain, that infuriating, mythic hero. Padraic Pearse had snatched those words for the motto of St Enda's college, the school he founded to turn schoolboys into patriots. 'Those aren't my own feelings, exactly,' Peadar said. 'I would rather have been remembered for persuasion than for combat.' He spoke as though his body already lay in a wet crevice in the graveyard.

'But why are you to go to Dublin when your men are here?'

'Orders from Commandant-General Pearse, who doesn't seem to be much of a favourite of yours. He needs men about him who'll be able to translate documents into Irish quickly when the Republic is recognized.'

'Oh, he's a cake that was iced before it was baked,' I cried, wild with grief and rage. 'Is it documents from every crowned head in Europe offering congratulations that that lunatic is expecting? He's playing to empty pockets if he does.'

Peadar looked at me sadly. '"Love is not love which alters when it alteration finds." Could I make you an offering of Shakespeare since Cuchulain is delivering smoke from your nostrils today? I've loved you through all the days of your life; the days when you wrote your irreplaceable songs and the days like this one when you weep at what those songs once strove to bring about.'

I would not be mollified. 'At least, my songs, even if they were misguided, reflected life rather than re-sisted it. I never glorified the dead above the living.' I was shouting now, flinging words like flints at the man I loved more than my life.

Peadar smiled his slow, gentle smile, a smile of unexploitable goodness. 'Reality is the imagination of the dead. That is the thought that won't let go of me.'

'So you let go of me,' I shrieked at him.

He broke into gulping sobs, buried his head in his bony arms until my rage became a sorrow as black as rage and I pressed his shaking body into my arms.

We stayed together until it was time for him to catch the Dublin train. We drank hot porter, mourning the flying moment, making plans for a future which we knew would not be shaped to include a life shared. We wheeled our bicycles to where the track divided. '*Mo ghrd thú*, I love you,' Peadar said.

'My soul is within you,' I answered and, in Irish, 'I am your constant friend.'

We kissed for the last time, and shook hands to give this parting the importance that was its due. Then I turned away from him, into the broken world of myself.

27

At night, I always put my bicycle in the coachhouse.
As I approached it late that evening, a bar of light
shone from beneath the door; one of the grooms must
have left a candle burning after he had done a routine
inspection of the vehicles it sheltered.

I pushed open the door and blinked in the blaze
of light from dozens of candles ranged on the rough
wall-shelves; great circles of light that throbbed and
merged and made the stone walls lurch. Seated in the
sociable, the low, open carriage used for summertime
excursions, his elegant legs crossed, Charles studied a
sheaf of pages on which were written the words and
tunes of my songs. He lifted an eyebrow at me in the
hateful way he had.

'Banality set to music, they are what I might have
expected from you — strange that I didn't guess the
identity of the mysterious Áinín Rua before now.'
He hummed a few bars of 'Waken Your Courage,
Ireland' and then threw back his head to savour the
tune as he might savour the after-taste of a fine wine
he had swallowed. He spoke with a sugary amiability
that was weighted with menace. 'Not bad, my dear,
it has the sort of easy thrill that would make men take
your part.'

I turned to leave but a warm, padded paw of a hand reached out and grabbed me by the wrist. Effortlessly, Charles swung me into the carriage and pushed me down on the seat beside him. He put his hands on my shoulders; I could feel their hot strength through my clothes, hands so strong that they could have lifted me between their two thumbs like the beer bottle that Charles had once lifted to win a bet, before my astonished child's eyes, that day at the pony show, when we had begun our vile collaboration.

'The RUC sergeant brought me these papers.' My husband's hands had me impaled as he spoke. 'He found something else too, although not the hidden rifles he'd been tipped off were buried beside that eerie, deserted lake, nor the local ghost with her barbaric and terrible cry.' He took his left hand from my shoulder and picked up a book from the floor of the carriage. It was a copy of *Fairy and Folk Tales of the Irish Peasantry*, edited by W. B. Yeats. Still using one hand, he flicked it open so that I could see Peadar's name written in his large, uncertain script on the flyleaf.

'You are nearly clever, but not quite, which is worse than being a fool. And you have acted stupidly – stupidity is the one real sin in the world since it is the only one that always goes punished, as you shall be, Áinín Rua.'

Each word seemed snipped off with sharp scissors; then he hunched his shoulders forward like a lion and his voice turned into a lion's snarl. 'You wrote songs of insurrection; you took a stranger to your bed. Were they ways you had of booting out your demons? Well, here's another way.' He began to hit me, batting me between his hands like a conjurer shuffling a pack of cards. Then he hauled me out of the carriage and began to tear off my clothes. 'You owe me luck money for giving you the horses; I'll take it my own way,' he said in a roaring whisper, and then, looking at me out of eyes that flickered madly like the candle flames above our heads, his body tensed and murderous like a lion awakened from its slumbers: 'You come from beasts and shall be taken like a beast.'

I fought him with all my strength. I screamed for Agnes who I knew to be in the uncomfortable room above, a room she hated, and hardly ever left. A saddle fell off the wall, a tin pail dropped from its hook and clanged onto the hard floor but Agnes did not come, although, as I struggled I could hear the creak of her footsteps on the boards and knew she was listening to my screams.

Hot candlewax dripped onto my bare thighs as Charles pushed them apart with a destroying touch. Inside my body, he made red war until I felt scraped out, eroded, as though nothing of me was left. Everything about me that had been light and spare and clean had been violated.

At last, Charles released my wrists which he had been clasping to the floor behind my head. He stood up and threw my clothes towards me. 'You should have contented yourself with learning Irish, my dear, Eye Rish, that useless badge of a beaten race.'

When I heard his footsteps on the cobbles outside, I opened my eyes. The candles had melted down to misshapen stumps, their smoky flames guttering. The feeble light disclosed that my legs were bruised purple and the power of Charles's fingers had crushed thick stripes on my arms. When I touched my jaw I could feel blood welling through my fingers. I put on my muddied clothes and shuffled to the kitchen door with bent shoulders and dragging steps like an old woman.

When Binnie saw me, her face seemed to shrink to the mould of its bones. She helped me to the settle and gave me hot whiskey. She put oatmeal poultices on my legs and said, 'Hell will never be full until he's in it.' Then I fainted.

'Damn the bit but it's all called off.' Festy made room for himself at the end of my bed among several dogs, and offered himself in the role of comforter. He slid his eyes off my battered hand as I offered him a peach from the luncheon tray that Binnie had brought up to me earlier, an invalid's tray with delicate, fussy dishes on it, of the kind that Binnie had once brought up to Harriet, a different kind of invalid.

It was Easter Sunday and everything was in a scrabble of confusion. On Good Friday, the *Aube,* a German boat bringing arms to the Galway Volunteers, had been captured, leaving the local revolutionaries with an arsenal composed of pikes and hayforks. Instructions were hard to come by. The Volunteers' messengers were the children of Countess Markievicz's Fianna Eireann. To unwatchful eyes, it looked like an Irish version of Baden-Powell's Boy Scouts: orderly, uniformed children, as full of notions of honour and duty and team spirit as an English cricketer. But the child members of Fianna Eireann were not trained to tie knots or layer twigs for a fire. Ambush and sabotage were the lessons they learnt; child-fighters in a secret war, who skipped about the country lanes with despatches hidden in the soles of their shoes, an inspired means of communication but, in the remoteness of Connemara, not always available or reliable.

Festy bit into the peach, letting the juice dribble down the front of his green tunic. 'Anyways, Peadar will be coming back now,' he said. 'Ah, the country is bunched and the glorious undertaking is put on the long finger. 'Twas Packy got the message from Ballinasloe, from his wife's cousin whose son heard it from Eoin MacNeill himself. There now, aren't you the happy woman at last?' He nudged me towards good fortune with a wink and a good-humoured shake of his head, a most unlikely man to be so disaffected by life as to be wearing the uniform of a revolutionary army, until you remembered that men such as he had only the impossible to hope for.

I lived in a swelter of death-like days, beyond hope of any kind, not noticing the bruises fading and healing on my skin. I thought only of Peadar and the end of love, a loss more violent than rape. It was his colossal absence that weakened me so that I could no more swallow the little steamed moulds that Binnie prepared for me than I could have crunched a shankbone. But Binnie would not indulge me as she had once indulged Harriet; she had had her fill of beaten, dejected women assuming the frailty of fine china that was fated to be smashed to smithereens. That Sunday evening she came into the room holding a favourite dress of mine, a thin, heathery wool with a purple velvet collar that stood up and then furled back in a pretty way.

'Who's to see to the vastation in this place if it isn't yourself?' She answered her own question by smacking the sleeping dogs off the bed and pulling back the blankets. 'Agnes has gone. The word is that she was seen at the station with no luggage except for a little stuffed wool horse of Malachy's in one hand and a ticket to America in the other that she'd bought with her separation money from the government. Horty will have a fine homecoming to empty rooms, and no loss to him either. Herself was so traitorous that the sneaking ways of her would put you in mind of the *droleen,* the wren, when she chirped and alerted the Roman soldiers to the place where our Lord was hidden in the Garden of Gethsemane.'

While she talked, Binnie emptied a jug of hot water into a bowl, laid out my underclothes and polished the silver back of my hairbrush against her rump. 'As for himself, there hasn't been a budge from him. Shut up in his study day and night and it's well for him, he that shouldn't be let out even at the end of a chain.'

I hadn't moved from the bed, even though it was cold without the press of dogs and blankets. I was studying the furniture in the room where I had slept for all my adult life and noticing, as though for the first time, how many pieces had legs that ended in the carved, sheathed claws of wooden lions: the triple-glassed dressing-table, a little cupboard whose sides were linked with looped garlands, even the flattened rosewood balls on which a tapestry stool rested were grasped in restraining paws. Binnie looked at me anxiously. 'I mind now a way that poor Nora had of getting you settled in yourself when you were

361

in fits of agitation before a pony show.' She held out her knotted hands to me. 'Get you up, woman, and come down to the kitchen. Life is always less despairful when you can see the kettle lifting on the fire.'

She helped me dress, then brushed my hair and braided it into a thick plait the way my mother had done when I was a little girl. In the kitchen, she took an iron that had been heating over the coals and offered it to me. At Shanvally, my mother had always made me do the ironing when I became tense and rowdy before a show day, itched by the terrible thought that the judges might be stupid or venal enough to favour horses other than mine. Holding the iron that Binnie gave me now was like having a hot, smoking hoof in my hand. I nosed it along linen sheets and damask napkins, the maids' aprons and my own thick petticoats. I drew breaths of the warm, sweet fragrance of metal on cloth. I smoothed out the crumpled thing my life had become and, as I ironed the evening away, I felt life returning to me, steady and rhythmic as the tidewater that teemed into the harbour. I slept well that night, with the smell of clean, hot linen in my nostrils.

On Easter Monday, the weather faired again, making the woods stand in a bluebell haze and the lake glint like crushed diamonds; the sort of day that would give hope even to the futureless. I went for a walk in the woods, noting the wild flowers and trying to remember their Latin names, the way the Ascendancy women did when they had come to house parties at Malina, tall, lovely women who seemed never to have anything more troublesome on their minds than the mild fear that they might trip over the exposed root of a tree and be unable to dance that night.

'*Viola odorata, monotropa hypopitys, orchis mascula.*' I murmured the unwieldy names like a grim, obsessive chant to keep my mind from Peadar's gaunt, dreamy face, Charles's brutal body. But the sunshine and concentration made me feel queasy and I came back after an hour or so, to see Festy rushing out of the house, leaning back so as to balance on his chest a pile of Charles's riding breeches. His eyes shone with fear and excitement. 'It's on, we're out!' he shouted. 'Redmond's National Volunteers have declared for the Crown but our boys have Athenry and Craughwell taken and the police barracks surrounded.'

'And the news from Dublin?' I crushed the sappy stalks of the flowers in my hand so that they oozed through my fingers.

'The tricolour's up for sure; it's all commotion and gladness.' He tipped his chin towards the pile of breeches in his arms. 'Uniforms are scarce on us. I'm taking these to give some of the boys a bit of dignity when they're on the march.'

'Take the horses, too,' I said. And when Festy gaped at me, I flicked my hand at him in a gesture of dismissal. 'Take them,' I insisted. 'They are mine to give. I've paid for them dearly enough, over and above their price.'

For three days rumour unfurled upon rumour: local men, with no weapons except for hayforks and rough enthusiasm, had captured the courthouse at Lisnagreve but, having no food, were driven back home by hunger some hours before the police arrived from Ballinasloe. Damian Dashwood had been arrested and imprisoned in a British warship in Galway Bay. The Germans had landed and the country was up. Sure, if you listened hard enough couldn't you hear the sound of their gunfire coming off the water? A curfew was to be announced which would force the public houses to close at 1 p.m. and Fintan Meehan was roaring terrible at the news and blaming the Volunteers for bringing the country to ruin.

I would have expected Charles to be out in the thick of things, but he stayed in his study, a lion in his lair, crouched and lumped in silence. The trays left outside the door were the only sign of his presence in the room beyond, the food on them hardly touched, the bottles of wine unopened. It was the maids who brought me news of the fighting in Dublin, although you could not call it news, those shreds and snitches of hearsay which they repeated in high, excited voices, their eyes round with wonder, as though they were reciting fairy stories, which, indeed, they might have been, since it was impossible for us to sort out the rock of truth from the mist of fable.

What they had heard made the saliva fizzle on their lips. Countess Markievicz, reckless and wonderful in the uniform of a colonel of Volunteers and a black velour hat quivering with cocque feathers, had captured St Stephen's Green, the largest square in Europe, with her army of women and children. She would not let anyone in except for the park-keeper, who came through the barricades twice a day to feed the ducks. Padraic Pearse, that mannered, morbid creature, had read a proclamation to a crowd that stood agape in front of the GPO, and raised the flag of the new Republic on the roof; the flag that put the white stripe of peace between the North's orange and the green of the southern counties. The entire city had been sliced through by the fighting, and looked like a battlefield in France, with smoking, blackened buildings, among which staggered delighted shawlies wearing furs and jewels from the looted shops of Upper Sackville Street. A tall, thin insurgent, a teacher of mathematics called Eamon de Valera, stalked the seething streets, wearing bright red socks, and handed out cigars to his men before leading them into the fighting at Mount Street Bridge.

The way that it reached us on the far side of the country at Malina, the fight for Ireland's freedom was a merry frolic, a holiday from real life, where not even a duck went hungry and women from the slums marvelled at the feel of stolen silk underwear next to their skins and stolen dancing slippers on their mottled, hillocky, bunioned feet. I clung to these extraordinary accounts of the Easter rebellion, these unreliable snippets of imaginary news for they seemed to have nothing to do with death or danger or terror coming to town.

Pearse's Republic could not last for many days more. The might of the British Empire, inept but powerful, would charge into Dublin soon; the disorderly, intoxicated city would be put to rights and the rebels sent home in a smirking, superior way, so that their brave deeds would seem questionable and embarrassing, a cabbage patch revolt which required as little daring as a schoolboy's raid on an apple orchard. Yet, in this odd, suspenseful interval, I listened to the maids' excited gabble feeling pleased and excited, forgetting, for hours at a stretch, that I had seen the war goddess in the guise of a hooded crow, hopping from one broken stone to another along the edge of Loch Áinín Rua.

Then, on Thursday, Damian Dashwood arrived at Malina. I looked at his face, feverish, mysterious and unrevealing and knew what he had come to tell me. He held a piece of paper in his hand as though it were scalding his fingertips. 'Are you able for it?' he asked me and, when I nodded my head, he told me how Peadar had died.

'There wasn't a finger put to him,' he said haltingly. 'He was in a house in Mount Street that our men had taken and it came under fire. But not one of the bullets that came through the window hit him. 'Twas the fault of our own guns, guns that were never meant for the use of saints and scholars such as himself and his friends.'

I knew the clumsy weapon that had been handed out to most of the Volunteers: the Howth rifle that had to be reloaded after every shot and whose barrel quickly became too hot to hold. A hopeless gun for clumsy, unpractised fingers.

A fellow-poet, made ardent and nervous by the whizz-whack of bullets around him, had picked up a rifle he thought to be unloaded and, perhaps because of his shaking, unreliable fingers, or perhaps because of the unexpected heat of the handle, had pressed the trigger. A bullet being in place, it had shot Peadar through the back of the head as he knelt before the barricaded window.

Mr Dashwood explained all this to me in a stern,

mournful voice that sank into an important whisper. He put a timid hand on my shoulder; I shrugged it off, remembering the hot, brutal grip of another hand that had seized it not many days since, although already it seemed to be something that had happened in a nightmare, just as the sight of Mr Dashwood holding a piece of paper did.

'They went out to wake up Ireland. After times will not willingly let what they did die,' Mr Dashwood said in his new, sanctimonious voice. 'Nobody can quench the Irish passion for freedom.' He bowed his head and was silent at last, although his foot tapped on the carpet as though he were shouting inside himself. He handed me the piece of paper – it was ruled and torn from a notebook and was much folded – and then he rubbed his fingers with his thumbs to rid them of the feel of it.

It was Peadar's will that he gave me. It had been found in the pocket of his tunic and brought westwards by a series of fleet-footed child messengers. It left me everything 'of which I am possessed and may become possessed'. When I saw his jerky signature on the page I ran outside and, holding on to a stone that stuck up through the soil, I vomited into a clear waterfall that fed Malina's lake.

The rain had begun by then, cold, slow and drenching, but I began to walk, circling the lakeside, my clothes and hair soaked and draggled, making up the story of Peadar's death, a story that I would be able to tell the child that I knew I was carrying by the sour aftertaste of vomit in my mouth.

Mount Street was where the Colthursts lived; it

might have been their house that the rebels had captured, locking the owners in the cellar, breaking the glass in the tall windows with their rifle butts before insufficiently barricading them.

I imagined the bullets coming through the broken windows like horizontal rain, sending shards of the Venetian chandelier tinkling to the floor, setting the grand piano jingling. I imagined Peadar's smoky green eyes seeing the unimaginable sights: James Connolly raising the Plough and the Stars over the Imperial Hotel, bright filaments of fire shinnying down the sky, and Dublin burning, burning, burning until it seemed that the spirits of our ancient warlords were abroad in the cinder-coated streets, giving the old order to their people to leave no city standing.

The rain slid over the ground in solid sheets when I finally returned to Malina but the fires of Easter week raged in my head, hot as hell.

28

'The terror is in the times.' I heard Father Casey's halting voice behind me as I leant my forehead against the cold wall of Morrigan's empty stall, pummelled by a bout of nausea.

For a moment, I thought the old priest had come to comfort me over Peadar's tragic, inept death. I wiped my mouth and turned to face him.

'These executions, the bitterness they're causing,' he said.

They were all to die. Pearse, Connolly, MacBride, all those who had declared Poblacht na hÉireann, the Republic of Ireland, from the steps of the GPO. I didn't care. I felt no pity for those responsible for my lover's death, the fatal farce of it. The British could kill every man in Ireland since none of them was Peadar Griffin. They could work double tides with their courts martial and firing squads and their detestable efforts to bring their turmoiled colony to heel with Cromwellian reprisals until all the birds were songless.

'It's what they wanted all along,' I said. 'Pearse and that crowd could sniff out an opportunity to make a blood sacrifice like a stag scenting the breeze.' I turned my head to the wall again as a wave of dizziness seemed to lift me off the uncertain ground.

'I have something to say to you,' Father Casey said. 'Will we go into the house?'

I should have liked to have taken him into the kitchen, to have had the soothing weight of the iron in my hand as I listened to his jabber which had always been irksome to me, but his voice was so strained and formal that I led him into the drawing-room, the place where he had once refused Christian burial rights to a sinless baby.

He shivered as he sat down. The maids lay in their beds weeping for the executed rebels and none of the fires was lit. Sharp, cold sunlight filled the room; motes of dust twirled giddily in the chill and the brass fire-dogs had a dulled, frozen sheen as they stood guard beside the empty cavern of the fireplace. The priest's red curl of a nose shone with cold and his scheming eyes looked bleak. I took pity on him and splashed brandy into a glass. He eyed me primly over its rim. 'Your husband is taking instruction,' he said, and winced when I laughed.

'Is it himself, the great irreconcilable? You'll be needing to keep a watch on the communion wine, Father, or he'll have it changed back into water on you.'

The priest made circles with the glass, slurping the brandy against the sides. 'He told me about the unfortunate situation in the coachhouse – ah, my poor child, the woe that is marriage – and wants you to understand that the measure of his love and trust in you was the measure of his anger. Rose Erris, he seeks your forgiveness.'

'I'll never forgive him, not until the clay is crammed

down my throat. He has you tantalized finally, Father. You've fallen for his conjuring tricks.'

'Try to understand.' Father Casey's voice was excited, blurting. 'We were born to our faith, he has chosen it. He knows that you no longer love him, that you loved another, but he accepts it as the cross he has to bear. He will tolerate it.'

'Come down out of that, Father. In the Irish language that Peadar wanted us all to return to, the word for tolerance doesn't exist. It doesn't exist in my husband either.'

'Ah, come on now, child. Give the man a chance to show he's a changed character in the years he has left to him.'

'We'll see how far his tolerance can be stretched soon enough; I am with child.'

The priest crossed the room with his bumping, old man's walk and fumbled for my hands. 'This is a blessing, a redemption, a cause for hope. I am delighted for you.'

'With child, but not by Charles. Another cross for him, Father, but he's lifting them as lightly as empty beer bottles these days, so he'll shoulder this one gladly. It will be something to forgive me for. He owes me that, at least. I've taken his malevolence neat for years.'

'You're very calculating,' Father Casey said, 'a real McCalla.'

'I am that. A McCalla always insists on seeing what's there in front of him, rather than what others try to wheedle him into seeing, that's why we're such good judges of horses. You want me to believe that my husband is a changed man and that I should stand before him and blink at his new pious lustre. I've another version of the story for you. I'd say that Charles's money no longer consoles him for his unhappiness; he's bored with it, he finds his own dashing exploits puny. He thinks it would be more exciting to be touched by God's fire and ice. Excitement has always been a disease with him.'

The priest flinched as though my words grated his sides. 'It will go hard with him, you know, having to admit the chaos of the soul when he's always had such a fondness for order and time-keeping.'

'And playing the mischief with those who loved him, and destruction and every kind of badness that there is to be had. He has done me a hundred harms and Harriet before me. To put religion on the likes of him would be like putting a saddle on a cow. There's no fit between the two.'

The priest flumped himself down beside me on the sofa and looked at me sadly out of his rinsed-out eyes. 'In the space of one lifetime who can work out a moral code? That is what our religion is there for, a way to discover what is good and what is missing. For God's sake, Rose Erris, help him.'

'Help him in this hopeless attempt to heal the festering disease in his soul? That would make Malina even more of a clearing-house of lies than it already is. But I'll do it, so, Father, for my baby, not for God. If Malina is hers from the start of things, perhaps she won't covet it later, this house and the hollow world locked in it, the way I did.'

The old man stood up and wriggled his hands in the air above my head like two white fish. He intoned: 'Take away our hearts of stone and give us hearts of flesh. Take away this murdering hate and give us thine own eternal love.' His eyes were closed so he did not see me leave the room and walk down the long, cold corridor to Charles's study.

I had expected to find my husband looking suddenly rapturous, radiant with the novelty of his newly discovered faith but, seated behind his desk, he seemed subdued and lessened, like someone shakily recovering from an illness.

'You have much to forgive me for,' he said in a maudlin voice.

I sat down in the chair facing him and swung my feet onto the desk, onto the exact spot where Harriet's photograph had once stood. 'There are scores to be settled, certainly,' I said.

'But you will stay at Malina?'

'I will so. To make a torment of your life. I'll be the cross you have to bear, and it's likely to get heavier.' I circled my hand over my stomach. 'I am carrying Peadar's child, the way that his memory will not be erased or silenced.'

Charles's eyes flashed wickedly and then the gleam vanished, as though it had been switched off. He nodded his head in the stoical way of someone who has convinced himself that life on earth is an endurance test for the heavenly one to come. 'So be it,' he said. 'I shall care for the child as though it were my own. Do you hate me?' he asked suddenly.

'No, I've seen what happens when hate takes charge of a life.' I got up and unhooked Josephine's portrait from the wall. I reached for the little dagger that Charles used to open his letters and tore the painted canvas across and across. Charles gave an unprotesting sigh as I tossed the brightly coloured strips into the wastepaper basket. He let his head droop on his chest as I rehung the empty frame on the wall. 'Now let us both come out of the exile of our pasts,' I said. I spat on my palm and held it out. He struck his against it. It seemed less full of blood and heat, less brisk. I sat down again.

'What happened to *Antes muerto que mudado* – sooner dead than changed?' I asked. 'What has made you take on the difficulties of a religious life, you of all people?'

He leaned forward intensely. 'Don't you see? I need difficulty like a negative ideal – difficulty, severity, austerity, the corrective of a life. It will be a way of keeping myself in check.' He put his face in his hands and the sunlight caught the signet ring on his finger with its engraved motto that had not stood the test of time. 'I want memory wiped out,' he growled through his hands.

I stood up to leave. 'Memory is about not forgetting what was done so that it cannot happen again,' I said. 'Without memory there is no morality.' The door gave a jumpy click as I closed it behind me.

After great pain a formal feeling comes. As I walked to the cottage where Peadar had lodged I remembered how my heart used to flap like laundry in the wind when I had come to meet him there and the way the air I breathed had seemed stolen, delicious. But the memory seemed to belong to somebody else and there was a bruising place where my heart used to be.

Martin Kenneally had died a few months back.

His empty cottage would stay so until its title deeds were resolved in favour of some faraway niece or nephew who would probably never return to claim this inheritance of thatch and limewashed walls and fishing-nets hung for safe keeping on the walls of the church. Already, the kitchen was powdery, sploshed with patches of damp, and a neighbour's old dog gnawed a cow's hoof in the place where Marty had kept his upturned currach. Already, in another place, Peadar's blood was dry underfoot.

I walked into the room that had once been his and wished that my arms had been strong enough to save him. Unbearable to look at his chair, his books, his bed – that same bed where I had held and been held, pulling his hip to mine, the old quilt soft against our skins. Once, in that bed, he had wound his fingers in my hair as he told me some old, sad story in our country's history. When I had yawned noisily, he had said, 'Never forget the past, you may need it again in the future.'

And now, carrying his child, I was not at liberty to disremember. This dear, dead love must be kept in my head, to be brought forth in stories to tell his daughter as soon as she could understand them. I took one of his clay pipes from a cracked bowl and sniffed the stale tobacco; I took his long, black coat – a coat you would be ashamed to offer to a tinker – from its hook, wrapped myself in it and lay on the bed, howling like a banshee. Then I got up and slapped my cheeks until they were dry. I could not undo things done; I could not call back yesterday. Peadar must be remembered without nostalgia, that fantasy which can never take place so that it maintains itself by never being fulfilled. I mixed some ink in a cup, filled the inkwell of the stained writing-desk and, taking Peadar's books from the shelf, one by one, wrote below his own scrawled name on the flyleaf of each the name of his daughter, Rosaleen.

In Ireland, every child is a precious gift. Our language has a different word to call the beloved child at every stage of its growth – *naoidheah, lanabh, malrach, piaste* – the child in the cradle, the child crawling on the floor, the child going to school, the child well-grown, so many gentle words, sweet as a kiss. When Rosaleen was born, tumbled from my body, in a rush of pain, lusty for the unsheltered world outside my womb, Malina filled with people again. The whole neighbourhood came to see this late, treasured baby girl, crossing over the carpet with exaggerated quietness on the tips of their toes, bringing gifts of butter and honey and lace caps with pink ribbons.

My daughter's eyes were the navy blue of every newborn. 'They will change, possibly,' Dr Parsloe said. 'She might get some hair on her head, too, if things go well.'

'Yes,' I said. 'Sliding green eyes, soft brown hair.'

'I wonder,' Charles said. He waved his hands over Rosaleen's face as she lay in the cradle beside me, as though he were conducting a performance. Her face glowed and her lashes fluttered from the heat of his hand. She smiled for the first time in her short life and went to sleep. Doubt held me from fingers to toes.

'She's perfect,' said Dr Parsloe, 'a real peach of a

girl, well worth waiting for. What's your secret, Rose Erris?'

'Tansy leaf tea,' I said.

The doctor twitched inside his immaculate jacket. 'These old remedies have never been proven,' he said.

'Desire, then,' I said. 'It was the desire for her that brought her to me.' Charles put his strong hand on the cradle's muslin frill and rocked it with great gentleness. 'She came by the grace of God and from the empty spaces left to chance,' he said.

Dr Parsloe frowned and snapped the brass clasps of his bag to show his distaste of the strange household we had become there, at Malina; the master of the house astonishingly wrapped up in the soft, clammy religion of the native people, his wife regressed to something primitive and stubborn. 'You will have the child vaccinated against the smallpox?' he demanded curtly.

'Of course,' I said. 'I am all for medical advance. If there were a vaccine to guard her against heartache I'd have you give her a jab of it too.' He gave me a narrow slice of a smile; he had never liked me. 'That's something that must be left to nature and nurture. Apply yourself to her nurture, Rose Erris. Nature being so very unreliable.'

At six weeks old, Rosaleen looked at the world through amber eyes; butted purposefully at my breast with her lovely, round head that was growing a gleaming fuzz, the colour of honey. Charles's daughter beyond a doubt. When he lifted her from the cradle, she made popping sounds with her lips which, although she was much too young to speak, sounded like Dada, Dada. The first time this happened, I wanted to snatch her out of Charles's arms and run from the house, the whole vaulted sprawl of it. Malina's cut-stone walls had become so repugnant to me that the cement that held them might have been mixed with blood. But Charles would have pursued me to the edges of the universe to snatch her back. Rosaleen was an unimagined compensation to him for the loss of youth and love; he was fiercely consoled by her milky warmth.

And to me, my baby at my breast, the future held some tenderness, although not that which I had expected. I had come to an accommodation between my duty and my feelings. I would stay; I would learn how to be lonely since the company I wished for was in the grave. After all, the art of living is to make do with what one has.

I sang to Rosaleen as I trailed up and down Malina's draughty passages, between the high, gilded walls that store up the cold and then spitefully release it. The baby against my shoulder was as warm as the kindled sod that warmed my hands as I carried it to school all those years ago – she has inherited her father's hot blood. What else has she inherited from him, I wonder?

The words of the song rocked her to sleep: 'Because it was him, because it was me. We sought each other out long before we met.' I paused at the tall window with its view of the lake where ducks nested in the reeds. The song became a prayer, one that Father Casey would not condone. I whispered it into her silky neck: 'May you be glutted with freedom, as your country may be. May you not die for Ireland but live and work for her. May you act always from your own will and centre.' Sustained by the nearness of my mouth on her skin, Rosaleen nudged her head deeper into my shoulder. Motherlove is said to leave the mother unrewarded, the daughter empowered. I can hardly believe that I, daughter of a horse coper, accept the one-sidedness of this arrangement so meekly.

29

April 24th, 1917. An anniversary has entered our lives, awkward and defiant. It is a year since the Easter Rising and little to show for the fervent dream of freedom that turned into the soiled reality of the firing squad. Little as yet but enough to make me believe that my daughter will grow up to see the tricolour fly on the masts of the yachts in the harbour and that she will learn a new word for her irresistible country: Eire, which means 'all of Ireland'.

Another sign of different times to come: Fergus Keane has repainted the outside of his shop, altered the white clay lettering so that it now spells out Ó'Caonaigh, the Gaelic version of his name that he has some trouble pronouncing.

Something else has gone along with the old letters that spelt out Keane's General Stores above the grimy window: the remote, serene and leisured way of life that belonged to the Ascendancy. They are leaving at last. Busho and Emmeline O'Cleary followed Leonora to England at Christmas, shaken by what people now call 'the crossness' of a year ago. Yesterday I met Julia Gibbons in Ó'Caonaigh's shop. She too is selling the estate that has been in her family since Strongbow's time, and was buying quantities of household soap to have the house scoured out for the Dublin solicitor who is to retire to it. She studied Rosaleen, who was being passed from one village woman to another, held high so that she could see out of the window. Julia admired the way the baby's tawny eyes shone as she watched the small, hushed waves collapse against the picrhead. 'She has her father's washed and polished look and I'd say the day will come when she will look as well on a horse as her mother docs. Take her up the mountain track tomorrow morning, Rose Erris. I have a farewell gift for her.'

I carry my baby up the mountain path in the canvas sling I devised for her, since I hate to have her anywhere except against my body. The day is as fine as it was this time a year ago. Birds swim in the sky; the mild, accurate bleat of the cuckoo carries across from the island in the bay. I pass an old woman coming down the slope with a young bull with moon-shaped horns. She smiles toothlessly at Rosaleen and spits on her head for good luck, as is the custom here. Near the top of Errisbeg I rest against a boulder and look down on the sight that has always had my heart torn within me: the silvery flash of dozens of tiny lakes, the bogland's watery lace, water that holds the image of time.

Rosaleen hears it before I do. She makes a little mewing sound of excitement and I turn to see a pony, Julia's pony, coming towards us, its step so sure that it seems to paddle the air. I walk to meet it until we are close enough for the baby to feel its breath on her cheek. She grasps its coarse black mane in her fat fingers, stares at its lovely narrow head, the flanks that shine with life, the folded nostrils and velvety lack of lips, the ears pricked to heaven. She listens, enchanted, as I give the low whistle which will make it follow me down the path and around the road that circles the lake and leads to home, leads to Malina.

THE END

THE ROSE TREE
by Mary Walkin Keane

'Beautifully written . . . it pulled me into its delicate world within a few pages' *Maureen Lipman*

From one summer's end to the next, you can tell the time by the number of cakes left on the shelves in Fitzgerald's Bakery. Duneen is that sort of town: what the local postmistress doesn't know isn't worth knowing. But things *happen* to people from Duneen.

Like Róisín McGovern. For her, the School Certificate equals escape from home, as well as from her role as ugly sister to the seriously glamorous Deidre. But even as a college student in Dublin, Róisín wears her childhood memories like an extra layer of clothing: the funerals; the journeys; the stories; the nuns; and, of course, the end-of-summer loonies' outing. Sometimes they all seem to mean more than the unfolding joys, tragedies and sexual adventures of adult life as a Dubliner. And ultimately they take her back where she belongs – home to Duneen – where her first BF (best friend) was a budding femme fatale and her second a saint in the making. And where the pastries still lie in wait on the shelves of Fitzgerald's Bakery.

The Rose Tree tells the story of a young woman making up for lost time. It captures perfectly the spirit and the rhythm of a seafront community in Ireland, in the days when jiving was all the rage.

'I laughed, I cried. I couldn't put it down. It's hilarious, moving and an out-and-out page-turner' *Patricia Scanlan*

A Bantam Paperback

0 553 40651 5

A SELECTION OF FINE NOVELS AVAILABLE
FROM BANTAM BOOKS

THE PRICES SHOWN BELOW WERE CORRECT AT THE TIME OF GOING
TO PRESS. HOWEVER TRANSWORLD PUBLISHERS RESERVE THE RIGHT
TO SHOW NEW RETAIL PRICES ON COVERS WHICH MAY DIFFER FROM
THOSE PREVIOUSLY ADVERTISED IN THE TEXT OR ELSEWHERE.

☐ 17632 2	DARK ANGEL	Sally Beauman	£4.99
☐ 17352 9	DESTINY	Sally Beauman	£4.99
☐ 40429 6	AT HOME	Charlotte Bingham	£3.99
☐ 40427 X	BELGRAVIA	Charlotte Bingham	£3.99
☐ 40163 7	THE BUSINESS	Charlotte Bingham	£4.99
☐ 40432 6	BY INVITATION	Charlotte Bingham	£3.99
☐ 40428 8	COUNTRY LIFE	Charlotte Bingham	£3.99
☐ 40296 X	IN SUNSHINE OR IN SHADOW	Charlotte Bingham	£4.99
☐ 40496 8	NANNY	Charlotte Bingham	£4.99
☐ 40171 8	STARDUST	Charlotte Bingham	£4.99
☐ 17635 8	TO HEAR A NIGHTINGALE	Charlotte Bingham	£4.99
☐ 40072 X	MAGGIE JORDAN	Emma Blair	£4.99
☐ 40298 6	SCARLET RIBBONS	Emma Blair	£4.99
☐ 40372 9	THE WATER MEADOWS	Emma Blair	£4.99
☐ 40321 4	AN INCONVENIENT WOMAN	Dominick Dunne	£4.99
☐ 17676 5	PEOPLE LIFE US	Dominick Dunne	£3.99
☐ 17189 5	THE TWO MRS GRENVILLES	Dominick Dunne	£3.50
☐ 40407 5	THE GREEN OF SPRING	Jane Gurney	£4.99
☐ 17207 7	FACES	Johanna Kingsley	£4.99
☐ 17539 4	TREASURES	Johanna Kingsley	£4.99
☐ 17504 1	DAZZLE	Judith Krantz	£4.99
☐ 17242 5	I'LL TAKE MANHATTAN	Judith Krantz	£4.99
☐ 17174 7	MISTRAL'S DAUGHTER	Judith Krantz	£2.95
☐ 17389 8	PRINCESS DAISY	Judith Krantz	£4.99
☐ 17503 3	TILL WE MEET AGAIN	Judith Krantz	£4.99
☐ 40206 4	FAST FRIENDS	Jill Mansell	£3.99
☐ 40361 3	KISS	Jill Mansell	£4.99
☐ 40611 6	SHEER MISCHIEF	Jill Mansell	£4.99
☐ 40360 5	SOLO	Jill Mansell	£3.99
☐ 17209 3	THE CLASS	Erich Segal	£2.95
☐ 17630 7	DOCTORS	Erich Segal	£3.99
☐ 40262 5	FAMILY FORTUNES	Sarah Shears	£3.99
☐ 40261 7	THE VILLAGE	Sarah Shears	£3.99
☐ 40263 3	THE YOUNG GENERATION	Sarah Shears	£3.99
☐ 40264 1	RETURN TO RUSSETS	Sarah Shears	£3.99
☐ 40582 9	THE SISTERS	Sarah Shears	£4.99
☐ 40771 6	UNKNOWN COUNTRY	Audrey Slaughter	£5.99
☐ 40651 5	THE ROSE TREE	Mary Walkin Keane	£5.99

All Corgi/Bantam Books are available at your bookshop or newsagent, or can be ordered
from the following address:
Corgi/Bantam Books
Cash Sales Department
P.O. Box 11, Falmouth, Cornwall TR10 9EN

UK and B.F.P.O. customers please send a cheque or postal order (no currency) and allow
£1.00 for postage and packing for the first book plus 50p for the second book and 30p
for each additional book to a maximum charge of £3.00 (7 books plus).

Overseas customers, including Eire, please allow £2.00 for postage and packing for the
first book plus £1.00 for the second book and 50p for each subsequent title ordered.

NAME (Block letters) ....

ADDRESS ....

....